THE
QUEEN'S
MEN

ALSO BY OLIVER CLEMENTS

The Eyes of the Queen

THE
QUEEN'S
MEN

AN AGENTS OF THE CROWN NOVEL

OLIVER CLEMENTS

LEOPOLDO & CO

ATRIA

NEW YORK LONDON TORONTO SYDNEY NEW DELHI

LEOPOLDO
& CO

ATRIA

An Imprint of Simon & Schuster, Inc.
1230 Avenue of the Americas
New York, NY 10020

First Leopoldo & Co/Atria Books hardcover edition December 2021

LEOPOLDO & CO/ATRIA BOOKS and colophon
are trademarks of Simon & Schuster, Inc.

For information about special discounts for bulk purchases, please contact Simon & Schuster Special Sales at 1-866-506-1949 or business@simonandschuster.com.

The Simon & Schuster Speakers Bureau can bring authors to your live event. For more information or to book an event, contact the Simon & Schuster Speakers Bureau at 1-866-248-3049 or visit our website at www.simonspeakers.com.

Manufactured in the United States of America

1 3 5 7 9 10 8 6 4 2

Library of Congress Cataloging-in-Publication Data

Names: Clements, Oliver, 1972– author.
Title: The queen's men / by Oliver Clements.
Description: First Leopoldo & Co/Atria Books hardcover edition. | New York
: Leopoldo & Co/Atria, 2021. | Series: Agents of the crown; vol 2
Identifiers: LCCN 2021002231 (print) | LCCN 2021002232 (ebook) |
ISBN 9781501154751 (hardcover) | ISBN 9781501154782 (paperback) |
ISBN 9781501154775 (ebook)
Subjects: LCSH: Elizabeth I, Queen of England, 1533–1603—Fiction. |
Dee, John, 1527–1608—Fiction. | Greek fire—Fiction. |
GSAFD: Biographical fiction. | Suspense fiction.
Classification: LCC PR6103.L448 Q44 2021 (print) |
LCC PR6103.L448 (ebook) | DDC 823/.92—dc23
LC record available at https://lccn.loc.gov/2021002231
LC ebook record available at https://lccn.loc.gov/2021002232

ISBN 978-1-5011-5475-1
ISBN 978-1-5011-5477-5 (ebook)

*To my sister Gwendollyn,
who keeps the lights buzzing,
the secrets silent,
and the dragons flying.*

*Hatfield House, Hertfordshire,
first week of November 1577*

The Great Comet is first glimpsed in the first week of November, in the twentieth year of the reign of Her Majesty, Queen Elizabeth of England. It is seen low in the sky above the western horizon and it is widely understood to signal the End of Days, a time when the Son of Man will come to sit in judgment on peoples of all nations, after which the seas will rise up, the sun will turn black, and molten fire will fall from the skies.

At Hatfield House in Hertfordshire, twenty miles north of London, the Queen already lies sick in her bed. She is sweating, her joints are aching, and her guts are coiled in knots. On hearing of the comet, she sends her physicians away and summons in their stead Dr. John Dee.

It is too late to send word today, though, and Her Majesty sleeps very badly that night, dreaming of boiling fire and screaming men, and when she wakes, she tells her lady of the bedchamber that she wishes to return to her palace at Whitehall, to be with her

Privy Councillors, and with her people of London, and to be close on hand when John Dee comes.

Her physicians and women advise against it, as does Sir John Jeffers, who is that day appointed her captain of the Yeomen of the Guard.

"The road is very bad," he tells Lettice Knollys, senior lady of the bedchamber, sent to communicate Her Majesty's wishes. "And the weather, too, and if Her Majesty is already ill . . ."

He trails off under Mistress Knollys's withering stare.

"Right," he says. "I will see to it."

So late in the morning of a filthy day of charcoal skies and teeming rain, he oversees the packing up of Her Majesty's immediate household, bringing with her only her most immediate necessities in five carriages—including the closestool carriage, for her relief en route—and they set out on the road eastward toward Waltham Cross, hoping to be in London before darkness truly falls.

But Jeffers is right: already at this time of year the road is dire, and a spring in the frame of the Queen's principal carriage breaks, and then a horse in the traps of her second carriage falls lame, so that must be left in Waltham Cross, and even before they reach the turn on the road south, just after noon, they have had to stop three times for Her Majesty to use her closestool carriage to void her bowels in comfort and privacy. Each time the convoy must stand waiting, eyes averted, while the Queen is guided from one carriage to the other, and there is much consternation as to which of her women Her Majesty is to have in her own carriage, and soon Jeffers hardly knows whether they are coming or going.

"We should have waited until tomorrow," his sergeant reminds him as they are forced to stop once more.

"Try telling Mistress Knollys that."

The afternoon turns toward evening, and as they approach the great forest south of Waltham, they find themselves stuck behind a farm cart piled high with filthy straw giving off a dense trail of steam.

"Only good for dressing soil, that," the sergeant says.

Jeffers shouts at the drayman to clear the road, and a bugle is sounded, but the hay cart is broad, and the road is narrow between the high banks of encroaching hornbeams. There's little the drayman can do but whip his animal harder.

The Queen's procession—now led by a humble cart—slows to a snail's pace and they travel for half a league or more like this until, at a dip in the land where the road enters a boggy stretch amid stands of tangled holly and bramble, the cart becomes stuck fast in glutinous mud, and the dray horse strains in vain to move it any farther.

"A turd in his teeth!" the coachman next to the Yeoman captain shouts.

Jeffers is just getting to his feet to do something—what he does not know—when two men hidden in the cart's straw throw off their cover and emerge like stinking ghouls. There is a moment when Jeffers stares, unable to believe it: they have arquebuses, and the steam rising from the hay was smoke from their lit match fuses. He lurches from the bench of the carriage just as the guns go off with two dull flashes and barks of powder burn. Jeffers leaps, and slams to the ground, just as the gun balls hammer into the face of the coachman who'd been sitting next to him, openmouthed. The man's head snaps back and he throws up his arms as he is flung from his seat.

Jeffers tries to rise up. But more shadows emerge from the trees above his head, at the side of the road, each with a burning fuse and an arquebus. Jeffers bellows incoherently and he tries to draw his sword. He struggles to get up the bank, slipping in the mud. He would throw himself in front of a gun for Her Majesty, but before he can move, a dozen flashes light up the canopy of leaves, and earsplitting thunder fills the air. Spikes of gray smoke stab out from the darkness, and ten or twelve holes are punched through the painted wooden panels of the Queen's carriage.

From their various perches on the other carriages, Her Majesty's Yeomen roar with rage and throw off their sodden cloaks. They drop to the ground to draw their swords, and as one they scramble up the steep banks of the roadside, but even before they reach the top, even before the gun smoke has roiled clear, the gunmen are gone, their weapons with them. They are like phantoms. John Jeffers leads the chase, blundering through the forest after them, stumbling on rough ground, whipped and snapped at by every kind of bough and branch. The gunmen have vanished silently into the darkness ahead, as if through witchcraft, leaving John Jeffers tangled in undergrowth, caught in thorns. He hears a strangled roar, of pure outraged pain and anger, and realizes it is coming from his own throat.

"Christ! Christ! Christ!" he bellows and he falls to his knees in the darkness. "Christ!"

He bangs his head on the earth.

"Christ!"

After a long while he stands. His men are gathered about, hands loose, swords drawn to no end. He hears his own heartbeat and their ragged breathing and the rain drumming on the leaves all about. None is even wounded save scratches across their faces. Jeffers has lost his hat. They are each stilled, staring, shocked by the calamity of what has befallen them.

It is the end of everything.

Jeffers gathers himself.

"Right," he says.

She might still be alive? The gunmen, they might have missed?

He takes a deep breath.

"Come on then."

And he leads the way back, his men falling into line behind in silence. It is like walking to the scaffold. Already he can hear weeping from the road ahead. A woman is wailing and the horses are snorting with fright. Over the sharp smell of burned powder comes something earthier, bloodier, something from the shambles.

"Get a lantern lit, for the love of God," he calls.

The women have the Queen's carriage door open. One of the women turns to him. It is Jane Frommond. One of the young ladies-in-waiting. Her palms are black with blood, and her dress soiled like a butcher's apron.

"She is wounded," she says. "A ball. In her shoulder. And also one in her stomach, thus."

She indicates her own belly. Jeffers's right hand twitches to cross itself. He fought Spain in the Low Countries. He has seen such wounds. He knows what they mean.

"We must find her a surgeon," another—Mary Sidney—says. "Get her to London."

The best course would be to make her comfortable, Jeffers thinks, to sit with her and hold her through this next hour, which will prove her last.

But they cannot be seen to just let this happen. They must be seen to be busy. So . . .

"Yes," he defers.

He orders his men to clear the hay cart from the road and sends a rider ahead, one of the boys from the back, on the best horse, to alert the Queen's household, to summon the Queen's surgeons, the Queen's chaplain, and the Queen's Privy Council, including, and most especially of all, Master Francis Walsingham.

CHAPTER ONE

Whitehall Palace, London,
same evening, first week of November 1577

S ir William Cecil, First Baron Burghley, stands in the darkness, in the middle of the great courtyard of Whitehall Palace, next to Sir Christopher Hatton, whom the Queen has recently appointed member of the Privy Council purely because—Cecil coined the rumor—he is an uncommonly graceful dancer. They are looking up at the Great Comet in the night's sky.

"There," he says. "Do you not see, Sir Christopher? Its tail points to the Low Countries."

Cecil is half joking, extending a hand of friendship to patch up what has been a bitter few months of rancorous factionalism in the Privy Council, with two parties opposed to each other on the matter of sending troops to help the Dutch Protestant armies against the Spanish and Catholic Dutch. Cecil had hoped the argument was ended, this last week, when the Queen at last made up her mind in favor of sending troops, deciding in favor of the faction led by Cecil and Walsingham, and against the faction led by Hatton. But Hatton is obviously not yet ready to accept defeat, nor the proffered hand.

"That might mean anything," he scoffs.

"No," Cecil tells him. "It means good Protestant Englishmen will soon be coming to the aid of their Dutch cousins, and that together we will drive Spain back within her own borders and, God willing, strike such a blow as will rid Christendom of popish superstition for all time."

He, again, is only half joking.

"I still believe it is a grave mistake," Hatton says, seriously. "We should not even be sending them money, let alone troops. It will deplete our treasury, and our numbers, and it will unite France and Spain against us. More than that, also, it gives succor to any subject who rises up against his rightful king. Her Majesty is sowing the wind, and she shall reap the whirlwind."

Cecil sighs.

"We've been hearing that same old refrain for years now," he reminds Hatton. "The simple fact is that if we let the Spanish crush the Dutch, they will. And then they will turn to us and crush us. There will be fighting, I know, and it will cost gold, and blood, but so much less if it is done now, and in the Low Countries, and mostly by Dutchmen. Spend now, save later. I am glad the Queen has finally seen sense."

Hatton blows out air.

"Twenty thousand pounds? Ten thousand men? It is the thin end of the wedge, Lord Treasurer."

Cecil knows Hatton hardly cares about the money. It is the old religion he hankers after. A return to Rome. And that is really why the Queen appointed him to the Privy Council: not because he has a well-turned calf, though he does that, but because she is naturally cautious in these affairs—or is too aware of the risks they involve—and Hatton is there to serve as a bulwark against Master Walsingham's zeal.

"Well," Cecil tells him, "it is done now in any event."

"We shall see," Hatton says. "There is many a slip between cup and lip."

Cecil wheels on him, suddenly furious. This argument has been had! It has been lost and won and now there is nothing more to be said.

"What do you mean by that, Hatton?"

Hatton is taller and younger, and infinitely more agile, but Cecil is Sir William Cecil, Lord Burghley, Lord Treasurer of England. And two Yeomen of the Guard are never more than ten paces from his side.

"Nothing," Hatton says, backing away. "Nothing, I do assure you."

Cecil growls and pulls his furs tight about his shoulders. He wonders at his sudden flare of anger. Perhaps because he knows Hatton is partly right? At the beginning, five years ago now, when the Protestant Dutch provinces first rose up against their Spanish Catholic king, the Dutch looked to the English for help—for money, or troops, or ships at least—but Her Majesty was too conscious of the divine right of a king over his subjects and was too afeared of offending the Spanish, and so she dithered, and it has taken Cecil and Walsingham five years to persuade her to help the Dutch, and though she now sees sense, there is no telling what she will feel next week. Or the week after that. And even if she stays her course, will the promise of money be enough to keep the fragile Dutch alliance together? The so-called Pacification of Ghent? If the northern Calvinists under William of Orange gain too much head, the southern Catholic states under Philippe de Croÿ will almost certainly revert to

King Philip of Spain, and then England is back to where she was, only having spent twenty thousand pounds and lost ten thousand English lives.

Until then, though, Cecil is content, and is wondering about returning home, since there seems nothing afoot that cannot wait until the morrow, when he hears bells tolling in the city.

"What in Christ's name is that? Fire?"

A moment later, Sir John Jeffers's boy—filthy, stinking, and tearful—is marched into the courtyard and brought before them.

"How now, boy, what is this?"

At the news, they retire at once, utterly incredulous, utterly dismayed, to the Privy Chamber where they question the boy, who stands almost incoherent and hoarse from shouting out the news as he rode through the city that the Queen is dead.

"You did not see her wounds?" Hatton asks.

The boy shakes his head.

"Captain Jeffers sent me here straight off, soon as it happened. Tell them she has been shot, he said. In her belly. By a dozen men with guns, in Waltham Forest. I saw the carriage. Full of holes, it was, sir, like a strainer. And her women were weeping and pulling their hair, and Mistress Frommond was with blood all on her hands."

He holds out his own to show them his leather-stained palms as if they were hers. His eyes are bright, as if he were mad, and he has lost his cap.

"But she was not dead when you left to ride here?" Hatton asks.

"I was not going to tarry till she was, was I?"

"Fair enough," Cecil supposes. He thanks the boy and sends him to the kitchens.

"Only do not dismay the cooks," he tells him. "We are in for a long night and shall have need of their services."

Then he sends for the Queen's surgeons and her physicians to be roused, and for messengers to ride for Robert Dudley, Earl of Leicester, and for Master Walsingham, also. He sends for more candles, and a fire to be lit. Finally, he sends for the casket to be brought up from the vaults below, and then he sits at the board and is still for a moment, save for his fingers that drum a rhythm from his childhood.

"Dear God," he says, more to himself than Hatton. "Dear bloody God. What now?"

Hatton says nothing. He paces like a cat in the shadows. Cecil can imagine his tail twitching. A moment later, a steward returns to usher in two footmen, carrying between them the casket Cecil ordered. They place it on the table and step back and set about lighting the fire and the candles. Cecil remains staring at the casket for a long moment.

He knows he should fish out that key from his doublet and start summoning all the messengers he will need to promulgate the news, to send out the letters contained therein: to George Talbot in his castle in Sheffield to alert him to post a heavier guard on Mary, Queen of Scots, who must be the likely focus of this plot to kill Queen Elizabeth, and probably at the heart of whatever comes next. He should send word to the Lord Warden of the Cinque Ports, and to Edward Clinton, Lord High Admiral of the fleet in the Narrow Sea, to warn them to expect an attack from Spain at any moment. Likewise to the governor of Berwick Castle that he must anticipate some incursion from Scotland. He should be mustering the city's militia and warning the Constable of the Tower to ready his keep for the arrival of a court without its Queen.

It is what they have planned to do, but really, now that it has happened, what is the good of all that?

Nothing.

It is useless.

Elizabeth Tudor is dead. Long live Mary Stuart.

Cecil continues to stare in silence at the casket on which the dust lies so thick it forms a wrinkled cloth, like fine felt. He cannot believe it. He cannot believe she is dead. Elizabeth, the Queen, who has been through so much and who meant so much to so many. The Queen in whom all their hopes reposed.

My God.

It is no surprise, of course. It has been long threatened, long expected, even, but however hard he has tried to imagine it over the years—and planned for it, as they all have—he has never grasped until now how it would feel. Even when she was stricken with smallpox back in 1562, he did not think she would actually, genuinely, *die*. After all she'd been through, the dangers she had weathered, when all around there were men desperate to kill her, it seemed too much an affront then, for her to go by her own bodily weakness.

Opposite him Hatton now sits in silence, waiting. There is a rumor—reliable, according to Walsingham, though denied by Hatton—that Hatton has promised Mary of Scotland that should Elizabeth of England die without heir, then he himself will be the first to come north to collect her; and that he will lead her south, carrying her Sword of State upright before him, into London and onto her throne of England.

And yet still he sits, with his long nose, and his sculpted beard, and his velvet cap with its band of gold-foiled pearls and pert white feather. There is cloth of gold, too, threading through the dark stuff of his doublet that catches the candlelight quite beautifully, and though he cannot be blamed for wearing such a thing on a night like this—for how could he have known what might happen?—nevertheless, Cecil does blame him.

He leans forward.

"Sir Christopher," he says, "is there not somewhere you need to be?"

Hatton looks at him defiantly.

"No, my lord."

Cecil sits back, satisfied he has caused offense.

"My Lord of Leicester should be with us shortly," Cecil tells him. "And Master Walsingham."

Hatton clicks his tongue against his teeth.

"Good. Perhaps Master Walsingham will be able to enlighten us as to how this can have been allowed to happen? All his devilish plotting and planning, his placemen in every great household in the land, his breaking of seals and meddling in other princes' affairs, and all for what? Naught!"

"But it is not such a disaster for you, is it, Sir Christopher?" Cecil goads. "Your only regret can be that you will not be afforded the chance to twirl and jig at the masque to mark Her Majesty's birthday, will you? Or perhaps you have in mind a different sort of dance—of a horizontal nature—with the new queen? Is that it?"

To his credit, Hatton appears genuinely startled by Cecil's suggestion.

"M-m-y Lord Burghley," he stammers. "I am . . . my objection to helping the Hollanders is not so . . . I would never countenance . . . Her Majesty's life . . . You accuse me of—"

Hatton is so shocked that he cannot form the words. Nor can he be sure of what exactly Cecil is accusing him. Nor, in truth, is Cecil, exactly, but he feels he has suffered a great wrong—*England* has suffered a great wrong—and that because of this infamous night, a woman is dead, and Cecil's lifework is in ruins. And there, on the other side of the table, with a handsome beard, gold-foiled pearls, and gold thread in his doublet, sits the man in whose favor the wind suddenly seems to be blowing.

Mortlake, west of London,
same evening, first week of November 1577

Dr. John Dee stands in his orchard with his friend and neighbor Thomas Digges, spyglass pressed to his eye, watching the fiery orb of red with its long, blazing tail of furious white.

"Whatever can it mean, sir?" Thomas Digges asks.

Dee does not take his eye from the glass.

"Perhaps, Thomas," he says, "one of its first tasks is to signal that since we have known each other for twenty years or more, and I count you as my friend and believe you to consider me likewise, it is time you called me by my Christian name?"

Digges thinks about this for a moment.

"Would the heavens expend such power on such a trifle, do you suppose?"

Dee lowers the glass to look at Digges.

"Now that is an interesting question, Thomas. How much power might it cost God to send a comet such as this? If He has infinite power—and He does—then might He not send any number of these comets, to remind mankind of any number of trifling things: to turn our shoes over at night so that the darkness does not pool within; to shut up our geese, too, less they fall prey to the fox; to—"

"—to pay the bookseller what he is owed," Digges interrupts, "so that he need have no recourse to the services of bailiffs?"

"Yes, that, too," Dee agrees. "But He doesn't do so, does He?"

"But if He did?"

"Then I would, of course, remember to pay the bookseller so that He need have no recourse to . . . to all the rest of it."

Dee passes Digges back the spyglass, and they are comfortably silent awhile, each tied up in his own thoughts. After a moment, Digges speaks, more serious this time.

"What do you think it really portends, John? Is it the End of Times, as Luther predicts?"

Dee exhales. Luther has made much of the coming of the end of the world. They all have, those Germans. It is as if they have a taste for it: fire, brimstone, sudden violent death. *Odd*, he thinks.

"Perhaps, perhaps," he says. "And look; its tail points eastward, toward the Low Countries."

Digges waits.

Dee goes on: "Johannes Trithemius reminds us that the angelic spirits rule the planets each for a period of 354 years, and it may be that this comet signals the end of one period and the beginning of another. So it may not signal the End Times such as Luther imagined, but the beginning of a new order, overseen by a virtuous angel. It may be that the world is set to become unified spiritually, and politically, under one Last Ruler. A time when all sins are wiped away, and we return to a state of purity such as we have not seen since Adam first ate of the forbidden fruit."

He is being optimistic. Digges is not: "But was a comet not also seen in the year of the Battle of Hastings?"

Digges refers to the comet seen above England in the year 1066, which presaged the death in battle of the last English king, Harold, and arrival on the throne of the French conqueror, William. Immediately the atmosphere clenches. Both men think of the throne's current incumbent: Queen Elizabeth, life and limb already threatened on all sides, and how she must feel seeing such a sign.

"Will you go to her?" Digges asks. "Go to Her Majesty?"

Dee has been wondering the same thing since he first saw the comet. He cannot for a moment believe that she is not studying it this very moment, just as he is—though in greater comfort perhaps, wrapped in sable, without the odorous Thames lapping at her toe caps—and he cannot for a moment believe she is not thinking of him, just as he thinks of her.

"If she calls for me, I will go, of course," Dee says, without needing to add the "but."

Digges says nothing. Dee passes him back his spyglass and the young man puts it to his eye.

"Or it might just as easily portend some great discovery," Dee goes on, trying to sound ever more hopeful. "Some treasure, perhaps? Or even, God willing, the end to our Great Work, the thing what we have been seeking all these years."

Digges lowers the glass.

"You mean the ore that Frobisher has brought?"

"Well, yes, that, too," Dee says, having forgotten the ore—nearly two hundred tons of it—which the admiral has brought back from the New World, from a sample of which Dee has had his alchemical assistant, Roger Cooke, try—with no joy, alas, yet—to extract gold.

"But I was thinking of something even closer to home."

He means, of course, the *lapis philosophorum*, the philosophers' stone.

Digges draws breath.

"Are you that near?"

"I am this close!" Dee laughs. "One more distillation, perhaps."

By which he really means ten times ten times ten. Digges is almost distracted from the comet by the news.

"But John," he says. "That is marvelous news! Congratulations, my friend! You will never need worry about booksellers' bills again!"

Dee smiles. Should it be so surprising, he wonders, that a man so interested in spyglasses should also seek to reduce the mighty to a trifle?

"The gold would be useful," Dee admits, "but it is the elixir of life, of eternality, that would be my chief delight."

Just then there comes a shout from the river. A barge.

"Who can that be at this time of night?" Digges wonders.

CHAPTER TWO

Whitehall Palace, London,
same evening, November 1577

The Queen's carriage has not yet reached Whitehall by the time Master Francis Walsingham, Her Majesty's principal private secretary, and his own private secretary, Robert Beale, are escorted into the Privy Chamber by four grim-faced Yeomen. Cecil and Hatton sit opposite each other at the end of the table in a pool of candlelight, and the atmosphere is sour.

"At last," Cecil says, lumbering to his feet. He comes to embrace Walsingham, and although he's a fat man with short arms, his fur-fronted grip is comforting, and at this moment, Walsingham needs comfort.

"God keep you, Francis," Cecil says. "Christ. God keep us all, for I fear we will have need of His grace soon enough."

"So it is true?" he asks quietly. Cecil nods. Walsingham steals a glance at Hatton, who sits in silence, face turned away.

"She is not yet brought in, but we have spoken to the boy. She is shot here and here."

He indicates.

"Enough to satisfy us only a miracle will save her."

Christ.

Hatton still does not so much as even look at Walsingham.

"Sir Christopher," Walsingham greets him. "God give you good evening. I am surprised you are not on your way to Sheffield Castle?"

It was Walsingham who discovered Hatton had been to see Mary, Queen of Scots, when she was in Tutbury. They had been permitted a private audience, Hatton's servant of the body later reported, two days after which Hatton sent out for an apothecary to come and dress his buttocks with certain salves, for his skin was much torn, "like he was one of them flagellants." Hatton has never, as far as Walsingham has yet been able to discover, been back to Tutbury, but that is only as far as he knows. Walsingham has, though, with his own eyes read Hatton's follow-up letter to Mary, pledging to be the first to be by her side, should Queen Elizabeth's last day dawn. Every man must live with one eye on the future, of course—there is no harm in that—but it has always puzzled Walsingham why Hatton thought Elizabeth might predecease Mary, given that they were roughly similar in age. Unless he knew something?

Only now does Hatton turn on him, furious.

"God damn it, Master Walsingham," he spits, "how could you let this happen? You are supposed to be a mole catcher! You are supposed to catch the bloody things before they come up! With your traps and your intrigues; your spies and your piss-sniffing seal breakers! But they have all been for nothing, haven't they? And by Christ so have you. All for nothing."

Walsingham sits.

"You wax passionate, Hatton," he says, "for someone who has conspired at this eventuality."

Now Hatton bolts to his feet. The stool falls back behind him. His fists bunch on the table.

"It is *Sir Christopher* Hatton to you, *Master* Walsingham!" he shouts. "And how dare you! How dare you accuse me of such a thing! I have never conspired at anything of the sort."

"You've envisaged it then. Go on, admit it, why don't you?"

"There is no one more loyal to the Queen than I. No one."

"Which Queen, though?" Walsingham counters. It is easy enough, he supposes, and if Hatton and Queen Mary have already come to an arrangement, then this evening might well be Walsingham's last chance to land such a cheap blow.

Cecil coughs.

"This is to little profit, gentlemen," he says. "We need to find what has happened, why it has happened, and now what to do about it."

"Ask him how it happened! Ask him why it happened!" This is from Hatton.

Walsingham opens his mouth to ask Cecil to ask Hatton why it happened, but Cecil's glare silences him. Besides, with a terrible lurch, Walsingham realizes that Hatton is right: he—Walsingham—has failed. He places his hands on the table before him. They feel like someone else's, those of a dead man. Perhaps they are?

"Do you know anything about it yet, Master Secretary?" Cecil asks. "On whose orders the murder is committed? On whose design the deed is done?"

And for the first time in many years as Her Majesty's spymaster, Walsingham has to admit he has no clue, and the realization makes him reel. He is nauseated, dizzy. He feels his guts turn, and vinegar sweat beads his brow.

"No," he says.

"No?" Cecil is incredulous. "*Nothing?*"

He shakes his head minutely. If he opens his mouth he will burp vomit onto the table.

Hatton half sighs, half laughs.

"By Christ," he says. "What have you been *doing*?"

Walsingham holds steady. Hatton is wrong to call him a mole catcher. He is a spider. He is a spider who has on Her Majesty's behalf spent thousands of his own pounds and many years laying over the land a web of gossamer, woven of many hundreds of strands of communication, between many hundreds of men and women, high and low, near and far, so that there is not a stirring in the realm that goes undetected, not a turning the tremors of which do not reach his office.

He knows everything.

Or so he thought.

Now he knows he does not.

And, by Christ, what else does he not know?

But now here is Cecil looking at him as if he hardly knows him. Cecil! Cecil who has relied on him as a cripple relies on his crutch. And Hatton, Hatton who comes to court to turn his *gavottes*, his *sarabandes*, his *saltarellos*; Hatton who eats sugar-crusted almonds and drinks Rhennish wine from silver cups while watching fresh-writ masques in the palace gardens at Greenwich; Hatton who strolls in shady bowers and sings songs of thwarted love while the Queen plucks plangently at her lute.

And meanwhile there are other men on the road in all weathers, in all seasons, in linen that at day's end must needs be peeled from saddle sores, and only so that they may work through the night so as to be back on the road again at dawn. There are other men who have to order disembowelings and beheadings; ligaments to be pulled and bones to be crushed. There are other men whose nights are racked by foul dreams, who wake half drowned in their own sweat. There are other men who have kidney stones, who walk with limps, who have gone nearly half-blind for the years they have spent poring over inky scribbles in bad light. There are other men such as Master Francis Walsingham.

And now they look to him to ask: *What have you done?*

"Failing, that is what you have been doing, Master Walsingham," Hatton continues on. "You've failed in your primary duty, which was to keep the Queen alive. And in failing her, you have failed the country; you have failed the reformed religion of which you claim to be so attached; and you have failed us. The only satisfaction to be gained from this is that you have also, and most crucially, failed yourself. Failed yourselves."

He includes Cecil in this, and Walsingham sees the temper of the room has changed. Hatton himself seems to puff up in size, like a gold-threaded toad, as if he is attracting all the power from Cecil and Walsingham. He wishes Dudley would arrive now, wearing some yet finer golden thread in his own doublet.

"Do you think Mary Stewart will thank any of you for all your hard work these last few years, keeping her under lock and key?" Hatton presses on, stating what is already all too well known. "Do you think she will forget the indignities and cruelties and even deaths you have inflicted on those who supported her and her cause while she waited to take her rightful place on the throne? Or do you suppose, either of you, that perhaps, instead, she will want your heads on spikes?"

It is strange, Walsingham thinks, that we who tried so hard to save Queen Elizabeth's life, in every way possible; we who upheld the law; we who upheld order: we will be the ones who will pay the price for her death, while those men—those wayside assassins—will soon be raised up to every honor. The only scrap of satisfaction he can cling to is that in having her cousin murdered, Queen Mary has opened a personal, private Pandora's box. When she is crowned queen, every Protestant in the land will wish her dead, and be licensed, by example, to see to it that so she becomes. Then he thinks: Ah, no. Mary will not reward the men who murdered her cousin. She will distance herself from them, publicly regret their actions, while reaping their reward, and she will probably have their necks stretched. At least, that is what he would do. Before moving on to settling scores with those loyal to Elizabeth.

But Hatton is still talking.

"And so the first thing we must do is bring Queen Mary down from Sheffield or from wherever you have her imprisoned, in state, with all the honor due the rightful Queen of England."

It is galling to see that Hatton has moved from low to high, from weak to strong, thanks to just one, albeit painful, afternoon spent with the Queen of Scots, and the promise that might have seemed rash at the time—or might have been given to facilitate his own escape—but now appears to be standing him in good stead.

"And then," he goes on, "we will begin the great and lengthy task of returning the country to the *status quo ante*, of returning the country to the true religion, to Rome, and of undoing all the damage done by the House of Tudor's flirtation with the so-called reformed religion."

Cecil's ordinarily plump and ruddy face has slumped on the bones of his skull, and his flesh looks like an old wall hanging: dusty, faded, and pocked with the depredations of moth.

"Well," he supposes, "we always knew it would happen one day, that we would be made to pack our bags."

"Bags?" Hatton laughs. "Bags? That doesn't begin to cut it. You will have to pack more than that. You will have to pack away your lives! Each one of you! And all your dark-cloaked espials and your foul, slinking intelligencers! Every grubby placeman on your Judas payroll! Because I tell you now that the revenge of the men whom you've oppressed and wronged, twisted, tortured, and killed these past years will be truly magnificent!"

Walsingham must get home, he thinks, back to the Papey. He must destroy all trace of the network he has spent ten years creating. He must above all destroy that ledger of names of his secret service: Drake; Raleigh; Marlowe; Frobisher; even John Dee. If those names should fall into the hands of Mary's agents, or even, God forbid, the Inquisition, then even the most awful days of the first Queen Mary's reign—when the very air of London bloomed savory with the taste of cooked meat, and Smithfield was spotted black with rings of fatty ash that dogs licked by night—that will come to seem like a day in May.

Cecil still looks gray, but not as gray as Walsingham feels. Has he any contingency plans? Walsingham wonders. A bag of gold under his bed? *I bet he has*, Walsingham thinks. *I bet he has a house in the Poitou perhaps: from the time of old King Harry's wars, encircled by a wall three-foot-thick, with a fish-stocked moat; and deep vaults stuffed with enough powder and shot, and that German wine he likes, to last him a year.* He imagines sacks of dried peas hanging from the rafters, along with smoked meats, and sausages.

Christ.

And what of him? What of Francis Walsingham? He has been one of the eleven thousand foolish virgins, he knows now. While others were feathering alternative nests, he was burning through his stock of candles on the Queen's behalf, never sparing a thought for himself or his family. He manages a rueful inner smile. One thing to be grateful for: he has run up so much debt on the Queen's account, paying his intelligencers and smoothing ways in foreign courts, that he is left with nothing a new regime might usefully take from him.

Save his life, of course, and the lives of his family.

River Thames, London,
same evening, first week of November 1577

Dee sits in the thwart of the barge, boat cloak on his shoulders, shirt collar untied, and takes the bottle he is passed.

"God's blood, John, what a thing. What a thing."

It is Robert Dudley, first Earl of Leicester, who has passed him the bottle that by now, as they approach Whitehall, is only a third full. "Did you predict this? Did you see it in the stars? Is this what that bloody thing means?"

He gestures in the lamplight toward the stern of his barge, beyond which—though how far beyond? That is a question, though for another time—the Great Comet hangs in the night sky, strangely cold, almost impersonal, and for a moment, Dee imagines it taking pleasure in the catastrophe it has wrought.

"I'd've hoped for a bit more notice, wouldn't you, John?" Dudley continues, shouting now as if to include the comet into their conversation. "A bit of consideration, given everything. I mean, I appreciate it; you're a star, or comet, but God damn it, she was a Queen! She was *our* Queen!"

Dudley takes the bottle back before Dee has had a drink.

"It is not that," Dee says.

"What?"

"Forgive me, Robert. I . . . I do not think the comet has anything to do with Bess's death."

"Don't call her that, John. Don't call her that."

Dee says nothing. After a while Dudley turns to him.

"You cast her chart, once, didn't you?"

Again, still, Dee says nothing.

"Did it say she would be shot dead in carriage? In Waltham Forest? In Waltham bloody Forest? Answer me. Dee! Did it say that?"

"Of course not. Also, such charts, as you surely know, do not work like that."

"Why not? Why don't they work like that? I think they do. You go to anyone else who knows anything about charts—that French man, what is his name, with his stone?"

"Nostradamus."

"Him. You go to him and pay him thirty livres and he will tell you exactly what you can expect. If the Queen had consulted him, he'd've told her—I don't know—not to take a carriage this day, lest some goddamned Catholic shooting party blast her to pieces with iron balls."

"Even supposing he could foresee that, which he could not," Dee says, "he'd not tell her it was so, because he would want it to be so."

"There you are. That is my point."

"Also, he is dead."

Dee is grateful that Dudley pulled his barge into the river's bank to see if Dee had heard the news, and to offer him a ride downriver if needed.

"Decisions need be made, John," he'd said, and Dee supposed this would have to be the same in every household in the land. With Queen Elizabeth gone, and another Queen Mary to come, perhaps it was time to dust off the crucifixes? Dig out the old prayer book and slide the new one into the flames?

Next to him, Dudley takes another drink.

"The thing about you, John, do you know? What it is?"

"No."

"Shall I tell you?"

"No."

"The thing about you, John, is that you don't give people what they want. You cast a chart, and you miss the fact that the person who is paying you to cast their chart is going to be shot dead in the week following All Saints, aged—I don't know. Do you see what I mean? Such a thing—a man, or a woman's, death—is a big deal. To them. Maybe not to you. But to them. It is what they want to know. And you do not tell them, do you?"

Dee wishes Dudley would shut up.

"So, do you see why someone might not wish to pay you? Or appoint you, say, royal astrologer?"

"Please," Dee begins. He does not want to go over this again.

"It is like your alchemy," Dudley rolls on. "You are—there is no doubt—the cleverest man alive. You know everything. And yet the Queen gives all her money not to you, but to some dwarfish little Dutchman, a known and blatant swindler. What was his name?"

"Cornelius de Lannoy."

"That is him. That was him. And do you know why she does that?"

God. Another time and he would be interested to hear Dudley's insight into that little puzzle.

"It is because he—that Dutch dwarf—said 'I can make you thirty-three thousand pounds' worth of gold. And I can do that every year. Year on year.' So she gave him everything he wanted! She gave him Somerset House and a pension of a hundred and twenty pounds a year! She gave him a house in the country and all the alembics and pelicans and Dutch glass and so on that a man could ever need."

"But he produced nothing!" Dee reacts. "They put him in the Tower!"

"That's right! But do you know *why* they put him in the Tower? It was Cecil. Cecil put him in the Tower not because they thought he was gulling them over his ability to make gold. They put him there because they thought he was *stealing* all the gold he was making! They thought he was making over eight hundred thousand pounds a year! They believed him, you see? Because he told them what they wanted to hear."

"Christ, Robert, this is not the time—"

"But what do you do when someone asks you to make gold?"

Dee sighs.

"It is not that simple," he says.

Dudley laughs.

"Exactly! You witter on about angels, and the kabbalah, and the True Elixir, and you talk about hidden languages and you will tell them that one plus two plus three plus four equals ten, as if that were something special, rather than mere coincidence, but do you know what? All anyone really wants is a practical, practicing magician."

"Whitehall coming up, my lord," the bargemaster calls.

Thank God, Dee thinks.

Dudley flings the bottle over the gunwale.

"Sorry, John. I do not know what has got into me. I just wanted you to know. I wanted to be honest. So that you know why she did not . . . make your life any easier. But she loved you, John. That is what I mean to say. She loved you almost best of all. Of us all I mean. Of course, it could never be. You know that. She knew that. You are a commoner, and by Christ, look at you, you dress like a bag of shit, but she . . . she always said, 'Where is my John Dee? He will know. He knows everything. He is my eyes.' I envied you. We all did. You spent all that time with her. In the Tower. You were fellow inmates! You were granted the liberty to take to the leads of the Bell Tower, and she— Well . . . They can't take that away from you!"

Dee does not remind Dudley that he, too, was in the Tower at the time. Though he was probably too distracted to follow Dee's early thoughts on the monad hieroglyph, or in fact pay much attention to Lady Elizabeth as she was then, for at the time Robert's father and his brother were about to have their heads chopped off, which preoccupies a man, and also he was desperate to avoid sharing their fate.

Instead, Dee thinks back to that time, those months, some years ago now, when he was appointed tutor to the girl who would one day, against many expectations, go on to become Queen of England. By Christ, she had been bright! Flame haired, and fierce, pursuing all avenues of inquiry, chasing down information, knowledge, wisdom, and insight as if she were a hawk after a plover. He had hardly had to teach her a thing, only point her in the right direction, and she was off. They had spent happy months, side by side, heads craned over books, lapping it up.

It had ended, of course, as these things always do. Well, not always. They do not *always* end in arrest, or at least not for casting horoscopes. She was eighteen at the time, six years his junior, and old enough to be the mistress of her own home, and perhaps she would have been, had the planets not pulled her in another direction.

"And then do you remember the time you saved her life?" Dudley goes on. "On her barge off Limehouse? While I was ill. And then—afterward, she spoke to Walsingham. He was to take care of you, she said, forever, but not—maybe not in the way that you would have wished. He was to— Oh I don't know. A secret service or something. You know what Walsingham is like. You talk to him about it. Christ, John, what is to become of us? What do the stars say about that? About us?"

Dee thinks he will have to remember all this later, pick it apart. Try to make sense of it. But Dudley is babbling. He is drifting from one sentiment to the next. The boat nudges the jetty and he staggers. Dee catches him.

"Where's that bottle. Christ. Did I throw it over?"

"It was empty anyway."

He helps Dudley up onto the gangplank where Dudley remains unsteady on his feet.

"River legs," he says.

He smells very headily of ambergris and alcohol and fresh sweat, but he is not as drunk as he appears.

"Come," he says. "Let's find Cecil. Walsingham. See what in the name of God they have to say about all this."

The Yeomen of the Guard all recognize Dudley and stand aside to let him roar past, Dee in his wake.

"Where is Cecil?" he keeps shouting. "Where is Walsingham?"

When they are shown into the Privy Chamber, Sir Christopher

Hatton is on his feet, haranguing Walsingham for forgetting to call him by his title.

"Give me my honor, Master Walsingham!"

Walsingham is rolling his eyes, but there has been some curious shift in the power, Dee sees. Then he remembers what Walsingham has been keen for all to know: about Hatton and Mary, Queen of Scots. He feels a further descent into horror. If Hatton is risen up, then it must be true. Elizabeth must be dead.

"What is he doing here?" Hatton demands of Dudley, pointing at Dee, who is not sworn in as a Privy Councillor.

"What are you doing here?" Dudley snaps back. "Still?"

"W-w-what the devil does that mean, Dudley?" Hatton stammers. "I am sworn in as a Privy Councillor."

"Yes, yes, of course you are. Just . . . whose? I wonder."

Across the table, Walsingham smiles. Does everybody know of Hatton's tryst with the Queen of Scots?

But Hatton laughs, too.

"There's no haste," he says. "I am enjoying this."

Dee hears them bickering, but he is hardly listening. He stands at the far end of the table, and though the light of the candles on the polished surface of the table is not bright, or especially distinctive, within it he feels something extra, some communication. He endeavors to be ever open to such things, to be constantly aware of the possibility of angelic communication at any and all times. It is only a matter of grasp, he oftentimes thinks, and then of interpretation, and of understanding the language in which the archangel chooses to communicate.

Dee feels unnaturally warm, and he believes that for the first time in his life, he is receiving messages from what can only be the angelic sphere. It is as if the burnished table were become a scrying stone, and Dee's senses are jangling, as if being roughened by a teasel. Until this moment he has always believed himself in need of an interpolator, someone to relay the angelic communication to him before he would be able to make sense of it, but now the table is concentrating the rays emanating from the angelic sphere and reflecting them back at him. Perhaps this will only ever happen in this time of extreme, cosmic crisis, and when the veil between the living and the dead is at its thinnest, around All Hallows, and when a comet appears, and when the soul of an anointed queen passes from one sphere to another, but now he seems closer than ever to gaining some understanding of the celestial emanations, which seem to be guiding his voice.

"No," he says.

The men stop their arguing for a moment and turn to him. He does not know what he has said, or if he is going to say anything more, or what that will be if he says it. It is as if some other power has taken his tongue, and his body is its instrument. His blood is like warm honey, his body strumming. He is suffused with light.

"What?" Dudley asks.

"No," he repeats. "She is not with them. She is not with the angels. Saint Michael. He— She is—"

He stops. His body cools. The light has gone. He is abandoned, bereft.

"Christ," Hatton says. "What is that fool talking about?"

The others watch Dee closely, waiting for him to continue.

But he is lost for words.

He could weep.

But then, from a distant part of the palace, some disturbance, and the movement of many feet, and the banging of doors, and then voices, urgent, strident. The men in the Privy Chamber turn to the door as the noise swells. It is like the ocean against a pebbled beach. It fills Dee's ears.

They stand as the door is thrown open and light spills in and the room is suddenly heaving with men, ruddy-faced and stinking of wet wool, horse, and sodden leather, who fill the space, burly in their breastplates, helmets, boots, and weaponry, and for a moment Dee believes they must be Elizabeth's murderers, come to complete the task of their assassination. But the atmosphere is all wrong, and after a moment they step back and there, at their heart, like a pearl revealed, stands none other than the person of the Queen herself: whole and unblemished, though her face is winnowed by care, and with illness, and exhaustion, but she is upright. She is alive.

"Your Majesty!" It is Cecil who speaks. Her chief treasurer.

"We thought you dead!" Walsingham almost shouts.

"Bess," Dee says.

Though tired and much shaken, the Queen shoots Dee a weary, warning look, but her attention is taken up by Dudley, who has fallen to his knees, and is shuffling toward Her Majesty, his arms outstretched, suddenly so violently incoherent he cannot say her name properly.

"Litsh," he says. "Lssss."

The Queen and her woman—is it Lettice Knollys?—step back. They look at him with a species of horror. Is he really intending to wrap his arms about her hips and press his face to her belly? She turns, and the men and women behind her part to let her escape the clutches of this drunk madman, and she retires, to her bedchamber, leaving Dudley on his knees and the room none the wiser.

"What in the name of God is all this?" Hatton demands of Sir

John Jeffers, who has pushed his way into the room as if he belongs therein.

"They shot at the wrong carriage," he says, almost mad with relief. "The Queen was traveling in her closestool carriage! She has the flux! The shits!"

CHAPTER THREE

The church bells peal from first light while the city celebrates in confused relief, and in the Privy Chamber of Whitehall Palace Her Majesty's councillors regather again, now in the gray light of dawn, to commence the inquest. The colored panes of the window lend Dudley's baggy skin a greenish tinge, and he sits with his eyes shut, sweating. Next to him Cecil is washed at least and appears the freshest of the four, juggling various tubes of paper with the disingenuous self-absorption of a man who has been let off a very big hook. Walsingham takes the seat next to him. He feels more than ordinarily fragile, as if he has fallen from a horse. His teeth pain him grievously, and his joints ache, and he cannot seem to think straight either. Like Cecil, he finds himself arranging and rearranging his papers on the table. Still, however bad he feels, he is instantly cheered by the thought of how bad Sir Christopher Hatton must feel, sitting isolated at the other end of

35

the table, his eyes fixed on the cloth, utterly abashed by last night's reversal.

Robert Beale is there, too, Walsingham's private secretary, but he is much vexed this morning because despite his best efforts to persuade the Privy Council the night before, the chance was missed to keep back the news that the Queen was saved and so observe how the plot was intended to develop.

"Had we stifled the news of her survival then whoever was behind the attempt would have shown their hand. We could have caught it, gripped it, and traced it back to the heart, to the brain!"

He is right, of course; Walsingham knows that. They all do. They are each of them much chastened by the events of the previous night, Walsingham because in the face of learning just how much he stood to lose had the Queen died, he panicked, and seemed to forgo all sense. Only Beale, relatively junior, with much less at stake, had kept his head.

"An opportunity has been missed," Walsingham now admits.

"Instead we must now . . . what? How do we even start after the scent of this plot? Now it is over and its participants have vanished into the night."

"This morning we have put out urgent word among every intelligencer in our pay among the papists we are aware of," Walsingham tells them, "and alerted those charged with watching Mary of Scotland for any unusual activity that might connect her to the gunmen.

"We've sent men up to question all the sheriffs, constables, beadles, night watchmen of both counties, and we will comb the same for any sign of the men. Judging by the holes in Her Majesty's carriage, there must have been a dozen of them at least. Such a party will have been noticed. It will have left a trace. Innkeepers, blacksmiths, couriers, they will have seen them on the road. Stables. Taverns. That sort of thing. We will find them."

"But how did they know to be there, at that very place, just then?" Cecil wonders.

This is a very good point. It is simple enough to stand by a roadside and blast a passing carriage with an arquebus, Walsingham supposes. A child might do it. But it becomes exponentially more complex the more men you involve in the task, and even more so if you have a particular carriage in mind, and more so again if that carriage is carrying the Queen of England, who is not expected to even be there, and who should not have been traveling that day at all. Were they simultaneously the luckiest—in that they were there, at the roadside, with guns that fired and balls that hit, as the Queen went by—and unluckiest—in that they ultimately failed—assassins alive?

"Some signal perhaps? Sent from Hatfield, to alert them that she was leaving?"

It is possible.

"I will send for the Steward of the Household for a list of all those under him," Beale tells them. "But we must also think of Her Majesty's people."

"We will have to question her women," Hatton supposes. "I am happy to pursue that for you."

Walsingham thanks Hatton. He is grateful for the help, because the Queen travels with enough men, women, and children to people a large village, complete with everyone from chaplain—four of them—to lackey, of whom she has perhaps twenty. That is quite some list to get through.

"In the meanwhile, to whom would she have first communicated her desire to leave for Whitehall?" Cecil asks.

"One of her women," Walsingham supposes. "Lettice Knollys is chief lady of the bedchamber. She will know."

They send an usher for Lettice Knollys, and while they wait, Walsingham's thoughts turn to the woman who was shot, who died in place of the Queen, in Her Majesty's carriage, even before they had reached the palace.

"Who was she?" he now asks. "Do we know?"

"Alice Rutherford," Beale tells them. "Daughter of Sir John Rutherford."

Walsingham knows of Rutherford. Of somewhere in Lincolnshire. Member of Parliament, unimpeachable gospel man, and now deserving of the nation's thanks and condolences.

"And she was but seventeen, eighteen."

There is a silence. Walsingham thinks of his own daughters. They are ten and five years old.

"Mother?" he asks.

"Dead in childbed with her brother. Rutherford never remarried."

"Poor bastard," Cecil mutters.

"We'll send her body up there before the weather turns. Closed coffin, agreed?"

There is a series of curt nods just as the usher returns from Her Majesty's privy apartments not with Lettice Knollys, who claims the Queen is too distressed to spare her, but with Jane Frommond, the girl in whose arms Alice Rutherford died. She is young—twenty perhaps—and taller than Walsingham, almost as tall as Hatton, and pretty in a clever-looking way, with hair just darker than honey. She is unaffected; one of those girls with chapped lips, and with skirts and sleeves of silk the color of polished gun barrels, a core of something less lustrous, with two strings of modest-sized pearls about her throat, and a miniature of the Queen on a gold chain around her waist that may be, but probably isn't, the work of Nicholas Hilliard. Standing at the head of the table, she looks each man in the eye as if she were equal to all. She has been crying.

"Please, Mistress Frommond, sit," Walsingham suggests. He would prefer his eyes not to be at the same height as her breasts, which are pressed upward by her new French-style bodice, reinforced, if his sources tell him no lie, by strips of whalebone and a thin line of star-bright linen that runs atop her bodice, leading the squirming mind where his has no time or right to drift at this present moment.

She does so, opposite him, and she seems shorter than them all when she sits. An optical illusion, Walsingham wonders, or more likely her legs are the longest part of her. She must make a very fine horsewoman. She is not so grand as some of the other ladies of the court, being only a maid of honor, rather than a lady of the bedchamber, or of the Privy Chamber, and Walsingham is somewhat relieved. The thought of trying to subject Lettice Knollys to questioning brings him out in a cold sweat.

He starts by asking after the Queen.

"She is much distressed by Alice Rutherford's death. More so than by the attempt on her life, I believe."

This does not surprise Walsingham. The Queen has always believed herself immortal, or unlikely to die any time soon, at any rate.

"But how was she before you came down from Hatfield?" Cecil asks. "It is understood she was not well."

Frommond nods.

"And still not. She can stray no more than thirty feet from the closestool, lest she must answer to her laundry maid."

"Really?" Hatton demands. He means: Might she really have to answer to a laundry maid?

"No," Frommond says. "A joke. Sorry. It is too soon."

She starts to cry again. It is, a bit, Walsingham silently agrees, though he smiles at the thought of it. He finds himself liking Frommond. Cecil passes her his kerchief. When she has dried her eyes and wiped her nose, and handed it back, Walsingham goes on.

"Was it something she ate?"

"Perhaps," Frommond agrees. "An oyster? They defy examination, for we cannot taste each one to see if it is sound."

Walsingham makes a note to forbid Her Majesty any more. Stick to salmon. He makes a mental note to have some sent to Sheffield, to Mary, Queen of Scots. See how she likes them. For the future.

They ask Frommond a series of questions about the household's activities that morning, and whether anyone might have had the chance to send some sort of signal to alert the gunmen of Waltham Forest that the Queen was leaving Hatfield that day. Frommond answers succinctly, and as she speaks Walsingham notes the clarity of her gaze, and for a reason he will not later be able to explain, he wonders what it would be like to wake up next to such a woman. He imagines a slice of sunlight falling from between the shutters and the curtains, refracting through one amber-hued iris. Afterward he supposes he must be getting old, because his mind does not touch on what might have happened the night before.

"And was there anything unusual about your preparations for departure?" he asks.

Frommond thinks for a moment, then shakes her head.

"You mean, did I see any . . . what? Men in capes disappearing through holes in the fence?"

She makes such a thing sound foolish, and Walsingham smiles, because that is almost exactly what he had in mind. Cecil, too, obviously.

"That is not so very farfetched a thing," he mumbles.

"So we are given to understand why the Queen decided to travel in her closestool carriage," Walsingham asks, "but why was Alice Rutherford traveling alone in the Queen's carriage?"

For the first time Jane Frommond looks ill at ease.

"There was no reason," she says. "It was the way things turned out. Four women in the back carriage, one with Her Majesty in the closestool carriage, and so one woman extra. Alice had been in the Queen's second carriage, but the horse was lame, and so the carriage was left at Waltham Cross, and Alice . . . well. The Queen would not have her in the closestool carriage alongside Her Majesty and Mistress Knollys, and there was no space in the back carriage, so it only made sense that she should travel in the Queen's."

Walsingham believes she is lying.

But why?

After that there seems not very much more to say. Walsingham thanks her and stands to show her through the door. He follows her through and closes the door behind.

"May I?" he asks as she pauses before setting off across the courtyard to the Queen's privy apartments.

"I hoped you would," she admits.

"Why?"

She continues walking in the cold November air. It smells strongly of coal smoke, and unless the comet really does signify the end of the world, it will soon be winter, he thinks. Winter. Christ, how he hates winter.

The courtyard is a pretty place, with low hedges shaped in an ornate pattern around graveled paths, and at its center, a sundial on a large stone plinth, as useless now as it is most of the time. They follow one of the paths, and he can hear her feet on the gravel, but not see them for her skirts. *She is only a little taller than me,* he thinks. *I mean; we do not look ridiculous walking together.* Her hair is neatly tricked in woven plaits and she wears no wedding ring. Walsingham wonders if she is betrothed to anyone and then wonders why it is he knows so precious little about the Queen's women. It is tempting to believe they sit all day stitching, or learning new dances, and yet that cannot be, can it? He waits for her to speak. At length, when they are farthest from any window, she does.

"Alice Rutherford," she says.

"Mmmm?"

"She was with child."

Walsingham stops. Ah.

"That is very unfortunate," he says, taking a pace to rejoin her side. "Did the Queen know?"

"She had just learned," Frommond now tells him. "It is why Alice was traveling alone in the Queen's carriage. Her Majesty had forbidden Alice into her presence. That is what I did not wish to tell you, before those other gentlemen."

"And Her Majesty was vexed?"

Frommond rolls her eyes.

"It is a mercy she was too ill to move."

Walsingham can believe it. It is well known that the Queen can barely stand when one of her ladies asks to take a husband, and she has been known to refuse permission if she believes the girl too young, or the marriage not advantageous enough, or if she has a personal dislike of the groom. And that is when things are done in accordance with correct procedure, but when they are not, her temper is legendary. Only this last year she broke Mary Shelton's finger with a candlestick when it was discovered she had secretly married Sir John Scudamore. But what would that rage be like if she discovered one of her ladies had fornicated out of wedlock?

"And how did she learn of the girl's state?"

"Alice used to be slender as a reed, which angered Her Majesty, anyway, but in recent days her laces needed to be loose tied, and she was oftentimes very green about the gills."

Jane stops and flutters her hands by her cheeks. It is a touching, obscure gesture. They resume their steps.

"And do we know the father?" Walsingham asks.

Frommond shakes her head.

"She would not even tell me, and I share a bed with her."

"So she was being sent home?"

"Not home. No. I think the Tower."

"The *Tower*?"

"It is what the Queen told her. Because she would not admit the name of the father."

Christ. What a thing. But he cannot see what this might have to do with the ambush. They walk on. Ahead two Yeomen guard the entrance to the Queen's chambers.

"Do you have any suspicion? As to the father. It will go no further, I promise."

Frommond shakes her head.

"But you must," he says, "if you share a bed?"

She shakes her head again.

"When do you think it happened?"

"How are you with an abacus, Master Walsingham?" Frommond asks.

"Tolerable," he supposes. "Oh. So about August?"

"It is just a guess."

"She would not even tell you when?"

Frommond shakes her head.

"Or where? But she would have been with Her Majesty, yes? And Her Majesty was—"

"On progress," they say together.

Walsingham sighs. Yet another reason to hate these yearly progresses, when each summer Her Majesty rouses her entire household, and they quit London and take to the road—three hundred wagons; more than two thousand horses; nearly four thousand men, women, and children, costing nearly eight hundred pounds a week in wages and horse fodder alone—to meander through the countryside, from house to house, castle to castle, like a biblical plague of locusts. They hunt. They dance. They enjoy masques and every other kind of entertainment. Last year they were at Bramshott with Edmund Mervyn, then at Brockhampton with John Caryll, then at Portsmouth with the Earl of Sussex, and then Her Majesty led them on up into the Midlands, leaving a swath of destruction and bankruptcies in their wake.

"So it could be . . . anyone?"

He gestures to include the whole world, or every man in it, anyway, and after a moment's thought, Frommond more or less nods.

"At any other time, I would find this man," Walsingham tells her. "And if I found that he had wronged the girl, harmed her in any way, other than the obvious, then, Mistress Frommond, please know that I would make sure he swung for it."

"But?" Frommond wonders.

"But—"

And Walsingham shrugs. He feels unutterably weary. She understands and gives him a long sad look.

"Yes," she says. "Perhaps I am a fool to care. I will leave you here, Master Walsingham."

He thanks her for her time and care and is wondering what else he might say to give her comfort when Robert Beale appears from across the courtyard. He is clutching some paper or other, his face very grim.

"Master Walsingham," he calls, holding up the paper. "A message sent down from Her Majesty."

CHAPTER FOUR

Mortlake, west of London,
second week of November 1577

In his sleeping hours, even four days later, John Dee surprises himself, for he does not dream of comets, nor of gunfire, nor even of his communication with the Archangel Michael, but of rivers, riverbanks, rills, weirs, and locks. He dreams of dams and watermills. On waking he is surprised to find himself having dreamed these dreams, and he wishes he would dream more of those golden moments when he was in the Privy Chamber in Whitehall, in communication at last with the Archangel Michael, but he knows it is fruitless to argue with his unconscious: the sleeping mind is resolute in its priorities. So he enters these dreams into his book of dreams, and interprets them to mean that his gifts and his talents are being checked from their true destination, and that some other force is using his power for their own purpose.

But what is this force? And what could their purpose be?

It is not hard to guess: Sir William Cecil; Francis Walsingham; Sir Christopher Hatton, all working against him seeing the Queen, against him seeing Bess.

But with the appearance of the comet, and with this communication from the Archangel Michael, it is now all the more important that he does see her. All his work, all his years poring through the tangled esotericisms of Johannes Trithemius's *Steganographia*, the triple thickets of Heinrich Agrippa's *Occult Philosophy*, and even Paracelsus's darkly impenetrable *Astronomia Magna* tell him that such signs are no mere coincidence. They mean something. They point to something.

And it can only be one thing: the coming of a last great age, when the world will be finally unified under one last Great Empress: Queen Elizabeth of England. To achieve this, for the sake of the whole world, she must begin by reclaiming her lost empire, Arthur's lost empire, in the Netherlands to begin with, with Holland and Zealand, and also Picardy, of course, but also she must show the world the genealogy that proves her to be the rightful heir to the throne of Castile; of Aragon, and of Jerusalem itself. Through these titles, she is heir to the rest of the world entire. The Last Empress ruling over the Last Empire. The British Empire.

Dee has spoken of this to Elizabeth before, of course, many times, and her reaction usually depends on who has her ear at court at that time. If it is Cecil, or Dudley, or Walsingham, she is more enthusiastic, but if it is this new man, this Sir Christopher Hatton, then she scoffs at him, and he becomes angry. But none of that matters now. The Great Comet, and the fact that the archangel is talking to him, if only briefly, means that the hour is at hand. She can delay no longer.

He must go to her. He must tell her this.

He closes his book of dreams and stops for a moment to

watch—through the open doorway into his workshop—his alchemical workshop assistant, Roger Cooke, take up a tiny flake of cinnabar on the very tip of a spatula and hold it over the very last piece of glassware that survives from Dee's time in Leuven. It is his favorite—his only—pelican, so called because its shape is supposed to resemble that of the bird, beak lowered to peck at its own breast to draw forth blood to feed its young, and it is set over a crucible, in which burns a piece of charcoal soaked in lamb fat. The flame is yellow and smoky, but steady, and the contents of the flask are bubbling nicely, even though Cooke has removed the glass lid, and vapor escapes. The cinnabar must be damp, though, or the spatula is, for the powder, so carefully measured out, will not slide off the metal and into the flask's open throat.

Careful, Dee says silently. *Do not for the love of God tap it on the side of the pelican for*— Cooke does so. The pelican cracks very gently. A tiny, high-pitched ping. Cooke looks up. Their eyes meet. Cooke puts the spatula down and comes to close the door in Dee's face. Dee is grateful to be spared the sight of the flask being emptied into the slops and thrown away with all the other glass that Cooke has broken over the years.

He remembers what Dudley had said about the Dutchman Cornelius de Lannoy, to whom the Queen paid all that money. De Lannoy had had the most beautiful glassware from the finest Dutch glassmakers, Dee recalls, beautifully clear, through which could be seen each successive change of the alchemical process, far superior to anything the English can yet manage, which he'd been back to the Low Countries to buy himself, wasting much time and probably much money. Perhaps there is still some of it knocking about in Somerset House or even the Tower perhaps? Though things tend not to last so very long there. He will ask the Queen.

He is looking for his coat when his mother brings him six coddled eggs in an earthenware dish.

"You must have your breakfast," she says.

He stops and smiles at her and sits back at his table. She watches him dip his spoon into one of the eggs. The broken yolk is very yellow.

"Knew you'd soon find gold, John," she says with her short-sighted, near toothless smile. It is not clear if she is joking, or not. Just as time has robbed her of her teeth, so it is with her wits, and oftentimes she speaks no sense.

"Not this time, Mother," he admits. "Next time perhaps."

"That's the spirit. Like your father, you are. Never give up."

But he is tiring of it now; tiring of his dire need of money, he has to admit, and he thinks if he could just conjure up one ingot, his life would be much eased. He might even be able to afford a scrying stone, such as that fat fraud Nostradamus owned. He has seen one, as fine an example as he has ever laid eyes on, that he believes might suit him, in a goldsmith's in Cheapside. It costs eight pounds, though, and where is he going to get eight pounds?

"Those men were back the other day," his mother tells him. "With the dog. You know?"

He thinks he does. Bob and Bill. Bill and Bob. Bailiffs.

"Did they say what they wanted?"

"They said they were collecting money for books," she goes on with another of her smiles. Her gums are as pink as a baby's, and her smile charming. He wonders what she thinks "collecting money for books" actually means.

"Were they, in fact, collecting money for a book dealer?"

She nods and smiles.

"As I said, dear."

"And did they say when they would be back?"

"This morning," she says, just as there is a thunderous hammering on the gate. "That will be them."

Dee puts his hand on her arm.

"Let me," he says. He supposes there will only be one of them at the door, while the other, with the dog, will have made his way to the orchard, to cut off Dee's path to the river. It will be slightly awkward, but if he is quick—he is up the stairs, into his bedchamber, and hauling himself out through the window and up onto the roof feeling just as nimble as the monkey that Bess used to keep, and with one lurching drop, he clatters onto the roof of the laboratory—tiled against fire—and claps his hands to the top ridge. His teeth rattle and pigeons take noisy flight, but he stays put.

"Ha," he says and clambers up onto the roof's spine. He sits astride it and shuffles along. It runs away from the house, almost to the wall separating his property from Thomas Digges's herb garden.

"Is that you up there, Dr. Dee?"

It is Roger Cooke, returning from the privy.

Dee holds his finger to his lips. Cooke, while clumsy, is not an absolute idiot, and knows—through bitter experience of oftentimes going unpaid himself—of his master's somewhat occasional finances.

The boom of Bob or Bill knocking on the gate comes again.

"We know you're in there, Dee!"

"He's not here!" Cooke shouts. "He's in Wales!"

"Yes, he is!" his mother calls. "I just this moment gave him his breakfast. Six eggs. And he has eaten but one!"

"Is that you, Goodwife Dee?" Bill or Bob calls. "Would you care to let us in so as we may see these eggs?"

Dee does not have much time. He gathers his cloak about his waist, wondering, again, why he wears it when a doublet and breeches would be much more convenient, and he stands, perched atop the spine of the roof, looking about him for a moment. It is one of those false autumn days that make you think the winter will be all right, with sunlight and light airs. From here he is able to see most of Mortlake: the clutch of the roofs gathered around the tower of Saint Mary's; the breadth of the river, her waters striped with all the weirs and the nets of trinkermen, and he pauses for a moment to consider if this is what his dream was referring to.

Too late he notices he can now be seen by Bill or Bob, whichever one it is in the orchard, and the man starts shouting and waving, and the bloody dog starts its barking, keen to reclaim Dee's wrist from which its jaws had to be pried the last time it was here. Dee sees he will have to hurry. He is in soft shoes, thankfully, and able to balance on the top beam of the roof, and even gain a little impetus as he runs. At its end is a drop as high as two men, but ahead is the branch of an ash tree that Digges himself used to use, when he was a boy, to climb over into Dee's garden to watch him as he went about his work.

Dee leaps, and for a moment he is airborne, like an angel he supposes, albeit one in black wool. He flies over the stone wall, and then drops, his palms smacking in the bough of the ash—grasping it, just—as his shoulders are wrenched almost out of joint. The branch shivers and yields, and Dee descends six feet or more before he is shook free and, with a certain amount of grace, delivered into a broad bed of late-cropping onions.

"Why, Dr. Dee! John!"

It is Thomas Digges himself, with a spade. Dee tries to find a joke about Digges and digging, but nothing good comes to mind.

"God give you good day, Thomas," he says. "Did you hear? The Queen was saved! The shooters targeted the wrong carriage!"

Digges smiles broadly. He had. Late-autumn sunlight warms

his handsome young face. Behind Dee's shoulder, over the wall, it sounds like the chickens are scattering.

"Dee?" a voice floats over, "you can't run forever. We are taking your samples today, pending your return of the two pounds, six shillings, and eightpence owed to Master Inglestone of Gutherons Lane."

"The bookseller?" Digges asks.

"A misunderstanding," Dee explains.

"Another one?"

"Another one."

"And which samples?" Digges wonders.

"Frobisher's, I hope," Dee says.

He wishes them more luck in finding gold therein than he has had.

"Can I assist you in any way this morning, John?" Digges asks.

"A coat, Thomas, if you have it, would certainly help, and some small coin or other?"

Thomas Digges lends Dee a coat, and a few pennies, and after somewhat open-ended further discussion as to the meaning of the Great Comet, Dee leaves his friend's property by the side gate that gives out onto a slipway down to the Thames, much favored by cowherds and their charges.

"Where are you going?" Digges asks.

"To see the Queen," Dee tells him.

"Like that?"

"Oh, she's seen me in worse."

Digges knows Dee and the Queen passed some time in the Tower together. A wherryman is drifting past on the river's flow, and steers over to collect Dee, who removes his shoes to keep them dry and climbs in. It is Jiggins, keen to discuss the attempt on the Queen's life—"aliens or foreigners"—and the Great Comet, which he thinks foretells the end of the world.

Dee disagrees.

"Well, what about that boy in Lincoln?" Jiggins counters. "Who is born with the face of a duck?"

"Why is it always a duck?" Dee asks.

Jiggins takes offense, believing you will get no sense out of Dr. John Dee, and the rest of the journey is conducted in silence save for the grind of the oars against the rowlocks, and the slap of malodorous river water against the wherry's planks. It is a busy morning on the Thames, but Dee takes note of every little craft on the move, and those that are not, including those still moored, taking on passengers from Hammersmith, and then the old bishop's palace in Fulham. As they round the bend, and turn northeast again, the river widens and Dee sees one of the Queen's smaller barges moving purposefully toward them, rowing against the tide. Not the Queen, surely? No. One of her household men on some official duty, accompanied by a half-dozen halberdiers in helmets. Dee watches them pass. He thinks about Bill and Bob carting away Frobisher's samples. What if they do find gold? Good luck to them.

The guards at the Watergate are very doubtful.

"You are never Dr. Dee," they say, and "What, *the* Dr. Dee?" and "Well, go on then, show us some magic." The one who asks to see some magic is the youngest, and most foolish, and the others step away from him. Dee likes to think they believe his reputation as a conjurer comes from his days at Cambridge, when he made a gold-painted beetle the size of a man appear to fly, but he knows, too, there is word put around about him being a conjurer of fiends, and a companion of hellhounds, and that his rivals—such as that Dutch fraud de Lannoy—point to his arrest in 1555, and how in the week after it, one of his accuser's sons went blind, and his other died.

News of his presence, and his person, too, is shuffled through steadily grander rooms, up a line of command, and eventually word returns from some distant privy room that the Queen will see Dee in her library, a room he knows well, though dislikes for having only one door. He is not trusted to make his way there, and four stern Yeomen conduct him to where he is met by a beautifully dressed gentleman usher who is startled to see him in his ill-fitting coat and mud-splattered shoes.

"It is what we wear in Mortlake," Dee tells the man.

"But Her Majesty—"

"Has seen him in worse. Come in, John."

She stands in pale silks in the middle of the gloomy room, alcoves of shelves piled with tomes to her left and right. Two ladies whom he does not recognize wait to catch her if she should fall, for she looks not much recovered from her ordeal on the road from Hatfield, or perhaps, Dee thinks, some longer-term malady. He makes his bow and she holds out a gloved hand for him to kiss.

"Please, John, may we—?"

She indicates a table and a bench in one of the alcoves and, standing behind it, hidden, with his back to the window, of all people: Sir Christopher Hatton, beautifully dressed in bloodred velvet, with a star-bright ruff. Oil in his beard.

"Hatton," Dee says.

"Sir Christopher to you, Dr. Dee."

"Oh yes yes."

Dee flaps a dismissive hand and turns back to the Queen, who has taken a seat a little distant, as if flagging at some inner effort. She appears diaphanous today, almost see-through, like the best porcelain from Cathay, held up to the sun.

"Bess—"

"John," she says, with a glint of steel. "Please don't. Please don't call me that."

He bows again.

"I'm sorry, Your Majesty," he says. "Forgive me."

He sees Hatton is about to say something, so Dee launches right in.

"But I have a proposal for you, Your Majesty. A plan. A plan to put an end to all these attempts on your life. Once and for all."

"Her Majesty is not in the market for any of your Last World Empire nonsense, Dee," Hatton interrupts.

Dee ignores him. So does the Queen.

"Go on," she says.

"The truth, Your Majesty," Dee continues, "is that all across Christendom, millions of virtuous men and women are content to pass their days herding their sheep, raising their children, and singing songs to their sweethearts as the sun goes down, but in among the virtuous many are a wicked few—of whom there are just as many in London as in Madrid, or Rome, or Paris, or Prague, upon my honor—who are not content to pass their days in God-given harmony, but must actively scheme to enrich themselves, to gain themselves more power, prestige, possession, heedless of the great cost in both health and wealth and happiness of the virtuous many."

"Pshaw!" Hatton barks. "A pretty speech. It is stuff and non-sense!"

But the Queen is listening, however discomfited, so Dee goes on.

"These wicked men will stop at nothing," he tells her, "and will stoop to anything to achieve their aims. Their preferred ploy is to trick the virtuous man into believing his neighbor is his enemy; that his neighbor means him harm. To distract the many from their knavish tricks, they whip up frenzies of hate and fear. They divide to conquer. They raise armies, send fleets, conjure up Inquisitions."

"It was ever so, John," the Queen murmurs. "Surely?"

"But that does not mean it should be forever."

The Queen and Hatton exchange a look. They know he is talking about men—and women—such as themselves.

"So what are you suggesting?" the Queen asks.

"I am suggesting we do not fight Spain. We do not fight the Empire. We do not even fight Catholics. We practice against their king, against their emperor, against their pope."

"I will not procure the deaths of princes, John. You know that."

Dee does.

"I am sorry, Your Majesty. I do not mean to practice against their bodies. I mean to practice against their minds."

Another pshaw from Hatton.

"Their minds?" the Queen prompts.

"We use their own greed and their own ambition against their own selves."

"And how do you propose to do that, Dee?" Hatton splutters. "Some of your magical powders? Or by telling on them to the angels? Or will you cow them with one of your giant golden beetles that can also fly? Lord save us, Your Majesty, this man's a clown."

Dee finds himself disliking Hatton, but that is quite an image, he thinks, and despite himself, he smiles.

"No, Your Majesty," he says. "We use science."

"Science! Ha!"

"Sir Christopher," the Queen growls.

Hatton bows, and remains silent.

"What do you propose, John?"

He takes a deep breath.

"There exists a book," he begins, "or a manuscript, rather, that is so secret it goes without name."

And he tells them of the manuscript of which he has heard,

written in the most extraordinary cipher, and filled with the most astonishing illustrations, that holds the key to the secret language of the angels, the knowledge of which will permit the adept not only to learn the nature of all the God-hidden structures of the world and skies beyond, but also to know—and influence—the thoughts of men, whosoever and wheresoever they may be.

"With this book in our possession," he tells them, "not only will England be preserved forevermore, but we will change the course of history."

Both stare, skeptical.

"Where is this book?" Hatton asks.

"Somewhere in Poland."

"*Somewhere in Poland?*" Hatton interrupts with a laugh. "Do you know the size of Poland, Dee?"

"And how much will it cost?" Her Majesty adds. She is ever careful with money, of course.

"I will get it for whatever I can," he promises.

Still she hesitates.

"Anyway," he goes on. "The point is not that we have the book. The point is that the book is *known* to exist."

"And—does it? Exist, I mean?" the Queen asks.

"I am not certain," Dee admits.

"Dammit, Dee!" Hatton exclaims.

"Dammit, *Dr.* Dee," Dee reminds him.

"Dr. Dee!" Hatton laughs. "We are under siege, hard-pressed on all sides. Her Majesty cannot spare a single man to go wandering off about the continent, looking for books that may or may not exist. Not even you!"

The Queen raises her hand.

"You overreach yourself, Sir Christopher!" she says.

He bows his head. Dee says nothing. He can hear the Queen breathing quickly. At last she speaks.

"It is not *even* you, John, whom we cannot spare: it is most *especially* you whom we cannot spare. We cannot stand to have you out of our realm. Without you by our sides we cannot rest easy."

"But Your Majesty! I cannot merely stand idle while men plot to kill you!"

"But you will not be standing idle, Dee," Hatton interrupts. "We have a task for you. Which is why we sent for you. We are in need of your particular talents."

Dee is about to interrupt, to tell them that it was his idea to come and see Her Majesty but he says nothing, and instead is taken over by a deep inner tingling. A strong, almost irresistible desire to help, but also deep caution: the last time a member of the Privy Council asked for his help, it led to his very near death on the sands under Mont Saint-Michel.

He therefore directs his question at the Queen, rather than to Hatton.

"So, how may I be of use, Your Majesty?"

He imagines that in view of their past friendship, she will know of his gifts, and call on his vast resources of recondite knowledge as to the movement not only of the planets, moons, and stars, but also of the communication of angels. Or will it turn on his interpretive ability to predict the future?

But she falters. A hand creeps to her belly and her face seems to change shade, to gray green.

"Tell him, please, Sir Christopher."

Hatton steeples his fingers.

"Her Grace," he says, "has had a dream."

A dream. Dreams are another area of his special interests.

"Go on," he says. He is keen to hear the Queen's, just as he is keen to tell her of his own: of rivers, watermills, locks, dams. Diversions, blockages, and checked potential. But Her Majesty will not meet his eye, and instead her gaze flits about the room as if looking for somewhere comfortable to rest.

"Her Majesty dreamt," Hatton answers for her, "of Greek fire."

He says it in a peculiar way, rolling the consonants. It sounds mocking and Dee wonders if he would do that were Her Majesty fully well?

"Greek fire?" Dee asks. Just that? He is disappointed.

"Yes," Hatton says. "Greek fire. Her Majesty dreamt that our navies made use of it to . . . to defeat the Spanish. In Her Majesty's dream Spanish ships are set afire, and the Spanish troops are made to burn in hell."

What kind of woman dreams of that? Dee wonders. Someone unwell, he supposes. Someone who has just this week survived being shot at. Someone who is perpetually besieged with worries and cares.

"It would do that," Dee supposes.

"What do you know of Greek fire, Dr. Dee?" Hatton asks. He is sneering. Dee wonders why.

"Well," he says with a shrug. "It was invented by the Jews of Syria, sometime before the fall of Jerusalem, and has been used by the Byzantines since to defend themselves against the Turk, both on land and at sea. It is a liquid, that once afire sticks to whatever it touches: wood, water, or skin, and it cannot be put off or out save with sand or—is it old urine? It is delivered using a pump and hose, though how those do not catch fire remains a mystery. The formula was lost with the Byzantines themselves, and no one has been able to re-create it since. Even those who captured supplies of it."

Hatton shoots the Queen a conspiratorial glance. She ignores it, but Dee sees where this is going: Hatton wants to use Dee's skills in some grubby little alchemical investigation into re-creating Greek fire. Greek fire: a substance that would no more bring in a new golden age of Adamic innocence, as to cause men to be roasted alive.

His spirits flag.

"Greek fire is not the way to defeat the Spanish," he repeats.

"But what of Her Majesty's dream?" Hatton asks. "Surely you do not doubt that."

Dee opens his mouth to argue the meaning of her dream, but does not even know where to begin. The room, already gloomy, seems all the more so as Dee's grander visions fade.

"But I don't— I do not have the right chemicals, the right tools, the right flasks."

He thinks of his broken pelican.

"Nor is my workshop set up for . . . for *fire*."

He thinks further of poor, dear, clumsy Roger Cooke, working in the room next to his library of precious manuscripts—nearly four thousand books, the largest library in England, painstakingly and financially ruinously gathered over the last ten years—with *fire*.

"No," he says. "I cannot—I will not—produce a method of roasting men alive, not even Spanish men."

"John," the Queen starts, her voice wavering. "Consider what they have done to us in these last days. Sent their assassins. But consider what they might yet do. Imagine what five thousand Spanish pikemen landing in Suffolk might achieve. We—whom you profess to love—are asking you to help us, to help this country you also profess to love, to safeguard all our progresses, the progress we have made in all the sciences, in geometry, astronomy, astrology, in religion. Do you wish us to return to the old ways? Worshiping graven images? Hoodwinked by monks? Ruled over by the bishop of Rome? All this progress lost? All this enlightenment that you yourself have helped bring about with your tireless exertions in natural philosophy, extinguished by a Spanish prince? All of us put under the Inquisition?"

Before Dee can answer, the Queen suddenly grips the arms of her chair and is quick to her feet. Dee and Hatton rise with her.

"Your Majesty?"

She looks panicked, as if she has heard something they have not. Suddenly her ladies are by her side, conjured from the shadows. She turns and retreats very quickly through a door in the paneling that Dee did not know existed, her exit covered by her ladies who retreat after her, glaring at Hatton and most especially at Dee, as if forbidding them to follow.

Dee and Hatton are left alone. They are silent a long moment, each asking himself if the Queen will rejoin them or not.

Eventually: "Shall we?" Hatton suggests, indicating the chairs.

"I do not think there is very much left to say, is there?"

"I am glad we are agreed," Hatton agrees. "Write up a list of the things you need from your workshop, and your house generally—a new shirt, for instance, would not go amiss—and I will have it all collected and brought to you."

"Collected? I don't need anything collected. I am going home now where I shall either change my shirt, or not, as I see fit."

Hatton smiles nastily.

"Dee," he says. "I know Her Majesty was asking you, but I am telling you: Her Majesty has tasked me with this, and I will see it is done, so if you do not agree, here, now, to help in this, then I will have you placed under arrest for conjuring treasure contrary to the Witchcraft Act, and from here you will be taken to the Tower, where you will either comply, or die."

CHAPTER FIVE

City of London,
second week of November 1577

Two days later and it is another gray morning, scented with the first real intimation of the winter to come, and Robert Beale walks eastward from Saint Paul's along Cheapside, with the gap-toothed bulk of the White Tower filling the end of the road ahead, and he wonders if it can possibly be true that the Dutch alchemist Cornelius de Lannoy bought his way out of its dungeons with gold? Would not the Queen, or Cecil, or Walsingham, or even the Constable of the Tower have thought to ask where he had it from?

Beale is on his way to Waltham Forest again to continue questioning the various sheriffs and constables of the area to find trace of the men who shot at the Queen, though as it stands he is not even certain how many he is looking for.

Most striking is the fact that the enterprise was planned in silence, with no word leaking out to alert any of Walsingham's paid placemen or any concerned subject. Ordinarily a servant might come forward. A groom, say, in the hope of a purse, or a farrier with an unpaid bill. And yet, nothing.

It is a mystery.

And something must be done. They cannot go on like this, and they cannot risk another drama such as the other night.

But what, though?

He is still tumbling ideas over in his mind when he hears a voice call his name, and there, standing on the corner of Gutter Lane, is an old friend: Nicholas Hilliard, goldsmith turned limner of the very finest miniatures to be found in Christendom. He is a handsome man, turning into his thirties perhaps, and today, surprisingly well-dressed, in sober black with a froth of linen about his chin, and an arch look in his eye. He has been working in Paris, where, from the look and feel of his cloth, he is doing well for himself.

"You are back?" Beale states the obvious, and, to confirm this, Hilliard makes an elaborate, sweeping bow in the French style.

"*Oui*," he says. "Until Christmas."

"And how is it over there?" Beale asks.

There is a flicker of something between them, a tiny signal both acknowledged and unacknowledged.

"Difficult," Hilliard admits. "But we go on."

He means for Protestants in France, especially in Paris, but also, that unspoken thing: both men serve Walsingham.

"Buy you a jug of something?" Hilliard asks. "And a pie? It is nearly dinnertime."

Beale has a long ride ahead, but he has never known Hilliard to buy a drink, so . . .

"Why not?"

They repair to the Mitre, much favored by goldsmiths, and Hilliard has to stop by the door to reattach his points, which have come loose suddenly so that his sleeves have slipped, and so Beale must go on ahead, and Hilliard asks for a jack of ale to go with his rabbit pie, and of course Beale must pay, and it is only then that he remembers why Hilliard is known as "Points." They find a space at the bench, and sit, and in his puzzling, west country accent Hilliard tells Beale how much he misses good English ale. Then he stops and looks more closely at Beale.

"You look perplexed, Robert? Something bothers you. Yet did not the Queen survive the attempt on her life?"

"She did," Beale agrees. "Thank the Lord, but—"

But the fact is that Beale still can not believe there is no plan in place for when Her Majesty does die, as eventually she must. All these years past they have been trying to solve the succession by trying to persuade her to marry and have a child, preferably male, so that there will be none of the upheaval that had followed after the Queen's father's death, and the Queen had given them hope that she might. That she could. That she would. And yet, and yet. The years are passing. She is still young, still beautiful, still able to bear a child, but it will not always be so. She will go the way of all flesh, and at this rate, when she does, her councillors will still be flailing around looking for a suitable successor. Meanwhile the next in line, the Scottish queen, Mary—a Catholic—waits in the wings, just biding her time, or, as is believed, already pulling strings to put herself at the head of a Spanish army marching on Whitehall, ready to reverse the clock and return England to the Church of Rome. All the excruciating birth pangs of modern England will have been for naught.

And so Beale has come to see that the methods of ensuring

the future that men such as Cecil and Walsingham prefer are not working, and will not work, and that their time must soon pass, and that coming men, such as he—Robert Beale—and perhaps a man such as Nicholas Hilliard, need to come up with a radical new solution.

But what though?

He asks if Hilliard heard anything of the attempt on the Queen's life while in Paris. Hilliard shakes his head.

"But it sounds like a homegrown weed? A thistle perhaps?"

"But the Scottish queen is under constant observation."

"There's a Spaniard, you know, or an Italian, who has devised a method to write a message on the white of a hardboiled egg without first removing its shell."

"It is why we coddle hers," Beale says.

"Do you? Well. If it can be done to an egg, why not a carrot?"

"A carrot?"

"For example."

Beale tries to think of Mary, Queen of Scots, with a carrot.

"Or a turnip," Hilliard adds quickly.

"Stop."

Details of the ruse that the Scottish queen perpetrated on Master Walsingham in the winter of 1572 are well enough known, and those that aren't known are freely invented.

"I forgot," Beale says. "You once painted her portrait, didn't you?"

Hilliard holds his gaze and nods.

Nothing is said.

The ale comes. Hilliard takes a deep draft. He shudders slightly.

"Not so certain I miss it after all," he confesses.

Beale asks him what brings him back to London.

"Ohhh, the usual," Hilliard admits. "Money."

He is probably there to see Master Walsingham, too, of course.

"You should charge more than three pounds for your work," Beale tells him.

"Of course," Hilliard agrees, "but then folks do say 'they are so small, Master Hilliard, and so why should they cost so much?' I had a man in my brother's workshop up the way there, some red-faced old soldier from Suffolk, whose young wife sits for me, and he tells me she is so beautiful, I should be paying her. I tell him the painting is so small, she should pay me."

Beale smiles.

"And is she? Beautiful, that is?"

"Ar," Hilliard says, nodding. "It's funny. This is her, look."

He slides a hand into his doublet and brings out one of his limnings, wrapped in a cocoon of silk and leather. He lays it on the table. Beale looks at it. It is very beautiful, with gilded edge, hardly larger than the ball of his thumb, and a woman in a plain dress, but with beautiful pearls that look so true to life, he might pick one off the painting's enameled surface, had he tweezers small enough.

The face, though, is not unfamiliar.

"Her Majesty," Beale says. He thinks Hilliard has made a mistake. But Hilliard smiles.

"I promise you," he says, "it ain't. Look. Just there, you see?"

He has a tiny thick lens with him that he holds over the face of the painting to reveal a tiny dark spot on the woman's cheek.

"A birthmark," Hilliard says, lowering his voice. "It separates her from the Queen, and in my humble opinion, though this is obviously a matter of taste, and secrecy, it makes this girl even more beautiful."

Beale stares at the painting through the loupe.

"Then why not just give her husband one of your old paintings of the Queen, with the mark dotted in?"

Hilliard pretends to be scandalized.

"Then it'd be like she were passing herself off as the Queen!" He laughs.

He pauses before he wraps the portrait up again.

"And she has the same beautiful hands, too, you know, though of course you cannot see them here. And she is alike the Queen in the rest of her person, too, as peas in a pod, you might say. Honestly, in the dark—"

He tails off and rolls his eyes.

"What's her name?" Beale asks.

"Ha! And that's another thing: it is Ness. Ness not Bess, do you see?"

"I do. Ness what?"

"Ness Overbury. Her husband is John Overbury."

Beale has never heard of him.

"Nasty old brute. Fought in the Low Countries and has never done anything he enjoyed more since. To think of his fingers on her flesh—"

"How old is she?"

In Beale's mind, a germ of an idea is forming against his will.

"She? About . . . I don't know . . . that perfect age, you know? Neither old nor young."

"Your age?"

"You put it so well!"

"And she's still there? At your workshop?"

Hilliard lifts up his mug to show he is drinking now, and in no state for fine work.

"No, they are in the Dolphin, in Saint Botolph's, waiting for this. I am on my way to deliver it now."

"Let me come with you. I would like to see this marvel."

Hilliard studies Beale sideways. He is a clever man, Hilliard.

He has been able to fool the Valois court that his French is only good enough for the chicken shop, no better, when in fact he spent two years of his childhood in Geneva and is fluent. When he is painting them he sits no more than two yards from men such as King Henry of France, or Francois, the Duke of Orleans, who is the man whom the Queen may or may not marry, straight-faced while they talk with their advisers how strange it is that someone so cunning at his art should come from such a benighted place as England, full of mists, foul brutes, easy women, and vile food. They will soon grow bored and overconfident, and as he does not react, their tongues will loosen and sometimes they will spill that which should remain constrained. Which is part of the reason he is there.

"What are you up to?" he asks.

"It is just an . . . idea."

CHAPTER SIX

Whitehall Palace,
same day, second week of November 1577

M istress Jane Frommond used to share the bed with Alice Rutherford, and so it is her whom Mistress Blanche Parry, mother of the maids, asks to gather up the dead girl's possessions from the coffer chamber they shared with the rest of the maids of honor and have them ready to be sent back to Alice's father in Lincolnshire, along with her body in its closed coffin.

"Some homecoming," Frommond says.

Mistress Parry lowers her gaze to the bed curtained in patched silk, and tidily made under its linen coverlet.

"Heartbreaking," she admits.

Alice Rutherford's position has become moot since her death. She is to be much mourned, but also there is no doubt that the Queen, even in her sickness, or perhaps especially in her sickness, ordered the girl out of her presence, and that she threatened that unless Alice admitted the name of the father, she—Alice—would bear the child—*rear* the child!—in the Tower, and that once the weeping girl had been escorted from the room by the Queen's ushers and a Yeoman, she had not been permitted back into the presence of the Queen.

"Why do you think she would not tell us the father's name?" Mistress Parry now asks Frommond.

It is a question Frommond had asked Alice herself, of course, many times before news of the girl's state was generally known: Was it someone we all know? Are you in love with him? Or did he rape you? And at each question Alice had shaken her head, and closed her eyes against the leaking tears, and Frommond told her that so long as she held out against them there was nothing she or anyone could do to help her, and Alice had sobbed and wept against Frommond's shoulder and said that she knew that, but still she would not—could not—change her course.

"Had she done so," Mistress Parry continues, more in the hope than expectation, "then I do believe Her Majesty would have taken pity on her youth, and her foolishness, and would have relented, especially if it were shown she was taken against her will."

Mistress Parry, as mother of the maids, wishes to believe that Alice was raped, that she was the victim of a crime committed by a man unknown, for this exonerates her from any failing in her duty of care for the poor girl.

"Because I did tell her," Mistress Parry bleats. "I did tell her, just as I told you when you first came to court, just as I tell all Her Majesty's maids of honor: the Queen is a worthy, chaste, and honorable woman and will tolerate nothing base, nothing wanton. There are temptations aplenty at court—many a fine young man with a shapely leg and a ready smile, always keen to sigh, and moon, and to send you verses and so on, but you—we—represent

Her Majesty, and if you yield to their charms and debase yourself, if you hold your chastity cheap, then you debase *her*, you hold *her* chastity cheap, and if that is the case then God help you for I shall not, no, nor none of us here."

All this Jane Frommond knows, for Mistress Parry has been saying it since Alice was proved with child.

"She never spoke to you about . . . about what had happened to her, or what she was doing? When you were in bed together?"

"We never spoke of such things," Frommond tells her, which is the truth of it in this instance. She has tried to think back to the summer, to think if there was a moment when Alice changed. She tries to remember if she ever saw Alice weeping, as if she had been abused or debased, but there never was. Nor was there a moment when Alice seemed struck by love, as the poets have it. She did not sigh over the moon and there was no suggestion of an absent love.

"She did not once mention a name?" Mistress Parry asks. "Of any man who might have led her astray? In her sleep, perhaps?"

Perhaps she did? But what would she have said? John? Every third man in England is John, and if he is not John, he is Thomas. And if he is neither John nor Thomas, then he is William.

Jane Frommond shakes her head and Mistress Parry draws breath through her teeth.

"Well," she says. "I am sorry for you. This must be hard on you."

It is, Frommond thinks, and unexpectedly so. To begin with there was the shock of the violence—the gunshots, and the blood—and she remembers the joke she so fearlessly made when addressing Master Walsingham, and Lord Burghley and Sir Christopher Hatton, but now she is suffused with sorrow, and she finds herself overbrimming with tears for her dead friend.

"Well," Mistress Parry says, "I will leave you to gather her things, and I shall send a boy to collect her chest."

The coffer chamber is on the third floor of the wing of the palace that houses the Queen's privy apartments. Long and thin, with two windows that give out over the courtyard, there are three curtained beds against one wall, and two presses—wardrobe cupboards—against another. The walls are plain whitewashed lime, but the ceiling is just boards on joists, and dust from the servants' rooms above drifts down to settle on everything below. Each of the unmarried maids of honor has a part share of one of the presses, and Jane Frommond has a coffer that fits nicely under the strings of her bed, when they are tightened. Alice Rutherford has a taller chest that does not fit under her bed, but sits at its side, and is usually covered in a worn scrap of Turkey carpet, and dust from the boards above.

Today, though, the carpet is pushed off, and it lies shed like an adder's skin at the back of the box, and there are scrapes in the thick dust on the lid where someone has scrabbled at it to get it open. Probably in the last day or so. *Strange*, Frommond thinks. Why should anyone do that? A servant perhaps? She will have to ask.

She lifts the coffer lid. It is made of some dark wood against moth, and within are a few of Alice's personal items: a comb with all its teeth; a silver hairpin as long and sharp as an Italian dagger; a slim hank of wool dyed vivid green; a fan (broken); and a small embroidery frame in which is stretched just a blank piece of linen. There is an out-of-favor partlet, an earthenware pot of some salve that smells of clove, and a nicely bound, not-much-thumbed copy of the Common Prayer Book, given to her—Frommond checks— by her father on her departure for the Queen's court before the summer the year previously. There are also some laces—grubby in lengths—and a few crumbs left of what might once have been a block of marzipan.

But there are no letters, nor other papers of any kind. This is strange. Frommond knows that Alice's father used to write from home in Lincolnshire, usually with news of her little brother, to whom she was close, and her dog, and with short descriptions of his hunting forays: who came; what they rode; what was caught; and among whom the venery was diced at day's end. Alice wrote to him, and not only to borrow money—though that, too: for cloth and new playing cards, which she was always losing; once a pair of needlework scissors she wanted to buy from the Royal Exchange—but because her mother had died birthing her brother, and her father had never remarried, and they remained close, and she wished him to know everything that she did. Frommond was certain she used to keep the letters in the coffer, as . . . well, where else would she keep them? But there is no sign of them here.

Perhaps she took them with her to Hatfield. In one of her bags? Frommond wonders what has become of them, since Alice must have had at least three, and Jane resolves to find them before—if— they are sent back to Alice's father with her coffin.

She restores the coffer to order and makes space for the clothes in the press that she and Alice also used to share: some linens; a pair of sleeves; a single dress the color of dried sage; and some hanging petticoats. Socks. Another pair of gloves. From the cloth rises the smell of Alice's scent, a distillation of lime flowers, but of the perfume itself there is no sign.

She takes out Alice's clothes and folds them atop one another in the coffer, and that is when she feels a tiny irregularity between the look and weight of one of her petticoats. There is a nodule there, some hidden thing within the length of the material, like a knot in wood, a seed within its pod, and she cannot get at it instantly. She must pluck away the cloth to find the opening. It is something stitched into the skirt's turned hem. The stitching is a simple blanket stitch, but broken a little along, so she must tease the weight of the thing toward the break and out into the palm of her hand.

It is a lozenge of dark gold, which, when turned over, reveals a picture of a young man, just his head and shoulders, before a sky-blue background. She takes the limning to the window. He is perhaps twenty, with reddish hair under what must be a velvet cap—a deeper red—on which is pinned some sort of gold badge, a very faint beard over a high but simple collar and a dark doublet. He stares back up at her with a sharp, challenging look.

Frommond does not recognize him at all, but she knows it can only be the father of the child. She feels warm with relief. Her cheeks flush as if she has been out in the sun all day. It is a love token. A token of love. So—Alice was a fornicator, yes, and deceitful and unchaste and unworthy, but she is dead now; she has paid a high price for her sins, and can this limning not prove that she at least loved, and that she was in her turn beloved? Can it not mean that she might have been betrothed to this man? Can it not have been the beginning of a happy story that went wrong? Can it not mean that her child was conceived in love? Is that too much to hope? Too much to load upon this simple little lozenge of gold, vellum, and paint?

She is still for a moment, the limning cupped in her hand. Tiny gold letters show that the painting was made last year: Anno Dm 1576. She wonders if the father of the child carries a similar portrait of Alice, done by the same hand, two for the price of one perhaps. Painted separately and slipped into a hand during a round of galliard, or during some other entertainment put on while they were on progress through the south this summer. Watching fireworks perhaps, or at a tilt. Or those acrobats, or the juggling clowns with their dancing dogs.

She compares the limning in her hand to the one she carries of the Queen on her belt, given to her along with a covered cup this last New Year. There are similarities in size, form, and color, but while the Queen is a wavering presence within her oval disk—as if she were copied from another painting perhaps, commissioned by the score to be distributed to Her Majesty's lesser courtiers—the image of this man, this boy, is pin sharp and pulses with life. He tilts his chin up, and he looks, what? *Hard*, she thinks. *Driven. Certain.* That is it. He knows what he wants, and it looks as if what he wants is something perhaps beyond the ordinary run of things. It is not a horse, for example, or a doublet inlaid with gold thread, or an income of more than forty pounds a year. Or perhaps she is wrong. Perhaps she is being fanciful.

She wonders how he will come to hear of what has happened to Alice, if he does at all, and how he will react when or if he does. Will she have already told him she was carrying their child? Much of Frommond wishes to believe that the boy knew Alice was pregnant, and that he will be heartbroken to learn of her death, but a sharper, harder part of her imagines he will feel some relief. He will not now ever have to pay for his great sin. Alice could never have been expected to hold her tongue in the Tower, could she? A day in its confines, even in the better apartments, would surely have broken her spirits. Or her father would have come to remonstrate, bringing her brother and her dog perhaps.

Then again, Frommond had always believed Alice a fragile little thing, yet she refused to divulge the father's name despite the full weight of the Queen and her ladies of the bedchamber. That must have taken great courage. And she looked them all in the eye as she took her place alone in the Queen's carriage in Waltham Cross. Alice might have carried her child to term and given birth, all in stoical silence, and then what would the Queen have done? Quietly let her go? Or held her until she was an old woman, her child fully grown, and no one quite sure who they were?

So who is the man?

She should show it to Mistress Parry, of course, and she is just turning to do so when the boy comes for Alice's coffer. He's twelve maybe, miserable and whippet thin. He takes off his cap and stands gripping it in both scrawny arms while Frommond hurriedly finishes packing it, pressing the clothes flat and closing the lid before wondering what to do with the scrap of Turkey carpet. This is when it strikes her very forcibly, very suddenly, that the carpet's removal and the traces of fingers in the dust must have been left by someone hurriedly going through Alice's possessions recently. Someone looking for something. Her few coins? Unlikely. The letters from her father and brother, equally so, but what about the limning? Could they be looking to retrieve that?

On impulse she shows it to the boy.

"Do you know this fellow?" she asks.

The boy pauses for a long moment before shaking his head quickly.

"Sorry, mistress, no one I know."

He is blushing, she sees, and supposes him shy.

"Not someone you have seen about the palace? Or on your travels? Did you go with the Queen on progress this summer?"

"I did, mistress, but—"

He shakes his head. He is anxious to take the chest and be gone. She slides the limning into her sleeve.

"Mind you," he says, "they all do look the same, them sort."

He means the gentles, rather than the commons.

"Where are you taking it?" she asks, nodding at the coffer.

"Stables, mistress, to be with her other bags and her . . . her."

He flushes deeper crimson at his clumsiness.

"I will come with you," Frommond says. She sets down the Turkey carpet. The boy cannot say no, and she opens the door wider for him to pass through before she follows him panting down some stairs she has never taken before, through the servants' passages and the salt house and the butteries and sculleries and so on, out into a cobbled courtyard in the center of which stands a dray horse having her rear shoe replaced by a bent-backed farrier.

"This way, mistress," the boy calls, and he leads her over the cobbles to a door as broad as a gate.

"If you wouldn't mind?"

She lifts a latch on a smaller door set into the larger door and stands aside to let the boy pass. A moment later the larger door swings open on oiled hinges: within are kept just a few of the Queen's carriages. Frommond's gaze is drawn instantly to the shadowy shape of the Queen's principal carriage, shrouded against the pigeons that roost on the beams above, but in the uncertain light let in through the archway behind, she can make out the holes blasted in its side.

She approaches slowly, as to a tomb, for this is where Alice died, but she stops before she is close enough to touch the punctured sides. She cannot bring herself to look inside. Her mind fills with disjointed, chaotic memories of the night it happened; of being the first to open the carriage door; of finding Alice mewling in spreading scrapes of her own blood; of volunteering to sit and hold her while they forced their way past the hay wain; of still doing so half an hour later, when she died, just as Sir John Jeffers had said she would.

Hearing the boy's final grunt of effort behind, she turns to see him slide Alice's coffer up onto the bed of another cart, and with a start she sees that Alice's coffin is already loaded aboard. She hesitates to approach this, too. It is not the first time she has seen a coffin, of course. Her own mother and father are both called to God, and her little sister, too, with the sweats, and so the length and bulk of the thing comes as no shock. But still though. She is within a handbreadth of Alice's cold flesh, and she cannot help but shiver.

Then she sees what she has come looking for: Alice's bags that she had taken to Hatfield, and the things she had with her when she died. She unties the points of the smaller of the three bags. Alice was not overtidy, but nor would she have stuffed her possessions into her bag like this, all jumbled up with no care. *Someone has been through it*, Frommond thinks, *for certain, and not a casual thief, either, because, look, here is Alice's mirror.* It was her prize possession. A thief would take that. And in one of the other bags she finds Alice's much-prized stomacher, stitched with pearls the size of a baby's teeth, and here is a glove, just one of her favorite pair, dyed as crimson as Christmas, to which a ring of silver is stitched against loss, but it has become separated from its twin, of which there is no sign.

"Has anyone come to look through the bags?" she asks the boy.

The boy shrugs and looks around to see if there is anyone to ask. There is none.

"Where is everybody?" Frommond asks.

"At the wake," the boy says with a catch in his throat.

"The wake? Whose?"

And then she realizes: the coachman. There was another that died that night, forgotten by men such as Walsingham, by women such as her.

"Was he—" She doesn't know what to ask. Was he much liked? A popular fellow? Did he sing with a true voice? Or did he beat his wife?

"My da," the boy says.

He hangs his head.

She gasps.

"You are not going to his wake?"

"I was. Mistress Parry caught me and asked me to do your bidding. Perhaps she did not know he was my da."

She tells him she is sorry for his loss, but he must go now and be with his family, and she gives him a coin, but he hesitates to take it.

"Go on," she says. He yields, but he is strangely reluctant.

"Thank you, Mistress Frommond," he says. "And I will keep a look out for your gent."

And he is off to the inn, leaving Frommond alone in the stables with the shattered carriage and the body of her friend in her coffin. She stands for a long moment, thinking, and then places her hand on the wood of the coffin, and she feels solemn and self-conscious at the same time.

"I will find him, Alice," she murmurs. "And I will offer comfort if I believe it deserved, but if I find he has used you, then I shall damn him to hell."

CHAPTER SEVEN

*Tower of London,
fourth week of November 1577*

A week has passed since Dr. Dee was brought to the Tower, and today is the sort in which London now seems to specialize: damp gray skies stained with coal smoke and an east wind blown straight in from Moscow. Dee stands on the south wall of the Well Tower, wishing for a fur cap—of any animal, a cat, a rat, he'd mind not which—and a lined cloak such as the Constable is wearing as he watches from a safe distance in the teeth of the Lanthorn Tower above. Still, with God's blessing, and a little luck, soon they should all be plenty warm enough.

"Ready when you are, Doctor!" Roger Cooke calls from his position on the bellows. He's standing about fifteen paces away, wearing a smith's apron of greased leather, and a steel helmet, with a visor, that he has borrowed from the armory. Even so, he is discernibly anxious, and as well he might be, Dee supposes, for this is their first large-scale effort in what has so far been a very hit-and-miss series of experiments to rediscover the secret of Greek fire. Between them, they have, for example, broken every one of Cornelius de Lannoy's beautiful glass flasks, and many more objects besides, including an oak table—burned to its feet—and two glass windows, reduced to slivers.

The Constable, a decent man, has been good about it, and Dee is grateful. His previous stints in the Tower have passed under lock and key and have been if not extremely uncomfortable, then not exactly a pleasure. Now, though, so long as he does not try to escape the broad confines of the Tower's curtain wall, he is at liberty to wander the grounds and the arcades of the bailey, following in the illustrious footsteps of the many men and women of honor who have in years gone by been afforded all the comforts of a royal palace, rather than its dungeons. Though they, too, give off their odor, and Dee finds himself avoiding the yard outside the chapel, where he knows the Queen's mother, among many others, met her end.

"Thank you, Master Cooke, yes, please, when you've a moment," Dee instructs.

Cooke starts his pumping. The bellows are of Dee's own design and require a great deal of effort; they make as much noise perhaps as ten swans lifting off from choppy water, but they are—to Dee's mind—extremely efficient. They force a great quantity of air along a stitched leather hose and down into a leather bladder that is placed within a double-butted firkin that is filled with their latest, and hopefully last, attempt at Greek fire. The firkin is otherwise sealed save for another hose that runs off the top for ten yards along the Tower's outer wall, and it is strapped to the battlement walkway by two hoops of iron that are themselves bolted to the floor of the walkway. As the bladder expands within the firkin, the liquid is forced up and along this second hose, which after a run of a few feet is raised up through a battlement and out along a bracket that Dee has had constructed from the stand for an arquebus, so that it stands proud of the castle walls, in case the liquid should dribble, rather than shoot out, and scorch them. At the end of the hose is a constricting nozzle that he imagines will need a tweak in future versions so as to control the liquid's flow, and below, thirty feet away on the other side of the moat, between it and the river, is a large pile of sand on which rests a broken bucket and a dead dog.

Cooke pumps away. There is much more thundering and batting of the leather, and then swooshing and gurgling, and the firkin judders in its constraints, and the second hose stiffens somewhat, and Dee, carrying a lamplighter's pole on which is fixed a lit match fuse, extends it from the battlements toward the nozzle whence the liquid he is already calling Greek fire now bursts in a wild ejaculation.

The fumes catch fire with a canine woof and for a moment flames dance in the air, and then the liquid itself goes up with a bellow. A spurt of roiling fire leaps across the moat to land very near the sand and the dead dog. It continues to burn on the water and it continues to burn as it splashes onto the stones of quay between moat and river. It continues to burn in the air as it shoots out from the castle walls in a smoking yellow line that reminds all men watching of the first time they ever pissed off a wall on a cold day, and Dee can hear cheering from all those gathered to watch, because, by Christ, it is quite a sight.

But then the flame goes back on itself, and the second hose catches fire, and the flames move almost impossibly quickly back toward the firkin of liquid in its iron hoops, and Cooke sees it at the same time Dee sees it, and both throw down whatever it is they are carrying and they turn and sprint along the walkway, one going east, the other west. Dee reaches the turn of the walkway and ducks inside just as the flames reach the main reservoir of the liquid left in the firkin. Cooke is not so lucky. The explosion is astonishingly loud in the damp air, like the Crack of Doom as the Constable will later claim, as the contents of the barrel and its iron hoops explode in a small, astonishingly powerful blast that is heard across Christendom and maybe even beyond. Every pigeon in the country takes flight as shards of wood and iron slice through the air. Cooke, with farther to run, and weighed down by the helmet and, it turns out, two smiths' aprons—one on the front, one on his back—is sent sprawling on the walkway before he can reach the cover of the Cradle Tower. Flames spread all over the wall, and every splash thrown by the blast lingers burning on everything it touches.

The Constable and his sergeants begin bellowing at their men to put the flames out with sand and urine in buckets they have been keeping separate from the solids, and after they've done that, the sizzling stench that rises up is very foul and catches the back of every throat. Black smoke fills the gray sky.

Cooke lies stunned as the flames lick along the walkways toward him. Dee can do nothing for him, for the walkway is made impassable with flames and now, also, a sizable hole over which, even if the surrounding parts were not aflame, no man could leap.

Cooke is a clumsy oaf, but he is a Christian soul, and he has his uses, and Dee does not wish to lose him, especially like this, in what might be said to be an accident caused by his own design. He races down the steps and across the yard into the Cradle Tower. He stamps up those steps and is out onto the battlements just as the flames place their first stealthy lick on the soles of Cooke's boots. Dee takes him by his leather apron's shoulder straps and drags him away. Cooke's soles are smoldering and his toe caps leave tiny traces of fire that pursue him into the doorway of the tower and then peter out in the darkness.

"Cooke? Cooke?"

Dee sees there is a sizable triangle of something black sticking from the rear apron, just below Cooke's right shoulder blade, and already blood stains the leather. But he lives, at least, for he is moving and groaning. Dee removes the shard—it is as hot as hell—and tosses it into the darkness where it lands with a clang.

"Well," Dee tells Cooke. "Not too shabby. A few tweaks, here and there, but not too shabby."

The Constable is less pleased.

"You have destroyed my walkway—look."

There is the smoking hole in the walkway, and the walls all about are pitted and soot stained, too, but the real damage seems to be on the outside, on the quay, where a crane ordinarily used to unload boats of the Grocers' Guild burns merrily away. The sand, the dead dog, and the broken bucket remain untouched.

"But it worked, didn't it?" Dee avers.

"Exactly as intended?" wonders the Constable. He is a dapper little man, with a shaped gray beard and strongly segmented skin, like a sea captain used to staring into the dazzle of sunlight on water, which is exactly what he was. He has removed his cloak and is in very dark blue worsted, and they are gathered by a fire in the first room of the Bell Tower.

"Not quite," Dee has to admit. "Something to do with the delivery system, perhaps? Or the mixture? More pine resin, less alcohol? More tallow perhaps? We will need new hoses, in any event."

The Constable cannot help.

"And how is your man?" he asks. He drinks from a pewter mug of something he has not offered Dee.

"Cooke? He's fine."

"His boots were smoking when last I saw him."

"An occupational hazard," Dee says. "Look, Constable, I do not want to be here any more than you want me here, and God knows I am sorry to have blasted a length from your walkway and burned a few things beyond your wall—"

"For which you will receive the bill."

"For which I will— Hang on. You can send that one straight on to Hatton, because he is the one who sent me hither to . . . to do all this . . . this nonsense."

"He is not making you burn down the Grocers' crane, is he? Not making you stink up this tower—a royal palace, don't forget—with your noxious emanations, or set our ears to bleed with all your infernal explosions."

"Constable," Dee starts, sounding reasonable, "I am trying to re-create a substance that is known only in myth, in legend, and in hearsay. I have spent days poring over every book to mention it, even in passing, but there is very little written, and certainly no recipe, or guide as to its constituents, and so I am—to a certain extent—feeling my way through five or six centuries of darkness and deliberate obfuscation here, and so given that, I hope you will understand that I cannot chart my path as flies the crow, and that I must, inevitably, err. And given that, I hope you understand that I cannot be held wholly responsible for any unintended damage or the very occasional casualty?"

The Constable sighs. Both men know they need to cooperate, and to make peace the Constable at last pours Dee some spiced wine.

"You have come a long way since your first efforts, Dr. Dee, I will grant you that."

"Thank you, Constable, and I hope to go further, but I believe we lack a certain element vital to our success."

"What is it? Lord Burghley has commanded me to supply you with all you need."

"Burghley? What is he to do with this? I thought it was Hatton who'd ordered me here?"

"Sir Christopher has been given responsibility for organizing Her Majesty's birthday celebrations, and in his stead, Lord Burghley has taken an interest in your . . . your doings."

Dee laughs. Of course: Hatton the party planner. But he is not sure he likes the idea of Burghley being involved in this Greek fire business. Burghley is altogether more effective an operator. He might actually be able to find the particular ingredient Dee does not want him to find.

"Well," he says. "It may not be easy. I do not think what I need can be found in this country. Nor indeed in all of Christendom."

The Constable is taken aback.

"Then what is it, and where can it be found?"

"It is something like an ore," Dee tells him, "but in liquid form, and is reputed to seep to the earth's surface in parts of Persia."

"Persia?"

Dee nods.

"And what is it called?"

"The scriptures call it 'thick water' and it is written—in Maccabees—that it is used in sacrifices for it ignites when the sun shines on it, which tallies with all that is written elsewhere, but that is as close to a name as I can find."

"Then . . . how will I even ask Lord Burghley for it?"

"He will need to find a Persian," Dee says.

"And where in all of Christendom will we find one of them?"

Dee smiles. *Exactly*, he thinks.

CHAPTER EIGHT

River Thames, east of London,
next day, fourth week of November 1577

Walsingham is in a barge with Robert Beale, being rowed upriver to see William Cecil at Whitehall, to break the news they have long expected from Piedmont: the Duke of Parma is marching his *tercios* north to the Low Countries and will be in Brussels or Antwerp within the month. Once the news reaches Croÿ and Orange, Walsingham gives the Dutch alliance a week at best. After that, the Low Countries will fall. And then: England.

By Christ, if only Her Majesty had not changed her mind. If only she had sent money, and soldiers! A gesture then, while the matter hung in the balance, and things might have tipped their way. Now . . . Well.

Now all they have is this Greek fire business, dreamt up by Her Majesty and entrusted to Dr. Dee to produce, and about which Walsingham is in two minds. On one hand he recognizes

Dee's talents and believes the man ought to be put to work, but on the Continent, taking the fight to the enemy, rather than toiling in the dungeons of the Tower. On the other hand, however, as Her Majesty says: let loose over the Narrow Sea, there is no telling the trouble he will drag the country into.

"Best keep him on a tight leash, Francis," is Cecil's refrain, and perhaps that is right, but how many attempts on Her Majesty's life will Walsingham need to foil or to fail before one succeeds?

If only they would let him take active measures!

Instead he has Robert Beale, and his various other agents, combing Hertfordshire and Essex for information about the gunmen of Waltham Forest, of which there is nothing, not one single trace of either hide or hair.

And nor has there been anything about the attack, not one single mention of it anywhere across Walsingham's entire network of informers and paid placemen: it has not been written about in any letter sent to France or in France; it has not been spoken of by any notable fireside in Spain; the emperor in Prague is ignorant of it, and the likewise Scottish queen remains in the dark. It can only be homegrown, then, even though he—Walsingham—has men in all the old households in England and knows everything about them: when they say Mass, and the names of the priests who say it, and the whereabouts of the holes in which they will hide when his men come knocking.

But there has still been nothing, and now, a week later, he and Beale are on their way to give this gloomy report to Cecil, whom they find not in his office, but in the palace gardens, taking in the frigid November air against the advice of his doctors. He is as broad as a house in his furs, and he carries a stick as if he were some burgher on his way to chapel in a Flemish painting, though his has a very fine silver knob on its end. He looks grim, and his face falls further at the news from Holland and from Hertfordshire.

"Well, we still have Dr. Dee," he says with a sigh, his breath visible in the air. "Though he has presented us with a pretty problem, too: Do either of you know of a Persian, by the way? I am in need of one. Or rather, he is. Dee, that is."

Beale manages a laugh.

"I sometimes feel like that, too."

Cecil looks at him doubtfully. Walsingham has three men working for him in the Ottoman court, but none in Qazvin.

"Why?" he asks.

"Dee requires some substance that can only be found, he says, in Persia."

"Persia?" Beale wonders. He makes it sound like the moon.

"Exactly," Cecil agrees.

Walsingham sighs.

"Anthony Jenkinson," he says. "He is all I can suggest."

"I did think of him," Cecil admits, "but is he still alive?"

"In Lincolnshire somewhere, but he may not wish to help. You, I mean."

"Oh, he's not still brooding about that letter, is he? Great God above, that was nearly twenty years ago."

This was when Anthony Jenkinson, then an agent for the Muscovy Company, had worked his way down from Moscow across the Caspian Sea and presented himself before the shah of Persia. He was the first Englishman ever to do so, and he carried with him a letter from Her Majesty greeting the shah as emperor over all the Persians, as well as the Medes, the Parthians, the Hyrcians, and the Carmanarians. This had caused no little offense among the Persians, for the shah had not been called the emperor since the days of Cyrus the Great, nearly five hundred years before the birth of Christ. Jenkinson, already on the wrong foot, never found the right one and came home after three wasted years, ruined.

"The Queen was ill-advised," Cecil admits. "Our information was out of date."

"You took it from the Old Testament!" Walsingham allows a rare laugh.

"He should have read the letter before he handed it over," Cecil defends himself. "Checked it against the observable facts."

"And break Her Majesty's Great Seal?"

"It has been done before. Anyway, Francis, will you send word for him? Or send someone to him, wheresoever he is washed up, to pick his brains? Master Beale, perhaps? Or go yourself?"

Cecil holds out a note.

"From Dee, via the Constable," he explains. "It is what he is after."

Walsingham sighs, takes it, and puts it in his sleeve. A cold rain starts spitting and Walsingham cannot face taking to the river again, so they take horses from the Queen's stable and ride instead, to the Papey, where there is the promise of gammon pie, warm wine, and a truckle bed for Master Beale. On the way they pass along Cheapside again, past the Mitre tavern, and Beale brings up the subject of Nicholas Hilliard.

"A very shrewd observer of the human condition," Walsingham agrees.

"He has been painting a woman named Ness Overbury," Beale tells him. Walsingham has never heard of Ness Overbury. He wonders how long those paintings of his take. Ten minutes?

"Have you seen the size of his paintbrush? It is this thin."

Hard to describe in thick leather gloves, but Walsingham takes his meaning.

"Anyway. What of this Ness Overbury?" he asks.

"Do you know of her? I met her and her husband the other day."

"I don't. Why? Should I?"

"I think you should."

Walsingham is aware that Beale is up to something, and they say nothing more of it until they are back by the fire, in the same seats they took when they heard the Queen had been shot. Some of that atmosphere lingers, Walsingham thinks, for Beale is looking very sober and anxious, despite the coming in from the cold giving him ruddy cheeks.

"Go on then, Robert, what is it?"

Beale reaches into his leather bag and after a bit of fiddling around produces a lozenge-shaped limning of the Queen, though she wears none of the finery of the other portraits that Hilliard has limned for her—the "Pelican portrait," for example—but a simple black dress with a ruff and a double strand of pearls and, do you know what? She looks all the better for it.

"Hilliard's, I presume?" Walsingham asks.

"Yes, I borrowed it from him the other day."

"Hmph. Very fine, but what of it? What has this to do with this Ness Overbury of yours, or her husband?"

"This is Ness Overbury."

Beale indicates the limning. Walsingham looks again.

"Hah. She is the spit of Her Majesty,"

"Except she has a birthmark," Beale tells him. He passes him the good magnifying lens from his table. Walsingham peers.

"Well, well," he says. He looks up. He is aware of Beale circling him, stalking him, pondering the best way to launch whatever it is he is about to launch.

"I was thinking," Beale starts, "about the other night. When we believed the Queen was dead, and Sir Christopher Hatton was all set to bring us down Queen Mary."

Walsingham suppresses a shudder.

"Go on."

"And I was thinking about the various thwarts that Her Majesty sometimes puts across your—our—various designs to ensure the safety of the realm, in the future."

Walsingham understands him to mean settling the succession. He gets to his feet to check the door. This sort of talk is unwise, even in a household such as Walsingham's. He checks the shutters and draws the hangings tighter.

"What I am proposing," Beale goes on, "is not a permanent solution to the problem, but a . . . a . . ."

He struggles to find the right word.

"A bandage," he lands on. "A dressing, such as soldiers use on battlefields, on wounds, until after, when they may perhaps show their hurt to a sawbones."

Walsingham is not yet the wiser.

"Well, let us say, for instance, the other night, when we thought the Queen was dead, and we were paralyzed. The only option was the very last thing any of us save Hatton wished to do, wasn't it?"

Walsingham agrees.

"We were lucky that night, because the Queen survived, but when it happens the next time—and there *will be* a next time—and there is still no better claimant to the throne than Mary of Scotland, what then?"

"We cannot conjure a successor, Robert, merely because we need one. Did the Queen's father not go to some lengths to find one, and—well, they do not just grow on trees. And we cannot just choose someone—not this Ness Overbury of yours, just because she happens to look like the Queen—"

He stops. The two men look at each other.

"Unless—"

Beale nods.

"Unless you mean not a successor, should the Queen, may God bless her, die, but a replacement? A continuation?"

Beale sits back.

"Exactly. Someone to give us time."

Walsingham throws himself back into his chair now. The possibilities and advantages of the scheme scroll before his eyes. The Queen but not the Queen. Someone they can get to marry; to produce a son; to send troops to the Dutch; to sanction money spent on the fortification of Plymouth and Southampton; to authorize the selling of guns to the Barbary Moors; to finally rid him of the thorn in his side that is the Queen of Scots, and take the war to Spain!

But no! It cannot be!

"Stop!" Walsingham cries. "Stop!"

He stands.

"Robert," he says, "for the love of God. Breathe no more of this. Put it from your mind. What you are practicing is against the life of the Queen. What you are suggesting is the blackest kind of treason."

CHAPTER NINE

Whitehall Palace,
the next day, last week of November 1577

The next morning the Queen eats some clear soup, and at last there is good news from the physicians who have been smelling her breath and her urine and have pronounced her person to be on the mend. Bells ring out, and there is much joy, though that is confined to the Palace of Whitehall, for outside there is snow in the air, and London is now shuttered against the winter.

Jane Frommond is in worsted and lambskin and a fine fur hat, and she is on a pony, a gray, and being led from the palace by the less-than-well-wrapped stableboy who had collected Alice Rutherford's coffer those weeks before. His name is John.

"Are you certain, mistress?"

"I am."

"Because it is mighty cold to be out and about on such a day," John tells her.

He has boots that are too large for him—surely his father's—but no gloves of course, and he cleaves to the pony, palms pressed flat against its neck for the warmth. They join the stream of traffic heading into the city: the odd cart with iron-hooped wheels, but mostly packhorses and donkeys laden with great sacks of muddy roots. Heads are bowed, shoulders are hunched, and body steam smogs the air.

They cross the Fleet and enter the city through Ludgate, and from the begging windows down at knee level come the usual pitiful cries of prisoners, hands stretched through the bars, begging for anything to help them live through the day, or get out alive. She usually gives one of them a penny, for she can run to that, but today the stink billowing from the windows is very fierce and grips her by her throat, and anyway, John tugs at the pony's reins, for he has no time for them.

"They stand as a fair warning not to get into debt, don't they, mistress?"

Ahead, even in this weather, there are more beggars, and the usual mob of thieves milling about by the conduit under Saint Paul's, awaiting a moment's carelessness from their victims, over-seen by the various sheriffs' and constables' men, though to Frommond's eye the villainous are indistinguishable from the virtuous, and the inchoate mass radiates menace. She huddles low. Wishes they had chosen a brown pony.

"Gutter Lane is just ahead, mistress," John says once they turn onto Cheapside. The street stretches down toward the Tower and is lined on either side by gold and silversmiths' shops; the atmosphere changes, and she feels less fearful. A little along, and there is a left turn, into a darker little street. Gutter Lane.

"We must find a man named Nicholas Hilliard," Frommond reminds John. She has asked one of the ladies-in-waiting whom she might ask more about having a limner make a portrait, and Hilliard was the first name that came to her mind.

John asks a boy of about his own age.

"Know a Nicholas Hilliard?"

"After commissioning a limning, are you, mistress? My master is half the price, twice as quick. Master Hilliard takes a month, costs a fortune, and his paintings are so small they cannot be seen save under the noonday sun on Saint John's!"

"We are after him in person," Frommond interrupts.

"All right, mistress, all right. His workshop's up on the right, but you'll most likely find him in the Mitre about now."

He nods back at the tavern, the way they have come.

Here is a pretty problem. Frommond cannot go into the tavern on her own, nor with John, for then who will guard the pony? And nor can she stand outside while John goes in, for fear of what might happen to a lady standing on her own on a street corner. They are about to ask someone to go into the tavern to see if they can summon Master Hilliard for them when a tall man comes walking very quickly up Cheapside in a very plush moss-green velvet doublet, but a shirt with what looks to be a burned collar; shabby breeches; and boots not at all suited to the weather. He looks somewhat harried and is carrying a bag laden with something heavy.

"Why, it is Dr. Dee!" John shouts.

Dee flinches, as if being hailed by a bailiff. Then he recognizes the boy John and offers a relieved smile.

"John," he says, "God give you good day!"

They shake hands, almost as equals, and Dee commiserates on the death of John's father, apologizing for missing his funeral for not being at his own leisure.

"I heard you was banged up the Tower," John says.

Dee looks startled.

"You did not hear it from Whitehall, did you?"

The boy is confused. Frommond, too.

"What do you mean?"

"Nothing, nothing," Dee says. He glances over his shoulder, then at Frommond, who waits patiently.

"Mistress Frommond," he says, "I recognize you from the night the Queen was shot at."

He removes his cap. He has iron-gray hair, cut close to the scalp, a livid scar working itself through one side, the result of a sword fight, perhaps, or of an experiment involving hot metal gone awry.

"I very much admire your coat, Dr. Dee," Frommond tells him, though her eye is drawn to that burned collar, and is it her imagination, or does he carry a strange sharp and foreign smell about him?

"Hah! This old thing? I will pass your compliments on to my tailor. He will like that."

He flicks the sleeve with his free hand. He is wearing a very fine pair of gloves, too: leather, the color of the best butter. Again, he cannot resist glancing back over his shoulder.

"Are you waiting on someone, Doctor?" Frommond asks.

"I am most especially *not* waiting for anyone, Mistress Frommond," Dee says, laughing. "But are you yourselves here for someone or something? Or is it the tavern? I myself am sometimes overtaken by a virtually unquenchable thirst for ale at this time of day, and often succumb. There is no shame in it, if that is your heart's desire."

"We are after a fellow named Hilliard," John tells Dee.

"Points the Painter? Nicholas Hilliard? Are you in the market to have him limn your likeness, mistress?"

"I am not. I would pick his brains about it, though, and we believe he is within."

She gestures to the tavern courtyard. It is a run-down sort of place, unchanged for a hundred years, since it was frequented by friars and their companions.

"Then let us go in," Dee says. "We are old friends, Points and I, though do not count on him to stand a round."

"I am not after a drink, Doctor."

They leave John with the pony and enter the hall of the inn. It is as untouched within as without, with a fire in its center and smoke that sifts up through the double height of the hall to escape from the roof above. Flitches of bacon hang from the rafters, letting slip the occasional bead of savory smoked fat to drop on the heads below. The friars used to like it, Dee tells her, and stood with their tongues out, making bets on whose tongue the drop would first fall. Around the fire is a horseshoe of long deal tables, their benches filled with men in worsted; and the smell of wet wool, burning coal, and frying pork is strong in the smoke-thick air. Faces look up as Mistress Frommond enters, for this is largely the preserve of men, and even the serving girls—who have knocked about a bit—look over with interest.

John Dee seems fairly well-known among the habitués of the Mitre, to some of whom he appears to owe money. Among them Dee identifies Hilliard, sitting slightly apart in conversation with another two, who divine Dee's intent and make way for him and Frommond to take a bench opposite the man whom Dee then greets as Points, but who introduces himself to Frommond as Nicholas Hilliard.

She removes her glove and they shake hands. His are long and cool, slightly grippy. He gives her the look with which most men greet her and she carefully bats it away. He smiles, not at all put out: if you do not ask, even without asking, you do not get.

"So what can I do for you?" he asks.

Dee suggests he buy them a drink.

Hilliard admits to being hard up.

"A temporary thing," he promises. "I am just waiting to be paid for a limning I have finished just this last week."

Even to Jane Frommond's ear, this sounds as if he might have said it before. Hilliard's gaze takes in Dee's coat.

"But you yourself, Doctor, you look to be prospering."

Dee laughs.

"I have been in the Tower," he tells them, "making use of their facilities."

He dips into the bag he carries and shows them a gold ingot.

Hilliard is amazed.

"You have done it? Made gold?"

Dee shushes him and rubs the coin with his thumb.

"Well, not quite," he admits. "It turns green after a day or two. Too much copper, perhaps? But yesterday poor old Roger Cooke broke the Constable's last alembic, so I am unable to tweak the receipt. Anyway, it is good for a day at least, as this attests."

He indicates the sleeves of his coat; his gloves; and then shows them a small pouch that he has, and in it, a beautifully polished flat red stone that fits sweetly in his palm.

"What is it?" Hilliard asks.

"A scrying stone," Dee tells them. "I have just bought it from a goldsmith for eight pounds."

Hilliard whistles.

"You do know that is theft, don't you, Doctor?" Frommond asks.

Dee swings his eyes her way.

"I think of it more as an I.O.U., Mistress Frommond. When tomorrow, or the day after, the goldsmith comes to see his gold is tarnished he will think to himself: *Bloody John Dee!* But he knows where to find me."

"He will have to join a queue, mind." Hilliard chortles.

As does Dee.

"And in the meantime," he says, "a man must live. Ale?"

"Wine, if you are buying," Hilliard says, nudging his cup forward.

Frommond has money of her own, though, real money. She signals to a serving girl and orders them a jug of warm wine against the cold, and an eel apiece, with sops. She has a pie sent out to John, who stands with the pony.

"So?"

So now it is Frommond's turn to delve into her sleeve to produce the limning of Alice Rutherford's . . . what? She still doesn't know what to call him. Man? Paramour? Rapist? Betrothed? She has no idea as to the nature of their relationship. Frommond watches Hilliard look it over. Her entire being is clenched. She so wants to hear him say that the work is his, and to tell her the boy's name.

He doesn't.

"Fine piece of work," he says. "Very delicate, the brushwork, and look at the boy's expression. You feel you know him. But who is he?"

Frommond deflates.

"I don't know," she admits.

"But you'd like to?" Hilliard asks.

Frommond sighs.

"Just because I am a woman, you assume this is some romantic thing?"

Dee is delighted.

"May I see?"

She shows it to him. He peers at it very closely.

"I am certain I have seen this fellow before. Where though?"

She stares at him.

"Was he a student?" he asks himself. "At Cambridge perhaps? Or Leuven? He is at the edge. Behind a shoulder? A servant? No."

He shakes his head.

Meanwhile Hilliard peers very close.

"That badge," he says. "It looks like a pilgrimage badge. Like the Catholics keep."

"Oh, I am certain he is not a Catholic," Frommond says, but she does not know why she is so certain.

"Anyway," she goes on, "please think on it, Doctor."

"I will," he tells her. "It will come to me in the night and I shall shout it out."

The wine comes. Hilliard apologizes for his earlier assumption.

"So it is not your work?" she asks.

"No. Not mine. If I were to guess, then it looks like the hand of Mistress Teerlinc."

Frommond has never heard of Mistress Teerlinc.

"Levina Teerlinc. Daughter of Simon Bening?" Hilliard says. "Surely you— No? Well, she took the place of Hans Holbein at court. She painted the Queen's father, her brother, and her sister, if I have that right. She taught me almost everything I know about the art of limning."

"And you think she did this? Where can I find her?"

Hilliard makes a clucking sound.

"You may find her body in Stepney, but her soul, alas, has risen to heaven, may God assoil her."

Frommond sits back. A wasted journey, a wasted jug of wine, and a wasted dish of eels, perhaps.

"But I am in touch with her son, Marcus," Hilliard goes on. "In fact, he is the one person in the whole world who owes me money." Hilliard looks at the limning once again.

"Fifteen hundred seventy-six," he says. "Last year. So if this is by her hand, it must be one of her last. Marcus will remember that, surely. He is also a painter—of sorts—and I believe he has preserved her workshop more or less as she left it."

"Would you take me there?" she asks Hilliard.

"We will both come," Dee announces.

"Have you nothing better to be doing, Dee?" Hilliard asks.

Dee smiles.

"People keep asking me that."

So Stepney it is.

"Are you sure you want to come with us, John?" Frommond asks the stableboy when she has paid the reckoning and stepped outside the tavern. "It is a long way out of your way?"

He is determined though.

"I will not let you down," he tells her and she almost laughs at how solemn he is.

When they reach Stepney, they find a handsome village, with a battlemented church named for Saint Dunstan, and Hilliard steers them up a rougher lane to a small, time-wearied house of two halls behind a garden, given over to a tethered pig. To one side is a shed with its rush roof slumped against a brick-built chimney from which slips a thin scarf of smoke.

"Marcus!" Hilliard calls.

When he comes to the door of the shed, Marcus Teerlinc is almost a Dutchman, in a long shirt, wooden clogs, and very close-set eyes. His large hands hang on very long arms and are smutted with charcoal.

"Master Niklaas!"

He suddenly seems to realize something because his pleasure

dries up and he steps back. Both Hilliard and Dee recognize the signs and laugh.

"I have not come for the money!" Hilliard tells him.

Teerlinc relaxes.

"Unless you have it?"

Teerlinc looks askance. Of course not. Hilliard laughs once more and pats Teerlinc on the back. Dee offers to help Frommond from her saddle. There is something in Dee's eye she likes. A companionable interest. She lets him help her down. John remains outside with the pony.

The shed is a workshop, lined with sagging shelves on which sit cobwebbed earthenware pots, bottles, jugs that might once have held wine, and scores of scrubbed-out brushes. There are saws and carpenter's tools on a workbench and in the vise a frame for a painting you can instantly see will never be square. A low coal fire smolders damply in the grate and there is a bank of candle stubs on the floor before a low bed that is covered with a surprisingly rich blue cloth.

"Still going at it, Marcus?" Hilliard asks.

"I do my best," Teerlinc admits.

He picks up a pair of owlish eyeglasses and studies Frommond, top to bottom, as if he were costing her by the inch. When he meets her eye, he takes the eyeglasses off.

"Sorry, mistress," he says. "It is a habit, of my trade."

"What is your trade?"

"Master Teerlinc makes woodcuts for printers," Hilliard answers for him. "Printers of the sorts of books you are unlikely to find in the Queen's library."

Teerlinc tuts.

"Are Chaucer and Boccaccio too lewd for the Queen?" he asks. "Is Dante?"

"Yes," Dee and Hilliard say together, laughing. To save her blushes Frommond thrusts the limning of Alice Rutherford's man at him.

"I am here to see if you can tell me about this. I hoped it might be your mother's?" At the mention of his mother, Teerlinc's face softens.

"Moeder's? May I?" He takes it from her and holds it to the light falling through the tall windows. He stares at it a long moment.

"Oh yes," he says, not looking up. "This is Moeder's all right. Her last. I remember it. I remember him."

Frommond feels a warming thrill of discovery. Whether she can believe Alice Rutherford died happy or died heartbroken depends on the word she is about to hear. Teerlinc keeps looking down at the painting. His face has hardened.

"Marcus?"

He looks up at them.

"Oh," he says. "Yes. I remember him all right. He drove Moeder mad, this one. He took her ages. He would come and go, and he kept unchristian hours. Here one day, gone for weeks the next. And in the end, he would only pay half or something."

"But *who* was he? What was his name?"

Teerlinc shakes his head.

"I never knew," he says. "I never met him. Didn't want to. Moeder, may God rest her soul, she said he gave off a vapor. That he was poisonous, like a serpent, do you know? She used to hate him coming, and I swear—and this sounds stupid—but I swear he drove her to an early grave. She was fine that day, I remember. Painting away. It was the last day he came. She was happy to be done with it, with him, and then that evening, a little while after he'd gone, and they'd had an argument about something. He wouldn't pay, though look at him: his clothes. He was good for it. And anyway, she just—she sat down, exhausted. Then she lay down and couldn't breathe. I fetched the physician, but by the time we got back, she was coughing up blood and there was nothing we could do to stop her, and she just seemed to spew up her lungs, you know? Her heart? So much blood."

Tears fill his eyes.

"I still blame him," he says. "I still blame this one."

Frommond takes back the illumination. Her spirits are sinking.

"But your mother must have kept papers," Hilliard presses. "Receipts? Bills? Even I do that."

Teerlinc looks around at the room—half helpless, half hopeless—at the shelves with their assortment of jars softened by spiders' webs.

"I don't know," he says. "Yes. Maybe?"

They start to look among the detritus of the old woman's artistic life. On her desk: All those brushes scrubbed out; all the dried-up pots of paint; the dusty palettes, long since scraped dry by one or other in a pile of rusting knives; the desiccated wishbone of a long-dead chicken; paint powders hardened to stone in their bowls. Tracks of mice and their shit and spiders' webs everywhere.

"This perhaps," Hilliard asks. He has found a leather folder on the workbench. Teerlinc leaps across to stop him opening it.

"No!" he says. "That is my work. For a . . . private collector."

Under the folder is another one, though, dusty, curled, and much nibbled by mice.

"Yes, try that," he says, clutching the newer leather folder to his chest. Hilliard opens it. Within are five or six sheets of paper and an old, ink-crusted pen. He stands back to let Teerlinc have the first look.

"Just descriptions of paintings," Teerlinc says. "Agreements to paint this or that. A bull and a gate. An old man and his stick. Here is an agreement with a gilder. Two portrait frames in miniature, oval. An agreement with a man for the tooth of a ferret."

"For burnishing silver," Hilliard explains. "But these are years old. Ten years, this one. She was still at court then."

Teerlinc shrugs. Dee is studying the wall of sagging shelves. After a moment he reaches across to a pewter mug. Within is a coil of paper, quite new compared to those nearly ten years old. He passes the mug to Marcus. Marcus plucks out the roll of paper between two fingers and reads it.

"Could this be it?" he wonders. "An agreement to paint two portraits in the new style, a man and a woman, separately, for five English pounds each, to be delivered and paid for before St. John's this last year."

"*Five* pounds?" Hilliard gasps. "May I see?"

Teerlinc shrugs and passes the bill to Hilliard.

"Oh," Hilliard says. "This is Dutch?"

Teerlinc nods.

"Moeder was always more comfortable in the old tongue."

"Does it say his name?" Frommond asks. "Who is he?"

"It is written here, I think. John Sterling, is it? Moeder's hand was never easy, and his mark is even worse."

She takes the paper. It is the size of a man's palm, and the words are written on a slant, in ink faded in parts to become almost unreadable.

"John Sterling?" she wonders. Perhaps.

"No."

This is from Dee.

"I remember him now: it is Jan Saelminck."

"Jan who?"

"Saelminck."

"Are you sure?"

"As I can be."

"Who is he?"

"A Fleming. He was one of Cornelius de Lannoy's assistants. The so-called alchemist. I knew I had seen him before."

Just an assistant, Frommond thinks, and she wonders what she had hoped for. That Alice's lover would prove himself a duke? An earl? Or just a lord? A poet, certainly, but this name seems mired in trade, and steeped in river mud, though she cannot help but be intrigued by his frequent absences. At least he was required here and there. At least he had plans, whatsoever they were. At least he was busy.

She runs a finger over his name. The writing is unadorned. Functionary. Unthinking. Unrevealing of anything, save, she now cannot help notice, an almost deliberate obscurity. An invisibility.

And why two portraits?

"Is there—"

"Ah," Dee interrupts, taking from the pewter tankard a clump of cloth. He puts the mug down, and then opens the cloth on the workbench. The content is revealed to him first, and he whistles. Frommond peers over his expensively clad shoulder. She feels a gasp in her throat.

It is Alice. Beautiful Alice. In perfect miniature, staring back out at the world from a bower of very finely realized lace, a jewel at her pale throat that Frommond has never seen before, and a smile, too, that is now lost. She speaks from the grave, to those willing to hear, but what is she saying?

"This is her?"

Frommond nods.

"Ahh," Teerlinc says, peering over. He smells strongly musty. "She I remember. Truly beautiful. She sat for Moeder, two or three times. Never for me. Moeder would not let me even ask. She was—"

Unattainable.

"But what is she even doing here?" Hilliard asks.

Teerlinc points to the limning in Frommond's hand.

"That is it. The boy! There. Look. They are a pair. A pair of paintings. Identical."

He puts them alongside each other to make the point more obvious still.

"I remember it now. They were painted together, the one for the other, do you see? As keepsakes. But when they were done, the bastard—excuse me, mistress—the bastard refused to pay the full price."

"It happens," Hilliard says.

"I wish I had been here," Teerlinc says. "But I was away that morning. Anyway, he offered only half the money agreed, five instead of ten pounds, so Moeder only let him have one of the limnings. She thought he would choose this."

He points to the picture of Alice.

"But he chose that."

He points to the one of the boy, to Jan Saelminck.

"He did not want her likeness, you see? He only wanted his to give to her, so that she thought he cared for her."

CHAPTER TEN

Seething Lane, City of London,
first week of December 1577

Walsingham and Beale have been in the saddle a week or more, on bad horses, on bad roads, in bad weather, but now they are south of Northampton, returning at last to London, and the comforts of their own beds, their own hearths, their own dogs. An escort of ten heavily armed men led by Sir John Jeffers, newly demoted from the Queen's Yeomen, follows two abreast behind, and what they think of it—of being out on winter roads in this weather—is not hard to gauge.

"Well, Robert, at least we have found Cecil his Persian," Walsingham supposes.

Beale grunts assent. It has been a fraught journey, with both men bruised and brooding from their confrontation at Walsingham's house in the Papey the night before their departure, and they had ridden in silence that first day, retracing Her Majesty's journey through Waltham Forest, stopping at each place the Queen's carriage had stopped on the way down to London, and finding nothing.

By late afternoon they were at Hatfield House again and in the fading light, Walsingham had insisted on another tour of the boundaries, as if they were beating the bounds on Ascension Day. There had been nothing new to discover, and they had come in from the cold and begun asking the same old questions to the same old people and getting the same old answers and after supper, both men had forgone their usual conversation and retired to their beds.

They were up again at first light the next morning, a breakfast of oats and cows' milk and small beer against a long day in the saddle ahead. They should have taken two days to do the seventy miles to Market Harborough, but they did it in one, and that evening when Walsingham dismounted before the inn in the marketplace, his legs buckled and he needed to be helped into the hall where they sat in silence and could hardly manage their ale.

The next morning, he was as stiff as a gibbet.

"I have been here before," he'd told Beale. "On Privy Council business, to interview a girl called Alice Bowker who may or may not have birthed a cat. A red one about yea long."

He'd mimed about two feet, and Beale had laughed, the first sign of a thaw. Then they had ridden together to find Master Anthony Jenkinson, previously of the Muscovy Company, the only Englishman ever to have journeyed to Persia, though his horizons are nowadays shrunk to those of Market Harborough.

He lived in a fine new-built house of unusual style, in among gardens, also of an unusual style.

"I thought he was supposed to be ruined?" Beale had asked.

"He was, a bit, but he got it all back. He is no fool, although—"

Jenkinson had received them wearing outlandish garb Walsingham guessed was Persian, with flowing silks gathered at his stout waist in a vivid red sash from which hung a curved dagger sheathed in what looked like mother-of-pearl. He wore a length of snow-white linen wrapped many times around his head, and on his feet: beautiful pointed slippers of leather the color of mustard. Under these beautifully shod feet were laid, one atop the other, Turkey carpets of the sort any ordinary man might hang on his wall, while on the wall were spectacularly fine woven silks depicting hunting parties, and elephants, and strange striped cats that were not even in the Queen's menagerie. While Walsingham and Beale searched in vain for a bench on which to sit, Jenkinson's servants—all young men, none native to Market Harborough—brought them sherbets and lumps of sweet, sugar-dusted gum that tasted of rosewater.

Walsingham and Beale had stayed with Jenkinson for two days, hearing tales of his many journeys, the first to meet the sultan of the Ottomans—from whom he extracted trade concessions generous enough to enrage the French and Portuguese ambassadors—and of the two he made while representing the Muscovy Company: down from the White Sea in the frozen north, to Moscow, where he befriended Tsar Ivan of the Russians—and acquired similarly wide trade concessions—and then farther south still, across the Caspian Sea, farther south and farther east than any Englishman was known to have ventured before, to finally reach the Sufi shah's great imperial capital in Qazvin, where after many months' wait, he had been granted an audience with Shah Tahmasp.

"If I am honest," Jenkinson had told them, "Tahmasp did not impress me greatly, though obviously nor I him, not with that bloody letter of Cecil's I brought from Her Majesty. You should have seen their faces once they had had it translated. Utterly bewildered. Who were the Carmanarians? The Hyrcians? They died out hundreds of years ago. Thousands! It is worse even than one of them coming to Whitehall and wondering why Her Majesty was not Boadicea of the Iceni, naked and stained in woad."

Walsingham had blinked away the image.

"Mind you, I do not blame her: it was Cecil who gave me the letter. Bloody fool. But I was a fool, too: I should have read what was in it first. Anyway. The shah didn't find it even slightly funny, you know? When I came before him I was instructed to wear shoes, which no one ever does inside in Persia, so as not to sully his holy ground, and when I left, unsuccessful in my attempts to please him, thanks to that letter, a man followed me with a bucket of sand, scattering it over my tracks so as to expunge them from the face of his earth."

At this Jenkinson's sun-battered face wrinkled into a laugh so hard it shook the jewel that he had placed in the crown of his turban, though Walsingham supposed he must have told that story, what, a thousand times?

Then they had got down to what Jenkinson had called brass tacks.

"Greek fire, eh? Well, the Persians called it Roman fire, since the Byzantines used it against the Turks, but I know what you mean. And this Dr. Dee believes he has discovered its parts, does he?"

They had showed him Dr. Dee's description, and the old man's face had wrinkled.

"I have heard of such stuff. In the south of Persia. They call it *naft*, which means just 'wet.' They use it like resin and set great pots of it aflame along the seashore to guide mariners away from rocks and shoals and so forth. But it gives off a terrible stink. Deadly to both man and beast."

"It does not sound overvaluable."

Jenkinson's eyes had narrowed and acquired a crafty mien. He is a merchant, after all, Walsingham had thought, a mercer, and a devotee to God and profit, in revolving order.

"It is like anything," Jenkinson had supposed. "It depends on when you want it."

Walsingham and Beale had looked at each other.

"Cecil says it is urgent—" Beale had started.

"Cecil?" Jenkinson had interrupted. "That little shitsnake!"

Walsingham had groaned inwardly

"He only acts in Her Majesty's interests," he'd tried. "And it is for the safety of the realm. And he will pay you for your troubles, of course. I would see to that."

"Ha! Like last time, you mean?"

Walsingham had wondered if he should tell Jenkinson that he is not alone in being owed by the Crown? He himself is still paying interest on loans he took out to pay for Her Majesty's embassy to Paris. Perhaps not.

"But we are not asking you to go to Persia for us," Beale had said. "We wondered if you still had any people there? Other merchants with whom you are in touch?"

Jenkinson had.

"In Moscow I have many, but at this time of year it is even worse than Scotland, and no man moves farther than the privy. If you are after this naft urgently, then the only way to get it before the ice melts on the White Sea in spring will be through the Middle Sea."

"But what about the Turks?"

Jenkinson had tipped his head and given them a curious, speculative look. *Were they joking?* he seemed to be asking himself.

"Now do you begin to see the depth of your problem? First you will need to find a willing supplier of this naft, which will not be easy, for whoever he is will have to either gain the permission of the shah to trade with a Christian—which will require a large sum in gold—or he will have to get around that law, which will also require a large sum in gold—for the risks run by the man who follows this path are very great."

Jenkinson had pinched the bridge of his nose, here, and clenched his eyes, as if remembering the sight and sounds of risks unsuccessfully run.

"And then," he'd gone on, "whoever your man is will have to find a way to smuggle his cargo—and we have not even discussed how much naft you are after—across lands controlled by the Turk. My God. And then, should that prove even possible, he will need to find a ship willing to sail the length of the Middle Sea, through waters utterly infested by pirates, and if not pirates, then Spanish, Venetian, or Genoese ships, through the gut of Gibraltar.

"Then," Jenkinson had continued further, "if your merchant manages to evade the Spanish guns on the island, or the gunboats from Cádiz, then they are into Portuguese waters, where at this time of year the main danger is not pirates or foreign men of war, but the weather: the great storms that rack the ocean, the waves that are taller than a church's spire that will drive you against every lee shore from Trafalgar to . . . to . . . to Tilbury itself."

There had been a long silence. Walsingham and Beale had exchanged one of those looks: *well, at least we tried.* Walsingham had been just about to tell Jenkinson that they were sorry to have bothered him.

"But that is not to say it cannot be done," Jenkinson had said. "That is not to say it cannot be done by the right man."

"And do you know of the right man?"

Jenkinson had smiled.

"Oh yes," he'd said. "Oh yes. But his price: it will be *astronomical.*"

Walsingham had thought of Cecil then, and of what he'd said.

"Her Majesty is willing to pay any price," he'd said.

"Any price?"

"Within reason."

"Hah! What does that even mean?"

"Any price then. She will cover your merchant with gold. Jewels."

"He is a large man, my merchant. A large Turkish man."

"A Turk? If the stuff comes from Persia?"

"Unless it goes through the tsar, it will have to come through the lands of the sultan."

Walsingham had thrown up his hands.

"I don't know," he'd said. "Whatever it takes."

Jenkinson had nodded. His eyes were very hooded, Walsingham had noted.

"You will have to pen the letter yourself," he had told them. "I will tell you what to write."

Walsingham had sat there, and Jenkinson's servants had brought him pen and paper, and Walsingham had written to this man—he was to leave the name blank; Jenkinson did not want to be cut out of any deal—as if he were himself a prince of England, a man of great renown and power.

"He will read nothing that is not come from an equal."

"Not even in the name of the Queen?"

"A woman? Are you mocking me? Write as if you are the Earl of Leicester. Write as if you are the Earl of Leicester's *father*."

"And he will like that?" Beale had wondered.

"He will respect it," Jenkinson had told them. "That is the only way to deal with this man."

So the letter was written in a high, commanding tone that was, Walsingham thought now, guaranteed to offend any man, scotch any deal. Before they left him, Jenkinson gave Beale a curved dagger that he claimed was made by the finest silversmith in the city of Boghar and Walsingham a small silk-bound book written in the language of the shah, which—again he claimed—must be read from right to left.

"Ingenious, no?"

Walsingham had thought not, but how would he ever know?

And so now here they are, riding south and gripped by buyer's remorse.

"Cecil will not pay whatever is asked, anyway, so it hardly matters," Beale consoles his master.

"That is true," Walsingham supposes.

They reach Dunstable that night and take a table in the hall of the inn, quiet at this time of year, with sharp beer and a fatty slab of pie, but a good fire and a keep who knows not to intrude. When they have eaten and pushed aside their dishes, Walsingham asks for another jug of wine and one last log for the fire.

"Robert," he says. "I have been thinking. About your scheme."

Beale looks at him closely. He says nothing.

"Who is this woman? This Ness Overbury?"

Beale is like a puppy.

"You could see for yourself, if you like? She lives in Suffolk. One of those villages."

He gestures eastward.

"We must be in London tomorrow," Walsingham says, "but— tell me: Is she even willing? Does she know what she might be letting herself in for?"

"I did not ask her," he admits, "in part because how would you put such a question?"

Walsingham sees what he means.

"But is she not already aware how much she looks like Her Majesty? Has no one told her?"

"She has never seen the Queen, or met anyone who has, except for Hilliard. I suppose she might know roughly what Her Majesty looks like, from descriptions given her by someone who might have glimpsed the Queen from the roadside, in a crowd say, but their impressions are always—"

He moves his hand in a circle in front of his face to signify the Queen's favored face powder, and her crown, and the rest of her finery, which tend to dominate any first impression.

Walsingham reverts to stroking his beard.

"Why do you think she would do it, do you suppose? Will she not see its dangers?"

"When the idea first occurred, I was unsure, but I could not rest until I had at least seen if it was possible. Then when I met her—she was staying at the Dolphin, by Bishopsgate—I was struck by her person. She is . . . full of life, full of curiosity. She is so hungry for something other than what she has, for something other than her everyday life."

"You sound—"

"What?"

"Nothing. Nothing."

There is a moment's silence.

"But you do realize what you are suggesting, don't you?" Walsingham goes on a moment later. "You sit here and tell me you are hoping to get someone to impersonate the Queen in the event of her death, and I know you, and I know what you mean, and I know that you mean nothing but good. But imagine what Hatton will think if he hears of this. Or imagine if the Queen herself hears of it. She will believe you aim to replace her with an altogether more docile character whom you may shape to your will. Have her marry you, why not, and you become king. Do you see? Do you see how your intent is open to misinterpretation?"

Beale does. He is not foolish.

"But that would be willful misinterpretation," he says.

Walsingham laughs at him. Perhaps he is foolish after all.

"That is what enemies do!"

"They need never know. Until it is too late."

"You— How would you even do it?"

"I have thought about it. We teach her everything the Queen is known to know."

"Every *thing*? Every *one*? Every *where*?"

"I do not say it will be easy. But she need not know everything. She need not fool everyone, completely. She need only fool us, do you see?"

Walsingham is stunned.

"Us?"

"You. You on the Privy Council. So long as she is plausible enough for you to maintain the lie, for as long as need be, then who else is there to challenge her?"

"Any number of people! Her entire court! Her ladies of the bedchamber, and their husbands; her women of the privy apart-ments, and their husbands; her maids of honor; her ushers; her chaplains; her physicians!"

"Most of them are already sympathetic to the cause," Beale claims. "And those who aren't can be sent away. Or changed. New ladies, new women, new maids, new ushers, even, or most espe-cially, new physicians."

Walsingham is speechless.

"It need only be for a month," Beale presses. "A year. Or, if it is working, however so long she is needed for."

"And at the end of it?"

Beale sits back.

"It is not intended as the end of the matter. It is a thing to give us time. Or it may be—it may be that the Queen does marry Dudley, say—"

"Christ, perish that thought!"

"Or Anjou."

"Hang on, isn't she already married?"

"Ness Overbury is, yes."

"Will her husband not have something to say?"

"He is sixty if he is a day. A brute. If she . . . vanishes . . . one night, say, it can be pressed upon him that she ran off into the greenwoods a-maying with some young buck."

"Really?"

"Such things happen all the time in Suffolk."

"Do you recall what happened to Lady Jane Grey? She attempted to disrupt the lawful succession and was queen for nine days before—"

He mimes the ax blow.

"But we are not setting Ness up as a new queen. We are keeping the one we have. Think about what happened this last time when the Queen was shot at: the whole of London believed her dead, with good reason, but the next morning we sent out word that she was not, and she was seen—within the confines of her own rooms, remember—and so life at court and in the city resumed as usual."

That is true, Walsingham supposes.

"But what if she had died? You heard Hatton: we would all now be under Mary, Queen of Scots, Rome, and in all probability the Inquisition. Unless we had someone like Ness Overbury to take the Queen's place among her women, a veil over her face, and restore and maintain calm for as long as needs be."

Walsingham lets out a long sigh.

"But the risks! And where would you conduct this exercise in high treason where men such as Hatton would not discover it?

Because he will smell something is up. And this scheme is aimed at his heart, you know? It goes against everything he has pinned his hopes on."

"It would need be somewhere out of the way. One of those small priories given up in the Queen's father's reign."

"Pfft. Plenty of them."

"And it would need someone to guide her, to educate her in as much as she would need to know, and how to act, to give you faith in presenting her as Her Majesty. I thought perhaps one of the Queen's tutors, someone who knows her as well as she can be known, and who knows what she knows, as well as a lady-in-waiting, or a maid of honor, to instruct her in court etiquette. Whom she is supposed to know and so on. Her little nicknames for people. That sort of thing."

Walsingham says nothing.

He thinks of Jane Frommond.

And then, oh Christ, of John Dee.

CHAPTER ELEVEN

Richmond Palace, west of London,
following day, first week of December 1577

It is still dark, and Sir William Cecil is still to have his breakfast, yet he finds himself once more in the Presence Room of Richmond Palace, once more on bended knee before Her Majesty Queen Elizabeth of England.

"He has *what*?"

"Escaped," Cecil admits.

"From our Tower of London? How?"

"He blasted a hole through the wall between the Cradle and the Well Towers."

She ought to be outraged, but the Queen cannot supress a smile.

"And how did he do that?"

"An alchemical experiment, Your Majesty, in search of Greek fire. I am yet to determine if it is judged a success or a failure."

"Ha. No one killed?"

"A swan."

"A swan?" the Queen repeats. She sits then, on the very edge of her throne, as if it were some bench in a hallway, and turns to look through the window, lost in momentary thought. Cecil stands in silence, his gaze directed at the steps before her. *Thank God we are alone*, he thinks, *and no one is here to witness this shame.*

"And where is he now?" she asks.

"It is unknown."

"Find him. We need him here by our side."

"But Your Majesty—"

"Lord Burghley, it has been a month since Alice Rutherford was killed, and we still know nothing about the men who killed her. They might have been phantoms for all we know of them. I understand you have your methods and Master Walsingham is pulling on every strand of the web you two have woven around our realm, but there are still more than a dozen men out there, armed with arquebuses who are ready, willing, and, for all we know, able to kill us. You have had a month and there has not been a single arrest. Not a single suspect. Not even a reasonable understanding of how it was organized, or how it happened. It is beginning to look to us as if you are prepared to tolerate attempts on our life."

Cecil throws up his fluttering little hands in alarm.

"Your Majesty," he begins again, "nothing could be further from the truth. We are doing all we can. We are following every trace. Combing every thicket. There is nothing more we may humanly do. It is just that—"

"It is just that you need a different way of looking for whoever did this monstrous thing. Which is why we now command you find John Dee; you are to consult him."

"But Your Majesty—"

"We know what you will say, Lord Burghley: you say it every

time his name is mentioned. We agree some of his schemes are unorthodox, but he has shown many times that his way of doing things—anathema to men such as you and Sir Christopher Hatton—works. Was it not he who told you we were not dead, the night we were shot at? Sir Christopher Hatton told us it was so."

Hatton? My God, Cecil thinks. *That snake has been having private audiences with the Queen behind my back. Perhaps he has been at her bedside these last weeks. Why have I not been told of this? Perhaps he has been nursing her back to health with vegetables he has had brought up from his own gardens. Special tinctures? Soups? Infusions? He will have to put a stop to that. Talk to Lettice Knollys.*

"He did seem to have some inkling," Cecil admits. "He believed the unpolished table acted as a makeshift scrying stone."

"You see? Do you have such a gift, Lord Treasurer?"

Cecil admits that he does not.

"Do you even have a scrying stone?"

"I have a polished table. Two or three of them, Your Majesty."

He has many more, in his many houses.

"But in yours you only see the reflection of your face, Lord Treasurer, at dinner. Dee sees the truth. The future. That is why I call him 'my eyes.'"

Cecil bows his head.

"So go out and find him, and then with his help find the men who shot at us. Find the men who killed our maid of honor, the men who killed our coachman."

Cecil bows as low as his padded old frame permits and reverses out of the door of the Presence Room into the company of Walsingham, waiting for him.

"You look frozen to the bone, Francis."

"A long trip," Walsingham tells him. He tells him about Anthony Jenkinson and his Turkish merchant. Cecil is pleased.

"Progress at least," he says. "And were you to tell me you have
caught the men who shot at Her Majesty, that you'd already had
them racked and hanged and drawn and that their bodies are now
quartered, salted, and dipped in tar, ready to be sent out to be
nailed to various city gates to serve as a treat for provincial crows,
then I would kiss you."

"Not quite," Walsingham confesses, stepping back. "There is
still nothing. They are like phantoms. They have come and seem
to have gone."

Cecil sighs.

"And now Her Majesty is asking after Dee, Francis, to come and
help, but he has recently blasted his way out of the Tower, and the
only trace I have of him is a report from an irate Cheapside tailor
swindled with gold that has turned green overnight. Have you, by
any chance, eyes on him?"

Walsingham shakes his head.

"I also find myself in the peculiar position of having need of
him," Walsingham admits.

"Great God above, why?"

Walsingham is shifting from foot to foot. He only does this
when he is uncertain of his course.

"For a reason I need discuss with you, if you have a moment?"

Cecil understands the need for discretion and inclines his
head.

"The garden?"

It is chilly, but away from the river, and in the thin sunshine,
not so bad. Dew sparkles on the yew, and underfoot the stones are
dark. As they walk in the inner courtyard, out of the wind, below
the windows of the Queen's privy rooms, Walsingham tells Cecil

about Beale's scheme. When Walsingham has finished his explanation, Cecil thinks while they pace, just their breath before them, and the sound of their shoes on the stones.

"The benefits are clear," is Cecil's opinion. "But it is laden with risk."

"Overladen?"

"Yes. But . . ."

More thought.

"We might," Cecil goes on, "apportion the risk."

Walsingham swings his dark eyes to Cecil.

"Go on."

"How well do you like Robert Beale?" he asks.

"Very much," Walsingham says.

"Pity."

Four or more paces. He waits for Walsingham to comprehend.

"Ah," Walsingham says. "But it is his suggestion, isn't it? His scheme."

Cecil nods.

"And if he wishes to pursue it, then—"

Cecil shrugs.

"You have committed nothing to paper?" he asks. "Nothing to prove your part in this?"

"Part in what?"

Cecil allows a flicker of a smile.

"And set a man to watch him, too. Someone you trust. To see this thing does not exceed proportion."

Walsingham agrees.

"And you might warn him," Cecil goes on. "Warn him that if the scheme is exposed, and if there is anything that comes close to implicating you, then the best you can do is give him a day's notice. Make it clear you cannot spare him, and that he must feel the full force of Her Majesty's wrath, as exercised through your offices."

Walsingham nods. He has the decency to look fretful.

"And there is a way we might make use of it, too," Cecil supposes. "Or at least, if the scheme goes awry, and we lose Robert Beale, a balm to ease the pain."

"Mmm?"

"You were suggesting Dee as a tutor?"

Walsingham looks up at him, and a moment later, a slow smile eases to the surface of his face.

"Thank you, Sir William," he says. "Wise counsel as ever. I will go and find him now: see if he is not up to something cabalistic in Mortlake."

CHAPTER TWELVE

Mortlake, west of London,
same day, first week of December 1577

Dee wakes before dawn surprised, once more, that he has dreamed again of water, and of a barge—a coal black one that lies moored in soft flowing water, amid wisps of autumnal mist—and in his dream he approaches it across the same dipping green water to find himself unable to scale its sides, and then he tries to think if he has seen the barge before. Is it an inkling of the future, or a reminder of the past? Some undone thing? Did he see it in the polders, perhaps, when he was traveling across the Low Countries, and in a trice he is distracted again by thoughts of Leuven, and of the friends he made there from all over Christendom.

He thinks of poor old Gemma Frisius, who died so young, but achieved so much, and who gave him a beautifully made set of his rings, in brass, just before he died, and which Dee has to this day; and he thinks of Gerardus Mercator, with whom he is still in touch, and whose maps he used to direct Frobisher across the Ocean, not only to collect the ore, samples of which Bob and Bill have carted off, but the Northwest Passage. And he thinks of Abraham Ortelius, who believed the continents drifted about the planet, and who is now appointed mapmaker to King Philip of Spain. Perhaps if Philip is patient enough, Dee had once laughed, Spain will bump into England, and there will be no need for an invasion fleet. Ortelius was always a dry old stick, though, and he hadn't thought that particularly funny. Nor was it, in further view.

Dee wonders what is happening in Leuven right now. Are the Spanish back in control? Will they enforce their placards against what they consider heresy? Will they impose the Inquisition on the university? What he would not give to be able to take a barge over there now—the coal black one from his dreams—and load it with all the books that will soon be burned, and all the men, too, if that is the case.

He is sickened by the waste of it, this diabolic war on knowledge, and he resolves, once more, to do something about it. He will go to Her Majesty again. Ask to be excused from the horror of making this Greek fire and petition to be allowed to pursue his other idea, a scheme that would not see men roast alive, but bring peace and enlightenment. He has in mind that his plan will persuade Her Majesty's enemies to beat their swords into plowshares, to meld their spears into pruning hooks. If only men such as Hatton and Cecil would listen, and let him talk to Her Majesty alone, he could persuade her, he is certain of it.

He swings his legs from the bed and picks his way across the teetering piles of books in his room. His eye falls on the scrying stone that has so far yielded him up not a single clue as to what the angels might have in mind. He is beginning to think perhaps the goldsmith might have rooked him, just as he rooked the gold-smith.

"John?"

It is his mother.

"What is it, Mother?"

"Do you want an egg?"

"Why not? If the hens are laying."

It is a beautiful, still morning, the river burnished, on the turn, reflecting the sky to the east in vivid indigo, but not yet too cold. That will come in January, and stay through February, feinting to withdraw in March, until finally April arrives to drive it away in a furze of new growth. *That is a long way off*, he thinks. *Winter to get through first.*

"You were out late again last night?" his mother asks as she tips an egg onto his bread.

"The comet," he says, indicating over his shoulder.

"Oh, that old thing."

He smiles, but then ponders her meaning. That old thing.

"It is a comet, Ma; the Great Comet."

"So long as the chickens are laying," she says, "it can call itself what it likes."

It is an admirable philosophical position, of course, though it seems limiting. He is about to take another bite when there is a thumping on the gate. His heart spurts, but he does not believe it can be Bob or Bill, unless they have adopted a new, less forthright approach, nor can it be the Queen's guard, come to haul him back to the Tower. They would come by boat and invest the orchard. You'd hear them from miles away. He listens as Roger Cooke goes to the gate and asks over its top who might be there.

"Huh?" he asks again, cupping his ear to the gate.

Cooke has gone a bit deaf, Dee thinks, and he wonders if exposure to explosions can deafen a man in the long term. Probably. He gets to his feet, egg spreading atop his bread, and steps out into the yard.

"Who is it, Roger?"

"It's a woman, Doctor," Cooke tells him. He looks panicked.

"Well, let her in," Dee suggests. Cooke opens the gate and there, of all people, stands Mistress Frommond, beautifully dressed in good boots and a dark riding cloak.

"Doctor," she says. "I hope I am not disturbing you?"

She is, of course, and the whole household, all three of them at least, who each insist she come in and then Widow Dee insists she take an egg, and ale, too, but Frommond regrets she has already eaten at Richmond Palace, from where she has just ridden. She is distracted, Dee determines, and after a moment she blurts out the reason for her visit.

"Will you come with me to Hertfordshire?"

"Hertfordshire?"

That is a day's walk, he thinks.

"You will think me strange but I have been wishing to revisit the scene of Alice Rutherford's death. Where she was shot."

She has deep amber eyes, and such an honest expression.

"And I would greatly value your help, for I have no servant to ride with me, nor friend to consult."

"Today?"

"If you are not busy?"

"But I have no horse," he points out.

"I have brought two, if you would care to look at them? Now? They are saddled and have teeth and hooves and so on. From the royal stable at Richmond."

As she is talking Dee sees Cooke over her shoulder. His eyes are very round and he is pointing in alarm toward the river. He mouths the name *Walsingham*.

"Excuse me one moment, Mistress Frommond," he asks.

He goes to the door of the library that offers a view of the orchard down to the river. Through the now bare branches of the trees he sees four or five of Her Majesty's Yeomen marching staunchly toward his house, following them the saturnine figure of Her Majesty's master secretary and his right-hand man, Robert Beale. Behind them is one of Her Majesty's barges, gangplank down, more Yeomen to come.

"So about these horses, Mistress Frommond," he says, returning and daring to take one of Her Majesty's maids of honor by the arm and guiding her more quickly than is polite out of the library, across the courtyard, and through the front gate, which he pulls close behind.

Two horses, as promised, saddled in red leather.

"Very handsome," Dee says.

He cups his hands on his knee for her boot, and with one hand on his shoulder she is up into the saddle with practiced ease.

"Should we give them some exercise, do you think?" she asks.

"Let's," he says.

They both kick on and are out and riding too fast along the road to London before the gate behind them swings open to let spill three of Her Majesty's Yeomen.

"You have no cloak, Doctor?" Frommond calls.

"I have the love of my Queen to keep me warm," he replies, though a few moments later he is just wondering if that will be quite enough to keep him alive on a journey to and back from Hertfordshire, when he sees, returning from market, Thomas Digges and his mother, both well wrapped against the cold, Digges in the luxurious velvet coat that Dee returned to him instead of his own after his time in the Tower.

"Thomas!" Dee calls, and he slows his horse to a gentle trot so as not to frighten the old lady. Politenesses are exchanged and blessings conferred and Digges is happy to lend his friend his coat again.

"Particularly if it comes back all the grander, as last time," he says.

Dee and Frommond ride on, eastward, toward Southwark and the bridge.

"What are we actually doing?" Dee asks.

"Riding to Hertford," she says.

"Did you know Walsingham was coming for me?"

"I overheard some of their conversation at the palace in Richmond this morning," Frommond admits. "They have some scheme in mind that involved your person, which I supposed involved your return to the Tower."

"Ha! Mistress Frommond, I am in your debt."

"I confess I am at a loss, Doctor, why you seem at odds with Master Walsingham, and he with you."

"Is that a question, mistress?"

"If you like."

Dee sighs.

"I do not wish to speak ill of any man, mistress—"

"But?"

"But I confess I find him stiff, and unyielding, and he guards the Queen's person—from me in particular—with unnecessary zeal, even going so far as, I believe, to have blocked my appointment as Astrologer Royal. He feels I am a bad influence on her. That I put notions he thinks foolish in her mind, and stir her up in a manner that does not suit his creeping ambitions."

"In what way?"

Dee is hesitant. He is not sure himself anymore.

"His mind is like a steel trap," he starts, "which is a good thing, for some things, but he is so fixated on plots, and intrigue, and all the nasty fingernail-pulling business of his trade that he lacks the time to look up. Or he lacks the imagination to speculate on what might lie over the horizon. The western horizon in particular."

"He deals in . . . what? Harsh reality?"

Dee looks at her again.

"You have been talking to him."

"He to me," she admits with a smile.

Dee laughs.

"That is a first. Usually he waits in silence for you to incriminate yourself."

There is a moment's silence. Dee thinks about Walsingham for a moment before he goes on.

"But, if I am honest, I do not think we are such foes as once we were. It is a habit, more than anything. We cannot bring ourselves to admit otherwise. We irritate each other, and oftentimes he flexes his power over my person too strenuously, such as today's scheme to return me to the confines of the Tower."

Frommond shakes her head and smiles. Dee wonders if she has any friendships such as that. Perhaps, he supposes. Less at stake, perhaps, but just as heartfelt.

"Well, it is a fine morning for a ride," she says.

He agrees and they ride on farther in awkward silence for a while until they reach the southern fringes of Southwark, when Dee notices that Frommond is weeping silently.

"Oh, Mistress Frommond! What is wrong?"

She tells him that nothing is wrong, but that since Alice Rutherford's death she has wept uncontrollably at the strangest moments, usually when she is most nearly content.

"I have cried a bucket's worth, I daresay," she admits. "It means nothing."

She waves away his attention and starts crying again. Dee thinks to remind her of Margery Kempe, the English mystic who wept all the time and drove everybody around her mad, but sees that story may not serve. At casual glance, Frommond appears so sunny and happy that it is easy to forget that she has recently had her friend die in her arms.

"And how long has it been since . . . it happened?"

"A month. To the day," she tells him.

"Ahhh," he says. "So a sort of personal month's mind?"

He pictures those among Alice Rutherford's friends and relations who were unable to attend the girl's funeral gathering a month after it, in the churchyard where she is buried, to share their grief and mourn their loss, and here is Jane Frommond, forbidden to join them.

"Are you certain you want to go back, though? To where it happened?" Dee wonders. "Might not a . . . a— Something else, be better?"

His eye falls on the bear-baiting gardens on their left. *No*, he thinks. *Perhaps not that.*

"It sounds foolish, perhaps," she says, "but I wanted to take the illumination of Jan Saelminck, and bury it. I wanted to bury it where it happened. Where Alice was killed. Now that I know he was not in love with Alice, and would not even stretch to keeping her likeness, I want rid of his. I intend to put it where it will be spoiled, just as she was. Does that seem strange?"

Does it seem reasonable? He doesn't know. He can't say. But

either it is the strange wild and sad smell that clings to the area around the bear gardens, or he feels some of her sorrow.

"No, Mistress Frommond," he says. "That sounds . . . appropriate."

On they go, into the crowded confines of the bridge that vibrates from the water against the starlings below, and the people are pressed very close. They move up on the left-hand side of the bridge, the only place in the kingdom where there is a rule about this, and it takes them twenty minutes of patient shuffling before they even reach the drawer bridge, in the bridge's middle, where an old house is being pulled down and they must stop while some beams are detached.

"What is going on?" Dee asks a workman.

"Making way for some house they are building over in Holland," the man tells him while they wait to let the dust blow over from a sack full of daub he has just tipped over the bridge's side. "Skillful little fuckers, they are, them Hollanders. Begging your pardon, mistress."

At long length they are let through, and Frommond asks about Saelminck.

"I did not know him save by sight," Dee confesses. "He was a sort of assistant, or manager, I suppose, of Cornelius de Lannoy, if that was even his real name, a swindler and false alchemist."

From the bridge they can see the Tower on the right; through the occasional gap in the houses. Dee wonders if they have fixed the hole he made. Probably not.

"Was he a clever little . . . what that man said back there?"

"Saelminck? Definitely. Well: they got out of the country together, with all the money they swindled from Bess, didn't they? But I wonder why he's back. Or was back, anyway. I wonder how they met. Him and Alice."

Frommond has wondered the same thing.

"They must have known each other more than a year, because of the date on the limning," she tells Dee. "But I suppose she was three months with child when she was killed, so if he is the father, he must have seen her this summer, when she was on progress with Her Majesty."

"That does not refine it much, does it?"

She shakes her head.

"Those progresses are very hectic," she says. "A multitude of people, all the time, and when we reach a place—one of those houses—it can be just like this, only the people are better dressed, and somewhat better washed."

She indicates the great jostle of people around the conduit in Gracechurch Street and the marketplace crowds of Eastcheap that stretch as far as Bishopsgate. At length they are out through the city gate, and past Saint Botolph's and Bedlam Priory, and they ride on, Frommond lost in her own thoughts, Dee treading carefully.

"What do you remember of the night the Queen was shot at?" he asks.

He hopes this will help.

"Every moment," she tells him. "It is as if I am living it whenever I close my eyes. It never stops."

Dee understands. He felt the same for a long while after leaving Mistress Cochet to drown on the sands under Mont Saint-Michel.

Gray clouds above now, a thin wind in their faces, and the forest ahead. Dee shivers. Frommond looks serious. The road rises and soon they are in the forest, deeper, darker, damper than he remembers, and it is strangely quiet: no birdsong even, and the road is deserted both ahead and behind. Dee shivers again. He is glad he has the coat. Frommond has turned deathly pale.

"We can go back. Come another day. When it is brighter?"

She shakes her head in its hood.

"We are nearly there. It is just —"

She nods ahead.

"There."

A desolate spot where the road dips into sludge between two high banks of black mud, tangled roots exposed, and above the underbrush is dense with crowded holly and tangled bramble. Dee draws the reins. Frommond slides from her saddle before he is able to offer help. Dee remains in his, watching. The bank still bears the marks of being cut about to get the hay wain out of the road. Other than that, there is nothing here to say what happened that afternoon a month ago. But Dee can see it all. Or almost all. Gunmen on both banks firing down into the road. They would have been waiting in the trees how long? All day? Or were they there every day?

"Master Walsingham believes someone sent a signal," Frommond tells him as if she might read his mind. "From Hatfield."

She ties her horse's reins to one of the bank's exposed roots.

"Does he have an idea who?"

"No."

Of course not, Dee thinks, or they'd've been racked half to death already by now.

"Anyone could have done it," Dee supposes. "It needn't have been anyone in the house. Someone waiting on the road nearby might have done it. On a good horse. He sees the Queen go by, and he rides ahead to alert the rest of them. But that would mean the rest must have been waiting nearby."

"They shot only the Queen's carriage. They knew which one it was, though it is not so very different in appearance from the others."

"A guess?"

She shrugs.

"And there was more than a dozen of them. A small army."

"They'd be conspicuous," Dee admits. "Someone would have noticed them."

"Master Walsingham has found no trace of them. He says he has spoken to every stable in every inn within a hundred miles. He says no one saw anyone on the road that day in any numbers. He is talking to forge masters and gunsmiths in both counties, and watches at every city gate, but no one saw a thing. He is calling them phantoms."

Dee dismounts. He scrambles up the right-hand bank and looks down. There is mud on his coat now. Digges will not be pleased, or rather, his mother will not.

"This is where they stood?" he asks. Frommond looks up at him and nods. She is very pale. She might faint he thinks. But then he imagines what it must have been like to be one of the gunmen up here, waiting, waiting and then the moment arriving and squeezing the lever of the arquebus, touching the match fuse to the pan of powder. *Boom.* He has never fired an arquebus. He has fired a pistol, but only at a lock. He might have missed that, too.

"And it was raining?"

"Heavily," she confirms.

Dee wonders how they kept their powder dry. He looks up into the trees' canopy. Then turns, with his back to the road.

"This is the way they ran?"

"I think so, yes. That is the way Jeffers chased them anyway. For all the good it did."

Dee helps her up the bank. She grips his wrist and allows him to grip hers.

"You are very finely dressed for a walk in the woods, Mistress

Frommond?" he notes with a question in his voice. She is. Not only is her cloak a beautiful blue, he sees she wears a very tight bodice as they do in the French court, with a stomacher, and even a farthingale. Her sleeves are voluminous, and she has long gloves though no rings.

"I was at court," she reminds him. "And had to move fast to beat Master Walsingham to your door in Mortlake."

"I am obliged, once again, Mistress Frommond, that you would think of me. It is not uncomfortable?"

"A little, but please, I am used to them now."

He wonders what she means.

She raps her knuckles against her bodice and produces a hollow sound.

"Whalebone," she says.

"Ah," he says. Yes. Whalebone stays. What a thing.

They turn away from each other. Dee feels a slight warmth at the mention of Frommond's underthings.

Ahead is a great impassable tangle of holly and bramble.

"Her Majesty's Yeomen got all torn up in it," Frommond tells Dee. He turns his mind to the Queen's Yeomen. He thinks of them in their breastplates and steel helmets, waving their swords and halberds about. Meanwhile the gunmen had mapped their retreat in advance. He can see it now, in the daylight that Jeffers was not afforded: a cut-through—a foresters' path, perhaps, or one used by fox and deer. It runs to the right. He sets out along it.

"And what about the horses?" she wonders.

"We'll not go far."

The path winds on, discernible only if you are not looking straight at it, even under the new drop of soft autumn leaves. It leads east, drawing him on, through stands of pollarded elm and then coppiced hornbeam; clearings of stunted, spindly hollies; then barren patches under a gathering of tall pine trees already marked with a cross of paint for the cutting of ships' masts. The ground slopes very gently down.

"Dr. Dee!" Frommond shouts. "Stop!"

He is so shocked he spins, as if attacked. She is reared back from something she has seen, at the foot of one of the firs. He hurries back.

"What? What is it?"

She says nothing. Her face is crinkled in horror, and something else. She points. Among the roots, tossed on the pine needles, is a scrap of something red. He bends to inspect it closer. A sleeve of scarlet leather, with a twist of fingers.

"A glove?"

He is about to pick it up when he surveys its status more clearly. It sits atop of a sausage length of shit that he knows instinctively can only be human. And there is something about the way the glove is twisted that tells him it can only have been used for one purpose.

He stands. Frommond is paler than ever. Her eyes are wide and for a moment she makes no sense.

"It's hers," she says. "It is her other glove. Alice's."

He looks at it again.

"Alice's?"

"They were her favorite pair," she says. "Given to her by . . . by someone—my God, *him*?—but Her Majesty would never have allowed her to wear them. So she wore them for fun, when we were on our own. I would recognize them anywhere."

Dee uses his toe to flick the glove from its resting place on the by-now-almost-gone-to-powder shit. The leather is faded in parts, but where it has not faded, it is vivid, cerise almost, and particularly striking.

"You are sure?"

She nods.

"I would swear on it."

"What in God's name is it doing here?"

She cannot say, nor can he. A wind is picking up. The treetops are beginning to whisper, gossiping in an urgent susurrus. Dee wonders, *Will trees ever be proven to communicate?* Via their roots maybe, touching in the deep damp dark. He wonders what they would tell him now. This puzzle—the mystery of the glove's appearance—makes his mind spin.

"We should take it," he says, though he knows not why. Better than to leave it here, anyway.

"And return it to her father? He will have noticed it missing, surely."

"Will he want it?" Dee wonders.

"It will clean up," she supposes.

After a moment he stoops to pick it up and shake it free of the clinging matter. He bangs it against the trunk and then is at a loss with what to do with it. He rolls it and slides it into his doublet.

"Let's go back," Frommond says. "I am worried about the horses."

"Just a moment more," Dee says.

There is something about the quality of the light ahead that invites him on. The trees thin ahead, as the forest ends, and he walks on, down the hill. She follows and in all they must have walked two thousand paces from the horses before the canopy opens, and there is gray sky above and willow trees and alders ahead, and underfoot it is squelching wet. He comes to a halt.

"What is it?" Frommond asks him.

"A river," he tells her. "It is a river."

A broad ribbon of soupy brown water, five yards across, fringed with desiccated rushes and teasels on either side.

They stare at it, and then at each other in surmise.

"Do you suppose Master Walsingham knows it is here?" Frommond wonders.

Dee supposes he has never even been up here. Why should he have thought to? *Walsingham is a spider*, he thinks, *not a bloodhound*, and then he wonders why Walsingham did not bring bloodhounds up to the forest the day after the shooting. Too much rain? Too much confusion? Too many footprints of Jeffers and his men, perhaps? And also, remember how Walsingham was that night? Almost mad with anxiety and fit for nothing the next day.

"The gunmen . . . they could have come up here by a boat?" Frommond wonders. "And left in it."

He hardly hears her. He walks on.

"Are you all right, Dr. Dee?" she asks.

The truth is that he is not. His head spins, or the world does, for he has been here before: in his sleep. This is what he has been dreaming about. This river. He turns to his right, and begins following it downstream, walking south, through marsh and sedge bog where teasels compete with bulrushes, and in the wind their dry husks and stalks and strange heads rub and hiss. Something is making a deep groaning whoop in the eye-high grass. After a moment a small barge—scarcely bigger than a wherry—steals up from behind, floating down the river under a much-patched russet sail.

Dee hails the pilot.

"What river is this?"

"River Lea," the man calls back in twangy English.

"Where does it go?"

"Stays where it is."

The man laughs at his own joke. There's a boy on board who also laughs. And a four-square dog that growls, whom Dee hopes cannot swim.

"Where does it flow from?" Dee risks. "Where does it flow to?"

"From up north," the man indicates. "Broxbourne and beyond. Runs into the sea at Leamouth, Isle of Dogs way."

The dog barks.

"Shut it."

Dee has never heard of the river Lea. The pilot isn't surprised.

"You will, though," he calls, beginning to have to shout as he drifts out of earshot. "If they ever finish that fucking lock."

"Which fu— Which lock?"

"Lock downstream. Them Dutch fuckers've been at it for months, but they've fucked off home now."

Those are his last words before he is gone and Dee and Frommond are left alone on the river's sodden margin. Frommond pulls a face.

"The Dutch are unpopular?"

"Well, there are a lot of them over here just now. Refugees from the war, but also they are marvelously industrious, and ingenious engineers. They know how to drain fens, for example, and build bridges and mills and weirs and locks and so on."

Dee tapers off and becomes transfixed by what he sees: the watermill, its wheel turning in the current. Downstream he can see more of them, undershot wheels turning slowly in the dawdling flow. Can it be here that his dreams have led him?

He sets off south, after the boat, stumbling along the river's uneven bank.

Frommond calls him back, but he walks on, heedless. He distantly notes her following him.

"Dr. Dee!" she calls. "I am only worried about the horses!"

"They will be fine!" he calls over his shoulder. "They are from the Queen's stable. Someone will take them back."

He is not completely sure about that.

"You would make a horse thief of me!" Frommond tells him. She has caught him up.

"I will vouch for you," he tells her.

Nothing seems so urgent as this.

"I have seen all this," he tells her. "In my dreams. Canals. Watermills. Locks. A barge."

At length they come to a pool where the same small barges are tethered to the stump of a tree.

"Are those your barges?" Frommond asks.

Dee shakes his head.

"Mine was black. And large. For coal maybe? And closed."

This is the tidal reach, and the tide is rising. Dee and Frommond walk on, and a little farther downstream they come to the towpath on the river's western bank, which they follow in silence for half a league or so. It is getting on for midafternoon now. They should definitely be turning for home yet still Dee presses on, with Frommond indefatigable in his wake, until they reach what he has been looking for: the site of the lock the Dutch are making.

Dee has an interest in this and admires the scheme: two tall frames are being built either end of a straight reach, with various winches and pulleys of the sort you see on boats, through which will run, one day, Dee supposes, ropes thick enough to lift and lower the huge wooden gates that are halfway through being laminated on the river's bank. Today though, work has stopped, and there is no one about.

Dee stares at the water.

"Is this your canal?" Frommond asks.

"It is," he says. "Or will be. Dreams are oftentimes more sugges-
tive than indicative."

But there, a hundred paces further down the river's bank,
moored to the trunk of an alder, is the barge. Forty paces long;
dusty black save for an oiled pine mast that is laid the length of the
roof of the cabin, thick as a man's torso. Loops of stained rope hang
from stanchions and along the top there are piled presumably the
sails in stained green canvas bags on which a man might happily
sleep. It is one of those that service the trade in coal between New-
castle and Calais, Dee supposes, the sort that creep up and down
England's east coast and then linger waiting for the right wind
and water to cross the Narrow Sea. It looks repelling, but from its
stovepipe curls the faintest wisp of pale smoke.

They stare at it for a long moment.

"The gunmen. Could they have lived here, waiting until they
got the signal Her Majesty was coming?" Dee wonders. "They
could have worked on the lock and no one would have thought
anything of them. No one would have even mentioned them to
any of Master Walsingham's searchers, would they?"

My God, he thinks, that is a deep plan.

"But are they still here? The boatman said they'd gone," Frommond reminds him.

"Maybe they have," Dee replies. He walks toward the barge,
drawn to it as if in a dream. He swims in air thick as water.

"Hello!" he calls. "Hello?"

There is a curious moment of sudden stillness, as if someone
has stopped doing whatever it was they were doing, but they had
heard nothing being done anyway. Is it that someone has stopped
breathing? No. It is a cat, turned from its private ablutions on the
cabin hood, to stare at them over its shoulder.

"What an ugly brute," Frommond says.

"Hello," Dee calls again. No movement. They look at each other. Dee raises his eyebrows. There is a log propped against the bow into which someone has adzed steps to make a rough gangplank. He climbs it and steps up on the little deck at the back of the barge. The cat rolls onto its feet and hisses at him. Gray tortoiseshell, its ear is ripped, and its eyes are yellow.

"Hello, boy," Dee tries to reassure it. More hissing.

"Bloody cat."

There are two doors over a hatch, with rope handles. Dee tugs them. Locked.

"Hello," he calls again. Still nothing.

He shuffles along toward the bow, along the footwide walkway until as he passes the stovepipe, he removes his cap and rolls it in a ball and stuffs it in the mouth of the tube. From the shore Frommond laughs in silence. Dee moves on to the bow of the barge, where there is another hatch, ingrained with dirt, and much scratched, that must lead to the hold. Two doors, wedged closed with an iron bar between two iron handles. He slips the iron bar and opens one of the doors. It is heavy, barred oak. The smell is a mix of bilge water and coal dust—very foul—and Dee feels his guts turn. He peers in. It is very dark, but with the hatch open, enough light sifts down into the hold and he believes he sees— Can it be? A pile of long canvas-shrouded tubes hanging like long sausages from the rafters of the cabin.

He looks up and takes a lungful of clean air.

"What is it?" Frommond calls from the shore.

Dee admits he does not know. He does not want to say they are the guns used to shoot her friend until he is sure they might be. He puts one foot on the rung of a ladder and looks up to see Frommond stepping up onto the deck. Alice was her friend. She wants to see what is to be seen.

"No," he starts to say; it is only a rope.

He stands, disappointed.

But then there is some violent percussive swirl of movement in the cabin below, a sudden drumbeat of action. The cabin doors burst open in a cloud of smoke, and a man looms on the deck behind Frommond. She turns to him in fright. He has in hand some fearful curved spike, some tool for turning logs perhaps, and he comes at her in pink-eyed rage. She turns and starts to run up the side of the barge, but he moves faster. The hook comes around under her chin, and she is yanked off her feet. The man lets the hook drop with her. She hammers to the deck, legs thrust forward, head twisted in the iron noose, its barbed point a finger's width from her ear.

"Who are you?" he yells at Dee. "Who are you? What you doing here?"

"Stop it!" Dee shouts. "You're hurting her. Let her go."

"Who the fuck are you tell me what to do? On this boat. Who are you? What you doing here?"

He sounds Dutch. Or is it Flemish? Or French. Not one of the Dutch fuckers, then? Or maybe it is the boatman's mistake. Very tall, with narrow shoulders and a rough red beard knotted under his chin, he is in a homespun shirt that reaches to his naked knees.

"Just let her go," Dee tells him. "Just let her go and we'll be gone."

But now the man has in his other hand a blade of something more than just an eating knife.

"Tell me what you doing!" he yells again.

Dee has to react. Find some way to pacify him. Perhaps ask him a question.

"Are you working on the lock? We are looking for your foreman."

The man looks at him with contempt.

"There's no fucking foreman."

"We're sorry," Dee says. "We've made a mistake."

"Big mistake. You—get in the hold. Now."

"I'm not—"

The man puts the blade to Mistress Frommond's cheek. Dee sees her skin part in a line of blood. She hisses and her boot heels scrape on the deck. Blood marks her linen collar.

"Get in hold," the man says. "Or I put out eye."

Dee backs to the bow, to the hatch of the hold. He is about to tell the Dutchman that he is not going down in that, but one look at the knife pressed below the jellied orb of Mistress Frommond's eyeball and he finds the top rung. He turns and steps down to find another, and another. The stench rises up around him to coat his tongue and fur his teeth. It tastes like crypt water. Down he goes. Four or five more steps. He turns and looks along the deck. The man is wrangling Mistress Frommond with his knees, as you might a sheep to the shearing cradle. She has both hands around the hook, keeping it from choking her, but it's the knife that's the real danger.

"Get down," the man shouts at Dee.

Dee slips and clatters down the last few steps. His feet sink in a kind of icy clinging ooze. He can hear the river thrumming softly against the barge timbers, and there come tiny high-pitched squeaks of protest to let him know he is not alone. Now the sky above is reduced to a square. He can hear the man's grunting, and Frommond's suppressed screams and her boots scrabbling on the deck. Then the shape of her blocks the square of light above and the man pulls the hook from her neck. It is a savage thing, and for a moment Dee believes he has cut her throat and he bellows with horror, expecting a shower of blood on his upturned face, but as

Frommond is pitched into the hold, her throat is intact, and her head connected. She crashes into Dee. Her outstretched hands pummel him, her head cracks against his cheek. Dee staggers. Three steps in the stinking ooze. But he does not fall. He holds her up, keeps them both out of the swill.

The hatch above is filled with the man and his hook and his knife. He is breathing heavily, his eyes mad and desperate.

Then it slams shut and Dee and Frommond are left alone in the stinking dark.

CHAPTER THIRTEEN

Old North Road, Essex,
second week of December 1577

It is the middle of December, when the days are near their short-
est, and after seven hours in the saddle Robert Beale and Nicholas Hilliard reach the little town of Great Dunmow, where they
stay in an inn just off the marketplace. They must share a bed with
Sir John Jeffers, and the room with the other two yeoman who ride
as escort, one of whose snoring shakes the timbers and wakes every
kind of vermin imaginable. The next day they take fresh horses,
along with the two from the royal stable they found on the road
up through the forest below Waltham Cross. Their finding them
there, just where the Queen had been shot at, has been a subject of
conjecture that kept them occupied all the rest of the previous day,
but to no profit, and the farther away they rode from it, the less
likely they felt they were to get to the root of the business.

"Tangled full of mysteries, that forest," Jeffers says now as they
set out to follow the old Roman road toward Bury St. Edmunds

through rolling hills quartered with hedged pastures and hamlets clutched around well-appointed churches of lichen gray stone. Each man is wrapped against the east wind that blows in their faces.

"Remind me why we are doing this again, will you, Robert?" Hilliard asks.

Beale has some sympathy for his old friend.

"You regret showing me your limning of Mistress Overbury?"

"Bitterly."

Beale laughs.

"I will make it worth your while, I promise."

He has not told Hilliard anything about his proposed scheme, and Hilliard maintains the fiction that Beale has fallen very desperately in love with Ness Overbury, which, in point of fact, he has. When he first laid eyes on her in the Dolphin, she was laughing at something someone had said, or something that she'd said, perhaps, and her face was turned in profile. When she turned to him, their eyes had locked, and Beale's breath was driven from his body as if by a huge, pillowed blow to the heart.

"I can't take your money for this, Robert," Hilliard tells him now, though they both know he will: first for having to endure John Overbury's aggressive, insulting jokes when he took Beale to the Dolphin to pretend he had not finished the limning as agreed; second for having then to lend the limning to Beale, for reasons Beale would not share; third, for having to make a copy of the original; and fourth, worst of all, for having now to ride six or seven days to deliver the thing because he had pretended it had been late finished.

"And I hate horses," he'd told Beale.

"All this is my fault," Beale had admitted, "but not that she lives in the middle of Suffolk."

And so on they go. The second day ends with overwatered ale

in a falling-down inn south of Bury; the third, final, short day at John Overbury's hall in a small village with connections to the disgraced Howards. The hall has seen better days, and the dogs are very thin. Overbury is surprised Hilliard has turned up so well escorted, but takes boorish pleasure being in the company of fighting men, and when he hears Sir John Jeffers fought in Flanders, he is more welcoming.

"Come to see my Ness, have you?" he barks. "You'll have to get up earlier in the day than that!"

He's not sixty, as Hilliard had once claimed, maybe not even fifty, but a soldierly, bluff man, of the sort to pride himself on telling it as he sees it through the calculating eyes of a clever pig. He owns Ness as he would an acre of woodland and resents every penny he must spend on her to see her flourish for other men's delight.

"We are on our way to King's Lynn, master," Jeffers has been told to lie. "And have ensured Master Hilliard's safe passage to your door."

The halberdiers believe they are Norfolk bound, too, and that they have been escorting Hilliard as a favor.

"You can stay in the barn for nothing," Overbury offers. "And there is room for your horses in there, too, though you'll pay for feed. Yours, too. Shut up!"

He cuffs a barking hound. As he is talking Ness appears at the doorway of the hall, framed by its light. She sees in an instant what she wants to see: a crowd of young men all turning to her, as daisies to the sun, among them Beale, and she knows why he is there, or believes she does, and there is a moment's catlike hesitation, as if she realizes she is on the threshold of something, and that if she pulls back now, if she takes a step back, then something will pass her by, be gone along the road, leaving her—where? But if she steps forward . . . She is wearing a loose linen hood, though her fine, sprung auburn hair escapes it, and she strokes a stray frond of it back behind her ear. Then she gathers herself and she steps forward, as if from the shadows, and into the light. As if from the past to the present, to the future. From what was, to what will be.

"Why, Master Hilliard, Master Beale"—she smiles—"may God grant you a good evening."

Overbury growls, like a watchdog, deep inside his chest. *Move not a muscle*, it means, *or I will rip out your throat.*

That night Hilliard shows them the limning.

"But I ordered a large one," Overbury says with a laugh.

Hilliard barely masks his sigh.

The haggling over the limning's price resumes the next day. Overbury has drunk too much wine the night before, swapping stories with Sir John Jeffers, and he is choleric this morning. He knows there is some other thing involved, and guesses that Beale wishes to see his Ness, and he will pay no more than two-thirds the price. Beale encourages Hilliard to hold out, and to string the negotiations out, for he cannot find a moment to be alone with Ness, and meanwhile the day is sliding by and Ness is busy about her tasks: in the buttery; in the dairy; in the smokehouse; and if they linger beyond tomorrow, it will come to seem like an occupation.

Early on the second day, with the use of a bone taken from the stockpot, Beale lures one of Overbury's mastiffs a decent distance from the house and then throws the bone into a sheep pen he has learned belongs to Overbury. He does not believe Overbury would ordinarily be called out to kill a dog among his sheep, but he might if it is his own.

Sure enough a boy comes running from the fields and Overbury will not believe it is his dog among his sheep until he cannot find it, and then he takes up his coat and hat and leaves his fireside to sort it. Beale is on his socked feet fast, and up the steps to the bedroom in which Ness Overbury is overseeing the turning of a mattress. He asks for words in private and the girls who are turning the mattress manage to keep their faces straight as they leave.

"Mistress Overbury," Beale begins. "I have a great deal to tell you, to ask you and very little time in which to do so."

She stands listening to his strange request, and as the winter light slides in from the unshuttered window, catching the dust motes, and falling across her alabaster skin, made only more beautiful by the beauty spot on her right cheek, she listens with her mouth slightly open, her teeth better than the Queen's, her hands by her side, and he badly wants to press his mouth on hers and as he has not the time to explain his proposition now, properly, persuasively, he tells her that he has one to put to her, and that it would be an incredibly valuable service, for the sake of her Queen and country, and God even, but that it would require her absolute discretion.

"You wish me to be involved with something—some scheme of which you cannot talk now, here in this room—and about which I am not to tell my husband or anyone else I know?"

She is mocking him, of course, and he cannot stop himself flushing furiously.

"Yes," he says, and he tries to reassure her his scheme is not as she believes, and that he means what he says about Queen and country, but it sounds absurd and he only tangles himself further. He tells her he needs to see her alone, with time to explain what it is he wants her to do—the fact itself, the act itself, and the ramifications that might stem from it—and that this needs be done properly for he cannot risk even mentioning what it is he wishes her to do without her expressing an interest in pursuing it, or feeling she mayn't for feeling her obligations elsewise forbid it.

"I will be in Bury St. Edmunds," he tells her, "until the day after the second market day this week coming. I will be staying at the house of the physician Dr. Paley, on the corner where there's a sign with three dogs, nearby the Angel inn. If you feel you are at least open to the suggestion then, please, come and find me there."

"It is a lot to grapple with," she says.

He agrees. But he can see she is breathing very fast and that her eyes are alive with the thrill of it.

"Come here," she says.

A week later, and Hilliard and Jeffers and the two yeomen have left Beale and ridden back to London, while he remains in Bury St. Edmunds. It remains bitingly cold, but dry, and he has the makings of a room to himself, under the thatch of the Angel inn, overlooking the old abbey gate. There is a cat for company, and a strong-smelling scullery maid who assumes he is a sodomite for he makes no move to touch her, but on the fifth day, Beale sees Ness Overbury, in green wool, with her two maidservants bobbing along a walkway in the marketplace like ducklings behind their mother. He has thought of nothing but her since the moment they kissed and pressed their bodies to each other in the room with the turned mattress. He has since masturbated four times a day, once twice more, and cannot now ride a horse without doing himself a mischief.

He gets to his feet and hurries through the backyards to the house of the physician Paley, who is one of Master Walsingham's men. Paley is elderly, somewhat deaf, and with vision that can only be hampered by the bubbles held in the finger-thick glass of his eyeglasses. Beale ushers him out of his rooms, and then out of the house, into his own backyard, before Ness can knock on his door.

Their first meeting is smeared and breathless, and as soon as
the door is shut and locked and they are alone in the small enclose
of Dr. Paley's consulting room, they tug at each other's points,
throwing their clothes aside, heedless of the things they send ascat-
ter: scales and weights; a glass jar for the sniffing of piss; bundles
of twigs; gathered leaves in linen bags; and a stone mortar of a
ruby-colored powder that is perhaps cinnamon bark. Before the
powder settles they are half naked, her thighs are wrapped around
his hips, and his cock is buried deep within her. They stare into
each other's eyes from a finger's width apart and breathe the same
air. They have exchanged not one word before he feels he must
withdraw, but she clinches him in her, and she whispers in his
ear that she is barren and though the words *we'll see* flit silently
through his mind, he is past caring and he comes in a great rush
and thinks he will faint with the pleasure of it.

She laughs and holds him while he gasps like a river-banked
fish, and she tells him that that is not how her brother does it.

He freezes stock-still.

She laughs more.

"It is a joke," she says. "About Suffolk people."

He manages a laugh and withdraws and rolls off her and col-
lapses on the floor next to her. He blinks away the sweat. The smell
of the ruby-colored powder is all around them. It clings to their
skin. After he regains his breath, he lies on his side, hand holding
his head, elbow on the ground and looks at her disarray. Her body
is very pale, with a fine spray of freckles, and a nipple that clenches
under his touch. He traces his finger across her belly, linking the
larger dots, like making figures from the constellations: here is
Ursa Major; Ursa Minor; Scorpio; Taurus; Virgo. He thinks: *You
might send a coded message on freckles such as this. A cipher. One of
those grilles Girolamo Cardano devised: you press it over an agreed*

text, and each perforation reveals a letter that you wish shown. But why not a shift, cut precisely, with each freckle and moles given a value?

She watches him.

"Well," she says. "What now?"

They do it again, less urgently this time, though it reaches its ending soon enough, and her ears and cheeks are set aflame and she clings to him with an almost frightening ferocity while her body writhes of its own accord. Afterward she lies on her back and trembles, breathing as if in pain, and she lets slip a single tear to leave a trail into the fine red hair at her temple.

"My God," she says. "I needed that."

He, too, is drained, enfeebled by something more than just his efforts. He can scarcely gather the strength to find her clothing and pass it to her, one tangled piece at a time, let alone his.

"You did not even take your boots off." She laughs. "Even my brother manages that."

He sits on the bench, she on the rushes. He watches her pulling up a sock and he tries to see her as the Queen. To tell himself he has just fucked the Queen of England. It is the sort of thing men would tell other men in the tavern, isn't it? *I fucked the Queen. I swived her good and proper.* But he cannot. He has fallen down a hole. He is lost.

When they are dressed, and they have righted as much of the physician's paraphernalia as they can, he takes the position of the physician, she the patient.

"So what is this really about?" she asks.

"*Really* about?"

"You cannot have come all this way just for that? However good it was."

He tells her. She listens.

"The Queen?"

He nods. She starts to laugh. She has hands just like the Queen. She holds one over her mouth when she laughs, just like the Queen. And her laugh: it is ... actually not like the Queen's. While he talks, her gaze dances about the place, and each time she identifies some hurdle or improbability, he has an answer for it. Except what to do about Overbury while she is learning how to comport herself as Elizabeth Tudor.

"There are two possible ways to get your husband out of the way," Beale tells her. "Three, really. The first is to find some venture that takes him away—a cloth fair in Antwerp, if Antwerp had not just been sacked. Amsterdam then. That is the coming place for cloth."

"He is an old soldier, he always says. If there were some ordering men to their deaths in muddy fields, then he would be there like a bolt."

Beale thinks: *Ireland.*

"What are the other two options?" she asks.

"If he were detained—in a prison say, then you might have good reason to stay in a house nearby. To visit him."

"And that is where you would be? In this house? With my tutors?"

"I would come and see you," Beale agrees.

"Come and see me!" She chuckles. She knows that is not what he really means. Her laugh really is not like the Queen's. "And what is the third?"

Beale does not want to tell her. Her eyes widen.

"You could do that? Kill him?"

Beale says nothing. He does not want to admit that he could have it done. But yes. She laughs again, quietly this time, and he can see her trying to picture her life without Overbury.

"Is it so bad?"

"With John? No. So long as you do what he says."

"Why did you ever marry him?"

"The truth? I was with child. He served the old King, with my father, and he claimed not to mind an experienced wench. That is what he said. He was already a widower, already getting on, with no children of his own and he has an income of forty pounds a year."

"What happened to your child?"

"Pffft," she says. "I miscarried a week after the marriage."

"So you were stuck with him."

"Yes," she says with a deep sigh. "I sometimes wonder if . . . if this is all there is to life. We cometh up and are, by and by, cutteth down. It sometimes strikes me that our souls are wasted in the pursuit of— I am not certain what. A new dress of red velvet?"

"But what of the rewards of heaven?"

"Oh yes, them."

She rights her hood and then stands to go. He is gripped with lust again, and would cast caution to the wind, but she holds up her hand to stop him.

"You are serious about this?"

She means the impersonation.

He nods.

"I will have to think on it. I will let you know."

"Of course," he says, disappointed. "It is no simple thing I ask of you."

"By Christmastide?"

He agrees.

"God willing we can keep Her Majesty alive that long," he half jokes.

She stands as the Queen can sometimes stand. It is only the

dark freckle on her lip that sets her obviously apart. That could be covered, surely. And she has none of the Queen's scarring. But the Queen wears so much powder that she might merely seem to be wearing more, or better, or thicker powder. Whatever would serve.

Before Nell takes her leave of Beale, she cups his cods and feeling them heed her call to arms, she smiles a strange hard personal smile of satisfaction. Then she is gone, leaving Beale as if boneless, as if bloodless.

"My God," he says. "My God."

CHAPTER FOURTEEN

Seething Lane, City of London,
third week of December 1577

It is late December, and Francis Walsingham has been confined to bed for ten days, on the rack of a fever his physicians say he must have caught on the road to Lincolnshire. They wrap him in henbane poultices, bury him under woolen blankets, and seal him in his room. Occasionally they return to ply him with a concoction brewed from verjuice and the liver of a baby bear they buy from the gardens in Southwark.

"He can have no more than a spoonful an hour or it will kill him."

The thought of his death is the only thing that keeps him alive.

Walsingham dreams of burning shipyards, and of drowning sailors. He dreams of an enormous Turk, buried upright in gold coins. He dreams of hard black bread, soft cheese in roundels, and of a baby crying like a peacock in the distance. On the tenth day of his illness he is well enough to be allowed daylight—winterish—

filtered through the murky glass of his window, and on the eleventh day, the window is opened a notch.

On the twelfth he is allowed to stand.

But on the thirteenth Sir William Cecil comes.

"We feared for your life, Francis," he tells him. "We prayed for you."

Walsingham acknowledges their concern—whoever they are—and thanks them for their prayers.

"What news?" he asks.

Cecil shakes his head.

"Bad first?" he asks.

"Bad," Walsingham confirms.

"Parma has reached Luxembourg."

Walsingham had hoped for some disaster on the way: an avalanche in some alpine pass; a sudden drought; a plague of snakes.

"We must pray he keeps to his barracks until the campaigning season."

"Amen to a hard winter."

"What else?"

"Do you recall Mistress Jane Frommond?"

"Vividly."

"She has gone missing."

"How?"

"She took two horses from the stables at Richmond—the morning we were there, before all your"—Cecil turns his hand over, to indicate Walsingham's time-consuming, inconvenient illness—"and has disappeared. The horses, though, have been found, hitched to the roadside in, of all places, Waltham Forest, exactly, according to Sir John Jeffers, where Her Majesty's coach was attacked."

Walsingham tries to make sense of this.

He can't.

"Have you searched the wood?"

Cecil looks affronted.

"I don't have the time to spend looking for runaway maids of honor, Francis. Your absence—it has proved an added burden."

"But anything can have happened to her, Sir William. We can't just—"

He starts to cough and his wife comes in. Cecil stands and is instantly placating.

"All is well, Ursula!" he says, his little arms out. "All is well. I have brought up an unpleasant subject, of which we will speak no more."

"Francis?" Ursula checks.

Walsingham gives her the best smile he is able. She has been through the wringer, and not just with his latest illness, he knows. At length she is content to leave them to it with reassurances from Cecil he will not be long, nor raise any more subjects likely to overtax her husband.

"Do not mention John Dee," she jokes.

Cecil throws up his arms in mock horror.

"Reassure yourself on that front, my dear Ursula," he says, "for there is nothing to say. He has rather gone to ground, and though I shall soon have to tear him away from alchemical books, I will ensure that he is kept from bothering your dear husband until he is restored to health."

This just about satisfies Ursula, and with one last concerned look at her husband, she takes her leave, closing the door softly behind her.

"What has Dee done now?" Walsingham asks.

"Ah, well," Cecil tells him, "it is not what he has done, it is what he is about to do. This is the only piece of good news I bear you: from Anthony Jenkinson. His Saracen has sent Her Majesty a barrel of the naft. A small one, as a sample of what is to come. Jenkinson says he—the Turk, whose name he will not share—is much smitten with what he has heard of Her Majesty."

"So soon?"

"Your man Robert Beale—he's been opening your messages while you have been so ill—believes Jenkinson has connections among the Marrano bankers, who have a carrier pigeon system to get a message from here to Constantinople in a week."

"What price is he asking?"

"Ah," Cecil says. "That is the strangest thing: I still do not know. There was a verse that came with the delivery, which Jenkinson says contains the terms."

Walsingham's eyeballs are starting to hurt again.

"A verse?"

Cecil has a small square of paper.

"Written in their language, but thankfully alongside what I believe must be a translation into Latin. I have given it to your man Phillips, in the event there is some underlying encryption, but he tells me that so far he has found nothing, and that he believes it should be read at face value. Would you like to hear it?"

"Not in Latin. I am not strong enough for that."

"I have translated it into English. It is a bit rough. As you know, I am no versifier."

"Go on then."

"See what you think of it," he says. "Remember, it is a first draft." And he recites it in his most sonorous tones:

> *"They say of love;*
> *the heart one day fell prisoner to a prince*
> *but long has mine been captive of*
> *England's twice-sceptered jewel,*

Wherein each facet the wise man may discern
heaven's sacred cipher,
And for whom the lion and the dragon
stay their course despite rough winds.
Oh Hoca! All faces gleam for us,
the sublime porte, the whole world's awe,
yet red grows the grief-scorched heart:
a poppy in the wasteland.
Now rain from a bounteous cloud doth slake
the parched heart's court,
And the unflawed gem must cross briny ocean wave,
the Pleiades to complete,
As a wine-bowl among friends,
time turns to us to savor its cup,
And oh! What wines we shall draw, my love!
What wines we shall draw!"

Cecil stops and looks at Walsingham. He is obviously very proud of his translation.

"What do you make of it?"

"Very nice," Walsingham says.

"Any ideas?"

"The sublime porte is the Ottoman court, in Constantinople, but who or what is 'Hoca'?"

"That I cannot tell you."

Walsingham struggles up on his elbows.

"And that is the price?"

"Apparently so."

"But there is no price mentioned. No marks or pounds. A jewel. 'England's twice-sceptered jewel.' If we can work out what that is, we will be halfway there, but what is it to be sceptered? To be hit with one? Twice? Whatever is ever hit by a scepter, even once? And why would anyone hit a jewel with one? Let alone twice?"

"I may have got my verbs muddled there," Cecil admits.

"And 'heaven's sacred cipher.' That sounds— Oh Christ. That sounds like Dr. Dee's territory. Though I do not have him down as a wise man."

"Well," Cecil says, "I have set one of my clerks going through Her Majesty's jewels, in case some idea occurs, and I will leave this with you to have a think about. Jenkinson says we must divine his meaning, and be ready to pay the full price on delivery, or the naft will go elsewhere."

"Elsewhere?"

"Elsewhere."

He means, perhaps, Spain.

CHAPTER FIFTEEN

River Lea, Essex,
third week of December 1577

There is a cell in the lowest level of the White Tower known as Little Ease that is so short and narrow that a man can neither lie, nor sit, nor stand in it, but must crouch in the darkness for days, weeks even, until he is dragged out to be tortured or taken to be hanged from Tyburn Tree. Dee, bent in the darkness with foul bilge water up to his ankles for he knows not how many days, has been thinking about this cell a great deal. He is wondering what it might be like to have the hatches of the hold flung open by some merciful gaoler and to be dragged across London to be half hanged, taken down, then eviscerated and butchered into quarters.

There are times when he would welcome it.

Somewhere in the darkness nearby is Frommond, and he believes she might welcome it, too.

"Perhaps that will come to pass, anyway," he muses. "Her Majesty takes as dim a view of horse theft as she does of coin-clipping."

Frommond usually says nothing during these attempts at light-heartedness. In fact, she has started to say less and less as the hours have turned to days and dragged on through nights of shuddering cold when they have had to cling to each other for warmth and huddle with teeth chattering, their bodies racked with shivers. Now though, with so little food for so many days, and with only half a canvas bucket of river water lowered into the hold each dawn, Dee can feel his own mental as well as physical strength beginning to wane.

He will have to do something very soon, but what?

"Why not just kill us?" Frommond had shouted in those early days. "Get it over with!"

During that first day they stood together, side by side, faces lifted, waiting under the hatch, gradually becoming used to their world of four lines of light, interrupted by six fat hinges, which they expected to expand at any moment as the hatch was lifted and they be let out. But as the light had faded, so had hope, to be replaced by outraged incredulity and then self-fueling, contagious rage. Dee had had to pull Frommond from bloody-ing her nails scrabbling at the underside of the hatch, just as she later had had to pull him from the bulkhead where he was bloodying his fists.

Both swore and drove each other to swear more, greater, more terrible oaths. Such blasphemies as might see either swing.

Accommodations had to be made. The realization they were trapped with each other came with that first dawn. Dee had to take a shit. Then Frommond.

"Look away!" She'd managed to laugh.

"I can't see a thing, Mistress Frommond," he'd promised, and it was true, though he could smell it and later something bumped his ankle, though that might easily have been his own turd.

That was then, though, when they hoped for a reaction from their gaoler: that he might speak to them; share his reasonings; create—or dash—hopes for a time when their world was not just this almost complete darkness of bilge water and slimy timbers, teeming with rats, but he has said not one word to them. They hear him going about his business in the cabin through the bulkhead: they hear his snoring through the night, him voiding his bladder and his bowels into the river at dawn; occasionally he talks to what must be the cat, though in what language they cannot tell.

At times there are no sounds, none of the subtle rocking of the barge to tell them their gaoler was even on board, and this was the time, to begin with, that Dee attacked the doors with his eating knife, to little profit save a broken blade. If only the arquebuses that he had imagined might be slung in the hold had not turned out to be ropes attached to what his tentative fumblings have revealed to be a sea anchor half submerged in the gritty stinking ooze of the bilge, then he might have— Might have done what? Shot the man as he lowered the daily bucket of water? With what powder, shot, or flame? Now the only things they have by way of weapons are the stubby handle of his broken knife, and Frommond's, which is so delicate it is hardly worthy of the name of knife.

He thinks about throwing the stub of his knife at the man when he opens the hatch at dawn. He could do that if he could stand upright, but the hold is too shallow to allow him to draw his arm back for that, and he could never get enough power throwing it underarm; and now that he has lost the actual blade somewhere in the bilge, it is useless anyway.

What he really needs is a crossbow, he thinks. That would be the answer. That would be the weapon of choice here. But who these days has one of them?

Early on the second day they felt the cat brush by them, come in through some secret way in the bulkhead timbers to set about the rats. Their screeching alarm was terrible to hear, and both Dee and Frommond lashed out in a frenzy as the rats scrambled over their faces and in their hair, but it was as nothing to the shrieks of the rat the cat caught, and both Dee and Frommond had to clap their hands over their ears until it was over. Dee wonders how it comes and goes. It will be some tiny gap between rib and timber scarcely big enough for its head. If it ate the rat in the hold, it would surely need to digest it before being able to slip back into the cabin.

"It is a strange thing to think of envying a ship's cat," Frommond says.

By the third day their spikes of rage had become intermittent, like flashes of lightning in a summer storm: sudden, intense, and then gone in moments, leaving behind a throbbing bruise of sorrow in their tow. Despair and the realization that they were being starved to death broke on them during the fourth day.

"We will die," Frommond had said.

"We are lucky to still be alive," Dee had suggested.

And this morning, when he wakes from his strange deathly sleep, wedged into one corner of the bulkhead and the hull, the fact that he is alive surprises and depresses him.

"Jane?" he whispers.

"Mmmm," she says.

"Listen."

There are voices. Two of them. On the bank maybe. He and Frommond throw themselves at the timbers of the hull side, hammering and shouting for help.

"We're here! We're trapped! Help! Help us!"

"Stop! Stop!"

Dee extends an arm to Frommond's.

They listen.

Nothing.

Silence.

Christ. Dee sinks to his knees in the murk, his face pressed to the timbers.

Frommond screams.

She has been bitten by a rat.

"I can't stand it! I can't stand it!"

Dee sloshes over to her and takes her in his arms. They hold each other not for warmth this time, but for human comfort. *This is what it is like to die*, Dee supposes, and he wonders why he miscast his chart so badly so as not to see this is the where and the when of his final days. He had for himself a long, long life, with much more travel, and a wife, and children. Perhaps that was wishful thinking? And yet—

The rats start screaming in alarm again and so the cat is back.

And it is only now that Frommond weeps. It is a tiny noise, no louder than a rat's squeak, but low and heartrending. Dee holds her clumsily in his arms. She still wears her cloak, for warmth, but his fingers press her back, and he feels for the hundredth time the vertical ridges of her bodice—loosened now, of course—and he finds his fingers tracing the whalebone from top to bottom.

He stops.

"Jane," he starts. "What is this whalebone like?"

She tells him.

"Hmmmm," he says aloud. "Do you mind?"

"It depends."

From there it is only a moment before he has her cloak off, and he is fiddling with the points of her bodice.

"Dee? What . . . are . . . you doing?"

"I need your bodice. Please."

"But I need it," she says.

He understands she has lost some of her wits.

"It is not for warmth, Jane, I promise. It will get us out of here."

When it is passed over, still warm, bearing Jane's smell, and while she huddles in her undershirt and cloak, Dee borrows her knife to slice the strips of bone from their fabric holds. One would break under any pressure, but there are ten, each about a foot long, and which, if bundled together, might be fashioned into a spring just strong enough for what he has in mind.

He sets to work, slicing his own coat into strips. He has become adept at knowing exactly where he put things, so has a strange sense of seeing in the dark, and he works fast before the four faint lines of light fade for the night. When it is done, he binds the whalebones together and when that is done, he has in his hands a foot-and-a-half-long spring.

"Ha," he says.

Frommond says nothing.

She is asleep. He hopes. *Christ*. What if she's dead?

He wakes her.

Thanks be to God.

He returns her bodice, or what remains of it, and makes her put it back on, with her cloak on top. She slumps back in her corner of the hold. He places the whalebone spring in his shirt.

But now he needs to retrieve the blade of his own, which when it first fell in the bilge he did not believe he would need. Now that foul bilge water is become even worse, but so is he. He is so depraved and filthy he is equal to it. He doesn't care now: he plunges both arms into the stew of bilge and their own waste.

He fumbles and feels things he will not try to identify. It is an exercise in anti-imagination, he thinks, such as the Russians use to cure hiccups when they run around their houses twice, not thinking of their word for *wolf*. It takes him a long while. He gags and lets spit trickle from his lips and gags again. His stomach clenches as if squeezed by a giant hand, and he vomits bile but he continues. There is nothing else for it. And at last his efforts are rewarded: the slip of the clumsy blade that he knows so well. Between his fingers.

"Got it!" He shows Frommond. "Jane! Jane! I've got it."

She says nothing.

He splashes over to her.

He shakes her. She flops.

"Come on, Jane. Come on! We will get out of this."

He does not add *if it is the last thing we do*, for if they do not— he does not even bother to finish that thought.

She mumbles something.

"Jane!" he shouts. "Jane!"

She moves. She reaches out, feels his face. Places her hand on his shoulder.

"I am all right," she says. Christ. She is like a drunk. She just wants to be left in peace to sleep it off, but she will not sleep this one off. He slaps her gently on the cheek.

"Jane! Jane! Keep awake! Keep alive. For the love of God! They cannot beat us! We must survive this night! Jane!"

"All right! All right, John Dee. All right."

He must leave her.

"Keep talking to me," he tells her. "Tell me something. Tell me something about Bess. About the Queen. How is she?"

"She's fine. Fine. All right."

Now he has two knife blades. It is not perfect, by a long straw, but it will do. It will surely work. Surely.

"Do you enjoy being a maid of honor?"

Dee sets to. Using the handle of his own broken knife he starts to tap his blade into the nose of one of the worn rungs of the ladder.

"It is not very interesting. I do not like sewing, or dancing, particularly, although I do not mind that. I do not like Sir Christopher Hatton though he is a very good dancer. He can spin on the spot and he does not grow dizzy. But he is—"

Tap tap. Tap tap. He stops. Listens for movement from beyond the bulkhead. He laughs.

"What is he?" Dee presses.

"Very agile. He can place his hands anywhere and everywhere all at once."

Dee continues his work. *Tap tap. Tap tap.*

When his own blade is firmly dug into the wood, he starts on Frommond's knife. *Tap tap. Tap tap.*

"Is that a good thing?" he asks.

Tap tap.

"Not always," she admits. "He can also position himself so that wherever you hold your own hands, you find you are cupping his cods."

Tap—

"That is clever," Dee admits.

After a while that knife, too, is dug in. He makes careful adjustments. Then he digs out the length of whalebone from his shirt, and to each end he knots a long piece of the hem of his beautiful velvet coat, leaving enough to tie the strips of ten-folded whalebone to the two knives.

He has, he believes, fashioned a sort of crossbow. But will it work? He pulls the cloth. The whalebone flexes then slides. He pulls the cloth tighter. Tries again. This time it thrums like the string of a lyre. But will it be enough?

He tests it first with a small piece of coal he finds in the stew by his feet.

He tries it as much as he dares and then releases it. The coal cracks into something above. The hatch? He can't say. He fiddles for another piece of coal and pulls harder this time. The coal hits something up by the hatch, harder this time, and ricochets back to clip him on the shoulder. *It doesn't exactly sting,* he thinks.

He finds the hilt of his own knife and places it in the string. He tugs the sling back a few inches farther than before, risking the whalebone bonds, and lets it fly. The handle leaps from his hands. It flies up and cracks into the rung two above the one in which he has dug the knives and falls and he hears it splash under the rung. He is past caring. He sloshes around and begins the search. He could drink this water now, he thinks. The stump of his knife handle is easier to find than its broken blade. He thinks to swap them over. Handle in the step: blade in the sling? He has time.

"Jane," he says. "Jane. Tell me more about dancing with Sir Christopher!"

"I danced with— He danced with me. He danced with me. A few months ago. He told me he was about to become very rich. Very rich. With money."

"Money, you say?"

He swaps the blade for the handle and makes further adjustments.

"Something to do with what he called getting into the alchemy game."

"The alchemy game? The alchemy *game*? Alchemy is no game."
She manages a laugh.

"His words. He has . . . has an admiral who had brought back gold nuggets from the New World."

Dee laughs absently. Frobisher's ore!

"Good luck with that one," he mutters.

Then he draws the sling back. This time the missile flies up and there is a curiously final thud in the wood of the hatch. No splash. Dee reaches up and there on the underside of the hatch, there is the knife blade, hanging—just—from the underside of the wood. He plucks it out and tries one more time, pulling the gut back and releasing it again. This time the flung blade digs into the hatch door by its corner. He needs all the strength in his fingers to pluck it out.

"Hah," he says.

He turns to her.

"Jane! Jane! Wake up!"

She will not.

He shakes her.

"Jane!" he shouts at her. "I am not about to let you die on me! Do you hear? Wake up! Keep talking!"

She does, very slightly, and all through the night he cajoles and nags her. In part because he wishes her to talk, and in part because he wishes to know more about Hatton and his alchemical games. It actually warms him. Makes him laugh. Gives him a gleeful reason to live. But Frommond keeps slipping away, and he must prod and goad and tease. He makes her hate him, but he keeps her alive, and she is still sensible the moment he hears the snoring through the bulkhead behind stop, and when, achingly slowly, the lines around the hatch begin to emerge from the darkness to show dawn is upon them. Now Dee must set her down and wait at the bottom of the steps for his last—his *only*—chance to get them out of here.

"You stay there," he whispers. "Say nothing. He must believe we are finally dead."

That will not be hard, he thinks. He crouches at the bottom of the stairs, half submerged in water, his beautiful green coat worn back to front to cover the white of his shirt, and he waits. The water makes him shudder, but he stays submerged in the silent dark, watching, waiting, attuned to every movement of the man in the cabin beyond the bulkhead. At last there is movement. The man is getting up, and there is always a long time while he says his prayers before he emerges on deck. Dee joins in, murmuring his own prayers that this will work. Then he hears the man come up on deck. He hears the man walking to the deck at the front of the boat to urinate loudly into the river. Dee supposes he must have had quite a bit of beer the night before, for the stream is long and loud. He does not take a shit this morning, thank God, but drops the bucket into the water then hauls it up and holds its rope in one hand while he scrapes the hold hatch door latch back with his foot. Dee can hardly breathe. He slowly stretches the cloth strap back, and he hears the whalebones creak. The man lifts the hatch, light falls into the hold, almost blinding him, but through the thinnest slits of his half-closed eyelids, he sees the man's shape as he stands with the bucket, and when he does not receive the usual barrage of abuse from Dee and Frommond, he grunts in surprise, and holding the bucket's rope in his right hand, and the hatch door in his left, he bends to peer down into the hold to see if, perhaps, at long last, his prisoners are dead.

And that is when Dee looses his homemade crossbow.

He does not see where the missile goes, but perhaps he hears something, a fleshy snick, and a cry that is cut off with the light as the hatch crashes shut in his upturned face. But Dee is on his feet the next instant, hauling himself up the rungs, nearly tripping on the whalebones, and he thrusts the hatch cover up and it moves and suddenly he is in dazzling gray light that seems to burn his eyes, but he can see just enough to make out a man staggering in the bow of the barge writhing with his hands clapped to his face.

Why Dee knows to look for the hook the man had used to move Frommond down at the side of the hatch he has no clue, but there it is, and a moment later it is in his hand, up above his head, and then he brings it down with an iron ring into the man's face, the curved side down. He wants to beat the man to death slowly, with as many blows as possible. He wants to shatter every bone in his face. He wants to knock out every tooth. He wants to break every rib; both arms; each hand and finger. He swings again and again as the man crumples into a blood-soaked pile of awkward limbs with a head that lolls to his belly. And even then, Dee keeps on beating. He wants to drive the man's spine into the deck, to shatter every vertebra, to disgust even that hangman of Tyburn with the mess he has made of this man.

And he screams while he does it.

And when it is over he stands for a moment, breathing hard, staring down at his repulsive handiwork, before with one last bellow of terrible rage, he flings the hook into the river as far as it will go.

Then he turns and he climbs back down into his cell.

It takes every shred of his being to do it. Every ounce of fiber. To descend once more into the black maw.

And with himself still gore soaked and blood shod, he walks

through that foul brew to where Frommond slumps unconscious in her corner.

"Jane! Jane! Jane!"

But she does not move.

He gathers her up with the last of his strength and he carries her to the rungs of the ladder and then, each moment a lifetime, he brings her up into the light.

CHAPTER SIXTEEN

London, last week of December 1577

I t is late afternoon when Robert Beale reaches home to find one
of Master Walsingham's men waiting on his step with a message
that he must make haste to the Papey.

"It is Dee," the message finishes.

Beale has been on the road for more than a week, to Suffolk and
back, and is bone weary, but he turns on his heel, and swings back
up into his saddle and rides to Master Walsingham's house with
the messenger mute by his side. He finds Her Majesty's principal
private secretary still in bed, with boils, drooping eyelids, and a
bottle of something that smells very foul.

"Dee," Walsingham tells him, "has been found."

Beale had no idea he had been missing.

"Oh yes," Walsingham says. "But no longer: the searchers
picked him up in a wherry this morning, coming upriver on the
rising tide, and in a very bad way, they say: half dead and screaming
his head off."

"What about?"

"None can fathom it, so they are holding him in the Bedlam. For his own good."

"Well, that will certainly do for him."

"Which is why I sent for you, though to be honest, Robert, you do not look overwell yourself? What is that bruise on your cheek? Did you fall from your horse?"

"I am tired, that is all," Beale tells hm. "I will go and find him."

"Thank you, Robert. And Mistress Frommond, also, if you've a mind."

"Mistress *Frommond*? She is there, too?"

"She was with Dee in his wherry and is said to be in even worse a state than him. If I am honest, when I heard your knock at the gate I feared it was a messenger to say she has gone out of this world."

Beale takes the letters of authority he will need, and four men, and sets a fresh horse north again, retracing his steps up Bishopsgate and causing the watch to let him back out in the name of the Queen. The old priory is up on the left, beyond Saint Botolph's. It is old, stone-built, and behind a tall stone wall, and though intended as a place of succor for those of addled mind—until God restores them to their wits, or calls them out of this world, and the latter is usually His first choice—it is run for the profit of one of the city's appointees, often a brewer, or a grocer, and staffed by those who in milder times might well be patients themselves.

He hammers on the gate, and once again instructs an answering voice to open up in the name of the Queen. Bolts are slid, chains unhooked, and a small door in the greater gate opens to admit him. He stands in what might have been a pleasing courtyard but there is not much to be seen in the lamplight.

"Where is Dr. Dee?"

The porter—of the sort who might pull teeth at fairs—guides him into the hall and up a small turning stair to a row of doors that were once the cells of the order's canons.

"Hold your nose," he tells Beale.

Beale does so.

They pass to the last doorway where the porter holds his lamp up to a slot in the door and peers in.

"Asleep," he says.

And he unchains the latch.

"Dee?"

Dee lies on a pallet, under a blanket. His eyes are open, but they do not follow the lamp, and they seem sightless.

"Is he dead?"

"Could be."

The tooth puller gives Dee a kick.

"For Christ's sake, man! He is not some prisoner. He is Dr. Dee."

The tooth puller retreats, crossing himself.

"Joseph and Mary," he says.

"Give me the lamp."

Beale takes it and bends over the body. The light reveals Dee as a skeleton, veneered in waxy skin, torn and bloody. He gives off the rotting grave stench you smell on the wind only in a plague year.

"I'm not gone yet, Master Beale," Dee says.

His voice is like the wind in dried reeds.

Beale almost drops the lamp.

"I heard you were?"

"Nearly, but not quite. If I keep absolutely still, and the old woman comes back with more ale, I believe I shall live."

"I will find her. Get her to bring some."

"No," Dee says. His voice is as fingernails on a bowstring. "Jane

Frommond. They think she is dead. But find her and give her ale by spoonfuls."

Beale is glad to step back from Dee. He finds the tooth puller in the corridor. "Where is the other one? The woman?"

The tooth puller clicks his tongue and half shuts one eye.

"Think you might be too late with that one," he says.

"Take me to her."

They descend into the vaults where Jane Frommond is already wrapped in a waxy winding sheet, on a deep stone shelf, in a cold room, ready for the priest and the cart tomorrow. Her feet are icy to the touch and the skin is like that of the bodies they find in the mud below the Isle of Dogs.

"She had on a nice pair of boots," the tooth puller tells Beale. "But ruined they were. By the wet."

He puts a great spin on the word *wet*.

"Help me with her," Beale tells him.

"She'll be stiff as a plank by now," the tooth puller says.

But she's not and together they slide Frommond from her stone shelf.

"Tchoff!" the tooth puller spits at the smell that rises from her.

They carry her up to a table in the hall.

"You can't put that there!"

It is an old man, emerging from the darkness with a hoop of keys on his belt and three teeth in his head.

"Fuck off," Beale tells him.

Beale wears a sword on his belt and has written authority from Francis Walsingham. He may do as he pleases.

"Get me ale," he tells the tooth puller, "and a spoon. And uncover that fire."

The tooth puller stamps away to the pantry while the old man removes the cloche from the embers and puts on a log.

Beale peels back Frommond's rough linen winding sheet. Christ. Jane Frommond is a peeled cadaver. But why isn't she stiff, as she should be?

The tooth puller returns with a mug of ale and a spoon.

Beale feeds Frommond, one drop at a time.

"Going down, in' it?" the tooth puller supposes.

"Have either of them said anything since they came in?" Beale asks.

"Only him up there," the old man says. "Something about a cat. All we could make sense of."

"Where've they been?" Beale wonders aloud. He looks at her hands. They are like bird's claws, but with what might be coal dust under her broken nails. Soaking-wet boots, coal dust, and the foul smell of putrefaction? Can they have been to *Yorkshire*?

He keeps spooning the sweet ale between Frommond's lips.

"Good-looking girl, this one was," the old man says. "And good clothes, what was left of 'em."

"Where are they?"

"Gone to the rag merchant," he says with a shrug. "They'll need boiling afore anyone can do anything with 'em, mind, that is for sure. Same with your gent's up the stairs."

They do not hear Dee until he is more or less standing with them. He has blankets wrapped about his naked body, and a far-away look in his eye.

"Rub her," he says. "Gently, from the hands and feet. Warm her blood. Her humors must be made to circulate."

"What are you doing out?"

"Shut up."

Beale begins to gently rub Frommond's hand.

"I ain't touching them," the tooth puller says of her feet.

"Then get out," Dee tells him, and he takes his place and puts his hands on Frommond's feet, his thumbs on the soles and he starts gentle circular motions. Skin comes off in his hands in wet, ghostly strips, like the flesh of rotting onions.

"Come on, Frommond," he whispers. "Come on. Do not leave me."

Then he starts a prayer in a language Beale has never heard. How long they keep up their work Beale does not know. More ale is brought, and more logs are put on the fire, and they keep rubbing, goading the life back into her until in the small hours perhaps, Dee at last says: "There."

And he sits on a stool, with his hands between his knees, and his head hung.

"Well, you tried," the old man says.

"You can only hope someone'll do the same for you, when your time comes," the tooth puller adds, "but when it comes—"

"Hush," Beale says.

He stares at Frommond's chest under its shroud.

"She's breathing."

There is a long moment of silence. Dee does not move. He might be dead himself now. The old man and the tooth puller stand as mute witnesses to a miracle.

"Get her another blanket," Dee mutters.

And then he keels off the stool.

It takes four days before they get any sense out of either of them, but by then reports have already reached the Papey of a man murdered on a barge on the river Lea, "like he was a victim of cannibals."

It is a bitterly cold Christmas Eve morning when Beale orders Sir John Jeffers to assemble with ten men to ride with him to

Waltham Forest, and then retrace Dee's and Frommond's tracks down to the river, and along its west bank to the barge where they are to meet the constables from Enfield whose job it is to identify the dead man and find his murderer.

"But it is Christmas!" Jeffers reminds him.

And snow dusts the land, but it matters not.

"You will be able to pick yourselves out a good yule log," Beale tells him.

It is a long ride with which they are already wearily familiar now, but today it is enlivened by an encounter with Sir Christopher Hatton, riding down from Hertford with a guard of perhaps twenty men, well turned out on good horses.

"You can never be too careful," he tells Beale. "Not these days."

Beale resents the implied slander of Master Walsingham, but says nothing.

"And yourself, Master Beale?" Hatton goes on, with the sort of smile that ordinarily comes with a tap of the nose. "You are up and down this road daily, it seems. One would think you have a woman stashed away from court somewhere and are become a lotus-eater!"

Beale flushes.

"I am busy about Master Walsingham's business," he mutters.

"Of course you are!" Hatton laughs.

"Not that it is any of yours."

"Quite so. Quite so!"

"Well, we will leave you now, Sir Christopher, and wish you safe passage to the city."

"Whatever makes you think I am bound for the city?" Hatton continues with his knowing laughter, and he tugs his horse into action, and Beale and his men, including the much-punished Sir John Jeffers, must make way to let them pass.

"Twat," Jeffers mutters. "As if we care where he's going."

But it is a bit of a mystery.

They carry on up the road and reach the forest where the shots were fired, where they found the horses. From there it is a walk down through the trees to the fringe of the marshes.

"In daylight I would have seen this path, as God is my witness, Master Beale."

Beale wonders if that is true. Probably.

They find the river, and turn right, and trudge along its sodden margins, crossing ditches and streams that supply various water mills. The river is black, made choppy by the east wind, and there is a constant low susurrus from the rushes. They pass small boats in a pool and then a half-completed lock that reminds one of the yeomen of a gallows. And then, at last, they find the barge. Two men—the constables from Enfield—stand baiting a crow that sits cawing on the barge's bow, as unwilling to yield its place as the men are to go aboard.

They greet one another and there are the usual comments as to it being a good day for it and meanwhile the crow keeps up its shrieking, and it is so cold that every time it opens its beak, a second tongue of steam rolls from within. Knowing what it guards, Beale wishes it shot, but a man with a halberd does the job with a stone and the bird flies to settle in a branch of the alder on the other side of the river.

The constables have scraped as much of the body of the dead man as they could from the barge's deck, and what they have is taken to Enfield, where it is to be buried, as a Christian.

"And we spoke to some of the other boatmen on the river," the older of the two constables tells Beale, "and they confirm the Dutchies doing the lock over yonder were bunking up in her."

He nods at the barge.

"Only they cleared off a while back, and there's only been one of them here since: a redheaded bloke—not overly friendly apparently—with a beard he wore in a knot under his—you know—chin."

He lifts his own, so that Beale will know what he means.

"Which we found," the younger continues, "in the front."

"So we reckon he's your dead man."

Beale nods. That accords with Dee's suggestion.

"Did you search the cabin?"

Of course they did, if only for what they might make off with.

"There was a loaf of that horrible black bread," the old one tells him, "and some orange cheese, which is what Dutchies eat."

"And some beer, too, sour with all hops and that."

"Nothing else?"

A blanket and that was it.

"Really?"

"He was wearing all his clothes," the younger constable explains.

Beale stares at them. The younger one admits there was a spoon they hoped might be silver.

"No guns?"

"Guns?"

They are genuinely at a loss and Beale has to believe them.

"What about the hold? Have you searched that?"

The two men shoot each other a glance. No. They have not. They do not know of Dee and Frommond's ordeal, so they have not thought it worth investigating. It appeared empty, they tell him, and stinks so badly that nothing that might be accounted as living can be down there.

"Even the rats chuck up."

"Nevertheless," Beale tells them. *After you*, is their reaction, and they step aside to let him pass. Beale, well wrapped with a cloak and scarf and woolen cap, pauses before he climbs the rough-made gangplank to the barge's deck. He looks around at the desolate landscape, all mist-shrouded rotting sedge and chill black waters, with that bloody gallows-bird cawing, and a dozen men in steel helmets gathered watching him as flecks of snow drift down from a goose-gray sky. He shivers, gathers his cloak more firmly about his shoulders, and steps aboard.

He looks in the cabin first. It stinks of cat and unwashed man. The constables were looking for anything to steal, he knows, rather than anything that might identify whoever lived there as the gunmen who tried to shoot the Queen of England, so they did not take the butt of their knife, as he does, and tap the bulkhead behind the cooking stone, where one plank is paler than its soot-crusted neighbors. Beale hauls the greasy old stone away from the wall and there, behind it, in the junction between deck and bulkhead, the wood is frayed between the planks. He inserts his knife into the wound and levers the plank out. It is as tall as the cabin is high. He can hear the squeak of rats and a sharp reek reminds him of his night with Dee and Frommond in Bedlam Priory.

He wishes he had a lamp, for within the cavity it is all darkness, and he is not anxious to be bitten by a rat or some such. He pokes his knife in. There is space in there. Quite a bit. He extends his arm into the darkness, all the way to the elbow, when his knifepoint touches something hard, like wood. He knows it is the frame of the boat. He runs the knife down. Nothing. If there were anything there, it has gone. He turns to use his left hand to search the right-hand side of the opening. Here, too— No. His knifepoint touches something that yields fractionally. Not the barge timbers. He withdraws the knife and stretches his hand. Something hard and slick. He grips it and draws out a tall package of greased linen. He knows it is an arquebus. He knows its attendant package will be balls, match fuse, and powder.

There is only one of them in the cavity, but there is space for many more.

He stands and carries the gun outside and leans it on the gunwale. The constables suggest that they would have found it had they known they were looking for such a thing, and Beale has some sympathy with that.

But now he must look in the hold.

He lifts the hatch and, even in this cold, is forced back by the stench. He claps his scarf to his face, and then steps down onto the first rung, and finds the makeshift slingshot of Dee's—still in place, dug into the nose of one of the rungs—but he steps over it, and climbs down to the bottom rung, for he has come for something else, on Jane Frommond's command. He waits on the bottom rung, scarf pressed to face, listening to the alarmed shrieks of the rats, until his eyes are more used to the dark, and then he steps gingerly into the stinking bilge brew and walks as carefully as he can to the far corner, the place he now thinks of as Frommond's corner, and, reaching up, he finds, just as she whispered he might, a small package jammed tight into the gap between the ribs and the bulkhead. Then he walks back and climbs the steps, pulling from the wood as he does so Frommond's knife but leaving Dee's, and her whalebones, where they are.

When Beale is back on deck he stops and looks down at the stained timbers in the bow, where Dee admits he battered the man to death. It has rained and snowed even in the last few days and hours, and much of the blood and gore has been washed away, but here and there are tannic splashes and stains to prove its passage, and in the gaps between the planks he is certain there must linger yet matter of interest to the crow.

He shudders again and looks down at the package Mistress Frommond has asked him to retrieve. A scarlet glove, balled tight, and within it, a tiny limning of a man in a fancy collar.

"All right," he says. "Let's go home."

CHAPTER SEVENTEEN

London, last week of December 1577

John Dee and Jane Frommond are moved from the Bedlam that afternoon. It is a slow process on carts with wheels swagged in horsehair, she to the coffer chamber in the Palace of Whitehall, he on a litter to Her Majesty's barge, in which he is rowed upriver to his house in Mortlake, to be met at the river's edge by his mother and Roger Cooke, with his eyebrows grown back, and by Thomas Digges and his mother, too, who instructs Dee not to think about her son's coat until he is quite recovered.

He is carried through the orchard up into his library and lain among his books, and the Queen has sent him a block of her best soap, as well as a box of oranges she was given by the Spanish ambassador but has found too sharp, and there is wood for his fire delivered from upriver, and bread and ale brought from Richmond Palace, and a yeoman is placed at his gate to deter any Bills or Bobs from bothering him for a while, at least from that direction.

At New Year's they are sent a cooked goose and savory cinnamon rice and sprout tops with almonds and a curious subtlety of sugar spun to resemble a boat that might or might not be intended to represent the barge, and then there are four bottles of Sir William Cecil's favorite wine. Dee rouses himself to sit upright on a cushion under a blanket, to be clucked over by his mother, and Thomas Digges brings over his mother to share in the dinner, and they bring with them a capon roasted with spiced mincemeat, and another bottle of French wine to which Dee's mother adds rosewater. They summon the yeoman from his post, who turns out to have a rough but unexpectedly charming singing voice, though his songs are all about the Cornish and what God wishes done unto them in punishment for some long-forgotten crime, and then Digges recites a poem he has made about the Great Comet, and then another that contrives to compare John Dee to Job of the Bible, and the barge to the whale, and that hints—without being able to be explicit about how—there might be a link between Job escaping the whale and John Dee escaping the barge through the use of whalebone.

It is not long after the last bottle is turned up in the bucket and the fire's embers are dying that Digges excuses himself and his sleepy mother, and Dee's mother and Roger Cooke soon drift off, too, and the yeoman decides duty calls and he must take a last turn of the property; and so Dee is left alone once more, sitting on a cushion in his best doublet and a hat of finespun wool. He begins to feel maudlin or melancholic and gets to his feet. His legs are still shaky, but he feels a powerful need for air, and he stops to stand for a while on the wooden walkway behind his house, looking down through the orchard to the river. It is ragged cloud tonight, with a gentle wind, and he thinks there will be a frost tomorrow.

He thinks about Jane Frommond. He has seen her once since he helped warm the life back into her: a glimpse as they carried her from her cell to the cart on a litter like his own. She had given him a little sign, a loosely clenched fist, that he took to suggest that he must stay staunch. Just thinking of her makes him smile. *Like a shooting star*, he thinks, and he scans the breaks in the cloud for a sign of the comet, about which he had almost forgotten until Thomas's poem.

He is standing like this when he sees on the river a lamplit barge, just such as the Earl of Leicester owns, come swinging around the corner, being rowed down from up river and he watches it slow and nose itself against the riverbank, and he wishes he had one last cup of wine. In the dark he hears a soft order, and in a pool of lamplight he sees a gangplank lowered. Who in God's name is this abroad on such a cold night and at a time when all good folks should be abed?

It is, of all people, Her Majesty, Queen Elizabeth of England, in a thick fur-lined cloak, and a silk-lined hood. She is alone, insofar as she ever is, unaccompanied by councillors or courtiers, but she walks within a loose square of Yeomen, as if some assassin might lurk behind the trunks of Dee's wizened old apple trees. Watching her come, Dee recalls that she still has left over from her coronation a red rug that is a yard and a half wide and nearly three-quarters of a mile long. It must come in parts, he supposes, and she might leave one with him, for just such an occasion as this.

He removes his hat and bows deeply. He has not, he suddenly smells, despite his best efforts, been entirely successful at removing the bilge scent from his lower limbs.

"Bess," he says. "Happy New Year."

He hears her growl.

"Dee," she says, "we will forgive you that breach of manners this one last time, in acknowledgment of your recent troubles, and what you have done for us over the years, but if you ever call us that again we will have you taken to the Tower and put in Little Ease for the remainder of your days."

"Quite right, Your Majesty," Dee tells her. "It is exactly what I would do."

The Queen laughs.

"John," she says, "we are mightily pleased to find you in such good spirits after your ordeals and are come to give you a New Year's gift."

She signals to a man lurking in the dark to step forward. He is a giant of a man and carries in his arms a small barrel bound in rope rather than the usual iron hoops, like a testament to the coopers' craft, that is obviously heavy with content.

"Some wine?" Dee hopes. "How kind."

"Not wine, John, but that which you seek for the production of Greek fire."

Oh. Christ. Greek fire. He had almost forgotten about that. It occurs to him that he has never had the chance to explain or apologize for the breach in the Tower's curtain wall. Perhaps now is not the time.

He thanks the Queen.

"But that much is not going to get us very far," he worries.

"It is merely a sample," the Queen repeats. "It has come from Master Jenkinson's Turk, as a mere taste of what is to come, brought *posthaste*, as a token of his goodwill, for he is said to esteem our person highly."

She widens her eyes and smiles, and he remembers she can be arch, Her Majesty, sometimes.

"Well, it is very generous of you to pass it on," he tells her. "Thank you. And perhaps put it down over there?"

The wooden walkway creaks under the giant's tread as he places the barrel by the kitchen door. The Queen is looking at Dee in expectation.

Oh God, he thinks. He has to give her something in return.

"I also have something for you," he says, "though—" But she looks at him with such expectation, such bright eyes, and then past him, into his library, where he keeps his cross-staff, his astrolabe, the globes that Mercator gave him, and Frisius's astronomical brass rings.

"Really?" she presses.

"Ummm," he says. "Well, perhaps I do. Yes. I do."

He turns, and then turns again, so as not to turn his back on her, and then he retreats awkwardly into his house to find a lamp to light his way into his library. *Where is it? That bloody useless scrying stone.* He finds it used to weigh down paper—bills, he notes, including one for the stone itself—but there is nothing suitable in which to wrap it. He will have to give it to her as is.

He does so.

"A ruby?" she wonders, holding it up to one of the lamps held by her men.

"Not exactly," he admits. "A scrying stone. In which messages from the angels may be read."

"Oh," she says. "Such as that possessed by Nostradamus?"

"Exactly."

"How does it work?"

Dee thinks back to his visions from the table in the room in Whitehall, the night she was so nearly killed.

"I once thought I knew," he says, "but I confess I am now uncertain."

"So it is a stone," she supposes.

"I will redouble my efforts to master its secrets," he promises.

She passes it to the nearest man with a lamp, and it is as if it never existed, let alone cost eight pounds, which Dee has, admittedly, yet to pay. The Queen now signals she is to be given some space in which to talk privately, and the Yeomen step back, and Her Majesty becomes, for his sake once more, a little more like the Bess of old.

"But honestly," she says, touching his arm, "thank you, John, for saving Mistress Frommond."

"It was the least I could do." He smiles.

"She is very dear to me, though she is a somewhat impatient stitch at needlework."

Dee can think of much more that he would like to add by way of praise for Jane Frommond, but knows the Queen well enough to keep it to himself. Instead he nods and asks after Jane's health.

"Very weak, and still she gives off that terrible smell," the Queen admits. "Though she has been washed in soap, top to toe. Bathed in the bath my father had built in Whitehall! But still. I wonder if she will ever smell clean?"

"It was very foul, that water."

He doesn't really want to think about it.

"Why do you think he kept you down there?" the Queen asks.

"It is a question I have oftentimes asked myself," he admits, which is true, about six hundred times a day when he was in the hold. "When we first found the barge, it struck us both that it was the best place for the gunmen to have lived while they waited to hear you were coming. They had a purpose and would not have aroused any suspicion among the local people. They might also escape easily, after the deed was done: down the river, hidden under a tarpaulin, say, with their guns. Then to a creek where they might climb out and disperse unobserved. Or even across the sea, perhaps, to Holland?"

"But the people of Holland do love us," the Queen tells him. She means herself.

"Perhaps the actual Hollanders do," Dee treads carefully, since he supposes that is no longer necessarily true since she declined to send them troops and money, "but there are others who value Your Majesty less highly: the Flemish, say, or the Walloons. They live in fear the Hollanders will drive Spain from the Low Countries and supress Catholicism just as much as we fear the reverse."

The Queen knows this.

"But why leave a man at the barge?" she wonders.

"That has likewise puzzled me," Dee confesses. "Perhaps the rest fled the county that night, but then, when they learned they had failed to kill you, they sent a man back there as a placeman, to hold it against another attempt on your life?"

The Queen shudders.

"If only you had not killed him," she says, "Master Topcliffe might have elicited the truth."

Dee says nothing. What happened that day on the barge is a matter between God, himself, and the dead man, he thinks, not Master Topcliffe, who is the Queen's torturer. A horrible-looking man with a face like two sides of well-aged beef, though of course that is hardly his fault. What is his fault is that he indulges his desire to torture men—and women—on the rack, or with the gauntlet, or in Little Ease, where a decent man would rather kill himself.

"And that being so," she concludes, "it is ever more vital that you complete your work on the Greek fire, for that way we will at least be able to defend ourselves."

Their gazes fall on the barrel by the back door.

"Need I return to the Tower?" Dee asks.

The Queen looks around at his own house: wood, wattle,

thatched in parts, filled with the largest collection of books in all England.

"Somewhere a little out of the way," she suggests, "with plenty of space to experiment. And with access to the river, or the sea, for its water. Should anything go awry."

He thinks Greenwich.

The Queen suggests the Isle of Sheppey.

"Any damage done will only improve the place."

Dee's heart sinks. Sheppey in January?

"This month?"

"Tomorrow. I will send a barge."

CHAPTER EIGHTEEN

Whitehall Palace,
second week of January 1578

It is past Christmas, past New Year's, even past the Epiphany when Master Francis Walsingham takes his first tentative steps in public on a pin-bright day; joined by Robert Beale, he walks down to the Custom House at Wool Quay, there to take a barge upriver to Whitehall. It is a journey he has made many times, but not having made it in so long, he notices the changes not only in Robert Beale—who looks worn out, with dark circles under his eyes—but along the way, too.

"I see they've finally pulled the tooth," he says, indicating the missing house on the bridge above as the barge slides under an arch.

They reach Whitehall as the tide turns and are taken by a gentleman usher to find Mistress Frommond not in one of the rooms in the Queen's privy apartments as expected, but out in one of the gardens, sitting on a stool in a shaft of thin winter sunlight and wrapped in furs and blankets lent her by Her Majesty and by Lettice Knollys, who has begun, Frommond tells them, to treat her as one of her daughters.

"Forgive me, masters," she says, "I was desperate for fresher air."

Her breath is a gauzy veil, and through it she is very pale, almost ethereal, her eyes remain like pure liquid honey in the sunlight, and Walsingham recalls his first thoughts of waking up in a bed next to her. Perhaps it is her lips: they are always slightly chapped, and it puts him in mind to kiss her. *The scar on her cheek is mending nicely*, he thinks, *though it will never be invisible.*

Greetings are exchanged and gratitude to God is offered up for her deliverance. She thanks them and asks after Dr. Dee, and Master Walsingham takes a certain amount of pleasure in telling her that Dee is restored to life and is about the Queen's business on the Isle of Sheppey.

"Oh," she says, disappointed. "I should like to thank him in person, though perhaps not now until he returns."

Walsingham sends for two more stools, and a table, and when they are produced, they sit and from his bag Beale brings out the things he claims Mistress Frommond asked him to find in the barge. They carry about them the distinctive reek of the hold, and Walsingham is pleased they are sitting out in the open. He waits to find out why they meant so much to Frommond, but she shows little interest in them.

"May I ask why you wanted them?" Beale must ask. "The limning I can understand, if he is someone to you, but a dirty glove?"

"The glove belonged to Alice Rutherford," she tells them.

Walsingham sits back.

A *momento mori* then? Well, why not?

"I found it in the forest," Frommond goes on. "Between the road where Alice was shot and the barge."

Walsingham sits forward and looks at it afresh.

"How ever did it get there?" he wonders.

Beale picks it up and examines it.

"I do not know," Frommond tells them, "but it was used as a privy clout."

She means an arse-wipe. Beale returns it to the tabletop.

Walsingham looks at it for a long while. Then he picks it up and spreads it out. One of the fingers is folded in. The index finger.

"Was that how you found it?" he asks.

She nods.

"May I ask you take your left-hand gloves off, both of you?" Walsingham asks Beale and Frommond.

They do: and Walsingham watches as both grasp the fingers of their left glove and pull. Beale's are looser, less fine than Frommond's and they come off first and easily. Frommond's are more delicate, like this glove of Alice Rutherford's, though a shade of yellow, and she must ease hers off, finger by finger. When they are done, each glove lies flat and perfectly formed. Why then is the finger of Alice Rutherford's glove completely inverted? It can only be deliberate.

"A code?" he asks.

There is a momentary pause for thought. Then Frommond makes a noise that is part sigh, part gasp.

"Yes," she says. "Look: five coaches. Five fingers."

He says nothing. Only looks at her intently. Frommond reaches for the red glove and holds it up by the tip of its thumb.

"The Queen's coach was the second."

Walsingham says nothing. Is this possible? Alice learns which coach the Queen is traveling in, pulls the corresponding finger of her glove in, then drops the glove out of the window for a man waiting at the side of the road on a good horse, who picks the glove up, its code and meaning preagreed and understood, and then rides to alert the men from the barge? They hurry up through the woods, and line up at the side of the road, and know exactly at which carriage to shoot. In the intervening time, one of them, whoever has the glove, is taken short. He has a shit against a tree, and leaves the glove there, in the wood, its purpose served, until later, Dee and Frommond discover it.

Beale shakes his head. This aspect of the plot seems to upset him most, and there is something peculiarly, and deliberately, degrading about it. It is as if they are insulting Alice, and the risks she took to let them know the Queen was coming.

"But then . . . why *did* she let them know the Queen was coming?" he speaks aloud. And now a tear trembles on Frommond's eyelid. Walsingham knows when to speak, when to stay silent. He stays silent and after a while Mistress Frommond points to the limning.

"That is the father of Alice's child," she says.

Beale's eyes widen. Walsingham had neglected to tell him Alice was pregnant.

"And who is he?" Beale asks.

"His name is Jan Saelminck," Frommond tells them. "A Dutchman who used to assist an alchemist, whose name I cannot now recall, but who was once imprisoned in the Tower."

"De Lannoy?" Walsingham supposes. "Cornelius de Lannoy?"

She nods. The tear retreats. She opens her mouth as if to ask something, then shakes the thought away.

"Well," she says, "that is why I asked to see you, Master Walsingham. I wanted you to know."

Walsingham takes a deep breath.

"How do you know he was the father?"

"Well," she admits, "I don't. No man can. But I found the limning hidden in Alice's clothes, here in the palace, after she was killed."

It is just about reasonable to suspect that Jan Saelminck might be the missing father, Walsingham supposes, but— Then Frommond describes her meeting with Marcus Teerlinc, Levina Teerlinc's son.

"The pornographer?"

"Yes. Saelminck commissioned a pair of limnings: one of him, one of Alice. But when it came to paying, he would pay for only one of the two: his to give to her. He was not interested in hers. He was not interested in having a keepsake of her."

"So he did not love her as she loved him?"

"I am surmising," she admits. "But the receipt for the limning is written in Dutch, and Marcus says his mother and Saelminck spoke that language together. And then, that night, Mistress Teerlinc died before a priest could be summoned."

"You think he killed her? Poisoned her perhaps?"

"Oh, I don't know," she admits. "Everything is conjecture, isn't it? Even John . . . Dr. Dee recognizing the limning. Is it really Jan Saelminck? Or just someone who looks like him?"

Beale raises his brows and catches Walsingham's eye. *Oh Lord*, Walsingham thinks, *Beale's intrigue with Ness Overbury*. He has not yet managed to raise himself to read the reports from Arthur Gregory, the man whom Cecil suggested Walsingham set to watch over Beale in case his scheme should warp out of proportion, and as a precaution against implication.

"But that suggests . . . that he seduced her months ago?"

"At least a year," Frommond says. "Look at the date."

1576.

Walsingham looks more closely at the limning. Now that he does so, he sees the boy is wearing a badge on his cap. It looks to his poor eyes like a pilgrimage badge, but there is something about its design that stills his heart.

"Robert," he says, "take a closer look, will you."

He passes the limning to Beale, who squints and frowns. Then he looks up and stares at Walsingham.

"My God," he breathes. "The Black Madonna."

And Walsingham knows the worst is confirmed. He feels a chill wind.

"The Black Madonna?" Frommond asks.

"The Guild of the Black Madonna," Beale clarifies. "You see the badge? On his cap. It is like a pilgrimage badge, such as any pilgrim might collect to show he has been to Canterbury, or Saint James's in Santiago de Compostela, but this one is different. This one is only given out to members of a guild of men who worship the idol of the Black Madonna in Halle, a town in Flanders."

Frommond frowns.

"They are the most . . . pffft."

Beale cannot find the words to describe the extremity of their commitment, which borders on lunacy, nor really can Walsingham.

"They are zealots," Walsingham says. "Dangerous unreasoning zealots. Worse than the Inquisition because they operate beyond the law. Not even Bloody Mary would tolerate them in England."

"And there is an oath they take," Beale continues, "to root out by fire the enemies of their idol, as they see her, or die in the attempt. Like the martyrs of old."

Frommond pales.

"And if they have their claws into Her Majesty—they will not cease until either she or they are dead. It is a death sentence."

"How many of them are there?" Frommond asks.

"No one knows. Oh Christ. That explains it. The men in the barge: they were guildsmen."

Walsingham nods.

"Well, there have been no further attempts on Her Majesty's life, have there?" Frommond asks. Walsingham allows there may not have been.

"Then perhaps he—Saelminck—has gone home? Back to Halle. Or perhaps he is already dead?"

She is an optimist. Beale shakes his head.

"No," he says, pointing at the limning. "Or, well, maybe, but look at the date again. This was a long-laid plan. Well seasoned. They waited more than a year before they struck. They wanted to be certain."

Beale is right, Walsingham thinks. Saelminck will have gone to ground again. He'll be planning something else. He'll never give up. Christ. What is he to tell Her Majesty?

"Why did he wait so long?" Frommond wonders. Walsingham thinks to remind her that he himself is not incapable. It is not an easy thing to attempt to shoot the Queen, because he, Walsingham, ensures that it is not. But perhaps there is a simpler explanation.

"Perhaps Alice would not do as he asked," he speculates. "Sooner, I mean? Or perhaps Saelminck only asked when he knew she was ruined—after *he* had ruined her."

"And even then," Frommond muses. "And even then, perhaps

she would only have betrayed Her Majesty *after* Her Majesty had threatened her with the Tower. Only then did Alice give him the glove."

They look at it now, a twisted relic of a dead love, a dead girl, and her dead baby.

Christ.

"Was it Saelminck whom Dee killed on the river Lea barge?" Beale asks. "Dee is said to have made a horrible mess of the man."

Walsingham can hear the squeak of hope in his voice, but Frommond shakes her head.

"He would have said something, surely, wouldn't he? If John knew him from the past, and when he came out of the cabin and first—"

She touches her neck. The bruises are faded now, but there is still the scar. She shivers. Perhaps it is the cold. The sun has dipped behind the stable block, leaving them in shadow, and Frommond suddenly looks as exhausted as Walsingham feels. But he has noted the easy use of Dee's Christian name. Well. Well, what? They were confined together for days. It might mean nothing. And yet.

"It is lucky for us, for us all, you found the limning," Walsingham congratulates her.

Frommond agrees.

"Especially," she goes on, "as I was not the only one who looked through Alice's belongings after her death."

She tells them about the finger marks in the dust on her coffer, and the gone-through bags on Alice's makeshift bier. Walsingham is very alarmed now. He feels there is a bird trapped in his chest.

"And nothing was missing? There was nothing stolen?"

"Nothing I noticed. There were some coins. And rings. Left behind. It might be that someone had been looking for something specific. Something hidden, perhaps, such as this likeness."

"Why did you not tell us sooner?" Beale asks.

Frommond thinks for a moment.

"You told me yourself, Master Walsingham, on that step there, that in ordinary times you might have the leisure to discover the name of the father of Alice's child, but now was not that time. Also, how could I know that he . . . that Jan Saelminck . . . might be connected to Alice's death? It was not until I found her glove, in the forest, and saw what was done to it, and by then— Well. It was too late."

Walsingham feels his grip slipping again. He thinks about Saelminck coming into the palace to rummage through a maid of honor's possessions, just as if he were some searcher at the docks.

"Can I be sure of this? You are saying that Saelminck was in the palace *after* Alice's death? Right here? At leisure looking for something in Her Majesty's privy rooms?"

Frommond nods.

"Or someone looking on his behalf."

Christ. That is even worse! Saelminck himself, or some bastard from the Guild of the Black Madonna! Prowling the palace! Walsingham can feel that vinegar sweat beading his forehead again. He stands.

"Double the guard, Robert," he tells Beale. "Lock this place down. Find out exactly who comes and who goes. Christ. Find out who's come and who's gone."

Beale makes another note.

"Now, Robert," he insists.

Robert coughs meaningfully.

Oh Christ. His deception of the Queen's person.

"There is no time for that now, Robert," Walsingham tells him.

But Beale is defiant.

"With respect sir, it is now more timely than ever."

Walsingham is momentarily taken aback by Beale's intransigence. It borders on disobedience. But by Christ, now of all times, perhaps he is right. Perhaps Walsingham has a field of blindness in this matter, and he should acknowledge it, and yield.

"Very well," he says, "I will see to it myself."

"I am happy to leave you to your deliberations," Mistress Frommond tells them, and she starts to gather her things, though she touches neither the glove nor the limning.

"I would be happy to see neither again," she says.

He puts them in his own bag and excuses himself, leaving Beale to pitch his plan to Frommond. He wants no part in that, and it is not as if he does not have things to get on with, he thinks, and he makes his way to Sir William Cecil's chambers to find him looking gloomy. He looks worse when Walsingham tells him about the Guild of the Black Madonna.

Cecil claps both hands to his cheeks.

"Those bastards? That is all we need."

He turns to stare at the flames in his chimney place.

"What shall we do?" he asks after a moment.

"What can we do? That we are not already doing?"

"But they might still be in the country. An enemy within, as if we did not already have enough of them."

"But these are armed and dangerous."

"Oh, that stupid oath. What is it? To root out by fire—"

"—the enemies of Her Grace the Mother of Christ, or something. Beale knows it."

"It is not as if anyone is an enemy of the Mother of Christ, is it?"

Walsingham shrugs. Cecil has put his finger on the nub of the stupidity of the rhetoric of this war between Catholics and Protestants.

There is a longish silence. Then Cecil sighs and tells him that

Parma is on the move. He means the Duke of Parma's army, the one that they'd hoped might keep to its barracks this winter, is out and on the march.

"Twenty thousand troops, ready for battle with the rebels, and we know how that always ends."

He rubs his eyes.

"Perhaps Hatton was right, after all. Imagine if we had sent troops," he goes on. "They'd be just another contingent in what is already an ungovernable hodgepodge of every country and creed."

The room seems to grow darker.

"Oh, bloody hell," Cecil says, sighing. "At this rate we will have Parma and his *tercios* in Westminster by Easter. Which is why this becomes all the more important."

He raps his knuckles on the desk, specifically on his draft of Jenkinson's verse. He reads out the first three lines:

> *"They say of love;*
> *the heart one day fell prisoner to a prince*
> *but long has mine been captive of*
> *England's twice-sceptered jewel,*
> *Wherein each facet the wise man may discern*
> *heaven's sacred cipher . . ."*

"It is this last line that seems to me to offer a way in," he supposes. "The poet is talking about a jewel—forget that it has been twice-sceptered for the moment—in which a wise man—by which I take him to mean an adept—may read heaven's sacred cipher."

"Yes," Walsingham agrees. *That is more or less what it says*, he thinks.

"So what is heaven's sacred cipher?"

"You tell me."

Cecil looks peeved. Then he moves some papers and finds a roll
to show Walsingham. It is a list of the presents the Queen gave and
received this last New Year: object, name of donor, and estimated
value. Cecil was given a cup with a cover, Walsingham notes, cost
estimated at three pounds. He gave the Queen twenty pounds in
gold. There is no mention of Walsingham's gift of two jars of green
ginger. Hatton gave her a gold cross, enriched with diamonds and
pearls, and a medallion with a picture of a man being pulled by
a dog, and on the back, certain verses. Walsingham thinks they
ought to summon Hatton to have a look at Jenkinson's verse. See
what he makes of it.

"Just because he dances a superior galliard, you believe he will
have a superior understanding of verse?"

Walsingham does not know why, but yes, he does. Cecil chews
the clipped stub of his pen for a moment before doubtfully making
a note.

"I will send him a copy, then. But anyway, I did not show you
the list for that. I wanted you to see, there."

He points:

"By Doctor John Dee, Shew-stone, £7 s6 do"

"Did you know that Dee gave Her Majesty his scrying stone at
New Year's?" Cecil asks.

"I didn't know he owned one."

"He doesn't anymore, if, in fact, he ever did: Master Bowes, a
goldsmith of Lombard Street, is petitioning for its return on the
basis that Dee bought it for eight pounds in gold that two days later
revealed itself to be . . . not gold. Anyway. Bowes's position is that
Dee never owned it and had no rights to give it away, even to the
Queen. I take his point but can only wish him well with that one."

"It cannot be the jewel mentioned in the verse?"

Cecil sighs.

"I hoped you'd say it must be. It's valued at only seven pounds and six shillings."

Walsingham laughs.

"Imagine."

"Do we know of any other scrying stones?"

"Perhaps we might use Dee's to divine that."

"Don't joke, Francis."

They continue to mull over the verse's meaning for a while, coming at length to no clear conclusion. As with the identity of Saelminck, it is, as Mistress Frommond would say, all conjecture.

"Do you suppose it might be something uniquely Ottoman?" Cecil wonders.

"To set a price this way? Or write the verse?"

"Both."

"I am not an Ottoman so I cannot say."

Cecil is disappointed.

"I think we need to get Jenkinson down," he decides. "Get him to talk us through it. Tell us who this man is."

"The Tower?"

"The Tower."

When the meeting is concluded Walsingham walks to the river, wondering where they might find a scrying stone that might approximate the value of a hundred and fifty tons of anything, and so he only hears his name being called at the third time of asking.

"Master Walsingham! Sir!"

It is an unknown, short, and poorly dressed man in faded lawyer's robes. He has an armful of papers rolled under his arm and no hat.

"Thomas Penyngton," he introduces himself. "I am clerk to the Court of Sewers."

He realizes his hat is missing.

"You are just the man I have been looking for," Walsingham tells him. Penyngton looks nervous. Perhaps no one has ever said that about the clerk to the Court of Sewers.

"I came as soon as I heard you sought me," he tells him. A roll of paper springs from his grasp. As he fumbles for it, another escapes. *He is like a mouse*, Walsingham thinks, and he imagines the clerk is probably happiest at home where he is fondly tolerated. Walsingham asks him about the work on the river Lea, specifically the construction of the lock below Enfield. He knows of it.

"Ah. That would be Master Honrighe you need to talk to. Garrett Honrighe. A surveyor, sir, and, being a Hollander, interested in water, or rather interested not in water, but in its want. He is interested in being dry, I should say."

Walsingham wonders if this Honrighe is also a member of the Guild of the Black Madonna. Not that Penyngton would know, of course, unless Honrighe wore the pilgrimage badge. He asks the clerk.

"No, sir," Penyngton replies, "no badges or anything of that sort. He is a very plainly dressed sort of man, sir. Not unlike your good self, sir, if I may be so bold as to say so."

Well, if you were a member of the Guild of the Black Madonna, you would not want it known, not in England, would you?

"So he is supervising the construction?" Walsingham asks.

"No, sir. Master Honrighe is the surveyor. He employs builders under contract to do the actual work. Why? Is there a problem with the lock?"

"It is nothing like that," Walsingham reassures him. "I merely wish to know the name of the builder of the lock, that is all."

"Are you thinking of having your own lock built? Is that it? I know Lord Burghley—"

"I merely need his name."

Penyngton is flustered and starts going through the rolls under his arm. Walsingham offers to hold those he has discarded. The second-to-last one the clerk looks at is the one he wants. He unrolls it. The writing is awkward and crabby, but after a moment he comes to the name.

"That's right," he says. "I remember being surprised at it now. It's a man called Henk Poos."

Walsingham has not heard of Henk Poos.

"Why were you surprised?" he queries, almost despite himself.

"Well," Penyngton says, warming to his subject and turning sideways to whisper from the corner of his mouth, as if imparting a great scandal. "Master Honrighe is a Hollander from West Friesland, you see, which is practically in the sea, and where all the best water engineers come from, but Henk Poos is a Fleming."

"And that is surprising how?"

Penyngton seems taken aback at Walsingham being so obtuse.

"Why, the Flemish are good with cloth, and wood, sir, not water! Furthermore, though, I saw that the two men do not like each other. I recall that from when I met them to discuss the works, and I very nearly told them the task must go elsewhere, and would have done so, had Master Honrighe not proved so insistent."

"So you have met Henk Poos? The man who is building the lock?"

"I have indeed, sir. A most unusual gentleman in our trade, for he is just that: a gentleman, such as yourself."

Walsingham dips his hand into his bag and in a moment has Mistress Teerlinc's limning.

"Is this him? Is this Henk Poos."

Penyngton peers close.

"Why, yes, sir!" he marvels. "That is him! The very spit!"

CHAPTER NINETEEN

Isle of Sheppey, Kent,
the second week of February 1578

I t is just past the old feast of Candlemas, early February, and still raining, when Dr. John Dee and his assistant, Roger Cooke, stand with their boots in the water's edge, their backs to the sea, and study once more the dismal gray lump of mud and weed that is the Isle of Sheppey.

"If there exists a more dismal place in all Her Majesty's kingdom," Dee says, "then I am yet to hear of it."

"Likewise Her Majesty, sir," Cooke tells him, "or she'd've sent us there instead."

Cooke believes the Queen has sent them here to Shurland Hall as a punishment for the hole that Dee blew in the Tower's curtain wall. Perhaps he is right. But Dee reminds him that the Queen's father and the Queen's mother spent a delirious summer here, away from London during a plague year, just before their ill-starred marriage.

"Never came back, though, did they?" Cooke points out.

"True," Dee concedes, "but that is not because they did not like the place."

They have brought with them from the Tower all the apparatus surviving their last efforts to create Greek fire, but they cannot get the thick black ooze of the naft to burn, even slightly.

"I believe we will have to subject it to a process of refinement," Dee supposes.

"Purify it, is it, sir? Right oh."

Cooke loves the process of purification because it will allow him to pass his time around the flame of the burner in the alchemical workshop that they have created in one of the stone barns just to the south of the hall, with a slate roof, that looks out into a courtyard which itself has become a hive of purposeful activity. In one corner is the workshop of Her Majesty's master cooper, who is sent them from Greenwich and is at work on a species of double-walled barrel Dee believes will cope with great pressures from the bellows that the thick-armed saddler with thumbs of steel is making from the pile of sheets of well-tanned oxhide in the workshop beside his. And a smith has been sent, too, down from Ripon, in the North, who despite hardly being able to understand English as it is spoken in the south of the country is able to follow Dee's complicated instructions to within the fraction of an inch, and has, he thinks, perfected Dee's design for the one-way valve, and a stand for it. The coming together of these industries in such an isolated spot has created a curious camaraderie, so that even in February the cooper, smith, tanner, and their boys are to be found gathered about the fire in the smithy, speculating on the true purpose of their shared endeavor, and making bets on the likelihood of its success.

"But for the love of God, Master Cooke," Dee tells him, "and of your own skin, and mine, please be careful this time."

Cooke dabs a knuckle to his cap and scurries away to unpack the rest of the new glass dishes they have been sent, wrapped in wood shavings and smuggled over the sea from Antwerp, which he is keen to get to work on chipping and cracking and staining with soot.

But he is destined for disappointment, for the very next day, on the very first attempt at distillation, they draw off what Dee believes they are looking for: a strong-smelling extraction that when held up to the light seems to make the air above it dance. A lighted splint makes a single spoonful of the liquid go up with a tiny woof, after which it burns with a settled yellow flame and a fat tendril of black, evil-smelling smoke that for a short while makes them both feel sick.

The problem is that this single spoonful has come from a cupful of the black sludge in the barrel, and after that first spoonful what they then manage to draw off from the cupful will not burn unless it is heated to a high temperature—impossible aboard a ship, say—and the fractions that come out of the condenser after that, while still interesting, suggest earthier applications than Greek fire.

"I fear we will have little more than a cupful from the whole barrel," Dee tells Sir Thomas Kemp, master of Shurland Hall, whom he knows to be in touch with Sir William Cecil.

"But it will work, won't it? You will be able to produce Greek fire? I can inform Lord Burghley that the price is worth it?"

"That must depend on the price," Dee supposes, "but there is definite potential. I will combine that which I have drawn off with the other elements necessary, and once the pump is fully trust-worthy, we will try it."

"On the beach?"

He means the strand of mud that stinks of fish guts.

"Such as it is, yes."

The system Dee has devised—larger in scale than that which burned the crane on Tower Quay—shows great promise. Practicing with just seawater in the barrel, which is itself buried in the mud, they have had four boys on the bellows, and though the hoses swell and writhe like foul leather snakes, they have so far held, and with Dee's newly devised nozzle, they have projected a stream of water that would shoot over the roof of any medium-sized parish church with height to spare, were there one to hand.

The next day they set about making a single barrel of the concoction Dee believes is most like Greek fire, and when it is done, they fill the reservoir barrel with all they have of it, and seal it up with fat hoops of iron, and bury it in the beach with its two hoses coming out of the ground as if a giant were stitching up the earth, and they attach one end to the bellows and the other to the nozzle on its fabricated stand, which must be dug into the beach, and then they wheel an old cart down to the tideline and stand waiting for the sea to rise.

When at last it does, and the water rises to the cart's axles, Dee gives the signal, and the boys set to work on the bellows, and with that same distinctive noise of ten swans rising from choppy water, the first hose swells and struggles to escape, and there is a curious noise from the buried barrel and some spectators take fright and run. But then the second hose begins to twitch and swell and then there comes the moment of truth: Dee releases the catch, the match fuse swings into place just as the first whoosh of trapped air is replaced by the liquid, and an arc of flame shoots across the water to engulf the cart. Everybody throws their hands up in fright or celebration.

"Like a fucking dragon!" Cooke shouts.

But it is over very soon. The lack of contents in the barrel means the spurt of liquid falters and fades and splashes across the mud like an old man's late-night urination.

Despite himself, Dee smiles.

"Look, Doctor!" Cooke calls. "It is still burning!"

The sand, and the cart and the sea all around it, is still alight. The water itself is afire.

"Go and try to put it out," he tells Cooke.

"Not likely!"

Dee does it himself, wading into the frigid sea to scoop a hatful of brown water onto the burning surface. The flames continue to writhe. He scoops more, and hurls it onto the cart, with no effect. He has made it, he thinks. He has made Greek fire.

He feels no joy, he feels only fear. He has created a terrible, terrible weapon, one that could change the course of the world. That will burn the flesh of men, women, and children; that will roast them alive; that will turn great cities to cinders; libraries to ashes, life to death. It is as if he has reawakened and ushered into the world an old species of being long since presumed dead— *Thanatos*, the God of Death—to walk the surface of the earth, bringing nothing but death and destruction.

Thank God, he thinks, that that is the last of it.

Robert Beale comes to the Isle of Sheppey two days later, having heard the news.

"It could not have come at a better time," Beale tells him. "The day after we heard word from Gembloux."

"Gembloux?"

"The Duke of Parma's army has crushed the Hollanders. It is the end of them, that is for sure. All the Low Countries will soon be under the Inquisition."

Dee exhales.

"So news of your Greek fire is very welcome. Even Sir William Cecil himself managed to smile when your name was mentioned."

"Then I am to be permitted home?"

Beale falters.

Dee sighs.

"Christ, Robert, have I not done enough here?"

"You have, John, you have. No one can fault you."

"But?"

"But there is something else with which Her Majesty needs your help."

"She need only ask," Dee says, because that is true. He would do anything for the Queen—even, if she asked, remain on Sheppey—but as he is thinking this, he feels the grip of queasiness. *My God*, he thinks, *I do this every time*: he assumes they call on him because they need him for his knowledge of mathematics, or the language of the angels, or his expertise as to the stars, and it always ends up with him involved in a task more suited to a goatherd or a dong farmer. It is a punishment, he supposes, visited upon him for pride.

Beale coughs and clears his throat. *He looks tired*, Dee thinks.

"It is somewhat sensitive," Beale admits, looking around in case they are overheard.

Well, Dee thinks, that sounds more interesting.

"May we take a walk?"

They walk down to see the blackened bones of the cart and grimy sand. They can still catch the whiff of the naft even above the timeless smell of the sea. Beale shows him one of Nicholas Hilliard's limnings of the Queen.

"Is this Points's?" Dee asks. "My god, he is good, isn't he?

But look: he has given her a blemish. Bess will not like that, not at all."

Beale explains that the painting is not of the Queen, but of Ness Overbury. Then he explains his proposal, and when he is finished, Dee is unsure he has understood the scheme.

"You are insane," he says.

Beale looks thunderously upset.

"In which article?"

"In the whole thing. No one will believe it."

"We hardly need convince a soul that she is the Queen against their will. So few people actually know the Queen; so few people have access to her person, and those who might detect she is not Her Majesty, or who we believe might be unsympathetic to our aims, she can send from her presence at whim. So long as her councillors remain true to her, then that is enough for anyone."

He is right there, Dee supposes.

"What of her ladies of the bedchamber?" he asks. "They must know her intimately. Dress her and nurse her when she is sick and so on?"

"She may pick and choose, surely? She might pick a new lady of the bedchamber, someone who does not know her so well, or someone inclined to our cause. Mistress Frommond, say."

"Ah," Dee says. "Mistress Frommond. And is she . . . involved?"

"She is," Beale says, though there is a flicker of hesitation to suggest he lies.

"And this Ness Overbury is willing? It is a deadly serious undertaking."

"She is. There is something about her. If she had been born a man, she might have achieved anything: become a bishop, say, or discovered the Northwest Passage, or both. I cannot describe her."

"She sounds— You sound—"

"What?"

"Very taken. With her?"

Beale flushes, but he does not deny it.

"It is not about how I feel," he says, and Dee half believes him.

He thinks for a long moment.

"How will it end, do you think?" he wonders. "Suppose the Queen lives until she is a hundred. Will you have Ness waiting there all that time?"

Beale has not thought of this.

"She might go back to her normal life . . ." he begins. His voice tails off. Dee sees that Beale does not want her to go back to her normal life, of course. He wants her in his. And how can Dee blame him for that? But this is a dauntingly risky tactic to get a woman into bed! It makes Dee admire Beale all the more.

"And you would want me to do what exactly? Teach her as I taught Her Majesty? I was not her only tutor you know. Roger Ascham must take some credit. Though I can see there might be a problem recruiting him."

Ascham has been dead ten years.

"Ness can already read and write—her handwriting is passable, but Her Majesty's hand is much changed in recent years anyway—and she has a little Latin, but no Greek. Or French or Italian."

"So marriage to Anjou is out of the question? Good."

"She need only know some geometry, a little algebra, the basics of astronomy and astrology, philosophy, theology—"

"But this would have to be done in the strictest secrecy," Dee thinks aloud. "If word got out—a whisper even—the suspicion of a suggestion of a word got out, then it would all be for nothing.

And if Bess discovered what you are about with Ness, my God—that does not bear thinking about."

Though that is what they both now do. The men involved would be hanged, drawn and quartered; the women would be burned at the stake.

"And supposing the scheme lay undiscovered until the moment—God forbid—the Queen dies. Queens do not die alone. There would be more physicians and bishops than you might shake a stick at, all looming over her, holding her hand and smelling her breath. And Mary of Scotland will surely have her placemen—Hatton, for example—waiting to bring her word the moment Bess is dead."

"New doctors may be found. New bishops."

Dee shakes his head to clear it. It is a foolish scheme, yet Beale is almost managing to make it sound if not sensible, then at least possible.

Dee asks if Beale believes in the Divine Right of kings and queens. Beale looks down at his hands.

"Do you?" he asks, looking back up at Dee.

"I believe in Her Majesty's Right," Dee tells him.

"But not Mary of Scotland's?"

Dee takes his point.

"And what have Walsingham and Cecil said?"

Beale says nothing.

Ahhh, Dee thinks. *Here we come to it.*

"They want no official part? They want to be able to deny knowledge?"

"Precisely."

What a pair of shits, Dee thinks. *Letting Beale take the risk while they reap the rewards.* But then he thinks: *There are some benefits he might reap that they cannot. My God, if Beale guides Ness through this, and she becomes Queen, then he—Beale—might ask of her anything he wants. He could become Ness's Lord Treasurer! Her husband! King. Then what would Walsingham say?*

He starts to laugh and looks at Beale afresh.

"So what is your plan?" he asks.

And with that, he realizes, he is become part of it.

CHAPTER TWENTY

Tower of London, last week of February 1578

I t is dawn on the last bitingly cold day of February, with a skim of ice turning the Tower's moat the color of spilled milk.

"It is almost inviting, isn't it?" Sir Christopher Hatton says. "You could dive right in."

"Be my guest," Francis Walsingham invites him.

They have arrived by chance together at the Lion Gate, both well wrapped against the cold, but Walsingham feels very homespun next to Hatton, who is done up like a peacock in royal blue, with gold and silver thread through his cloak and cap; his beard oiled and trimmed to a point.

"You are very brightly turned-out for the Tower?" Walsingham comments.

"I am summoned to Whitehall later," Hatton tells him. "By Her Majesty. After being too sick to celebrate her birthday last year, this year she wishes to mark the date with due ceremony."

"Ah, yes. I had forgotten you are become a party planner!" Walsingham tells him. "At last a job for which you are qualified! And will there be some dancing, do you suppose? A galliard or two, maybe? A pavane, perhaps?"

Hatton flushes.

"I am glad you are recovered strength enough to mock me, Master Walsingham. I quite feared for your life this last month or so, and whenever I met your man Robert Beale, he, too, looked drained of life. I feared it might be something contagious."

Walsingham is carrying a new packet from Arthur Gregory, the man set to watch over Beale and his scheme, and he reminds himself that he must open it and read it, if only to make the money he pays Gregory seem worth it. He is also carrying a message from the clerk of city works, who reports that he has personally been to every worksite in the city, whether commissioned by the board or not, and has found no sign of Saelminck, nor Hank Poos, nor anyone who had worked with him, nor indeed many laborers from the Low Countries, for they have mostly—along with Garrett Honrighe—packed up and gone home for the winter. He is not sure whether to be encouraged to hear this or not. Can the Guild of the Black Madonna only work in the summer months? He doubts it, but by God that would make his life easier.

The gate is opened, and Walsingham yields precedence to Hatton, who is, Hatton reminds him, a knight of the realm, with precedence, and they walk in silence while Walsingham costs him by the inch: just shy of forty pounds, he thinks, including boots and hat and sword. *Where is he getting that kind of money?* What was it that Cecil had said? A new venture with one of the merchant adventurers, perhaps? Or was it just Frobisher? Frobisher and that worthless ore that he brought back? Perhaps that is it. He will have to set a man on him. In fact, why not Gregory? He smiles at the symmetry.

In the Constable's lodgings, they find Cecil is already gathered around the table with the Master of the Board of Ordnance and the Constable of the Tower, and the atmosphere in the room, with applewood on the fire and warm wine in the good silver jug, is more convivial than might be expected for an inquiry the outcome of which might be the racking of a man. It is the verse, Walsingham supposes, and the prospect of taking receipt of the naft.

"We are discussing storage of the naft," Cecil cheerfully proves him right. "The Constable here fears its incendiary properties and is not keen to have it kept in the vaults of Her Majesty's Tower."

"The masons are just today finishing up the repair to the damage Dr. Dee inflicted last time he was here," the Constable appeals to Walsingham. "Listen."

And sure enough, through the window they can hear the tap-tap-tapping of the hammers as the masons shape the final stones to fit the hole Dee blew in the wall.

"And that was before he had the naft!" the Master of the Board of Ordnance adds. "What in all of Christendom will he do with it when he has that?"

There is some gentle laughter.

The Master of the Board of Ordnance is a pleasant, innocuous little fellow, appointed by Cecil to be immune to too much bribery.

"But we are counting our chickens," Walsingham reminds them. "It may be that Jenkinson is as much in the dark as to what is required as we are."

Copies of the verse are brought out and shown around.

"Well, Sir Christopher? Any thoughts?"

Hatton is hesitant. He blushes and stammers and then talks of the love that the writer must feel for a prince.

"A prince? You think this is a woman writing?"

"Isn't it?"

"There are no wrong answers, Sir Christopher," Cecil soothes. "We are all of us in the dark here."

"Well, there are wrong answers," Walsingham points out. "If we come up with them, someone else will get the naft. Most likely the Spanish."

Hatton tells them he likes the last line. Cecil's gaze flicks to Walsingham. *See?* he says without saying it.

"Let's get Jenkinson in here," Walsingham says.

Word is sent to the Bell Tower, where Jenkinson has passed a comfortable night. Though when he comes to the Constable's room, you would not know it.

"Do not touch me!" he shouts. "Do not so much as lay a fucking glove on me!"

He is addressing a six-foot Yeoman of the Queen's Guard, one-third his age perhaps, who carries at least three weapons with which he might eviscerate Jenkinson. More than that he has two other Yeomen of the Guard with him. That is nine ways, right there, in which Jenkinson might die.

"Master Jenkinson," Cecil tries to soothe, "please, sit, join us. No one is going to touch you. Unless you want them to."

"What do you mean by that, you godless old fuck?"

Cecil rolls his eyes. Jenkinson is not dressed quite so strangely as when they rode to see him in Market Harborough this last year, but still wears a turban of white silk over a loose hood and a tunic of the same material that falls from his shoulders to the ground. He wears gloves the color of grass in May, and a black cloak of what must be the finest wool ever spun.

"Are you not content with wasting three years of my life, Cecil, you now want a week more? Is that it? You have me dragged from my own bed by these men who would shame a camel with their habits, who make me sleep in manacles and share their foul food."

Cecil's patience snaps.

"Oh pipe down, Jenkinson," he rumbles. "Or I will have you gagged."

Jenkinson—face stained darker than needs be, and with charcoal lining his eyes—sits.

"Now we've got your terms here"—Cecil prods the verse on the table—"but can make neither hide nor hair of them. So you tell us now: What is it your man wants? And speak plain, man. None of your . . . heathen oddness."

Jenkinson, tired from his long journey perhaps, or intimidated by being in the Tower, now makes a fatal misjudgment. He laughs. It is a sneering sort of laugh, as if he pities Cecil, as if pities them all. He pities them for the crude clumsiness of their dress; their ugly shoes; their warm wine in dumpy pewter cups; their ruddy red, winter-bitten faces; their gloves that fit like shoes; their ignorance; their insularity; their lack of sophistication. He pities their pretensions. He laughs as if there is nothing they have that he wants, that their power is beneath him, and they cannot touch him.

It is interesting, Walsingham thinks, to see how men react to this: Hatton sees the situation through Jenkinson's eyes, and is mortified and ashamed of himself and his pretensions, which now seem not quite enough, as if he is playing dress-up as a grown-up, while Cecil swells as does a bull before it charges. Had Hatton been the senior figure here, then Jenkinson might have carried the day, but Hatton must defer to Cecil. This is Cecil's meeting, and so it is Cecil who bellows.

"Topcliffe! Topcliffe there! Send for Master Topcliffe!"

Topcliffe has been waiting. He bustles in, a young man with slack, drinker's cheeks, and a face that you'd not guess would belong to a man who pulled other men apart and raped their wives and daughters as they stood forced to watch while balanced on a beam with their arms chained to the wall behind their backs. His assistants, though, my God, you would not wish to meet, not just on a dark night, but ever. Two of them: one enormously stupid, and slow, but hugely muscled, like a circus giant on whose forehead a third eye is usually painted; the second a skinny, sniggering weed with ratty teeth and a boneyard pallor. The big one, hands the size of plates, clamps Jenkinson in an undeniable grip and though Jenkinson flails, he is like a child in the giant's paws and can do nothing but kick his legs in the air and shout and scream "Habeas corpus!" as he is bundled out of the Constable's lodgings.

Walsingham laughs.

"Habeas corpus," he repeats, but Cecil is still inflamed.

"I will tell you what is not right. Him. Laughing at us. Well, you saw! You saw, didn't you? We gave him every chance. We met him as a gentleman, here in your chambers, Constable. Not in some dungeon. What gives him the right to be so high-and-mighty, to scorn us! Merely because he has been to Persia? Those Persians were right to have nothing to do with him! I wish to God we had not either!"

Being in a room with someone who has recently behaved so impetuously, Walsingham thinks, is like being drunk in the company of a drunker drunk: it sobers you up. He wonders what it might be like to go to Persia. It might make him laugh at men such as Cecil, too.

"Well," he says. "Let us see if we can at least save his life."

He takes up the draft of the poem, and he follows the still-shouting Jenkinson across the inner ward—where it has begun snowing again, very fine flakes from a pewter sky that needs a polish—and up the steps of the White Tower and then down, again, into the lower dungeon where the rack is kept. The atmosphere is instantly repelling and can be felt like a miasma, a definite presence, and Walsingham finds himself holding his breath.

In the room, where lamps burn sickly in sconces, he finds he does not want to even look at the instrument itself, where Jenkinson shouts and kicks within the frame, pressed down into its embrace by the giant while Topcliffe and the rat-toothed assistant tie his wrists and ankles with strong rope.

There are drifts of straw across the floor to help soak up any fluids, and a coffer, on which lie such tools as would horrify a farrier.

When they are done with the knots, Jenkinson lies spread star-shaped on the floor, his wrists tied fast to one end of the bulky oak frame, his ankles to a winch at the other end, and the giant turns the winch, and Jenkinson is straightened, though his back still rests on the floor. Walsingham signals him to leave it at that for the moment.

Jenkinson is red-faced and breathing very hard.

"Master Jenkinson," Walsingham says, "I am sorry it has come to this. I expect you are, too. All we want is some information."

He imagines such words have often been spoken here, but this does feel like a situation that has bolted beyond control, and that if they might just sit down, and discuss what is, after all, only a verse, then any further unpleasantness—let alone a man having his arms torn from his shoulders, his legs from his hips—might be avoided.

"I know nothing of it," Jenkinson tells him.

"Nothing at all? Nothing about the imagery and so forth? We don't care about meter or rhyme, Master Jenkinson. We are brutes, as you say. All we want to know is what it means."

"You will have to ask the man who wrote it," Jenkinson mutters.

"Ah! Now that is interesting. Who did write it?"

Jenkinson says nothing. He seems to regret having suggested this line of inquiry.

"It is a bit late to be thinking of protecting your contacts, Master Jenkinson."

Master Topcliffe stands by, ready for Walsingham's nod. Walsingham nods. He turns the winch handle and the ropes creak. He stops it off with a wedge. Master Jenkinson is not yet off the floor. It is hardly a comfortable position for an old man, but not too bad.

"Give us a name to go on, Master Jenkinson. We will not cut you out of the deal. You will get whatever is coming to you."

The rat-toothed assistant laughs.

"Get what's coming to you," he repeats, reversing its meaning.

"Can you get him out?" Walsingham asks Topcliffe. The man looks distraught, but goes clumping up the steps.

"So who is it, Master Jenkinson? Who is the poet?"

It is a curious thing about the rack, Walsingham thinks. Some men spill their secrets merely knowing it exists, and these are the men Walsingham as often as not has admired most: clever men who have considered their strengths, and come to terms with their weaknesses; imaginative men who can foresee what being pulled apart might be like. Others believe they will be able to resist the pain, or feel they are strong enough to hold themselves together, and as often as not these men have their minds broken before their bodies. A third kind he is yet to meet: those who die without word or regret.

"Oww," Jenkinson says.

It is comical.

"Come on, Master Jenkinson. This is stupid. You are enduring this for what? Some money? You already have enough. Surely the amount you hope to make from this cannot be so very great. Or is it . . . what? The chance to humiliate Cecil? Is that worth it?"

He gives the signal. The winch and rope creak. Jenkinson hisses. Topcliffe frowns. He mouths to Walsingham that Jenkinson is still not yet off the floor.

"Master Jenkinson," Walsingham tells him. "You have endured about as much as most men can in one session. You have shown great courage, but surely now is the time to give up the name. I do not believe the poet—whoever he may be—would expect you to endure so much for so little."

Jenkinson thrusts his jaw out. He can still take some more.

"Oh, for Christ's sake!" Walsingham steps into the frame and slaps Jenkinson's cheek, hard enough to sting. "Tell me his fucking name, you fool!"

He makes to slap him again.

"All right! All right! I will!"

Back in the Constable's lodgings, Cecil is now shamefaced.

"Well?" he asks.

"Sokollu Mehmet Pasha."

Cecil throws his pen down and sits back, incredulous. Both the Constable and the Master of the Board of Ordnance are at a loss. Hatton is gone, off to see the Queen, to organize his party.

"What is that?" the Constable asks.

"He is the grand vizier of the Ottomans," Walsingham tells them. "The most powerful man in the empire, after the sultan."

There is a long silence.

"What in God's name does that mean?"

Walsingham says nothing. He paces the floor and then stops to stare out of the window. The masons are still there, silent about their business, as if the atmosphere of the Tower has cowed them, and their usual whistles and chat is all dried up. *My God*, he thinks, *what* does *it mean? The grand vizier of the Ottomans?* He feels he has taken hold of what he believed to be a snake only to discover it is the tail of a tiger. Far from playing this Turkish merchant of Jenkinson, he knows now that he—and England—are the plaything.

"This will require some thought," he says.

"Well, well," Cecil says. "That explains why the verse does not ask for gold. The grand vizier can have no need of that."

"But Jenkinson knows nothing more? He cannot tell you what the unflawed gem actually is?"

Walsingham shakes his head.

"He was only ever trying to keep his commission," he tells them.

"But Sokollu is an Ottoman? What was all the business with Persia?" Cecil wonders.

"Jenkinson was just trying to bump the price up. Apparently, there is naft enough in Ottoman lands, in the south, as he told me, around a city called Basra."

"Crafty little devil," Cecil says. It is a compliment.

"He was trying to get his three wasted years back," Walsingham supposes.

"And is he left alive?" the Master asks.

"Oh yes. He's fine. Scarcely quarter of an inch taller than when he arrived."

Cecil laughs his quiet hissing laugh.

"Bloody hell," he says. "Bloody hell."

"So what next?"

"We open up our own lines of communication with Sokollu," Walsingham tells them. "I cannot promise the same speed as Jenkinson, but I have three men in Constantinople, and now we know who he is, we can find out just what it is he really wants. What that infernal verse means."

He feels a huge weight lifted from his shoulders and wonders what it was. *Uncertainty,* he thinks, *that was it.* Now he knows whom he is dealing with, he can see a clear path.

"I will tell him: yes, he can have whatever he wants. Some damned unflawed gem."

The meeting ends, and Walsingham walks with Cecil and the Constable through the inner ward under snow like falling feathers, and Cecil congratulates the Constable for getting his masons to work in winter.

"Mine downed tools in November and buggered off home to Holland."

Walsingham thinks of Jenkinson and of the road he will have to take home to Market Harborough, and he thinks with pleasure of the few steps he will have to take before he is by his own fire in his house in the Papey.

CHAPTER TWENTY-ONE

Sulgrave Manor, Northamptonshire,
second week of March 1578

"A bit small," Robert Beale apologizes.

He and John Dee are in Sulgrave, a hamlet to the southwest of the town of Northampton, and staring at the hall Beale has rented for their purposes, through the offices of Her Majesty's private secretary, which is as grand as his off-the-books budget can encompass.

"It will do very nicely," Dee supposes, because so long as it has bench and table, and a peg on which to hang the girl's hornbook, then he will be able to teach this Ness Overbury just as much as he ever taught Bess Tudor. Well, enough to get by, in most events, anyway. Elsewhere there will be stables and kennels and a mews for the hawks, he supposes, and if Ness cannot yet pull a bow as well as Her Majesty, then God willing there will be time and space enough for that, too.

"What do you make of it, Mistress Frommond?"

"It is like my father's house," she tells them. "Though we had no arms above the door."

She indicates those of Her Majesty: the English lion and Welsh dragon attending the quartered leopards and fleur-de-lis that someone has had embossed into the stone that looks gray in this light but will probably be golden in the sunlight. Dee smiles.

"*Semper Eadem,*" he reads. "Always the same."

"Or not, in this case," Frommond comments with a laugh.

Frommond has ridden with them from London, having sworn never to travel by carriage again, and on the road a little distance behind come two carts, laden with the books and clothes and furniture they believe they will need to complete their task.

"Quickly then," Beale says, and he kicks on and leads them into the small courtyard.

The owner of the house comes out. No servants.

"Master Travis," he greets Beale.

He is a bony, spare old fellow, with bad teeth and a head like a horse.

Beale swings out of his saddle and shakes his hand.

"Master Washington," Beale says, "these are my servants. Master Perkins and Mistress Drummond."

"Right," Washington says, but he shakes Dee's hand with a horny palm the size of a malt shovel, and he removes his cap in respect to Frommond, who looks nothing like any kind of servant he can have ever seen.

"Stables are around the back."

A thin rain starts to fall. The carters unload their baggage into the buttery and are gone with enough time to reach Northampton by curfew. Washington leaves them to their business. The house is old-fashioned, with two chambers above the hall, and a bed in one of them.

"Ness had best have that," Beale says.

There is no glass in the windows, only shutters on ropes.

"I will sleep by the fire, if no one objects," Dee tells them.

Frommond likewise.

"And me," Beale says.

The house has not been occupied over the winter and it needs warming.

"When does Ness come?" Dee asks again.

"I will ride to fetch her in two days."

"And what have you done with Overbury himself?"

"It was hinted that a knighthood was in the offing if he volunteered to help Henry Sydney massacre the Munstermen in Ireland. Which should take him a year or more at the very least."

"If he doesn't get killed himself."

"Yes," Beale admits, "well, fingers crossed."

He is Uriah the Hittite to Beale's David, Dee supposes.

"And what does he think his wife is up to while he is off about his travels?"

"She is with her sister's family in Ely."

"That is very modern."

They spend the next two days clearing mice droppings and warming the stones of the house. They keep the windows shuttered against word of what they are doing leaking out.

"What have you told Washington?" Dee asks.

"He believes you to be an alchemist."

"I am. Well. I could be."

A woman is to bring them bread and ale, and to cook dinners that she is to leave in the buttery, and take away linen, but she is to come no farther. Beale will see to the chamber pots and to the privy.

"Is that needed?" Dee wonders. "I thought we had come all the way out here because we can be sure that not a soul hereabouts has ever seen Her Majesty in the flesh."

"I do not believe we can be too careful," Beale tells him.

Dee and Frommond have hardly spoken of their confinement in the barge. They walk awkwardly around each other, allowing each twice as much space as each needs. Only once have their hands touched, accidentally. When Beale departs to ride across country to fetch Ness, they are left alone. In the evening they sit by the fire, as if they have been married for twenty years.

"This is not as good as the barge," Dee suggests.

"No," Frommond agrees, "it amazes me that people still choose to live like this, when they might starve in the dark, up to their ankles in a freezing soup of their own making."

"Don't forget the rats."

He sees her hand go to her face, her fingers tracing the long scar on her cheek from the boatman's knife. He wonders how long it will be before she becomes used to it. A month? A year? Ten years? He himself is already used to it: it gives her an air of mystery, he thinks.

A while later he asks why she is helping Beale with this scheme. She cannot quite say.

"I suppose I wanted to do it to thank you."

"Me?"

"He said it was your idea."

"Bloody Robert."

"Then why are you doing it?" she asks.

Dee thinks.

"It is because," he says, after a long while, "Bess—Her Majesty— is brilliant. She is beautiful and brave, and the cleverest woman alive, but there is something within her—a caution; a reservation, perhaps—that stops her being the best she could be."

"Could that arise, do you think," Frommond proposes, "from the experience of having her father have her mother's head chopped off when she—Bess—was three?"

Dee laughs.

"It may do," he agrees. "If you grow up believing that anyone you love can be taken from you in a snap of the fingers, and that someone you love can, in the same snap of the fingers, reveal themselves as a monster, then perhaps the lives and loves of ordinary folk are like to be a closed book to you. But whysoever she is as she is, she is still as she is, and in this state of frozen watchfulness, she shakes her head and watches opportunity after opportunity pass her by. She needs to be forced to act."

Frommond nods.

"To do what?"

"To end this war. Against Spain and the France and the Vatican. To change the world order. To replace the malice of the few with the virtue of the many. We could do it. I proposed—I tried to propose—a scheme to the Queen, which I believe would soon have the crowned heads of Christendom beating their swords into plowshares. But she would not even listen."

"You sound . . . angry?"

Dee admits he is.

"But I could never be angry with Bess for long. I love her with all my heart, and would do anything for her, if she would just let me. Sometimes I believe she will. It is as if it is on the tip of her tongue to say yes, but then up pops Hatton, or Cecil, or Walsingham, and we are back to the same old ways of failing."

At moments like this, Dee becomes terrified by how much rides on Queen Elizabeth's shoulders, on her life.

"Without her," he says, "we are all dead. All hope is dead."

Frommond nods.

"Well," she says, "we must do what we can."

Ness Overbury arrives two days later, hooded against the heavy March rain and brought by a carriage hired in Bury St. Edmunds. Dee and Frommond are in the hall and hear the iron-hooped wheels on the stone of the courtyard.

"Here we go."

For some reason Dee can feel his heart in his throat. It feels as he imagines it might to meet a long-lost twin. They stand in the doorway and watch Beale help Ness down from the carriage. Frommond sighs.

"He'd best try to not touch her like that if she becomes Her Majesty."

Dee had always supposed Beale and Ness to be lovers, but now, presented with the fact, he tries to think what it means.

"It cannot go well," Frommond announces.

They step back to let Ness across the threshold in blue velvets, her hood lined in sage green to set off her red hair. She looks at them, in silence, and then tips back her hood. The same pale skin; the same broad forehead; the same slightly beaky nose; and crucially, devastatingly, the same dark, amused eyes, with the same soul-searching intensity. All that sets her apart from the Queen is a dark beauty spot, just there, above her lip.

My God, Dee thinks. *My God*. He catches Frommond's gaze before he says a word, and Frommond need only raise her eyebrows.

"Mistress Overbury," he says.

"Dr. Dee," she says, "and Mistress Frommond."

But her voice! It is enriched with a strong, almost direct country burr that in all other circumstances would be delightful, but here, in someone intending to imitate the Queen, becomes a hurdle. And the way she moves! There is none of the birdlike restraint or tight control of the Queen, but a fluid, knowing occupation of space. She knows what her body is for, it seems, and the effect it can have, on men especially, and she tilts herself toward Dee, who is suddenly overwhelmed by a powerful desire to see her dance, at the very least.

Beale looms into view. Water drips from his cloak. He looks exhausted.

"Well?" he says. "What do you think?"

Dee laughs. Assessing a woman is usually at least somewhat covert, but with Ness Overbury, it is like inspecting a horse. He almost asks to see her teeth.

"May I see your teeth?" Frommond asks.

Dee and Overbury both laugh. Her teeth are neat and square, and ivory colored. Her laugh is throaty and unrestrained.

"That need not matter," Frommond tells them. "Her Majesty tries to hide hers, so you need only follow her example. But please, Mistress Overbury, I beg you: never laugh like that."

"How should I?"

Beale attempts an impression that only makes the other three laugh. Then Frommond tries but starts laughing genuinely.

"I'm sorry," she says.

"Well," Beale admits. "We have plenty of work to be getting on with."

And so they set to, trying to turn Ness into Bess, each taking a turn to show her what the Queen does in any given circumstance, and how she might do it, from the moment she opens her eyes in the morning, to closing them at night.

"But why?" Ness keeps asking. "Why should she bother with this? Whose idea was that?"

And it is, as often as not, a good question. Why has all this ceremony accrued around the person of the Queen? Each additional ritual is become like a barnacle on a ship's hull, building up to slow Ness down, so that even though she wakes at dawn, she is not ready to face the day until two hours later, when she emerges encrusted with powder and so trammeled about in linens and silks that she can scarce breathe, and so utterly bored to tears that she would rather die than sit with Dee and discuss the things in which Her Majesty is passionately interested: Euclidean geometry; the Georgics; the works of Seneca, the astrology of Ptolemy; Greek grammar; the lost empire of King Arthur; the necessity of a National Library; the appointment of, and a pension for, a royal astrologer, or rather, an Astrologer Royal.

Ness's mind is not as sharp as the Queen's, nor her intent a quarter so serious, and she is unwilling to follow Dee on what even he must acknowledge are his more arcane and abstruse intellectual excursions, but she has a gift for languages, and within a week can have a conversation with Dee in Latin.

"*Quod homo amat virginem?*"

The man loves a girl?

"*Mirantur quod virginem sed iunior puellae est quam in homine per decem annos et a superiore genere in familiam.*"

The man admires the girl but the girl is younger than the man by ten years and is from a higher class of family.

"*Puella amat homines,*" Ness says.

"The girl loves the men?" Dee says.

"*Puella amat homo,*" she corrects herself.

Ah. The girl loves the man.

"*Ipsum bonum,*" he says.

She is a very good mimic and can intuit a meaning that Frommond cannot fully express by the mere alteration in the position of her hand, or her gait, and during the first week they make such progress, so that when sitting and doing needlework, say, Ness is able to modulate her body and her voice to look and sound exactly like the Queen, or as alike as Dee and Frommond and Beale can remember. She is still somewhat too vigorous in her movements when walking; she enjoys her food too much; she fills her clothes to a distracting fullness; and of course her skin lacks the pitting of smallpox scars, but given time there is hope that they might, just, if necessary, perfect the pretense.

But it is not easy, especially for Ness, who is very easily bored, and is almost violently impatient of any constraint or inactivity.

"Please, for the love of God, just let me be," she yells sometime in the second week, and they must let her walk off into the orchards that surround the house, tailed at an indiscreet distance by Robert Beale, who brings her back an hour later, face flushed, with mud on both their knees, and then in the third week she cries out that if this is what being Queen is like, then she wants no part in it.

Sometime in the fourth week she tells them that this is even more boring than being at home, and that Beale had promised her adventure. He had told her that he had once met a man who had been to Persia. Her eyes actually glistened with a yearning to be elsewhere.

In the fifth week she refuses to get up, and Beale must coax her out of bed, though she will not dress in any finery, and Frommond, whose task it has been to wash her in the morning so that she becomes used to it, comes down the stairs thoughtfully.

"Jane?"

"Hmmm?"

The first buds are on the trees in the orchard now, and the rain is letting up, and the grass is a vivid shade of green, and Dee thinks of home. He wonders how his mother will be getting on. He has left her in the charge of Cooke and asked Thomas Digges to pop his head around the door now and then, to see how she does, but he finds he misses her, and trying to teach a reluctant student, however beautiful she may be, the rudiments of algebra, which she does not care to learn, is not what he had in mind when he joined Master Beale in this enterprise.

"Do you hear from Master Walsingham?" Dee asks Beale.

"Occasionally."

"Has there been any word on the men who shot Alice Rutherford?"

"Nothing," Beale tells him. "Master Walsingham hopes the gunmen have gone home . . . back to Halle. After the shooting they probably took flight down the river to Leamouth, and from there, well, anywhere."

"Really?" Dee asks. *That is quite a risky thing to hope*, he thinks. He wonders if there is something Beale is not telling him.

"In a sense their task was complete," Beale claims. "They gave Her Majesty such a fright that she did not send the Hollanders any troops or money, so . . ."

He trails off. It is wishful thinking, both know it. Beale wants the gunmen to have thought that, but if they were members of the Guild of the Black Madonna, they will have rather died than failed. Perhaps they are dead, then.

"So the danger has passed?" Dee, probes, disingenuously.

"It has never passed, John," Beale admits.

Time passes slowly for some, but quickly for Dee, who is enjoying this leisured lease of pleasure spent with Frommond and Beale, but it is one morning in perhaps the sixth week, when Dee is taking Ness through the early books of Dante, and she is reading aloud while he paces the room that he sees—through the window—someone in the orchard. A man, furtive and prying.

Before he can move, he hears Ness groaning, and he turns to see she is bilious.

"Oh God," he says. "*Really?*"

Her answer is a hard-earned splatch of beige vomit on the floor between her feet.

"Master Beale! Master Beale! Come in here, please!"

Beale feigns ignorance, but Ness manages a laugh.

"Come on, Robert, they are not fools."

In those early days the whole house had been shaking with it, Dee restrains himself from reminding them. It is probably the only thing that has been keeping her here.

"When is it due?" he asks.

"August," she supposes.

They are all four silent for a long while, each trying to discern what this new development means to their intrigue.

"Nothing, perhaps?"

"But what will Master Overbury have to say?"

"I can tell him it is his."

"*His?*" Beale gasps.

"Why not?"

"Because the child is *mine*!"

Ness looks at him as if he is a fool, a child.

"But I am married to John."

Beale leaps to his feet and lurches out of the room, the house, as if himself seeking somewhere to vomit.

"What's got into him?" Ness wonders.

He is gone all afternoon. Dee waits to talk to him about whoever it was he saw in the orchard. A glimpse of a man it was, or he supposes it a man, sliding behind a tree. Whoever it was did not want to be seen.

Meanwhile Frommond teaches Ness to shoot a bow.

Bloody hell, she is good at that.

Dee stands watching, waiting for another glimpse of whoever it was he saw that morning in the orchard, but there is nothing all day. Was it Washington himself perhaps? Come to spy on his tenants?

When Beale gets back it is nearly dark but Ness is still out there, alone, patiently shooting arrows with an almost deadly accuracy, waiting for him, to show him what she can do.

By the fire within, Frommond asks Dee about John Overbury.

"Twice her age," Dee tells her. "And not overly agreeable, according to Beale, but he would say that, I dare say."

They hear Ness's booming laugh. When the two come in they are arm in arm and smiling. God knows what sort of arrangement they have managed, but their amity lasts late into the night.

"I do not know whether to be scandalized or not," Frommond says.

"It will certainly make for a livelier court," Dee supposes. Then he wonders whether that comment is treason. Probably. "Though that is not to say I would wish a livelier court," he makes clear. She laughs.

He tells her about seeing the man in the orchard.

"No apples to steal, are there?" she queries. "Perhaps he was some local, wondering what we are up to."

"Could be," he agrees.

She makes a noise to suggest a ghost has just walked down her spine. They draw the shutters tight and bar the door, but they do not see the man again, and Dee begins to suppose that it was just a curious local, perhaps, and the matter is dropped.

"Dogs," Frommond says in the middle of the night. "That is what is odd about this place: we have none."

The next morning they get one, from the brewster's husband: a lurcher pup, almost blue black, with a pale chest and a wonky eye, and Dee takes to it.

"I shall call him Francis."

He sleeps at the foot of Dee's mattress and grumbles in the night.

The next day, a constable calls, come from Banbury. He's a young man with very ruddy cheeks, with a green vest and a stout stick.

"John Samson by name," he tells them.

He wants to know why they have taken up the manor house in place of Master Washington but have yet to attend Sunday Mass at Saint James's? His voice is sonorous, rich with hay-and-muck scent, and he sways from side to side, craning to look over Beale's shoulders into the hall.

Beale tells him they have been ill but are now recovered, and he thanks Mary Mother of God it was nothing serious, and that seems to satisfy the constable, who probably feared they were Anabaptists, and he retreats.

"But we are on notice," Beale tells them. "Will you and Jane go to the service on Sunday at least?"

Most mornings thereafter Ness is too sick to attend any lessons, and so Dee and Frommond walk in the orchard, dew on their boots, watching Francis chase bees and the spring unfold.

"This has been nice," he tells her.

She agrees.

"It cannot last much longer, though, surely?" she asks. "I feel I have taught her all I know."

"Robert has the lease on the hall until Saint John's."

"But that's more than a month!" she says.

He cannot decide if that pleases her or not. On balance, it does.

"Will you stay?" he wonders.

"I promised Her Majesty only that I would be back for progress."

Progress is in August.

"Will you go with her?"

"That was my promise, so . . . yes. I suppose I must. Will you?"

"Me?"

"Yes, why not?"

"I have never before. Also I am not much of a dancer, if I am honest. When I do, things around me tend to get broken."

He is thinking plates and cups and benches and windows.

She laughs.

"I should like to see that," she says.

Dee is also thinking that he likes to go to Wales in the summer, to tramp through the valleys in the footsteps of King Arthur, to sleep by streams under the stars, rather than into the formal straits of the court in progress.

"Well, there is always her birthday," she supposes. "There will be dancing at that."

That is the beginning of September. The Queen takes her birthdays seriously, for having reason more than most to be thankful she has survived another year.

"I will be back for that," Dee says, "if I get an invitation."

He did not last year, but then she was ill.

"Still, though," he says, "we might have two months of this."

Sunlight dapples the bank where the may is already fading.

She breathes deeply, and with some delight.

"I can still smell the hold, sometimes," she says. "As if it is soaked into my skin."

She sniffs her fingertips.

They walk on for a bit. Christ, he is happy doing this. He tries to think what else he would be doing: trying to eke the gold out of Admiral Frobisher's stubborn ore, he supposes, or perhaps he would be readying himself to go to Wales. He wonders if, when this is over, that is what he will do. He should go back to London, of course, back to Mortlake, but there is nothing to stop him going west, straight from here. It is early in the year, but he has all he needs. Yes, he thinks. He will do that.

The next week a letter comes from Overbury, forwarded from Ness's sister in Ely. He is wounded, it tells her, by an exploding arquebus, and she is to send him money for his recuperation before he comes home. Until then she is to pay not one penny more for some delivery or other, and that she is to evict some tenants and sack a reeve. Ness writes to him in Munster to tell him he is to be a father. Her handwriting is much improved, and they must roughen it up a little. Beale leaves the house again, and later that day, just before noon, Dee believes he sees the same man in the orchard, this time watching Beale, who paces the gravel by the stockfish pond and pulls on his hair.

Dee slips out of the house, but by the time he is there, the man is gone.

This time he does tell Beale. Beale is alarmed. More so than Dee would have imagined. He wonders if they should leave the hall, go back to life.

"How much more is there to teach Ness?" he asks.

"A great deal," Dee supposes, "though perhaps her head is full?" Beale ignores the unintended slight.

"I would have liked to test her on someone who knows the Queen somewhat, but she will soon start to show too much."

They watch her shooting a bow in the garden and there has been a definite shift in shape. Dee tries to clarify his thoughts on Ness Overbury. At one point he felt a troubling lust for her, but this soon gave way to frustration at what he thought was her frivolity, and her inability to concentrate for more than a few moments at a time, which led, he has to admit, to a mild dislike of her, but that has faded, and now he is powerfully fond of her. She is like a well-fed cat, he thinks: playful, affectionate, curious, and self-reliant, but also apt to drift away about her own pleasures, caring nothing for no one. She lacks the intensity, and the storminess of the Queen, but then, as Frommond says: she has not had her father prosper by having her mother's head struck from her shoulders before a cheering crowd of hundreds.

"It would be too risky to try it on someone who did not already know of the scheme," Dee tells Beale. "It will have to be Walsingham, or Cecil. They both know."

Beale shakes his head.

"They would never agree to meet her. Not until—God forbid—Her Majesty dies."

"Then who?"

"Honestly? No one. But try telling her that. She is itching to try her act on some unsuspecting fool."

"Don't let her."

"I won't."

But Beale does. It is not his fault. It is a misunderstanding. Lawrence Washington comes uninvited while Ness is in as close to full regalia as they can manage in clothes that have been bought, begged, borrowed, and stolen, and she sits on a stool, framed in the doorway between house and kitchen garden, holding, to signify the scepter and orb, the first of this year's beetroot in one hand and a willow wand in the other, and on her head Beale's cap for a crown. Her face is blank with powder, and Ness is, for once, trying to keep a straight face. It is in imitation of a painting of the Queen's coronation that hangs in the Presence Room in Whitehall.

"My God," Dee tells her. "It is not half bad."

They hear Francis bark the moment before Washington comes around the corner, into the kitchen garden just as if he owns the place—he does—and he draws up short and stares at the spectacle. Ness sees him first, over Dee's shoulder, and starts to try to juggle with the ball and scepter.

"We are mummers," she calls out. "We are rehearsing for a pageant. For the Queen's birthday!"

He looks very doubtful.

"I am Athena, the goddess of wisdom," Ness improvises. "These three shall be my attendants, and if you should see us when they, too, are fully dressed, and upon our stage, you would believe yourself back in ancient Rome."

Athens, Dee says silently.

There is a long moment of silence.

"Right you are," Washington says, and he touches his cap. He thinks they are just mad.

"Can I help you, Master Washington?"

"Came to say John Samson—the constable—says there's been sightings of a man around here and abouts. A stranger. Thought he might be connected with . . . with whatever it is you're doing."

He gestures at Ness. They look at one another before shaking their heads.

"Nothing to do with us, Master Washington. Is there any description?"

"No."

When he is gone, they let out their breaths.

"He didn't even recognize me!" Ness laughs.

"One day you are going to meet someone who actually knows what Her Majesty looks like," Beale tells her, "and then we will be in trouble."

But Dee thinks about the stranger.

"Who is he to us, if he is also a stranger to them?"

They look at one another, and then hurry inside the hall.

A period of cautious confinement follows. Either Beale or Frommond is usually at a window, watching the margins of the garden, the orchards, the outbuildings—waiting. Sometimes Francis barks for no obvious reason. Ness becomes even more frustrated but her embroidery improves. It rains all week, so that makes it easier.

Then it is June and Ness is six months pregnant and can no longer move as the Queen moves, but she sits and listens to Dee try to teach her as much geography as he knows, and the importance of tides, and the rudiments of metallurgy, and Frommond teaches her how to cheat at primero, and at piquet, and how far she might take advantage of her position as Queen to push a dice.

That night, the middle of June, the Great Comet fades to nothing. Dee takes Frommond outside to show her.

"What is it?"

"Nothing."

She is silent for a moment or two.

"Well, that was interesting," she tells him.

He thinks back to his friend Digges, suggesting the comet might have a personal message to bring, or a personal warning.

"The meaning of such messages are oftentimes opaque," he tells Frommond.

He hears her smile, though that may be impossible of course.

No word from Overbury, though Beale hears from Walsingham: another massacre in Munster.

The next day, at dawn, they see the watcher again.

"Is it the same man?"

Dee thinks so. None of them can stand the thought of sitting hiding in the hall until Saint John's Day.

"Ness will never wear it," Beale admits.

She is asleep upstairs.

"Besides, we should find out who he is and what he wants."

So Frommond keeps Francis within, while Dee takes the hunting bow, and Beale his sword, and they leave the hall by the front door, under the arms of Her Majesty, and part: one goes one way up the track, the other down it, and each makes a loop around the property to enter the orchard from its far end. Dee nocks his arrow and feels his pulse in his teeth. *My God*, he thinks, *I am hunting a man*. He steps into the shade of the rough hedge. The grass here is beaten down to make a path. Above the loamy hedgerow Dee can smell stale urine. *Has he moved in?* he wonders. He steps forward. And there, suddenly, in the shadow of a tree: the man in black. He looks young and broad, with a saddlebag over one shoulder, in a dark doublet and breeches, with worn riding boots and a sword designed for more than mere decoration. He stands with his back to Dee and is peering up at the house, careless of what unfolds behind. Dee sees Beale approach through the trees from the other side. Beale signals that Dee is to shoot the man in the back.

Dee has knowingly killed only two men. One: a Spanish priest in the crypt of the Abbey of Mont Saint-Michel who would have killed him, and two: the man who kept him and Frommond locked in the hold of a barge. He has never considered shooting a man in the back, even with a hunting arrow, until now, and he finds he does not like the thought of it. Besides, do they really want him dead?

Beale is mouthing at him. *Do it. Do it now.*

Some sixth sense alerts the man that his death is being contemplated, or perhaps he catches a glimpse of Beale from the tail of his eye. He turns sharply. Dee draws the bow and looses. The arrow flits through the sun-dappled space and catches the man's shoulder. He shouts with the pain and turns to find Dee, and seeing him, he draws the sword and comes running at him, swinging the blade.

"You fucker!"

Unarmed, Dee thrashes the bow wildly, just catching the blade, clipping it so its edge flashes past his ear and then his shoulder. The man barrels into him, and they both go flying. Dee lands on his back, the man atop him, jabbing the fingers of his left hand toward Dee's eyes. Dee, stunned and half blinded, tries to buck him off, but the man is strong as a bull, and desperate. Thank God, just then Beale comes with his sword. He chops the man across his back. The man cries out and lets Dee go. He arches upright and lashes out at Beale. Beale parries the blow, stops the sword.

"Who are you?" he shouts.

The man reels away, on his feet now, and he stumbles into the bushes. Just then gunshot noise fills the clearing and the swordsman staggers backward into sight and falls by Dee's still outstretched legs. His chest is a terrible mess of glossy blood. He lifts his hands as if to pat the wound, or stanch the blood, but he is dead before they reach it, so they drop to his sides.

Beale stands motionless, staring. Dee, too. A man steps out of the shadows of the trees, in dark wool, carrying a still-smoking handgun. He touches his cap.

"Master Beale," he says. "Dr. Dee."

"Oh Christ," Beale breathes. He lowers his sword. "Gregory."

Dee's heart is still racing.

"Who are you?" he asks, lifting himself on his elbows.

"This is Arthur Gregory," Beale tells him. "Probably not his real name. One of Walsingham's men."

Beale turns to Gregory.

"Why did you shoot him? Now we'll never know who he was."

"I was trying to save your lives."

"I had it in hand," Beale tells him.

Gregory scoffs.

"What are you doing here, Arthur?" Beale asks.

"The boss sent me."

"To keep an eye on us?"

Gregory shrugs. Of course.

Beale grunts.

"Of course."

"And now we need to hide him in case Washington heard the gunshot. Come on, help me."

Beale and Gregory grip one of the corpse's bloodied wrists, and together they drag him through the long grass up to the house, leaving a broad, bloody trail, a sword, and a leather bag that Dee collects and takes up to the hall.

"My God!" Frommond breathes as she lets them in.

Francis starts whining.

"Shush, Francis," Dee tells him. "It is just a dead man. Nothing to be worried about."

They dump him before the fire, face up. There is a hole in the sole of his boot, as well as the one in his chest.

Gregory takes a seat. He is sheened with sweat.

"Not used to it," he admits.

He could almost rest his feet on the dead man's chest.

"Who are you?" Frommond asks.

She means Gregory. Introductions are made.

"And who's he?"

Now she means the dead man.

"No idea. But he's been watching you for weeks. And then . . . he was getting away. If he'd had half an inkling of what you are up to— Christ. I do not dare think about it. And, anyway: I didn't mean to kill him."

Dee opens the man's bag. There is an apple in it—very green— and a leather flask of liquid. Also, a purse of very few coins, and a letter.

"What does it say?"

Gregory, who had been sitting a moment earlier, snaps the letter from Dee's fingers. Dee is outraged.

"This is a matter for Her Majesty's principal private secretary," Gregory tells him. That does not soothe Dee, but after he has read it with a frown, Gregory passes it to Beale, and he sits back in the chair with a loud creak of protesting wood. Beale reads the letter.

"Oh Christ."

Dee collects the letter from his fingers.

It is written to a John Rhys—the dead man, presumably— instructing him to "keep eyes on and bring to the light so that it may be discovered as to its true purpose and intent, the most recent activities of Master Robert Beale, late in the employ of Master Francis Walsingham, who has this day taken up residence in Sulgrave Manor, in our county of Northampton, and to send word posthaste once the purpose of the said design is revealed."

Dee reads it with mounting alarm, but it is only once reaching the last line that he sees what Gregory and Beale have seen.

"For and on behalf of Sir Christopher Hatton."

Christ.

At that moment, the door resounds to three hefty blows.

"Open up! It is John Samson here! Constable of the county!"

CHAPTER TWENTY-TWO

London, third week of June 1578

Francis Walsingham is on the river again, and the weather—
being warm and sunny, with a light breeze from the west—
mirrors his mood perfectly, but after landing at Wool Quay and
walking up through the city, he finds Arthur Gregory waiting
at his gate, looking done in. He bears a message from Robert
Beale. One look at his face, and Walsingham knows it contains
bad news.

"What is it?"

"You'd best read it yourself."

Walsingham opens it and finds the contents encrypted.

"Come on, Arthur," he says. "It will take an hour or more to
decrypt this. Just tell me what it is."

Gregory refuses. This cannot bode well.

"Wait here."

Gregory nods and retreats toward the kitchens as Walsingham
climbs the stairs to his chambers, swearing under his breath. He

unlocks the three locks and then locks them behind him and settles down to decrypting the message hidden in Beale's rushed and rudimentary substitution code. When he has finished transposing, half an hour later, he sits in his chair, unable to move, as if buried in rubble.

Between them—Robert Beale, John Dee, Jane Frommond, Arthur Gregory—they have managed to kill two men—one a constable, the other belonging to Sir Christopher Hatton—and they have managed to reveal—to Sir Christopher Hatton of all people!—that they have been plotting to replace the Queen with a woman who looks like her.

Walsingham picks up his decryption and looks at it again. Can he have gotten it wrong? Can he have gotten this sentence wrong?

"But all not lost as Ness now with child & not like HMQ."

HMQ is Her Majesty the Queen. So one of them—he cannot stand to do the sums, but he instantly knows that it is Beale—has also managed to impregnate the woman whom they've been teaching to imitate the Queen?

Walsingham sits in the chair and tries to recall an intrigue that was more doomed to disaster. Perhaps that is what the comet signified. If his memory served him right, the word *disaster* comes from "bad star" in Latin.

He returns to the decryption: they have gathered up all their possessions and quit the house in Northamptonshire, it goes on, and Dee and Frommond are coming back to their own lives in London, while Beale has taken Ness back to her sister's house in Ely, and there awaits instruction from his wise master, by whom he means Walsingham. He signs off as being a good and humble servant.

By Christ, Walsingham thinks, he ought now to turn on him. Have him arrested before Hatton starts pulling on the strings and finding how well-connected they are. Christ. That is what he must do. He must cauterize this wound now. Protect himself. He stands, and paces, around and around. He can hear the boards creak under his feet as if he were in a ship at sea. He knows that if he moves against Beale now, he will be signing not only his death sentence, but also Frommond's, Dee's, and this Ness of theirs. And Arthur Gregory's, too.

My God! He suddenly realizes that he has never read any of Gregory's reports. In his defense, he is sent about a hundred reports a day, from all over Christendom and beyond, and Gregory's never seemed as if they might contain anything of instant import. He finds them now, slotted away neatly, each still sealed. He breaks open the first: and there it is, the first inkling that Beale and Ness are lovers, meeting in a physician's house in Bury St. Edmunds and that afterward Beale walks as if he has been bled of a pint or more blood. He alerts Walsingham that Ness looks very similar to Her Majesty, insofar as he has glimpsed her, though Ness is altogether more of a country woman, who rides rather than go by carriage. Gregory approves of this, though adds that this is not to disparage Her Majesty.

The messages continue to relate their meetings, and their toll on Beale, who has clearly, as Gregory writes, become "cuntstruck." At one point Beale is seen falling asleep in his saddle and falling from his horse. Gregory writes to ask if he should continue to follow Beale, who is like a ram to ewe, or Ness, whose husband must suspect she is engaged in lewd activity, for she returns from Bury St. Edmunds "much flushed and mussed about with." Of course, Walsingham does not answer, so Gregory continues following Beale, to and fro London and Bury St. Edmunds, always reporting the same, until in a flurry of excitement, he reports that Beale is moving Ness across country, to a village in Northamptonshire, with John Dee and a woman he as yet cannot identify.

And it is here, after a couple of weeks, that Gregory first glimpses Beale's design: "They aim to turn this Ness Overbury into

Her Majesty and have dressed her far above her station and she is learned to walk and move in ways that do ape the Queen." Two weeks later, after a period of time during which he had nothing much to report save that they and he are still alive he writes urgently to say that someone else has arrived to watch the house and its occupants. A week later it strikes him that he has seen the man before, on the road somewhere, and he thinks perhaps it was at an inn near Great Dunmow in Essex and then once more in Bury St. Edmunds.

Walsingham can feel pressure building up between his ears. In a flurry now, he gets up, and unlocks and relocks his three locks, and then bellows for Gregory, who appears from the shadows of the hall like a whipped dog that knows it is about to be whipped again.

"Walk with me," he tells him.

Gregory breaks from the shadow like a drop of treacle off a spoon and together they walk down to the Custom House and take a barge for Whitehall.

"One of Hatton's men?" Walsingham shouts when they are in midriver. "*And* a constable?"

"It happened very quickly. There was no choice."

Christ.

"What did you do with the bodies?" he asks. "No. Don't tell me. How can you be sure Hatton knows?"

"I can't, but the man was carrying this."

Gregory shows him a letter instructing John Rhys to keep eyes on Robert Beale.

"It was worn like that when we took it from him, so he must have had it awhile. If he'd been sending reports back—and if Hatton had been reading them—then Hatton must know."

Jesus. Northampton is Hatton's county, too. He has property there. Did Beale not know this? Find out in advance? Christ.

Walsingham gets Gregory to tell him everything. It takes until they arrive at Whitehall and he almost runs to find Cecil, bursting into his chambers with scarcely a knock, and only then, too late, does he realize Cecil is not alone.

Oh Christ. Of all people. Hatton. Cecil in black, Hatton in a sober shade of blue, as befits a man on the business of government rather than party planning.

"Ah! Here he is in person," Cecil says of Walsingham. "Sir Christopher was just talking about you, Francis, and I told him I was certain you would have an explanation. One of his men has been following your man Robert Beale, he tells me, but has recently gone missing."

Walsingham must think on his feet. Must play for time.

"Gone missing, you say? And he was following Master Beale? Why? Why in God's name was he doing that?"

"Don't try to slip out of it, Master Walsingham," Hatton tells him. "I became concerned about Beale last year, when he was behaving so erratically after the Queen was shot at in the woods."

"And a woman died, if you recall, Sir Christopher!"

It is desperate, Walsingham knows, and even Cecil raises his eyebrows in surprise. A bold move, he seems to suggest, to try to deflect it that way. But Hatton is above that sort of thing and ignores it.

"And then I kept meeting him on the road north, always evasive, hiding something, so I set a man to follow his trail, to see what that might be because at the time I suspected he might have slipped your oversight and was up to some foul intrigue of his own, but then I heard he was still coming and going from your house in the Papey, and so I saw that you had not lost control of him, but that he was doing your bidding."

"Bidding? What are you talking about? Card games?"

"Shut up, Walsingham," Hatton snaps. "And this was confirmed within just a few weeks, when Master Beale was seen meeting the wife of a man named John Overbury at the house of a physician that I know you employ as one of your snouts, rootling around for anyone you deem insufficiently zealous as regards the practice of your faith."

"I am sorry, Sir Christopher, I do not know what you are talking about."

"You may not, Master Walsingham, but I do. I know that some arrangement was made with this woman, John Overbury's wife, and that then John Overbury was subsequently sent to join Henry Sydney, fighting for his Queen and country in Ireland, where I understand he has been wounded, while you pursued your diabolic plot."

"Hatton—"

"Sir Christopher Hatton to you, Master Walsingham. Please give my title, as I would give you yours."

Cecil pulls an eloquent face, but nothing more.

"So with Overbury out of the way, your man Beale was seen running away with the man's wife, to take a house in the parish of Sulgrave, in Northamptonshire, not twenty miles from my own house, and it was here that it was revealed just how black and treacherous your scheme really is, for that's where you had Dr. Dee, and Mistress Frommond—that maid of honor who made such a poor impression on us after the Queen was shot at—waiting for Overbury's wife, and why?"

"Why?"

"Because Mistress Overbury looks just like Her Majesty! You were training her to *replace* Her Majesty!"

"These are serious charges, Sir Christopher," Cecil intones. "Have you any proof?"

"I do!" Hatton says.

But there is a slight slide of his gaze, a lick of lips, and a rub of the fingers on the expensive stuff of his breeches, and Walsingham knows he is lying.

"What is it?"

Hatton hesitates.

"Look, Sir Christopher," Walsingham says, all reasonableness now. "I do not know anything about this. If Master Beale has done as you say, then I will be the first to sign his death warrant, but until I have some proof..."

He trails off.

Hatton says nothing.

"Do you have the girl?" Cecil asks him. He's leaning forward, the benign old snake. "This woman whom you say Francis is training up to replace Her Majesty?"

Hatton admits that he does not.

"But I know where she is," he tells them. "I know where she may be found."

"Well then," Cecil says, "let us hurry there at all speed."

He hardly moves.

"Where shall we go, Sir Christopher?" Walsingham joins in. "Where shall we find her? Will we need many men? Horses? Should I whistle up to the Tower for a pair of manacles?"

Hatton rises above him, figuratively and literally, standing to collect his hat and leave the embrace of Cecil's chamber.

"That is a kind offer, Master Walsingham," he says, "but given the circumstances I believe I had best bring her in myself, don't you?"

"But haven't you a party to be organizing?"

Hatton shoots Walsingham the sort of look he can laugh about now but will come back to him in the short hours.

When he is gone, Cecil turns his unsettling eyes on him.

"Well, Francis," he says. "A pretty pickle."

CHAPTER TWENTY-THREE

Isle of Ely, Huntingdonshire,
third week of June 1578

Robert Beale sees the minster at Ely rising out of the fens from twenty miles distant.

"We will be with your sister by nightfall," he tells Ness.

She nods, or perhaps it is the state of the road that makes her nod.

"Would you like some ale? I have a little left."

She closes her eyes and this time she definitely shakes her head. Beale stoppers his flask. He hates traveling in a coach. It is unmanly. He should be riding ahead, to warn Ness's sister that she is to expect a guest, but he does not wish to leave Ness alone with her thoughts, though perhaps his loyalty is misplaced, for he has been unable to distract her from them, and she has resisted any attempt at conversation since they left Sulgrave in such a hurry.

"We had to kill him, Ness, I promise," he repeats.

She does not even look at him but keeps her gaze fixed on the linen-covered window, through which the flat marshy land can be sensed as a low smear of greenery. She is very hot, impatient, and her belly is a drum on her slender frame.

"You have said not a word since . . . since we left."

And she doesn't now.

It was a horrible moment, he can see that. Ness had come down from her chamber to find Arthur Gregory throttling the constable in the hall, in front of the heaped ashes of the fire, and the constable was making the most terrible sounds and his heels were drumming on the floor. And it had taken so long. Frommond was bent away, with her hands clapped to her ears, and Dee, too, had turned his face from the sight.

Beale had not noticed her standing there until she fell back onto the steps as if her legs had been taken from under her. She'd hit her head on the wall, and by the time he had reached her, five strides across the flagstones, Ness was shaking as if in the grips of the deadliest kind of ague, as if she, too, were being strangled by Arthur Gregory. Beale gathered her up, cushioning her head as best as he could, and he held her until the shaking stopped, after which she seemed to fall into the deepest sleep from which she would not wake. She had snored very loudly, and once the constable was dead, they left him and came to stand around her, waiting, watching.

Eventually the snoring stopped and for a moment they thought she had died, until, with a start, she woke. He—Beale—had been so pleased that he kissed her on the lips and it must have seemed to her that he had forgotten the two dead men that lay a couple of paces away, on their backs, staring blank eyed at the roof beams.

"Get away," she'd said, and her eyes had deepened and become wild. Her nails flew to his face and she'd scratched three deep grooves in his cheek before he'd managed to throw himself back. Frommond and Dee had been a soothing influence on her, and

Frommond had coaxed her back up to the bedchamber while Beale stanched the blood with his cuff.

"Christ," was all Gregory had said.

After that they had sought and found the best place to bury the two men and set about doing so, the three of them taking turns to dig while Frommond sat watch over Ness. By the time the hole was deep enough, it was dark enough to drag the bodies out: Hatton's watcher first, then the constable, who had deserved to die the least and so was to be put on top. They had flopped the corpses into the hole, and while Dee had said a prayer, they had covered them with earth and then, when the hole was full, they had tamped it down and covered it with ivy borrowed from a nearby wall. The moon was up, and a fox had barked as they walked back to the house.

"So would you call that a good day's work, d'you think?" Dee had asked Gregory.

Gregory had said nothing.

The next morning, the household had broken up. Dee and Frommond had waited with Ness while Beale rode to Banbury to hire horse and carriage and a man willing to take them to Ely. It had taken all Beale's remaining gold, and some of Frommond's besides, because he looked so untrustworthy, with scabs on his cheeks and terrible gravediggers' blisters on his palms.

Then Dee had left on his own, walking westward, and a tearful Frommond had helped a tearful Ness into the carriage and then mounted her own horse and rode alongside them until they reached the road for London, where she'd left them, joining a party from one of those northern houses, riding south to join the Queen on progress, and Beale, left with a silent Ness and a suspicious carriage man and his lackey, had felt powerfully envious of their parting. Gregory had long since slipped away with word for Master Walsingham.

And so now here he is, with Ness and her swollen feet and belly, and a tear-stained face. She sniffs all the time and is lost in her own misery, and Robert feels bruised with shame. He cannot imagine what Master Walsingham will say. He cannot imagine what he will say to Ness's sister, the woman who hoped she was helping her sister get away from Overbury. Beale had only ever tried to do the right thing, and now here he was, returning her in this state.

The silence lasts until they reach Ely.

"Here," she says, pointing, and he knocks on the carriage roof.

Ness's sister lives with her husband and three children in one of a row of houses on a lane Beale will come to know as Cat Lane. Her husband is a mercer, and she keeps the shop at the front. The shutters are down, and the children and neighbors come out to see the carriage stop. Beale gives Ness one last tight smile and tries to grip her hand. She flinches and pulls hers away. After a moment, he gets out.

Claire, Ness's sister, has three children and spends her days on her feet, so she is an older, worn-out version of Ness. She comes out of the shop and onto the lane, in a dress of nubbly blue wool with a linen apron and hood over the same reddish hair as her sister's, and opens the carriage door. The driver just sits and stares at her, and his boy takes the opportunity for a piss.

When she sees Ness, she gasps.

"Oh dear Jesus! Ness!"

Beale comes to help. He wishes Claire would tell him to get away, call him a viper, a lewd monster, a fornicating devil, a ravisher of women, a damned soul, anything that would allow him to take his leave, but she doesn't. He believes she knows that that would be to offer him the easy way out, and that staying will cost him most.

"Help me," she says, and they edge Ness from the carriage and across into the house. Two of the children sense the mood, but the third is a simpleton, and comes to gad and caper about in front of Aunty Ness, telling her she has become fat, and asking why she is crying when she should be happy to see them, until the other two return to take the child away.

They get Ness into the house and into the back room, behind the shop where there is a table and stools around the cooking fire, with its new, brick-built chimney. They sit her down and Claire makes some sort of brew with herbs and bread sops and all questions go unasked.

Eventually Master Vernier, Claire's husband, arrives.

"What is she doing here—oh."

He sees Beale.

"Master Vernier, God give you good day."

Vernier—very narrow, clerkish—is quick to assess the mood of the room, and though ordinarily he might simper and defer to Beale—who is from London, wears a sword on his waist, and is of the sort to look down on Vernier if he were to even notice him—today, with Beale looking diminished and seeking his help, the man sees a chance to take revenge for all the past slights he has ever received. And here, too, is his sister-in-law—stuck-up Ness after whom he has always lusted, though she only ever treated him with an indifference bordering on disdain—sitting in his house, ruined, just as he always said she would be.

"Oh dear, oh dear. What have we here, then, hey?"

His voice is thin and nasal, like a fly caught behind a mesh.

Claire turns to her husband with effort.

"Nigel," she says, "Ness will stay with us here a few days longer, just until she is quite well, with your permission, before she goes back to Overbury."

"Oh, she will, will she?"

"With your permission?"

And so it starts, a grim, disheartening process of attrition, obviously wearyingly familiar to Claire Vernier as she tries to extract an
unexpected favor from her bitter and vindictive husband. Meanwhile Ness sits there, an object to be haggled over, and Beale sees
tears dripping from her cheeks once more, but he is too sickened
with guilt and shame to move. He knows he has no rights or standing here, and that if he were to say anything, they all three would
turn on him. The children, too, even the simpleton, who is staring
at him as if they are old friends met by chance.

"Look," he says, when he can stand it no longer, "I will find
an inn."

He means for himself but they think he now means to take
Ness from them, and for wildly differing reasons they do not want
this, so they turn on him and accuse him of having done enough
already and telling him that he has not been able to look after her
when she was healthy and what now can they expect of him that
she is heavy with child and that her time is coming fast? He has no
answers.

"Go," Ness says. Her voice is very low.

Beale takes his chance and is out onto Cat Lane with scarcely
another word. It is only when he reaches the marketplace that he
realizes he is weeping. He misses Frommond. He misses John Dee.
He even misses Francis the lurcher. They have been his constant
companions these last months, never judging him as he lost his
head over Ness, always there with quiet consolation when she
threw him out of her room. Now, though, he has not a friend in
the world it seems, and no money, either, even had Ness taken him
up on his offer of finding an inn.

A thin, welcome rain starts to fall.

What has he done, he asks himself.

He knows he must seek out Master Walsingham. He needs to

find out how much Sir Christopher Hatton knows about Ness, and what can be done about it. He sets off south in the early-evening light, down the hill toward the fens, and it is only as he leaves Ely and is in the marshes that he realizes what he has really done: he has used Ness as a pawn, a sacrificial pawn, just as Robert Dudley's family used Lady Jane Grey as their pawn, and it will surely end the same way: only with Ness on the pyre, instead of the block, unable to deny she looks like Her Majesty, because her guilt is written into her face, her body, the color of her hair. He has turned her into a weapon against herself. A spark to light her own pyre.

He cries out into the evening, something incoherent.

And if Hatton knows she exists, he will know *why* she exists— to thwart him—and so he will bend all his might to find her, because with her as proof, he can bring down not just Beale, but also Walsingham and maybe even Cecil.

He stops on the road and turns back to Ely. Not a light can be seen after curfew, but the moon is up and he is certain he can make out the distinctive shape of the island rising up from the fens with its minster atop.

My God, he thinks, *Ness*.

He has to get her away, away from everything, away where she cannot be found.

He starts running, back the way he has come.

CHAPTER TWENTY-FOUR

Mortlake, west of London,
second week of August 1578

Dee is back from Wales—unsuccessful, sunburned, wiry, and as broke as ever—standing at his gate, studying the large pile of black stone that recently has been dumped against his wall, when he feels a hand like a bear's paw descend upon his shoulder, and a rough voice in his ear.

"All right, Dr. Dee?"

There is a strong smell of raw onions.

"Bob!" Dee cries.

"Bill, if you don't mind, Doctor. Bob is in your orchard, in the event you've a mind to take to the river. What a nice little dog. Have a name, does he?"

"Francis. He's a lurcher."

Bill bends to stroke Francis and tell him what a good boy he is and so on, although Francis is more eager to cock his leg on the samples that Bill and Bob have brought back for having found them valueless.

"So how much is it this time, Bill?"

"It has mounted up in your absence, Doctor, I am afraid to say. There is the original outstanding sum of two pounds, six shillings, and eightpence owed to Master Inglestone, booksellers of Gutherons Lane, and then there is three pounds round owed to Master Truefitt, tailor, of Lombard Street, for a coat of green velvet, and also I regret to say there is the sum of eight pounds owed to Mr. Bowes, goldsmith, of Cheapside, for a showstone, whatever that may be."

"But that is more than most men earn in a year!"

"Yes," Bill agrees. "Quite some shopping spree that one, eh, Doctor?"

"I have some gold within the house."

"It isn't the stuff that turns green two days later, is it?"

"Hmmm. Does it do that? Well, well. Obviously I have not quite perfected the process. And the samples you took, you had no joy with them?"

"None at all, Doctor, as you see. And it turns out there is a great deal of this stuff on the market right now, so unless you have some real gold about your person, Dr. Dee, then I am regretfully going to have to take you to Ludgate."

"In manacles? Really? Surely there is no need for that."

"I'm sorry, Doctor, but it is as Bob would say: trick me once, shame on you; trick me twice, shame on me."

"Bob is a very wise man, obviously, but listen, Bill, may I at least put my bag down, kiss my mother, and introduce Francis to Master Cooke, who will be looking after him while I am at your pleasure?"

"I don't see why not, Dr. Dee, since you are a gentleman of your word. Only I must insist on the manacles."

"I'll just—"

"No, Doctor."

"But—"

"It is these or I can't let you go in, sad to say, Doctor."

Dee holds out his hands, watched by Francis, with his head cocked in puzzlement.

"It is a bit strange, Francis, isn't it? But there we are."

Bill applies the manacles and locks each one.

"My God, Bill, are these silver?"

"They are, Doctor. Clever of you to notice, and nothing but the best for you. We took them as a lien from an Edinburgh gentleman who was a familiar of the Queen of Scots, so there is a good chance these could have been worn by herself, as part of her costume no doubt, for a masque or some such."

Bill shows him the key. It is decorated with a thistle.

"Well. Goodness, Bill. What an honor. Now, if you'll excuse me? Come on, Francis, let us go and meet Johanna Dee, whom I am honored to call Mother, and Roger Cooke, whom I am honored to call Roger Cooke, and who, unless something turns up in the next moment or two, will be looking after you until I can raise thirteen pounds, six shillings, and eightpence. Would you do the honors, Bill?"

Bill knocks on the gate.

A moment later Cooke's voice floats over.

"Who is it?"

"It is me, Roger, John."

"Why, Dr. Dee, you have acquired the knock of a bailiff!"

The gate is unlocked. Cooke sees Bill.

"Oh."

"Not too long now, Doctor, if you've a mind, for we must get you to Ludgate before curfew."

Dee brings Francis in and closes the gate on Bill, who remains standing outside, implacable.

"Quick, Roger, we do not have much time. Fetch the jar of *salis amoniaci* and the spirit of niter. We are in need of *aqua regia*, fast."

They have made *aqua regia* fairly often in the past, so called because it eats through noble metals, including gold and silver, and they make some now, creating the distinctive red liquid in the last of their crucibles and a humble glazed jug.

"How have you been, John?" his mother asks from the kitchen while they work. "You look tired."

When it is ready, Cooke spoons the *aqua regia* onto the chain link of the manacles. The fumes are very repellent and Dee turns his face from them.

"Keep going."

It is not a quick process, but they have made a strong solution. Bill bangs on the gate.

"Come on, Doctor! Time is fleeting!"

"Shall I get that?" his mother wonders.

"No, Mother! Leave it!"

The banging continues.

"He is very insistent," Dee's mother says.

"Not yet, Mother!"

He pulls his wrists apart and Cooke spools more acid in the chain.

"It is not working quite as fast as I hoped. I think we may need an ax."

There is one with which they chop wood. Does he trust Cooke? He would have to place his hands on the block and let him swing at the gap. More hammering on the gate.

"Doctor!"

"Shall I let him—"

"No!"

Dee looks at Cooke. Well, he will have to trust him. Just then, with one last effort, the chain snaps.

"Ha!"

Dee is up the stairs and out on to the window before his mother can even open her mouth to ask if she should let Bill in. He scuttles along the ridge of the roof and leaps to catch the bough of Thomas Digges's tree without so much as a pause to look at the river or consider the possibility of building an observatory, and he smacks his hands on the bough of the tree and is duly deposited neatly into the presence not of Thomas Digges happily digging for onions, but of Bob and his dog, and another man with a big stick with a gnarled root end.

"You broke the queen's bracelets!" Bob shouts.

"I did not break them: I dissolved them. There is a—"

The gnarled root end makes sharp contact with his head, and Dee feels the world slide and tip away from him.

He wakes up to a kind of hell: Ludgate prison for London's debtors, at night; in the light of a single lamp burning an unhealthy flame, he sees a seething mass of men and women and children, each trying to find space to lie among piles of filthy straw that soak up the broad slough of ordure snaking its way through the middle of the low-roofed, overcrowded room. Rats and insects devour the quick and the dead alike, and the stink of corruption is thick and infernal.

The first thing Dee notices is his manacles are much tighter, and much heavier, being made, he presumes, of iron or steel, and he bitterly regrets his foolishness with the Queen of Scots' bracelets. His head still rings from the blow from the bailiff's stick, though, so he believes himself well punished. A man, who might be dead, lies with his head on Dee's ankle. He hauls himself free and brings his knees to his chest and tries to sleep till dawn. He knows all the tricks to parceling time.

Is this worse than the hold of the barge? He has somewhere dry to sit, he supposes, but he does not have Frommond for company, and thinking of her gives him a kind of strength. Where will she be now? Back in Whitehall, he supposes, subjecting the Queen's court to her cool gaze. Or, no, preparing to go on progress.

He raises his head.

Christ, he thinks. *I need to go to her now.* He tries to stand, to make his way to the lamp by the cell door. He treads on people and on things he does not wish to think about, and he is insulted and lashed at by vengeful prisoners, and at the door he uses his manacles to hammer on the planks and shout for a guard and everybody in the vicinity tells him to shut his mouth and stop his hammering or it will be the worst for all of them because the guards will come and when they come they will lay about anyone and everyone they can reach with their clubs, but Dee will not stop shouting that he is John Dee and that he needs to see Francis Walsingham.

And just as predicted the guards do come and they lay about anyone and everyone they can reach with their clubs, including Dee, and then they slam the door again, and Dee is at it again, and this time the reaction is even swifter, and eventually Dee sees that he is bringing nothing but more misery on all those about him, and so he slumps to the floor, his back to the door, battered and bruised and bloody, but despite it all he does not despair, because this will pass. This must pass. It must.

And it does, perhaps.

Sometime later—it could be dawn, but how can he know?—he is woken by rough hands pulling at his collar.

"Get the fuck out the way," someone spits at him.

But he can't. He is pinned against the door by the press of inmates and can scarcely move a muscle. In the uncertain light he is face-to-face with a bald man whose nose is so broken it has migrated halfway to his ear. The back of Dee's head is pressed to the door, and he can feel the boss of each nail pressing into his back. Then the door starts to open and he is forced into an even closer embrace with the man with the nose who turns out to be a woman who cackles at him and accuses him of being a dirty bastard. A mood of frenetic jollity seems to grip the crowd about him like a madness, a dance of death, and he can make neither head nor tail of it, until the door is finally open enough to allow the throng to spill out and he is carried helpless as a nutshell in a stream out of the room, along the corridor and up the steps to another room that is at least graced by natural light coming from two broad windows set high in the wall, and it is to these windows that everybody rushes as if to escape. But the windows are barred and through them he can see the legs and feet of passersby, and then he sees where he is: the begging room of the gaol.

The clamor starts, with everybody pressed to the window shouting at those going by.

"Please, mistress, I beg of you, a penny!"

"Master—a penny for charity's sake!"

Dee lingers at the back of the room.

"Shy beggars never prosper," a guard tells him, and Dee supposes that is true, but like most men not born to such situations, yet finding themselves in them, he believes something will happen to take him from all this.

But it doesn't, all that day, while he stands there waiting for he knows not what, and then come evening, his stomach in knots from hunger, it is time to be locked up again, forced into that foul cellar.

The night passes with Dee standing upright. At one point he dozes, but he is ready at dawn to be among the first to fight for a place at the begging window, hands shoved through the grilles, palms open for anything and everything, which includes spit, and worse, but no coins, or bread, and every inch of space at the window is fought for, a constant wrestle, all day, and for what?

Nothing.

He believes he will see someone he knows pass by. He believes in his heart that he will see Frommond. He continues to believe this as he is elbowed and pushed aside and he endures a second day without food and there is only a trough of water brought in buckets from the Fleet, already tainted by the city's waste, and now made turbid and foul by the hands and faces of others who've dipped and splashed in it already. The next day he is so desperate he is no longer shy and he makes off with a head of broccoli that so nearly ended up in a small, grubby child's hands, and he keeps it for himself and tears at it with lupine wrenches and he curses anyone who approaches and he knows he has become as bad as any in here but he does not care, because he has just realized that it is August and that the Queen is already gone on progress around the country, and with her: Frommond.

Christ, he thinks. *I must get out or I will die in here.*

For all his talents, all his knowledge, Dee has nothing that will allow him to turn himself into a cat, say, and slide between the bars and be away. That is what they might expect of a conjurer, a companion of hellhounds, a summoner-up of wicked and damned spirits. What did Dudley tell him that time on the boat? That common people feared him not because he made that giant golden beetle fly when he was at Trinity, but because it was known that in the weeks after he was accused of witchcraft in 1555 the children of

one of the men who accused him of it fell ill, and one of them di
He has always been mortified by that, but perhaps now is the ti
to pray upon it.

It is easy enough. Tell a guard that he—Dee—has laid a cu
on the life and family of the man who allows him to die. Remi
him who he is first, of course. Then, when he has purchase on tl
guard's ear, offer to read his chart. Remind him he once read tl
Queen's chart. Offer the same to any guard interested in what the
future holds. They will not pay him in money, but privileges, an
so the futures he predicts had best be good.

The guards in Ludgate are dispiritingly mundane, with few am
bitions beyond being made rich through the work of others and t
sleep with other men's wives. It is easy enough, but it is charlatans
work, for none of the guards can be sure of the year they were born,
let alone the hour of that largely unhappy event.

Still though. The first day he earns bread, and ale, and a piece
of cheese. The second day, as word of his services spreads among
the guarding community, he is moved to a room upstairs, above
sewer level, and allotted a part share of a still somewhat verminous
mattress he must share with a pepperer with a shop of Bucklers-
bury, who all through that first night whispers sweetly in Dee's
ear, though that is as far as he goes. The third day: pen and paper,
and some dried ink that he can resuscitate with spit. But it is only
on the fourth day that he achieves what he set out to gain: the
freedom of the leads.

"Come on then, Doctor, out you go."

It is a thick summer's morning when he steps out onto the roof,
hemmed in only by the low gray wall of the battlements, and he
has his note—promising untold wealth if whomsoever finds it can
alert Her Majesty that her servant Dr. John Dee is unfairly taken
up and put in Ludgate—already wrapped around a decent-sized

onion, ready to be launched onto Fleet Street should he see some-one he knows, or, even, anyone mildly receptive.

It is not a water-fast plan, but it will have to do for now.

He is not the only one granted license to stand on the roof, of course: there are a couple of women, who look as if they have been here awhile, and a family, eating cheese. In the shady corner, though, is a group of men, young, like guildsmen, perhaps, squat-ting together, each of them with his back to the wall, and alert, and when they see him, they look up. Often when you meet a group of people you are at a loss as to whom to greet first, but with this group there is no choice. He is a young man in a bloodred cap, with a badge—one of those pilgrims' tokens—in the brim. He has a thin reddish beard and a level, determined look in his challenging gaze.

It is Jan Saelminck.

CHAPTER TWENTY-FIVE

Francis Walsingham has not slept well since Saint John's and once again he wakes at dawn to the sounds of the water carriers greeting the dong carriers as they pass one another on the street outside his window. He lies for a while, trying to distract himself from thoughts of Sir Christopher Hatton's men combing the country in search of Robert Beale, working in a steadily widening circle from the village in which Ness lives—lived?—with John Overbury, whom Henry Sydney has written to say has been wounded in Ireland, perhaps by his own men, and is not thought likely to survive. If that last bit is true, Walsingham muses, then it is the only aspect of this whole intrigue that has gone according to plan.

If Hatton finds her, what will he do with her? This is the question that has haunted him over the last month and a half. What would he do if he were in Hatton's place? The obvious thing would be to use her to bring Beale down, and with Beale

Walsingham and Cecil, too. But a moment's thought and he can see that if Hatton could turn Ness to his own purposes, then she might become *his* weapon. And a moment's thought further, and Hatton could see that the best thing to do would be to do both things: destroy Beale, Walsingham, and Cecil, in that order, and then insinuate a biddable Ness onto the throne of England. Then: marry her.

So Walsingham has his own men combing the counties also looking for Beale and Ness, and others pursuing Hatton's men as well. He is almost certain that Hatton has men pursuing his men, too. It is a twisted circus, with the nation's intelligencers tailing one another around the country, and meanwhile, what of the men who are *really* trying to kill the Queen? What are the men of the Guild of the Black Madonna up to? Merely because Saelminck cannot be found does not mean he has given up and slipped back over the Narrow Sea to Halle, does it? He might have gone back to Halle, along with all the other Dutch and Flemish builders going home for winter, but he—and they, the guildsmen—might well have come back with the returning tide of refugees who have fled Holland and come to England after the disaster of the Battle at Gembloux, when, as predicted, the Duke of Parma's cavalry smashed William of Orange's mishmash of Protestant volunteers. Could Saelminck and his guildsmen have come back with them? Could they be calmly working away on some building project right now, all just waiting their chance to step away from their tent, or hovel, or barge, to collect their guns, and shoot Her Majesty down? To root her out with fire?

Of course they could.

The clerk of city works has sent Walsingham list after list of unpronounceable names—none of them Henk Poos or Jan

Saelminck—though that means nothing, of course—and the clerk of the sewers has likewise been in touch, and neither he nor any of his men have had sight of the man.

And meanwhile the Queen is on progress, in Hampshire this week, at the house of God knows whom, a vast snaking army of porters and carters and every other profession under the sun. Robert Dudley, the Earl of Leicester is with her, and sends word that it is all as secure as possible, but there is no doubting it is not as secure as having her locked in Windsor.

Walsingham catches the smell of kitchen fires already thickening the heavy summer air. London is bad this time of year, and he doesn't blame the Queen for wishing to be elsewhere. He gets up without waking Ursula or the children, and he pads naked to the next-door room to rub himself down and get himself dressed. In his study he finds the messages that have come overnight: one from Brussels, encrypted; one from Malta, encrypted; one from Cádiz, encrypted; one from the French ambassador's house in London, encrypted. But there is nothing so far—again, still—of Beale or Ness Overbury.

Beale is clever, of course, and he must know that Hatton will be after him, but Walsingham still wonders why he has not sent further word. Does he believe Walsingham has already cut him off? He tries to think what Beale would do, but each theory is dissolved into nothing by the condition that Beale is with Ness Overbury, and that Ness Overbury is with child. They must be like Joseph and Mary, he supposes, plodding from town to town with an ever-dwindling supply of money and options.

He sets to work decrypting the messages, discovering nothing he wishes to know, until a fresh slew of messages is brought up to him midway through the morning, including one from Cecil in Whitehall, that bears just a single word: *naft*.

My God, he thinks. It is here. Finally. The rest of the naft.

He gets up, slowly, and finds his doublet, and summons his servants to walk with him through the city back down to the river, where he expects to see a trireme with a lateen sail and woodwork painted vivid crimson, but finds only just another battered merchantman standing out in the river while the tide turns.

Master Jenkinson is there already, still in his alien clothes, come, perhaps, to meet his contact, and to see that he is not even at this late stage cut out of the deal.

Walsingham offers to shake his hand, but Jenkinson will not allow it.

"It didn't hurt!" Walsingham reminds him.

The sun beats down, shadows are short, and Walsingham sweats, even in his linens. The merchantman is swinging with the tide now and will be alongside the quay shortly. Walsingham looks across at the ship's crew, some of whom line the gunwale, staring across the dipping, dingy waters of the Thames at the Tower. What do they make of it, these men from the Levant? He turns to look at it himself. Impressive, surely, he thinks. It has withstood hundreds of years and will withstand many more, so long as Dr. Dee is kept away from the match fuse. The repair to the hole he blew in the wall is still visible as a patchwork of dark mortar and stone.

Upriver, Cecil's barge comes sliding through an arch under the bridge, oars folded back, and then tacks toward Tower Quay. When it abuts the quay, Cecil defies his age and nearly leaps out. He is like a child promised a treat and he comes scurrying down the gangplank and along the quay, patting his little soft hands together in gleeful anticipation. And sure enough, the Constable of the Tower comes, as does the Master of the Board of Ordnance.

"Is it really here?"

"This is it," Cecil beams.

The ship is warped to the quay and tied off to the bollards, her sailors staring down at them with dark eyes from dark faces, and each man has on his head a turban of grubby linen, and soon a crowd is gathered all around and high above, on the Tower's battlements, where men line the walkways, there to see the Saracens.

"Let them gawp, Francis, let them gawp! Let them spread the word! The sooner the Spanish ambassador hears we have taken delivery of the naft, the sooner King Philip will know, and the sooner he will draw in his horns."

"But we still don't know the price," Walsingham reminds him.

Cecil sighs.

"I have been going through the lists of the Queen's jewels," Cecil tells him. "There is a ruby, as big as my knuckle, and flawless, but I am buggered if I can discern heaven's sacred cipher in any of its facets, and nor is it so famous your man Sokollu will have heard of it. Have you had word of him from any of your men in Constantinople?"

"Only background stuff: that he was born in the Balkans and was forced to convert to Islam as a boy, but now he lacks for nothing and has a harem to rival that of the sultan."

Cecil whistles.

"Lacks for nothing eh? Bloody hell."

"But he holds the English nation in high esteem."

"Well, that is something, I suppose."

"And keeps a painting of Her Majesty that some merchant gave him on his wall."

Cecil is no longer listening. A gangplank has been lowered, and after a moment, four men in very finely worked silver breastplates and helmets from which hang long plumes of horsehair, cautiously step out and down onto English soil. Each carries a blade like a halberd, and a sword, and they are dressed as Jenkinson was the day they nearly racked him.

"Perhaps this little chap will be able to tell us something," Cecil says.

At the top of the plank, paused for a moment to survey the scene, stands a man clothed in plush velvets and silks that are each a variation on the color of an apricot, or a peach. He has extravagantly puffed breeches and something red without obvious purpose on top of his voluminous turban that might signify great rank, or not.

A boy unrolls a carpet before him and he steps very cautiously out onto the gangplank in pointed leather slippers.

"Can this be Sokollu Mehmet?" Cecil asks Jenkinson. It is the first time he has acknowledged his presence.

Jenkinson jeers at his ignorance.

"Of course not. Sokollu Mehmet Pasha would not come like this. Christ, he is a greater man than you have ever even glimpsed! When he rides out, no one is permitted to look his way, and he rides with such a troop of cavalry that the earth quakes and the dust does not settle for a day."

Cecil makes a dismissive little hoot.

"Well, who is this then?" he asks.

"His name is Mustafa Beg. He is a dragoman of Constantinople, sent by Sokollu Mehmet Pasha to secure the payment to which you have agreed."

Cecil mumbles that he has agreed to nothing. Jenkinson can scarcely control his trembling rage. It seems he has much at stake. Beg is followed down the gangplank by five or six men who are almost as equally colorfully dressed as he.

"Thank the Lord that Hatton isn't here to see this lot," Cecil murmurs. "He'd be off to his tailors before the sun is set. Still, let us be polite."

Jenkinson bows very low, almost to the ground, before Mustafa Beg, but Cecil is not so limber and manages only a long nod of the head. Walsingham follows Cecil's example, and many words are spoken but none are understood.

"Just ask him where the naft is," Cecil instructs Jenkinson.

"You have not grasped the situation, Cecil," Jenkinson tells him. "You can't just dismiss him like that. Mustafa Beg represents Sokollu Mehmet Pasha. For all intents and purposes, he *is* Sokollu Mehmet Pasha."

"Not just some merchantman, then?"

"No. For the here and now he is the grand vizier of the Ottomans. Ordinary men and women are forbidden to look at him on pain of having their eyes put out."

"Well, why does he wear such bright colors then? He should follow Master Walsingham's example here and wear black."

Cecil knows how to be very irritating.

"So what rank is he? Can't call him King Beg. Lord Beg? Sir Mustafa? Doesn't sound right. Doesn't sound Christian."

"Call him Vizier," Jenkinson suggests. Meanwhile Vizier Beg is disconcerted by something.

"Which of you is Lord Walsingham?" he asks in halting Latin.

It takes a moment to realize what he is asking.

"*Lord* Walsingham?" Cecil wonders, turning to Walsingham. Walsingham flushes.

"I may have exaggerated my status in my letter," he admits. "Jenkinson said he would never deal with a mere master, or even a sir."

"Quite right. What else did you put in it? I do not believe I saw a copy."

Walsingham says nothing. He put in all sorts of grand nonsense, now that he thinks about it, all at Jenkinson's suggestion. He almost made out that he was King of England.

"And where is your Queen?" Vizier Beg asks.

Cecil is taken aback.

"Why?"

"She should be here. If she is not here, I am not here. We are not here."

He gestures around them, meaning, Walsingham believes, him, his followers, and England. There is consternation among the men behind him. They are craning their necks about looking for something. As if expecting something. Can it be Her Majesty? Are they expecting the *Queen*?

"What are they saying, Jenkinson?" Cecil asks.

"They are saying they will not show us the naft until they have seen the Queen."

"I suppose he has come all this way."

"But she is on progress!" Cecil reminds them. "She'll not be back for two weeks or more. Then again, it will give us time to raise the money or find the jewel or whatever the bloody hell it is he wants. But what shall we do with him, in the meantime? I was expecting someone in the line of—I don't know—a guildsman. Do we need to put him up in a gentleman's house?"

"He will stay aboard his ship," Jenkinson says. "And he asks only for fresh water, and supplies of lamb meat, onions, and peppers."

"Seriously?" Walsingham asks.

"Also: charcoal."

"I think we can run to that," Cecil supposes. "Make it so, will you, Lord Walsingham? I will put you in charge of entertainment and so forth. Keep him occupied, won't you? Show him the bear pits perhaps?"

Walsingham is about to tell him that he has no time, that he must find Beale and Ness Overbury, but Cecil is looking stubborn.

"And find out what exactly he wants for the naft."

Oh Christ, that accursed verse.

CHAPTER TWENTY-SIX

South of Ely, Huntingdonshire, August 1578

I t is August now, and Robert Beale and Ness have stayed away
as long as possible, living almost as vagrants in the house of an
old friend from his student days, set back from the road, outside
a village a few miles north of Cambridge. Now, though, Ness's
time is come, and they must leave it, and return to Nigel Vernier's
household on Cat Lane in Ely, to the care of Ness's sister, Claire,
who will know of a midwife, and of a nurse, and of a priest to baptize the baby when . . . if . . . , God willing, it is born.

And so Beale has used the very last of Ness's gold to hire a carriage and they are grinding slowly over the sunbaked road, heading
north.

"I never want to see that house ever again," Ness tells him. "Do
you hear?"

He does, and he agrees, for these last few weeks have been a
species of torment, a penance for their sins, with the sun beating
down unforgivingly all day, drying up the well, trapping him and

Ness within a house that even through the pitilessly short nights has remained so hot that resin oozed from its timbers. Ness's body has burned just as hot, hotter yet perhaps, and Beale has spent his days and nights drawing bucket after bucket of water up from the river half a mile away and bringing it back to pour over her and sometimes he would swear the water hisses when it touches her.

But now, with her labor pains racking her womb, they are at last on their way to Ely, and it comes as a blessed long-sought-after relief. It is only ten miles, but it feels like a hundred, and with every jolt of the wheels on the road Beale believes it will be proven they have left it too late, and that somehow the baby will be shaken loose, and that he will have to deliver it himself.

"Some women," Ness tells him again, "go into confinement . . . months before the baby . . . is due."

He reminds her that he would have taken her to her sister's earlier, if only she would have been prepared to spend a moment longer under Nigel Vernier's roof than needs be.

"Oh Christ," she says, "I should rather birth in a ditch like a ewe than be beholden to that man."

Beale has no idea what will come next. He has put that out of his mind until after the baby is born. That is what she has told him to do.

"Who knows if I will live through it anyway," she has told him.

And she's right, of course: it is safer for a man to go into battle than for a woman to childbed.

"All will be well, Ness," he has told her, and he tells her again.

That is easy for you to say, she need not say.

When they arrive at Cat Lane, Vernier is there, in the shop, looking through the bolts of linen with another man of a similar ilk.

"If he says one thing," Beale tells Ness, "I will run him through."

She grips his arm as another contraction grips her.

"I do not . . . think . . . there will be time . . . for you . . . to run him through."

He says nothing, but hurries her into the house, into the room at the back where it is at least blessedly cool. The simpleton is in a dress, playing with a doll. Claire comes from the garden, flushed, with a great pile of linen dried stiff as boards. She gives up a great cry and hands Beale the boards and shouts for the maid to set the water to boil and to fetch the cunning woman.

"You: out," she tells Beale, and he leaves, out into the garden, where chickens are crouching in the dust under the apple tree and he joins them in the shade and wonders what in the name of God to do now.

While he stands there the simpleton emerges, eyes the color of the sky, skin the color of dust, and passes him a message that has perhaps lain in the house for a month, dirty with finger marks. It is from Master Walsingham. Just a few terse words, unlarded by love or even friendship.

Do not come home. SCH seeks N through all of England.

It is unsigned.

"When did this come?"

The simpleton cannot say, of course, and just then the air is rent with the first agonizing cry of what will turn out to be a long day and an even longer night.

Beale sleeps as best he is able under the apple tree and is woken well before dawn by a cockerel crowing from perhaps a yard away. The lamps have been on in the house all night, and Ness's cries have become like those of a wolf. Beale rises and shakes himself and retreats to the privy and beyond, where the cries can torment him no longer.

At last, just before noon, it is over.

Claire Vernier comes to the door. She has in her arms a bundle of something, and though she looks worn to the bone, and somber as ever, she carries the bundle in the way women do, and he knows he has a child.

He comes running.

"A boy!" Mistress Vernier says.

"And Ness?" he asks first. "Is she—"

Mistress Vernier nods.

"Oh yes," she says, as if it was not even that bad a labor.

Ness is lying on the maid's straw mattress in the middle of the kitchen. She is covered in sheets of linen and looks pale and vague and exhausted but alive and happy, with her hair wrapped in linen, and an old lady is bustling about gathering more linen that is steeped in blooms of rose-red blood. Beale kneels next to Ness and takes her hand, which is, at last, cool to the touch.

"A boy," she says.

He cannot stop himself smiling.

They have discussed names all summer long and have chosen John.

At that moment there is a disturbance at the front of the house. A raised voice. Mistress Vernier, still carrying the baby for them, stiffens. Ness's fingers clench his.

"What is it?"

The voice, from the front of the house, in the shop: she knows it.

"Where is she? I know she is here!"

Every face tilts to the light.

It is John Overbury, back from the wars to find his house empty and his wife with another man, now come to bring hell. He stumps through the shop, bringing with him a lingering stink of sulfur and rotting flesh. He has a terrible wound to the face and has lost an eye, a powder burn from an exploding arquebus. His other eye is mad and wild.

Behind him scuttles Vernier.

"A woman should be with her husband," he bleats.

Beale draws his sword, the last thing of value he owns, and he steps between Overbury and his wife.

"There you fucking well are!" Overbury cries and he lunges at Beale with a short blade that Beale very nearly does not see in time. He feels the blade burn his ribs as he leaps aside. He lashes across Overbury's face with his own blade but Overbury has been killing men, women, and children in Munster for a year, and despite his wound, and his age, he is as quick as a snake. He ducks the blow and turns and slashes at the back of Beale's leg. Beale dips his knee and feels the blade in the flesh of his thigh. Christ! He is going to lose this fight. He throws himself back as Overbury's left fist catches him above the ear.

He has to keep him at sword's length but Overbury is relentless. Beale dances back, away. He knows not to look at his own blood.

"Stay back!" he shouts.

"Fuck you pipsqueak little fuck!"

Overbury storms at him again. Beale is forced farther back. He trips over a bucket of blood by Ness's feet and goes sprawling. He keeps hold of his blade and scrabbles back. And now the worst thing: at the door, Mistress Vernier, carrying Beale's son, whom he has not yet even held, steps forward, between them, and faces Overbury down.

"Don't you dare," she growls at him. "Don't you dare bring your foul hatred into my house, into my kitchen."

But it is too late for that. Foul hatred is already here. It always clung to John Overbury, like a stink, but John Overbury is recently come from Munster, where men dash babies' heads on cold hearthstones before raping their mothers, and with his recent pain and humiliation, his hatred and his foulness have only intensified, and what he sees here in Mistress Vernier's arms—his wife's child by another man—is the quintessence of all that he hates in the world and so it is nothing to him—nothing—to dash the bundle of cloth-wrapped flesh from his sister-in-law's arms and set about her with his fists, she whom he has always hated for the bloodless way she has been superior to him all the time she has known him, while Ness screams in helpless, hapless horror.

And that is when Beale is on his feet and the blade in his hand is suddenly true and purposeful and with a quick step and a thrust, it is through the devil Overbury's windpipe and out of the back of his neck, and for a moment, blood seems to float in the air, lingering in droplets, a pink mist in the beam of light that falls from an aperture. All movement ceases. Overbury is stilled, pinned in midair by the blade in his throat, until Beale withdraws it, and then Overbury slumps to the ground, with a great loose sigh, like an old horse's fart, as if his soul is finally relieved to be free of his cankerous fleshly body.

Beale drops his sword. He stares down at the body as dark blood slicks across the flagstones in jerky rushes.

After a moment he turns away, to Ness, who has picked up her baby, and has it clutched to her, wrapped in his sheet, and she is hunched over it, shuddering, and Beale bends to crouch by her and he tries to take her in his arms, but she is locked stiff, unyielding to his care, though that is all he wants to be able to give.

"Ness," he whispers. "Ness. All is well. He is gone. He is dead. He can harm you no more."

But she is shaking still and will not raise her head. She is closed to him.

He glances up at Mistress Vernier, seeking her help, but he sees she has her hands to her face and is staring down in horror not at the devil Overbury's sprawling corpse, but at Ness, and the boy in her arms, and when Beale looks down again he sees it: the blood. A badge of it dabbed across the sheet that is stretched across the crown of his son's head. He feels a stab of alarm. He tries to prise Ness's fingers from the boy, but her hands are like claws, clutching him to her, and it is only when Beale attempts to force her that her silent howl finds its voice in a desperate, tearing screech.

"By God, Ness! Let me!"

But it is too late for that. Something has happened. When Beale finally wrests him free of the grief-maddened mother, the boy's body hangs broken in his hands. A break. A fracture. The boy is dislocated. Limp. Broken.

He is dead.

How do you live after that? Beale will never be able to explain, other than to say he did not die. Time passed. The screaming stopped, for a bit, at length, and he was faced with a series of very urgent practical problems that required solving there and then. He must get up. He must take his son with him, and he must take Ness, and they must be gone from the house, from Ely, before the hue and cry is raised and the whole town is turned out to find him.

He picks up his son, first, gathering him in his sodden birthing sheet that is now become his winding sheet, and he puts him in the bucket nestled with the bloody clouts and rags from his birth. He covers the bucket with a cloth as you might a pail of milk to keep away the summer flies. Then he wipes his sword on a piece of the devil Overbury that is not covered with blood from his torn-open throat, and then he resheathes the blade. He straightens his doublet, takes a deep breath, and turns to Ness. She has slipped back into the same blank fog as before, when she saw Arthur Gregory throttling that poor constable to death. Beale is glad. It means, he hopes, that she is in some way isolated from the pain of what has just happened.

Mistress Vernier is still kneeling. Her head hangs, her hands hang. She might be saying her prayers before putting her neck on the block. Beale puts a hand under her arm and tries to lift her but she is a dead weight, and he lets her be.

He turns back to Ness.

"Ness," he says. "Ness. We must go. We cannot stay. The hue and cry. It will come any moment."

She understands not a word.

"Help me," he tells the simpleton, but the child turns and runs out into the garden where the chickens are. The midwife, or cunning woman, or whatever she is, or was, is long gone, as has Vernier.

Beale gathers Ness's clothes where he sees them and sits her up. She is startlingly light, as if the effort of giving birth has burned away all her heft and weight, and she is no more substantial than a bundle of hot twigs wrapped in linen. He places another shirt over her first and then a smock. He has not much time for niceties.

"Come, Ness, come," he whispers.

His ears are cocked for the hue and cry.

"You cannot!" Mistress Vernier whispers from behind. "You cannot take her."

"I must," he says. "I must. She will die if she stays."

"She will die if she goes."

Beale pauses, and looks at Ness, the woman whom he has ruined. He thinks about her on a pyre.

"I must," he repeats. "I must or she will be burned alive."

Mistress Vernier says no more. He turns to see what she is doing. Nothing. Only staring at him as if he were no better than the devil Overbury. Perhaps she is right. Perhaps he is no better.

He turns back to Ness. All strength is gone in her. She is too weak to move, but it means she cannot resist. At length she is dressed. She can just about stand, though by God she is weak. He puts her in the settle by the sweet-smelling fire and then gathers up all that he can: Overbury's heavy purse, the bucket containing his son, and he then stoops to lift Ness to her feet. He believes if he can get her out of Ely, he . . . they . . . stand a chance.

Outside in the lane it is very bright, but deserted save for a very fine horse, laden with a saddlebag, tethered to the post of the over-hang. It can only have been Overbury's. Beale approaches as gently as he can but the horse is nervy and has been treated badly. Beale must soothe it before he can help Ness up onto its saddle. He needs her to hold the bucket before he can swing up onto the saddle be-hind her. She does so, blankly. He swings up. The horse backs and shudders. It is not going to be a comfortable ride. He hopes he will be able to find a carriage on the London Road.

"Come on then," he says and they plod slowly out of town, still deserted, and out on to the Cambridge Road. Tears fill his eyes. Ness is keening. The weight of his son is nothing, in the bucket. South. Or north. It hardly matters. He must just be gone. He looks around and remembers when he was once horsewhipped by his father. He'd wanted to plunge his buttocks in a trough as he ran just to get away from the pain. It is like that now. He runs without running. He looks without seeing. Water, perhaps? A river? The Great Ouse. It will take them northward, to King's Lynn.

But then he sees the four men coming riding toward him, and he knows there is nothing he can do to stop them. This is where it must end. He can make no more amends.

"Christ, Ness," he tells her, "I am sorry."

He should kill her, of course. That is what Walsingham would suggest. It would end any contagion of the conspiracy and save her much pain later on at the hands of men such as Richard Topcliffe, but he knows his heart is too faint for such a thing. He is too human, too weak. He reins in the horse, very gently, and diverts himself with making sure Ness is as comfortable as she might be, though what is the point, really?

The men sweep along the road toward him, cloaks flying, dust pluming. They know who he is, he is sure of it. The slow their horses to a trot and come to a stop before him. They are wearing masks against the dust of the road. One of them peels his down.

"Beale!" he says.

Beale feels his legs give way.

By Christ, it is Arthur Gregory.

CHAPTER TWENTY-SEVEN

Hampton Court Palace, Hampton, west of London,
August 1578

Jane Frommond stands at the window of one of the privy apartments at Hampton Court Palace and watches Master Walsingham lead a company of men up from the river, some of whom are so exotically dressed she can only believe they are players come for a masque, yet they carry themselves with a wonderful serene dignity, and it is Walsingham and his small party of secretaries and guards who look flustered and discomfited.

"What is it, dear?" Mistress Parry asks.

She tells her.

"What on earth is he doing here? He must know Her Majesty is on progress?"

"Perhaps we will find out?"

Mistress Parry gives her an arch look over her embroidery frame.

"Sorry," Frommond mutters.

Blanche Parry sighs.

"No," she says. "I am sorry. It is good of you to stay to keep me company. I know you would rather be with Her Majesty."

Before Frommond can deny it again, Mistress Parry launches into a description of some of the adventures she had on past progresses, when she was younger—and not ill, which she is now—which Frommond has heard before, but is happy to hear again, because she likes Mistress Parry, who is, she knows, a cousin of Dr. John Dee, of whom she has been thinking a great deal recently.

Where is he? she wonders. Having been in his company for so long, she misses him and wonders why he has not sent word to her or come to see her. She has not been to see him, true, but that would not be proper, and she only did it once before because Master Walsingham and Lord Burghley were planning to arrest him again.

"Perhaps I will go and see what they are up to."

"You do that." Mistress Parry smiles.

She does, and Master Walsingham is pleased to see her.

"I did not know you remained behind."

She explains what she is doing there, and Walsingham explains what he is doing.

"The dragoman does not seem overly impressed?" she asks.

"No," Walsingham admits. "I understand Constantinople is rather grander in scale. Anyway, this makes a change from the bear gardens."

He gestures at the palace.

"But what are they even doing here in England?" she asks.

Walsingham looks evasive. *He is ashamed of himself,* she thinks. *What for? Not having mastery, that is it.* But then he seems to come to a decision.

"Mistress Frommond," he says, "perhaps you are the one to help."

She cocks her own eyebrow this time, not just because he sounds so costive.

"I admit I am loath to commit," she tells him. "The last time you and Master Beale asked my help it was merely to teach a girl how to accept a curtsy and that ended in a bloodbath."

"Yes," Walsingham admits. "That."

They walk in silence for a while, he with his hands behind his back, footsteps on the gravel. It is another warm day.

"Go on then," she says.

He blows air through his nostrils.

"Thank you, Mistress Frommond," he says. "Can I ask how are you with verse?"

"Verse?"

"Its meaning?"

She understands words, she tells him, yes. He fumbles for his bag, and then within.

"Where is it? Ah. Here we are."

He shows her a verse. She reads it. She thinks it somewhat cold and formal and cannot quite understand what it is meant to be. Is the poet in love with something or someone perhaps, that he—it is definitely a he—believes should be passed to him like a shared bowl of wine?

"Perhaps some context would help," Walsingham supposes.

He tells her about the naft that Dr. Dee requires for the Greek fire.

"This verse describes the price they are willing to accept for it."

"Is that ordinary?" she wonders.

"Nothing about this is ordinary," Walsingham admits with a sigh.

"Have you asked him? The dragoman?"

"Of course. He merely smiles enigmatically and laughs and I am left feeling a fool. Perhaps I am a fool?"

She ignores his fishing for praise and concentrates on the verse.

"Twice-sceptered is an odd thing, isn't it? What is it to be twice-sceptered?"

"The very question I asked myself."

"I mean, what is a scepter?" she wonders aloud.

"A staff," he tells her. "A king's symbol of sovereignty."

"Or a queen's," she reminds him.

"Yes, yes," he agrees with a slight edge of impatience.

She reads on, looking for something else to catch her attention.

"The lion and the dragon," she says, and she thinks of her time walking with John Dee in the yard at Sulgrave Manor, and of how they had stood that first time and looked up at the eaves under which the owners had painted the arms of Her Majesty, including on the left a lion, and on the right, a dragon.

"*Semper Eadem*," she says. "Always the same. Never changing."

He frowns and looks at her and then at the verse where her fingers are pointing.

"Staying the course?" he asks.

"Why not? And look. Twice-sceptered. It does not mean England's jewel has been twice sceptered—whatever that means—it means England's jewel *has* two scepters."

"But what *is* England's jewel?" Walsingham asks. He is frustrated. Frommond cannot stop herself laughing at him.

"Don't you see? England's jewel has two scepters means that England's jewel has two kingdoms."

Walsingham closes his eyes and tries to think what that might mean.

"Is it some metaphor I do not get?"

"No. It is literal. She has two kingdoms. England and France."

"She?"

"Her Majesty always refers to herself as a prince, doesn't she?"

Walsingham agrees. It is something on which the Queen insists.

"She . . . is . . . a . . . prince," Frommond continues. "She is *the* prince."

She slaps the piece of paper with the back of her fingertips.

"And she does have two kingdoms, doesn't she?" Walsingham muses. "England and France."

"So the poet says being in love is like being a prisoner of a prince, and his heart has been captured by a jewel—by which he cannot mean a ruby or a sapphire, but a woman, surely?—who has two kingdoms and rules over them by Divine Right—heaven's sacred cipher—with the lion and the dragon being her arms, never changing—*Semper Eadem* is her motto—despite the perils she faces from abroad."

Walsingham is looking sick. He claps his head as if to drive out pain and knocks his cap off, down his back to the ground.

"He wants *Her Majesty*? That is his price?"

"So it would seem," she says. "Yes, look. I am not sure what *Hoca* is—a person perhaps?—but the poet seems to say that everyone envies him, or is in awe of him, but he is secretly sad, and the only way to cure his secret sadness is with . . . with Her Majesty crossing the sea to— Well, I do not know anything about constellations, you would have to ask Dr. Dee about that—but to complete the Pleiades—perhaps he has a collection of stars or something that is incomplete?—and then it will be his turn to drink from the wine bowl, and that the wine will be delicious."

She finds she is blushing, but Walsingham stands aghast.

"Christ," he says. "Christ. Christ. Christ."

He starts running back toward the barge.

"Where are you going?"

"I must see Cecil this moment."

"I wanted to ask you about Dr. Dee!"

But he is gone.

CHAPTER TWENTY-EIGHT

Ludgate Gaol, City of London,
last week of August 1578

No one ever believes prisoners' stories, particularly when they are so farfetched as his, but John Dee's persistence finally pays off and he is taken up the stairs to see one of the wardens of the gaol.

"I know the fellow you mean," the warden tells him, "but there ain't nothing I can do about it, because he is gone."

"*Gone?* He is on the leads."

"*Was* on the leads. He has paid off his debts it seems, or someone has paid them off for him, and he has left this very morning. Shame. He was an agreeable fellow, and never did no one no harm, from what it seems?"

"He shot at the Queen and murdered one of her ladies of honor."

"Did he now?"

Blank stare. It is none of his business.

"What about the other men? Those others with whom he always sat?"

"Them Dutchies? They have all likewise paid their ways out this very day! One after the other they came in. I was joking with them that perhaps they had all placed a wager that had come good!"

It is not much of a joke.

"Listen, you have to let me out of here, today."

The warden's eyes seemed to twinkle in their folds of flesh.

"Hoohoo! Dr. Dee, you are a one!"

"I mean it. That man—he told you his name is Jens Blenk—his real name, or one of them, is Jan Saelminck, and he is here to kill the Queen. Francis Walsingham has been combing all of Christendom looking for him and his men, whom you have just this morning let go."

The warden has to admire their ingenuity.

"What a place to hide! Right under their noses!"

"Yes, yes. That's not the point. The point is that I need to get out."

"Why don't I just toddle down to Whitehall or wherever Master Walsingham works and tell him myself? Claim a nice fat reward, go and live in Kent and farm cats or some such?"

"Because he would never listen to you."

"And he'd listen to you?"

"We don't have time for this, Warden! Saelminck may be planning to try to kill the Queen even now!"

The warden throws up his hands.

"I am not going to let you out, Dr. Dee, and that is final. I will send word through the usual channels that you suspect that a man of interest to Master Walsingham was here, but now, owing to your arrival and identification of him, he and his—accomplices, shall I call them? Yes—he and his accomplices are left the gaol having paid their debts and are no longer—"

"Hang on! It was not my fault!"

"No? You let them know you had identified them."

"And I tried to tell you then but you would not listen!"

"If we listened to every Tom, Dick, or Harry's reason as to why he she or it should be allowed to walk free, Doctor, then we'd never get any work done."

He's a fat man, in a leather jerkin, with arms like boiled hams, eating an onion.

"What work do you even do?" Dee cries in exasperation.

"Enough," the warden says. "Now off you toddle."

He waggles his fat fingers.

Dee could bite them, but he tries to think. What to do? Walsingham must learn that Saelminck was here and is now roving about London. He must learn that his accomplices are with him and have been since . . . since when? Dee doesn't know. They were able to pay for preferential treatment, that is for sure, since they were not in the gaol's sewer room, and they did not need to fight for space at the window from which to beg. Dee knows that the upper rooms of Ludgate are supposed to be almost palatial and that these gatehouse prisons are as stratified as some of Roger Cooke's more successful distillations. Saelminck and his men could have been holed up here for months, years even, happily undetected, and it was only when he caught Dee's shocked stare, and knew he'd been identified, that he paid whatever his debt was and left. Dee decides that if he ever gets out of here alive, he will not let on to Walsingham that it was he who alerted Saelminck that he had been spotted.

But Dee needs to get out, or he needs word to get out to Francis Walsingham.

He scrapes the message from his last piece of paper, smelling strongly of onion now, and with the scrapings of the ink from its pot, he changes his words and pens the letter to Walsingham, telling him that Saelminck has left Ludgate, with at least five men, and they are now at liberty in the city. He signs it, wraps it back around the onion, and ties it in strips of linen torn from the sleeve of his shirt. He is about to go back up onto the leads, to try to launch it onto Fleet Street when his way is barred by one of the wardens.

"Not you."

His credit is up. He must return to the cellar. *Christ.*

Dee opens his mouth to tell the warden that he has cursed the children of the man who sends him to the cellar, but something stops him. There is danger in this sort of thing, he feels. Also, does this oaf have children?

The warden pushes him toward the stairs that lead down to the sewer room and from which wafts the thick stench.

"I can't," he says.

"'Course you can."

"I have to see Francis Walsingham, right now."

"Stow it. The only thing you're going to see is my fucking fist."

Dee would class himself as a lover rather than a fighter, but he is not having this. He can't. Vivid imagery of the man on the barge comes to him, and he wishes he had a boat hook with which to dispatch this one. But no. Instead the warden pushes him sharply. He must run to keep his balance. Then he turns and lets the warden come at him, and then slides out of his way, catching his ring of keys and tugging the man past his outstretched boot. But the warden is set foursquare, solid as a bullock, and does not move.

He carries a club, too, against just such an event, and he raises it now. Dee backs away. The warden advances.

Just then there is a barked shout.

"You there!"

Both men stop dead still. The passageway behind the warden's cocked right arm is suddenly filled. Five men, well dressed, led by the senior warden, the very man who dismissed Dee a moment earlier.

"Here he is." The senior warden is smirking. "Safe and sound, just like I told you."

Dee recognizes none of the five men exactly, but he knows their type. Walsingham's? Cecil's?

"You Dr. Dee?"

"I am."

"I'm sent by Sir Christopher Hatton to see you safely delivered from this . . . this place."

Hatton? *Hatton?*

"What does he want with me?"

"Daresay you'll find out."

Both wardens step back. Dee straightens his much-soiled doublet.

"Right," he says. "Lead on. I bid you farewell, my friends. Master Warden, and junior warden. I will mention how helpful you have been when I see Master Walsingham."

It is on the tip of his tongue to predict for them that their lives will be short, blighted by violence, death, and disease, and end in miserable poverty, but perhaps they know all that anyway. And, after all, they are only doing their jobs.

The leader of Hatton's men is John Buckfast. He is a Northampton man with great presence, but little curiosity.

"I don't care what your business with Francis Walsingham is. I serve Sir Christopher Hatton and as far as I am concerned, that is that. You are coming with me."

He has a very firm grip on Dee's arm, just above the elbow, and they march out of Ludgate, and along to one of the houses on the Strand, beyond Saint-Dunstan's-Without.

"Mind your backs there. Coming through."

At the gate the porter admits them, and Dee is taken across the gravel past the door of a very fine, brick-built house in the new style, with gables and very good glass in the windows. Behind the house is a garden, likewise newly laid out, and slightly sparse where the lawn and hedges are yet to fill out. New trees are planted and beyond is a long pink brick wall, punctured by a gate that leads, Dee must suppose, through to the river. Hatton stands to one side, on the lawn, with a knot of gentlemen in riding boots, watching some sort of workman fiddling with various contraptions that appear at first glance vaguely alchemical. Dee can smell gunpowder. As he is being led to them, there is a flurry of movement, and a hissing sound, like an angry goose, that sets Dee's hair on end, and then something shoots up into the air, a hundred foot above, and explodes with a riot of red stars. Everybody in the garden flinches, but when nothing seems damaged and no one is hurt, they are delighted, and congratulate Hatton as if it is he who has done something marvelous. The noise of the explosion was so sharp Dee can still hear it echoing, and a flock of pigeons is awhirl about the garden, shadows flitting on the grass as the smoke dissipates.

Hatton notices Dee.

"Well, well," he says, stepping back, as if he might catch something from Dee. As well he might, Dee supposes. Hatton is in blue linen and vermilion silk, while Dee has been wearing the same clothes for a week or more.

Dee thanks him for getting him out of Ludgate.

"I hope you prove worth it," Hatton tells him.

Whatever is he talking about? Dee wonders. Anyway, there is no time for that. He tells Hatton he must find Francis Walsingham, urgently, to tell him about Jan Saelminck. At the news that Saelminck is in London, Hatton seizes up. He is like a rat faced with two traps, Dee thinks, and trying to plot his own best interest gives his eyes an animal quicksilveryness. Should he alert Walsingham, and perhaps save the Queen, but go uncredited? Or should he look for Saelminck himself and claim credit that way? Or should he just sit on his hands and see how this develops?

Dee has never quite shared Walsingham's view of Hatton: Can he *really* wish the Queen gone? When she raised him from nothing? Surely he can expect nothing greater from the Queen of Scots? Unless—?

"I will send word to Master Walsingham," Hatton decides. But his voice is too loud. *He wants it broadcast*, Dee thinks, *like seeds of truth, when it's obvious he's lying.*

"I can go myself," Dee presses. "Let me through the gate and I can be at the Tower within the hour."

"No, no. No need. I will send one of my own men. In the meantime, I have something else I need from you. Something important."

"What can be more important than the life of the Queen?"

Hatton grows petulant.

"I have said I will send word, and so send word I shall. I did not spring you from Ludgate to have you argue with me, Dr. Dee. Now, there is something I need you to see."

"What is it?"

Dee is suddenly in no mood for this. He needs to be gone, but Hatton's men linger, and he feels the shadow of their grip on his arms. He has no choice but to follow Hatton across the nascent lawn and through some trees to find—picturesquely half hidden under a smock of climbing ivy—a small building set against one of the side walls. *It would make a perfect laboratory*, Dee thinks. But that is not what Hatton wishes him to see. He wishes him to see something piled against its wall, covered in green sailcloth. A guard in blue stands over it. *Not much of a job*, Dee thinks. Hatton nods, and the guard puts aside his halberd to pull the cloth back.

Dee smiles.

"Well, well," it is his turn to say.

Frobisher's ore.

"Where did you get that?" he asks.

"A bailiff's sale or something. I am not certain."

Dee thinks of Bill and Bob. They will have kept some to sell, he supposes, and dumped the rest back at his gate. Then, when the first lot sold, they would have been around to reclaim the rest. It will have gone some way to expunge his debt he hopes, and he wonders, idly, how much they would have got for it.

"What do you make of it?" Hatton asks.

What do I make of it? Dee thinks but does not say. *Nothing.*

"I am familiar with it" is as far as he will commit. "I have been working on it for some weeks now, trying to extract gold."

"With no luck?"

"These things take time."

He cannot see where Hatton is going with this. Then something triggers a memory: Frommond, in the barge, telling him that besides being a fine dancer with a shapely calf, Sir Christopher Hatton was also a buttock-cupper and a breast-squeezer, and that he was also going into what she had called "the alchemy game."

"I have a man," Hatton confesses, "who tells me he can do it."

Dee is taken aback.

"Who?"

"His name is Cornelius de Alneto."

Dee laughs.

"Cornelius de Alneto? A Dutchman about this high?"

He holds out a level hand. Five foot perhaps. Unusual for a Dutchman.

"With eyeglasses?"

"He is— Yes."

"His real name is de Lannoy," Dee tells Hatton, "and he is also a charlatan and a fraud."

Hatton rears back. No man likes to admit that he has been rooked, which is how de Lannoy got away with it the first time.

"He is not! He is not! He has already shown me what he has extracted from this small sample: over ten pounds' worth of gold!"

Dee knows the old phrase: you cannot accumulate if you do not speculate. De Lannoy will have fronted the ten pounds' worth of gold to prove his worth, and now Hatton is digging into his purse—probably looking to borrow more even—to buy more ore, and soon he will be bled white.

But Dee hardly cares about this. He is now thinking of Saelminck. Perhaps he has slotted back into his old master's intrigue? Imagine that: hiding from Walsingham in Hatton's household! The Hebrews have a word for that.

"Does he have an assistant? This de Alneto?"

"How should I know? Christ, Dee, I do not look at, let alone talk to, let alone know, if someone has an assistant. Yes. He must have hundreds."

"May I meet him?"

"De Alneto? No. He is gone back to Flanders, to buy the specialist glass that he needs. He tells me English glass is not clear enough to see through."

Dee smiles to himself. *Oh yes, that is de Lannoy all right.*

"So what is it you want from me, Sir Christopher?"

"I am told, or rather de Alneto has been told—by your man

Roger Cooke—that you have access to a great deal more of this ore. And since you are unable to extract the gold, it is no good to you."

Dee wonders: *Is that quite how this sort of thing works?* And as soon as Hatton has finished speaking he, too, seems to realize the mistake he has made in telling Dee the amount of gold de Alneto/Lannoy extracted from it.

"I do have some," Dee says with a laugh, "as it happens."

This is probably no longer true. He does, though, know where to find it—a lot, lot more: two hundred tons of it, in a warehouse in Deptford. That it is not his, yet, and more properly belongs to the Board of Ordnance is neither here nor there.

"How much are you willing to sell it for?"

Dee has no clue.

"How much are you willing to buy it for?"

That, to him, sounds mercantile.

But before Hatton can shape his answer, a man bursts from the watergate, ruddy-faced and urgent. One of Hatton's. He comes running to Hatton and thrusts a tube of paper at his master, who opens it, reads it, grips it in his fist, and then curses and hurries away, following the man back through the watergate, and onto the river, leaving Dee standing with the guard and his pile of worthless rocks.

CHAPTER TWENTY-NINE

———⟡———

Hampton Court Palace, Hampton, west of London,
same day, last week of August 1578

Robert Beale and Arthur Gregory buried the baby themselves. They had to. No priest would have done it on hallowed ground, for there was never the time to baptize the boy before he was murdered, and so they stopped in one of those small villages with a flint-faced church and a square tower, and they dug the hole themselves, the second grave he and Arthur Gregory have dug together, though this time with tears in their eyes, and they laid the boy down as best they could, and then covered him with warm red soil and Beale was choked with the misery of it. Ness could not get out of the carriage and Gregory said it was better that way.

Then they continued south, until they saw London again, and they rode past the Dolphin, the inn where they had first seen each other, a lifetime ago, and to the Papey, only to discover Master Walsingham was not there, but in Hampton Court, and so they rode west, and now here they are, arriving at the palace, her bricks glowing ruby red in the sunset, and they are hardly off their horses before Walsingham emerges to greet them.

"Robert!" he cries, and he comes down the steps before Beale has dismounted, and Beale cannot stop himself weeping to see his old master, and for once Walsingham's spine unstiffens and he holds Beale and Beale feels the prodigal son and cannot help weeping silently. When it is over, for now, they stand apart, but still holding each other.

"Robert," Walsingham says, "someday, there will be a time to mourn for all this, and a time of silence when we can sit and think and talk about what has happened, but that time is not now. Matters are pressing."

They turn to the carriage in which Ness remains unmoving.

"How is she?" Walsingham asks.

Beale shakes his head.

"She is broken beyond words. I have taken her from everything. This time last year she was one thing; today she is another."

Walsingham nods.

"She is certainly that. Hatton is combing Christendom for her. Did you see any of his men on the road?"

Beale did. Gregory took the reins of the coach, and with authority borrowed from Her Majesty's principal private secretary, he was able to defy their questioning, while Beale rode the long way around, riding alone through the fields and woods, weeping, mostly, and wishing there were a way to undo the last year, to forget he ever met Nicholas Hilliard and ever saw that accursed limning.

"I have to tell you, Robert, that she will never be safe."

Beale is desperate. He had hoped Master Walsingham would have a solution.

"We can change her appearance," he pleads against the sense of what he's saying. "She is much changed already."

And she is, but the awful thing about it is that in these last months she has lost much of the fulsomeness of her figure, and of her character, and with them gone, she has become even more like the Queen.

The coach comes to a stop. Beale moves to open the door, to reassure Ness, but Walsingham stops him.

"She cannot stay here, Robert. You know that, don't you? She cannot stay with you. Or you cannot stay here. You must take her away. Where I do not know. She has no home. Nor will you have a home, so long as you are with her. She is a danger to herself, a lethal, excruciating danger to herself, and the same to anyone who seeks to assist her."

Beale feels himself emptied like a husk. Hollowed out, cored. He feels so dirty, and guilty, deserving, even, of a traitor's death for what he has dragged her into.

"What . . . what do I say to her?"

Walsingham does not know.

"Do you love her?"

Beale is startled by the question.

"What has that to do with it?"

"Everything."

"I do," he says.

"And she you?"

Beale shakes his head. That ended, when? When she saw him standing by, watching while Gregory murdered the constable? Or during the months that followed, in that house while she was too sick to move, and they broiled in the heat? Or when he could do nothing to stop her baby being dashed to the floor of Mistress Vernier's house? Or perhaps it was not just a single event, but something that unfolded slowly over the last year. The way these things do. Was it when his promises of life and adventure were revealed as lies, and bit by bit came down to her being holed up in a house that was like an oven from which she was not permitted to venture because men were combing the countryside looking for her, so that they could take her, and torture her, and put her on a pyre and burn her to death as a traitor? Or was it ever really there in the first place? She was ever jealous of Frommond and Dee, and their easy companionship. *Why do we always have to fuck each other?* she had asked him, and he had had no answer, other than to try to fuck her.

Oh, Christ. He might vomit at any moment.

"What shall I do? What shall I do?"

"There is a solution?" Walsingham tells him.

"Anything."

"Well, that is for her to decide," Walsingham tells him. He looks incalculably somber. "But may I speak to her alone?"

"If she will let you," Beale agrees.

Walsingham gives Beale's arm one last clutch.

"You must needs be strong, Robert."

CHAPTER THIRTY

Hampton Court Palace, Hampton, west of London,
same day, last week of August 1578

Walsingham taps on the carriage door, and then, hearing no answer one way or the other, he opens it and steps up into the darkness of the interior. He takes the seat opposite the woman about whom he has heard all too much, and looking at her now, he remembers the time he once saw a tiger, crammed in a wooden crate, in Basel. He had not expected it to be there, and he has never forgotten the shock of exchanging stares with something so imperious, so other worldly, and he feels something of that now, as for the first time he lays eyes upon Ness Overbury. She sits, utterly still, utterly composed, staring at him with ice-cold command and he feels his breath forced from his body.

"M-m-y God," he stammers, "you are—?"

He cannot bring himself to look at her as he would to a normal woman, not even as he would the Queen. He hardly dare ask if she is the Queen, in case the question is impertinent. After a moment, it seems she has seen enough, and she turns away and looks through the linen covering of the window. It is a gesture of disgusted disappointment more damning than any the Queen could make, and he feels himself compelled into utter darkness.

He gathers himself.

"Mistress Overbury," he starts, "I am most heartily sorry for the losses you have endured these last few weeks. There is little I may do to assuage the pain you feel, or the hurts you have suffered, but the truth is, and I am ashamed to have to admit this, you are only at the very beginning of your troubles in that regard."

She sighs so distantly he can hardly hear her.

"Sorry," he says. "Perhaps you know all this?"

"I do."

She even sounds like Her Majesty.

"He has made me this way," she goes on. "He has turned me into this. My very existence is evidence of my crime."

Walsingham scratches his chin.

"He is not a bad man," he says.

"No. He is not a man at all. He is a boy. A child. He saw something he wanted and he took it."

"You might have said no."

She laughs a bitter little laugh.

"So," she says, "I am to be condemned to burn because I gave into temptation. Because he flattered me. Because I hated my husband and he—Master Beale—promised me a way out of my strictures. He promised to take me away from sheep fields and tallow fat, from Suffolk, from endless abuse of my husband—from my life. And he told me I would be doing something great and good. And now because I believed him, because I believed *in* him, I am to burn on a traitor's pyre?"

"There is no profit in us arguing who has done right, and who has done wrong," Walsingham tells her. "Perhaps Robert's idea was a good one. Or perhaps his mind and your mind and all our minds I daresay were clouded by considerations other than . . . than they appeared. But the fact is that now we are all in an infinitely perilous position, and what we do now matters more than what we did then."

"You sound as if you have a suggestion, Master Walsingham."

He laughs, unable to believe it.

"You really, really can sound like Her Majesty."

She looks at him unsmilingly and he has to look away.

"So what is it?" she asks. "Your suggestion?"

He hardly knows where to start, and if he were not so conscious that time is passing so quickly, he would refine his approach, and take his time, but today he has no such luxury. All he can do is remind her of that spirit which Beale once saw in her—that she might be a bishop, he had said, or discover the Northwest Passage—and then emphasize the perils and pain she now faces—

"Or?"

"Or there is a chance you can escape all this, and by doing so come into infinitely more than anything which Master Beale promised you."

She is silent, but there is a flicker of interest that marks her apart from the Queen.

"Go on," she says.

When it is done, when Mistress Overbury has heard him out and listened to his proposal, she had been silent for a long while before shrugging and asking "why not?" and he did not tell her why not. Walsingham still cannot quite believe it, but he sends Arthur

Gregory to the Tower, to prepare things there, and he dismisses all the servants from the palace and summons Mistress Frommond to him in one of the Queen's privy chambers. When she comes, she is hesitant.

"Mistress Overbury is come," he tells her.

"I saw Master Beale, by the river. He looked . . . distressed."

"Yes, well," Walsingham says. "Not as distressed as Mistress Overbury."

Frommond does not pretend to understand him.

He tells her about the child. Light flees from the room.

"Dear God," she says. "What a thing."

Walsingham nods.

"That is not the least of her troubles," he goes on, "but neither is it the greatest: the greatest is that Sir Christopher Hatton knows Arthur Gregory refused his men permission to search Mistress Overbury's carriage on the road from Ely, and so he has appeared with fifty men at my door in the Papey, believing she is to be found there. He is on his way here, now, with yet more men."

He shows Frommond a piece of paper that he tells her is a message from the Papey.

"Then we must get her away," Frommond says.

Walsingham agrees.

"But where?"

"Surely you have some place she will be out of harm's way?"

"Not really," he says, "unless—"

"Unless?"

"Unless. Well. I have a stone," he says "with which I might kill two birds, Mistress Frommond, with your assistance?"

She waits. He tells her.

She won't do it, of course. In fact, she is astonished he should even ask.

"No! She cannot have agreed! She must be out of her wits!"

Walsingham admits that may be the case, but that is just how it is. They cannot give her months in a darkened room eating lettuce soup.

"Will you talk to her?" he asks.

Frommond is shocked.

"Will *I* talk to her? Will *I* talk to her? If I talk to her, I will talk her out of it."

"What alternatives will you offer her? Dry wood or green wood for her pyre? Chains or ropes? Will she—and I am sorry to be saying this in front of you, Mistress Frommond—want Her Majesty's torturer, Master Topcliffe, to rape her or not? Vaginally or anally? Or both? I am sorry to use such rough words before you, Mistress Frommond, but those are the only other realistic alternatives you can offer her."

Frommond stares, thunderstruck.

"But what will they do when it is discovered Ness is not the Queen?" she asks. He almost smiles. She has made the first step his way.

"How well do you know your gospel, Mistress Frommond?" he asks.

She shrugs.

"As well as any man ought."

"The Gospel according to Saint Matthew, chapter six, verse thirty-four?"

She thinks.

"Ah," she says. "So that is it? 'Sufficient unto the day is the evil thereof.' That is your justification for this? You will cross that bridge when you come to it?"

He holds out his hands.

"It is all I can do, Mistress Frommond," he tells her. "By the time it is learned Mistress Overbury is not Her Majesty, they will be in Turkey, too late and too far away to act against us, even if they wished to, and by then we will have the naft."

"But what about her? What about Mistress Overbury? What will they do to her?"

"Nothing that we would not, if she did not go with them, don't you see? And there is a chance—a likelihood—that they will take no action. Why should they? She is a personable woman. She is able to look after herself as well as any man I know."

Is that true? He does not suppose so, but it does not matter. He must do what he must do to protect the realm, and its Queen, and Mistress Overbury must likewise do what she must do. She is being given a chance to live, and she must take it.

"In a calling such as mine, Mistress Frommond," he tells her, "there oftentimes comes a moment when a situation needs to be resolved. Things need to be pushed. People need to be pushed. I am not suggesting that Mistress Overbury is expendable, but at the same time, I am afraid she is. I need her out of here, you see? I need to ensure that she cannot implicate Robert Beale in this, who in turn would implicate me, and hence Sir William Cecil, whose departure, should he fall, will leave Her Majesty as prey to any old huckster such as Hatton."

"But it is you whom you wish most of all to protect, isn't it?"

Walsingham sighs. What does she want of him? Acknowledgment?

"Yes," he tells her. "I wish most of all to protect myself."

He wants to add more but knows when to remain silent. Anything now will only give Frommond purchase and allow her to start the cycle of conversation over again.

After a moment Frommond registers defeat and sighs.

"What is you want me to tell her?"

"Prepare her for it. Dress her for it. Pack her a coffer to take with her. Soothe her nerve."

"Oh, do you think she will need it soothed?"

Walsingham sighs.

"I know it is a big step, Mistress Frommond. But Dragoman Beg is delightful company, and do not believe the tales you hear of Ottoman barbarity: in many ways they are infinitely more civilized than we. He has set aside the master's cabin for her, for example, and it is— Well, a month or so at sea, in such luxury, might well be what would do Mistress Overbury most good."

Walsingham has seen the cabin. It is more comfortable than anything Mistress Overbury can have ever known. There is silk even on the deck. Such opulence! Does that mean anything? He doesn't suppose so, but it shows good intent, or enough of it to cleanse his conscience.

"The tide turns at six o'clock, Mistress Frommond. It would be best if we were ready to set off then. Can you see that she is dressed appropriately? The first impression she makes will be the one they remember, so can you apply all her antimony and lead to some effect?"

He means make her look exactly like the Queen. Frommond nods.

"Take jewelry—not her best—from Mistress Parry. There is to be a ring on each finger, and a diadem in her hair. But Mistress Frommond, if I may, please ensure that no one, not one solitary human being, not even a dog, lays eyes on her, yes? Find her a boat cloak and ensure she is well covered and when it is done, open a window and hold up a candle. I will come for her then."

Frommond looks helpless, dispirited, and sad.

"One thing, though," she asks, before she goes, "why ever would a man name the possession of a woman as a price for anything, especially a queen?"

Walsingham remembers that letter, the one he wrote to Jenkinson's then unnamed merchantman: What did he say? He wishes he had kept a copy for he remembers the comically grand tone of his words, as if it were he who was the real power behind the throne, and the Queen, Her Majesty, was a dispensable figurehead. Perhaps he is to blame for putting the idea into Sokollu's mind?

"I cannot say," he tells her.

But she knows there is some age-old thing here—women as chattels—and she nods slowly and turns and is gone about her business. Walsingham watches her go. *What a woman*, he thinks. Then he thinks of himself: *what a man*, and he is ashamed, but not so much that he will change his course, and so he, too, turns and sets off toward the river, where Cecil's barge—a luxurious thing, with sixteen oarsmen, and Mustafa Beg will not bother too much with the differences in the livery badges—waits ready to take Ness to her appointment with destiny.

CHAPTER THIRTY-ONE

London, same day, last week of August 1578

Dee leaves Hatton's house on the Strand through his well-appointed watergate and hails a wherry.

"Why, hello, Dr. Dee!"

It is Jiggins.

"You are looking somewhat ill-used, Doctor."

Dee's linen is filthy.

"Never mind all that, Jiggins, just take me to the Tower."

"Can't do that, sir. Not till the tide turns. The bridge'll be impassable."

This is a common enough reservation, for when the tide is coming in, the weight of water through the arches can flow as a weir.

"As near as you can make it then."

"It'll be an extra penny."

"I will have to pay you when next I see you."

Jiggins rolls his eyes but agrees.

"Lot of action on the river today, Doctor," he remarks as he leans on the oars to take him out into the flow. "Sir Christopher Hatton and a barge full of his men going up and down like turds on the tide. And Master Walsingham, too."

"Do you know where is he?"

Jiggins does not. Dee has him land him under the bridge at Drinkwater Wharf and he clambers up the steps and heads east: Thames Street, Billingsgate, Petty Wales, and finally the Lion Gate where he is met by the Yeomen of the Guard, eking out the shade in their broad-brimmed hats.

"What do you want?"

"To see Master Walsingham."

"Well, he is not here and if he were he would not— Why, it is Dr. Dee! Well bless my soul, look at you, sir. I hardly recognized you. You look like shit."

"Thank you. Do you know where he is?"

"He is not here, sir, but his man Master Gregory is within, sir, fixing things up for this evening, if he would serve?"

Dee has no time to wonder what is happening this evening. Gregory will do. He will understand the gravity.

"I need to see him."

Gregory receives him in the Lanthorn Tower. Dee tells him about Saelminck.

"Christ," Gregory breathes. "When was he released?"

"This morning."

"And how many of them were there?"

"Five or six, I suppose?"

"Why did they leave?"

"How should I know? A visit from a rich uncle from Bruges?"

Gregory looks skeptical.

"He saw you'd recognized him, didn't he? That's why he left."

"You'd best hope that's why," Dee tells him. "And not because he has a task at hand."

Gregory takes his point.

"You have to tell Walsingham," Dee tells him. "He has to cancel it."

Gregory nods.

"He's due here on the turn of the tide," he says. "Can it wait?"

It will have to, Dee supposes. Gregory suggests a wash and some fresh linen. Dee accepts and when he is washed and in new—to him—linen, he returns to find Gregory drinking ale. Dee thinks it must be about five o'clock. He is starving. What a strange day.

"What have you been up to then?" he asks. "The last I saw you, you were digging a grave for two men you'd killed."

"I've had to dig another since," Gregory tells him. "Ness lost her baby."

Dee is silent for a while. Christ. Poor Ness. Poor Robert.

Some bread arrives, and some wine, and Dee eats. From the window Gregory indicates the hole Dee made in the wall, mended now, though still obvious.

"Most prisoners just scratch their name."

"Happy days," Dee replies. They seem a long time ago now, forever linked in his mind to meeting Frommond for the first time.

"Anyway," Gregory says. "It is good you are here. The naft has come. Just this last week. An Ottoman from Turkey or somewhere

brought it, though it is yet to be unloaded. But Master Walsingham will want you to crack on with it."

"No," Dee says.

Gregory laughs.

"Why not?"

"Do you know how dangerous it is? Having a weapon like
that?"

"Do you know how dangerous it is *not* to have it? The Dutch
are about to be swept into the sea and then the Spanish will be
here, and everything you hold dear, all your precious books and
your learning: they will become a crime. You'll be whipping yourself to a pyre in Smithfield, just for believing the earth revolves
around the sun."

"It is still too dangerous. That it exists. The Spanish know
we have it, don't they? They will be setting their alchemists to
work on divining its secret, and there will be a race to own it,
and perfect it, and it will set us at one another's throats for all
time."

"We are already at one another's throats, Dee. Have you not
noticed? Your head is too often in your books!"

"I cannot do it," Dee says.

"It is too late for that. You are like a woman with child deciding
she did not wish to do the deed in the first instance."

"I may still say no. Listen: no."

Gregory smiles and gestures at the walls that enclose them.

"Look where we are! Look where *you* are. You've no choice."

Dee is silent for a moment.

"Look, Dee," Gregory goes on. "There are thirty barrels of naft,
aren't there? You are not going to make enough to set the world
alight. You will manage two or three barrels perhaps?"

Dee thinks ten.

"How much of a difference can that make? It can burn a fleet, yes. But no more. Its real power lies in the fact that the Spanish know we have it, that is all. That is what will keep them at bay. It is a deterrent. A defensive weapon."

"But what if—I don't know—it falls into the wrong hands? What if you lose it? It is stolen?"

"From here?"

"You know what you and Walsingham are like. Anything might happen."

"That is why it is being kept here, in the armory, in the Tower, guarded by two hundred Yeomen of the Guard."

"What about all my equipment? Where is that?"

"Safely stowed below. Along with all your tubes and barrels and bellows and so on, all brought up from Sheppey. All under lock and key. All under the watchful eye of the Constable and his Yeomen."

Gregory peers back out of the window, up at the sky, as if trying to guess the time.

"Anyway," he says. "Finish up. Tide's turned, and Walsingham will be here soon. You will want to see this."

They wend their way up the Lanthorn Tower to join the guards on the battlements of the now-repaired southern wall, overlooking the moat and the quay where Dee set fire to the crane. Across the moat, on the quay, are lined up perhaps a hundred Yeomen, turned out with arquebuses and halberds, standing to attention in neat blocks. They face the ship that is tied there, and running through them is some of that famous red carpet, left over from Her Majesty's coronation.

"What the . . . ?"

The ship tied to the quay is an ordinary-looking merchant-man, though it is tidier and cleaner than any Dee has ever seen, ever, and nor is it stacked high with cages of pigs, goats, chickens and so on, or peopled with lounging toothless sailors. Instead there are carpets on the deck, and what must be soldiers, a dozen of them perhaps, helmeted, and in long robes, carrying polearms.

"Is Her Majesty coming?" he asks.

Gregory smirks.

"Wait and see," he says, pointing upstream. Dee shields his eyes against the setting sun. Under the bridge, through one of the middle arches where water throngs the fastest, comes a barge. Sleek, black, beflagged, with eight oars either side.

"Cecil's?"

Gregory nods. The barge steers toward the quay below them and bumps gently against the pillars. Bargemen leap out and tie her up. There is a shout on board the merchantman, and a stir: her soldiers take positions, and the cook douses the fire with a couple of buckets of water. Someone hurries to the captain's cabin below the foredeck. A moment later a party of men in colorful robes emerge like peach-colored peacocks. On Cecil's barge, the gangplank is laid out, covered in yet more red carpet, and on it, in a boat cloak, a woman whom Dee would swear is the Queen, save she comes with no fanfare, just a very small crowd of courtiers, including Sir William Cecil and Francis Walsingham.

"Christ," Dee says, "is that . . . *Ness*?"

Gregory says nothing. Dee watches in silence as Ness hesitates, turns to look about the place, as if for someone—Robert Beale perhaps, whom once she loved—fails to find what she is looking for, and then turns to stare at the ship on the quay ahead. She gathers herself. Cecil comes forward to stand alongside her—like a noble taking his daughter to meet the man he has arranged she should marry—and together they walk to the ship's side. The men in flowing robes have spilled out onto the quay, and as she comes they do not just bow, they lie on the ground. It is the same with the soldiers.

There is a comical moment, when Ness and Cecil stand there, not knowing what to do. Then one of the men shuffles forward to kiss her feet, and Dee can imagine what the real Ness might say to that. But he cannot gauge from the tilt of her head, or the angle of her shoulders what she is feeling now.

"Puellam in nave questus est?"

Is the girl getting on the boat?

Gregory says nothing. He probably does understand Latin, but instead he lets out a long sigh. Below them the men have left a clear path to the gangplank that leads up onto the deck of the ship. Ness steps out along it.

"Why?" Dee asks.

Gregory still says nothing, but he grips Dee's arm, and points at the bridge, from under which comes another barge.

"There," he says.

Coming around the shadowed headland of Rotherhithe, her oars working thunderously against the turning tide, is another barge, smaller than Cecil's but still quite something. Dee sees the familiar flags streaming from the bow.

"Hatton."

"Hatton."

Two more barges follow behind, both stuffed with soldiers.

"She just has to be aboard," Gregory says. "In the cabin would be best. But aboard is good enough. For her, I mean."

They watch as Ness places one foot on the gangplank.

"Go on," Gregory whispers.

"But why?" Dee asks.

"Some verse," Gregory tells him. "The Ottoman wants the Queen in return for the naft. Cecil can't give him that, can he? So your Ness is the next best thing. She wants to go, Beale says."

"She *wants* to?"

"Nothing for her here, now, is there? Family all dead and a death sentence hanging over you? Not what anyone wants, is it?"

Dee supposes not.

"Besides, she'll live in a palace, won't she? A harem. Not so bad. Better than Suffolk."

"There is that," Dee mumbles, but bloody hell.

"Don't be so soft, Dee. These sorts give their daughters away to men they've never met, just for a couple of hundred acres of marshy sod."

Ness hesitates at the top of the gangplank. She stumbles very slightly and then turns to survey the land of her birth for perhaps the very last time, and there is something in her stance that is just as regal and fine as Her Majesty would manage. She sees Dr. Dee standing at the battlements. Their gazes lock, and they look at each other for a long time. *What is she thinking?* Dee wonders. She reminds him of one of the stories from Malory's *Morte d'Arthur*, though he cannot recall which, and it seems as if the barge has become a bier, and that Mistress Overbury is sacrificing herself for love of her fellows.

"Christ, Dee, look at you!" Gregory laughs. "She's not stepping onto the scaffold! She's not about to have her head lopped off, and here you are all somber. Ten pounds says she's back in our lives in three years with some stories to tell."

Dee shakes his head, because it does not feel that way. *She is a good woman*, he thinks, *ill done by, and behaving with grace and courage.* It is all you can ever hope for.

He raises his hand in farewell. She nods. Then removes the hood of her cloak to let the lamplight fall upon her red hair and catch the jewels in her diadem, and she steps aboard the ship.

Gregory breathes out a great sigh of relief.

"There," he says. It is done.

CHAPTER THIRTY-TWO

Tower of London,
same day, last week of August 1578

S ir Christopher Hatton's barge has nowhere to tie up, and so
must use Saint Katharine's dock, and by the time he is out
and hurrying to discover just what is going on, and perhaps to try
to arrest Ness Overbury, she is on a foreign ship, and he has no
immediate jurisdiction.

"I know what you are about, Walsingham!" he shouts. "Get her
off! Her Majesty demands it!"

But Cecil, next to him, makes that soft noise of regret and
tells him that the Dragoman Beg comes as an ambassador from
the Sublime Porte, and that diplomatic niceties forbid a boarding
party.

"This ship is like the diplomatic bag," he tells Hatton. "And Beg
is in the bag, don't you see?"

He laughs, a soft powdery laugh, and Hatton can only grind his
heel in the grit.

"Christ, Walsingham," he says. "I know what you have done. What risks you've taken; the lies you've told; the deceits you have practiced."

Walsingham can only laugh at him.

"You only know the half of it, Hatton!"

"You will give me my title, Master Walsingham. You will address me as Sir Christopher, Master Walsingham!"

Cecil, standing by in fog-gray linen, steps forward to usher Hatton away, back to his barge, to head downstream, so that he may be with Her Majesty in Greenwich, putting the finishing touches to the celebrations planned for her birthday.

"What have we got planned, Sir Christopher?" Walsingham overhears him asking.

Walsingham steps back into the shadows and watches for a moment as the ship's hold hatches are opened, and the porters and sailors set about getting the naft onshore. He can feel its curious smell tingling in his nostrils. He remains until the final barrel of naft is unloaded, and bales of English cloth, which the Ottomans will probably not want, are loaded aboard in their place, more as ballast than anything else. When it is done, and the holds are battened down, and the ropes are about to be cast off, Mustafa Beg comes to the gunwale.

"Good-bye, Lord Walsingham! Good-bye, England!"

He is a funny little man, Dragoman Beg, and Walsingham has enjoyed his enthusiastic company.

"You will take care of her, won't you?" he asks.

What will he say if Beg says no? But Beg is shocked at the thought he might not. Beg smiles.

"She will be in a heaven on earth!" He laughs. "Much better than this place! No offense."

None taken, Walsingham thinks.

The ropes are cast off, and the ship shivers in the running river as it is dragged out into the current by two boatloads of oarsmen, and in the very last of the late-evening sun, Ness appears on deck much swathed in a new, even finer cloak, of carmine red, to give a parting wave to England, and to her past life. Walsingham raises his hand to her.

She does not even look at him.

He drinks wine that night, two bottles of it, and sleeps as he has not for months. The next morning he feels groggy, as is to be expected, but after a stout breakfast of pork and eggs and a pint of small beer, he attacks the pile of messages with vim, surprised to find nothing very much to disturb him save one from Cecil to tell him the Queen still dreams of fire.

He walks to the Tower through late-summer sun, to find that John Dee has already started work processing the naft, and the man himself sitting on a bench with his back to the armory, sunning his face next to the open doors of the vault. There is a lurcher puppy by his feet and Dee occasionally calls out to his man Roger Cooke who is doing all the work, reminding him how to re-create the Greek fire recipe they perfected on the Isle of Sheppey: "Hotter!" "Stir it for as long as it takes to say the Lord's Prayer twice!" "Don't breathe it in!" Cooke is tending a fire under a large iron tripod, from which hangs a curious-shaped glass beaker that spits steam from a long spout, and he is surrounded by the ingredients he needs, including tallow, honey, olive oil, dragon's blood ("for color"), and a breached barrel of the naft, which, Walsingham supposes, explains the smell, and why the guards on the battlements have taken cover against the possibility of another blast.

Dee has lost weight, of course, and has a prison pallor, but the lurcher is the color of smoke at night, and will be very handsome.

"What is his name?"

Dee smiles and tells him. Walsingham just sighs. It is a compliment, really.

"How does it progress?"

Dee raises his hands to indicate, as far as Walsingham can tell, sorrow and resignation.

"Gregory told me you had been having reservations," Walsingham says.

"Mmm."

Next to Dee, another man—young, scholarly—is rubbing fat into various pieces of equipment, including a set of bellows as big as a bull, an equally large barrel, much hooped-about with iron, and two thirty-foot-long snakes of stitched leather each end capped with a brass flange. Dee is reading from a weighty book the title of which he is not keen for Walsingham to learn.

"And what about you, Master Walsingham? Any joy?"

He means with Saelminck. Walsingham sighs.

"None. He seems to have vanished, or blended back in. I have never known anything like it."

"Have you spoken to Hatton?"

"Not about Saelminck. Not since I got his note to suggest that you had been doing my job for me, and that I should have known he was there all along. And so on and so on. Christ, Dee, I hate that man. I wish him nothing but ill."

"I suppose you could always say you did have Saelminck in custody, couldn't you? But there is something else: about Hatton, and Saelminck. You remember Cornelius de Lannoy? The little Dutch fraudster for whom Saelminck worked? I believe he is now working for Hatton."

Walsingham sits on the bench next to Dee.

"As an alchemist?"

Dee nods.

"Then he might know where Saelminck is?"

"He might, though he is gone back to Flanders, to buy glass."

Walsingham laughs. He remembers that ruse. Still, he thinks, he will order a search of Hatton's property while the man is in Greenwich with the Queen.

"De Lannoy calls himself de Alneto now," Dee goes on, "though he has kept the Cornelius."

"De Alneto is his real name. De Lannoy was his alchemical name. If that is a thing?"

Dee allows it might be.

"So what is he doing for Hatton?"

Dee hesitates before answering: "Something alchemical."

Dee is up to something, Walsingham grasps, but what? Despite his other obligations, Walsingham is intrigued and decides to wait him out. Dee is no good at this and gives in after barely five breaths.

"You remember the ore that Frobisher brought back from the New World?"

Walsingham laughs again. That! He has not thought about it since it was unloaded with such fanfare, only to defy every effort, including Dee's, to refine so much as an ounce of gold from it.

"He claims he can derive gold from it?"

"He *claims*."

Walsingham studies the ground between his feet for a moment. Now it is Dee's turn to be silent next to him.

"Will he come back to England, do you suppose?" Walsingham wonders.

"Only if he can find more ore."

"Which we have. We can offer him as much as he likes: there are nearly two hundred tons of it."

Dee nods.

"But Hatton will smell a rat if you offer it to him," Dee goes on. "It will be better coming from me."

Walsingham smiles. So that is what he is up to! Negotiating his slice. Well, why not? He will only spend it on books. But it is a surprise. John Dee involving himself in grubby commerce!

"You are certain he will find no gold?" he asks.

"The ore has no value save that which a fool is willing to pay."

"So you are suggesting we assist de Alneto to defraud Hatton, and then arrest him?"

Dee shrugs.

"You could put it like that."

"My God, Dee," he says, "you have made me smile. How much is Hatton willing to pay, do you think?"

"How much are you willing to take?" Dee counters.

Walsingham remembers de Alneto/Lannoy went very high with his promise to Cecil and the Queen. That is what took them in.

"I will not take less than ten pounds a ton," he decides. That is two thousand pounds from Hatton. "Anything that you can agree above that, we split, agreed? It will be your fee for all this."

He indicates Roger Cooke sweating in the inner ward. Dee accepts this with a limited nod of agreement. *Christ, he is ungrateful.*

"Well, I will leave you to it, Dee," he says. "I'm to meet Cecil and Hatton to discuss final arrangements for Her Majesty's procession. I think they'll have to change in the light of Saelminck's— what?—escape?"

Dee nods. And Walsingham is just moving off when Dee calls out, as if something has just occurred to him.

"Oh, Master Walsingham?" he asks. "Will I get an invitation?
To Her Majesty's birthday?"

Walsingham is surprised.

"Do you *want* one? I did not have you down as a dancer?"

Dee pulls a face.

"I would say I was a pretty good dancer."

"Well, well," Walsingham says. "I tell you what, Dee: If you get
all this naft turned into Greek fire before her birthday, then I will
make sure you are on the list, how does that sound?"

Dee cocks an eyebrow.

"Will Mistress Frommond be there?"

"Ahh." He chuckles. "So that's it. We'll see."

"He wants fireworks," Cecil tells Walsingham when he finds him
at his house on the Strand. "They are like comets, only man-made,
and multicolored, from Cathay. Guaranteed to burn down the
city."

"We can forget about them," Walsingham says with some glee.
"Remind the Queen that she has been dreaming of fire."

Cecil twinkles with pleasure at that idea.

"And he wants a procession from the Tower through the city
to Saint Paul's, and then on to Westminster. He is suggesting the
usual players' stages on the way, and he has gone for an Arthurian
theme, in respect of Her Majesty's heritage."

"Let me guess: Hatton as Lancelot? White chargers and so on?"

"It certainly plays to his strengths."

"Well, anyway, we cannot have a procession through the city.
Not with Saelminck's whereabouts unknown. It will advertise her
route more certainly than any red glove. Or maybe we can, and *not*
have her ride down them?"

"Try stopping Elizabeth Tudor riding down a street of adoring commons."

Hmmm.

"The best we can manage is a procession along the river," Walsingham suggests.

Cecil's eyes widen in alarm.

"You cannot have forgotten last time?"

"It was not last time," Walsingham reminds him. "Her Majesty has been up and down the river a hundred times since. Even past Limehouse."

Cecil thinks.

"I suppose she would be less of a target in a barge than were she in a carriage, or on a horse, dressed as Guinevere. Hatton will be furious but I suppose he might have his mummers and their stages moved to line the river? All along the quays and so on. They might still play for Her Majesty as she passes."

It is a pleasure to unhorse Hatton's plans. He is, as predicted, furious.

"I cannot expect a man of your status to know the meaning of the word *majesty*," he shouts at Walsingham, "but for the future be certain to remember that majesty does not cower!"

"It is not cowering not to wish to dress up as Guinevere, Sir Christopher."

"I will consult Her Majesty!" Hatton shouts. "I will tell her that this change of plan is your idea, and that it is malicious, capricious, and cowardly and the result of your own failures to capture the men who shot at her carriage, nearly a year ago to this day! It is a tribute to your rank incompetence."

He storms out of the room.

There is a long silence. At last Cecil speaks.

"You know he's right, don't you, Francis?"

Walsingham does.

"It is not for lack of effort, I promise, Sir William."

"Well"—Cecil sighs—"we have several days until her birthday. We can make an announcement at Saint Paul's Cross that she is to come upriver . . . when shall we say? Early evening? To catch the tide. More dramatic that way. And perhaps permit one or two fireworks?"

Walsingham reluctantly agrees, as a sop to Hatton, but only from Whitehall.

"So that gives you nearly a week, Francis, to comb every warehouse and dockyard on both banks from the Tower to Westminster, just in case Saelminck is holed up somewhere like last time. Do you think you can manage that? You will have the Yeoman of the Guard at your disposal, of course."

Walsingham thanks him.

"You are a great one for giving a man enough rope, aren't you, Sir William?"

Cecil laughs. His little fat fingers patter across his desk like a spider.

Thanks to Mistress van Teerlinc's limning Walsingham is able to show the Yeomen of the Guard the likeness of the man they must be wary of, and once they have each seen it, he divides them into two companies, a hundred men each, and for the next week they work their way up both banks of the river. On the northern bank, led by Sir John Jeffers, they move from the Custom House on Wool Quay, all the way through the city, including the Steelyard, and down the Strand to Whitehall and then through the houses that line the bank all the way to the Palace of Westminster. Two Yeomen are left every two hundred yards, so as to ensure nothing changes between the search and the passage of the Queen. The same on the southern bank, though this is an altogether muddier affair, for the bank here is given over to fields and pastures, and is perilously marshy, and Francis gives command of this job to Robert Beale, as a punishment. Again, two men every two hundred paces.

There is no sign of Saelminck.

Is that good? Or bad?

Can it be that Dee's discovery of him in the Ludgate gaol has put off some plan of his, and he has returned home to Flanders or wherever he came from?

Who knows?

All Walsingham can do is pray this is so, and he goes to bed on the night before Her Majesty's birthday believing he can do no more.

CHAPTER THIRTY-THREE

Tower of London,
the day of Her Majesty's birthday, September 7, 1578

B ut Walsingham is woken before dawn by a thunderous hammering on his gate. *Nothing good can come from this,* he knows. The night watchman is still with them, and a servant comes running up the stairs carrying a lamp. Walsingham meets him on the landing of his own chamber. Later, he'll remember that he tried to keep the boy from waking his wife and daughters.

"What is it?"

"The Tower, sir! It's the Tower! Broken into, sir! It's been broken *into*!"

"*Into?* Someone has broken *into* the Tower?"

Walsingham wonders if this is some sort of cretinous joke, the sort of thing Leicester would get up to.

"The Constable said you'd want to know right away."

Walsingham is nearly naked.

"All right," he says. "All right."

When he gets to the Tower, the sun is risen enough to see by. A single guard at the Lion Gate, looking . . . what? Odd.

"Where is everybody?" Walsingham asks.

"You tell me, sir."

Walsingham ignores him and enters the inner ward. Ahead is a knot of men, gathered around the wall in which Dee blew a hole. The hole has reappeared, and alongside it, the rocks, prised from the wall.

"Mortar never set, sir," one of the men says. "Told them at the time. I said: it's too fucking cold—begging your pardon—for mortar to set."

"Master Walsingham!" Someone is calling him.

Behind, over by the lodgings of the Master of the Board of Ordnance. The doors to the vaults gape open. Walsingham turns and walks toward him. He feels otherworldly. It is revealing itself to be a beautiful morning. A pink sunrise. Not even the ravens cawing can spoil it. But they don't need to.

"It's gone," the Master says. "All of it."

Oh Christ. Oh Christ.

"And his machine. All the bellows and pipes."

Walsingham can hardly think straight.

"Where— Where were the fucking *guards*?"

The Master looks at him incredulously.

"All along the river, Master Walsingham. As you ordered."

Walsingham steps down into the vault. He cannot believe it. It must be a mistake. Was it put somewhere else, perhaps? But no. The Master shakes his head. He is further along in his process of acceptance than Walsingham. But every barrel that Dee had drawn off from the naft, gone? It is offensive to his eye.

"And he stoppered the last barrel only yesterday, too," the Master says. "Dee. Before taking a barge home, he said, to the comfort of his own bed."

Walsingham turns and trudges back up the ramp and out into the inner ward. He goes back to the hole in the wall. The thieves dropped a couple of beams across the moat, along which they must have rolled the barrels. He steps out through the hole and walks along a beam. The moat is refreshed at high tide, but it is low now. On the other side he sees their tracks in the dust. It has been a dry summer and the grass is brittle. He can follow them, slipping slightly down onto Tower Quay. From there, a boat of course. And from there?

Christ.

Anywhere.

Walsingham stands with his hands on his hips and stares up and down the dimpled length of the Thames. He imagines—what? That he will see the thieves sailing away with his Greek fire? *Stop*, he will shout. *Stop! Come back!*

He feels a type of savage fury. He wants to strangle something. Himself even.

But then, he thinks, *At least now we know why Saelminck lingered in London: to steal the Greek fire. Cecil was a fool to make it known we had it.*

My God. What is he going to tell Cecil? What is he going to tell the Queen?

Let someone else tell them? Or try to control the story?

Oh Christ. Is it too late for that?

He must go and find Cecil. He will be at Whitehall.

Walsingham has no time for a wherry. He will walk. He sets off. At times like this he misses Robert Beale. He imagines Beale misses him, stuck over the river in Rotherhithe. He walks purposefully: Stockfishmonger Row; Thames Street; then over the Fleet on the covered bridge and behind Bridewell Palace onto Fleet Street. He is sweating and muttering to himself as a man out of his wits.

"They will put you in Bedlam, sir!" one of the Yeomen of the Guard calls out.

Fleet Street, Temple Bar, the Strand.

Elsewhere the day has that peculiar stillness that often comes before a big event: as if the place is holding its breath. He cannot describe the umbrage he feels, the personal offense he has taken against the thieves. He feels lost, floating, spinning as a cork in a millstream. What has just happened? Did someone plan to steal the Greek fire back in— When did they rack Jenkinson? January? February? Was it that long ago? Or was this an opportunity seized? He thinks again of the stern bluff of the Tower's curtain walls; its towers; its moat. No, he is suddenly certain: this was a long time in the planning. He thinks of those bloody masons—working away silently, and of how he believed they had fallen under the Tower's oppressive spell. *My God. It was probably Saelminck there himself!* He could have been the foreman, knowing the mortar would never set. It was like keeping a key! And all he needed to do was wait! Wait until the Greek fire was ready and then, just when it was, and Walsingham had reduced the Yeomen of the Guard to a skeleton crew—because he thought Saelminck planned an attack on the Queen—he struck!

Finally he is here, at Whitehall, in a muck sweat.

"Why, Francis," William Cecil greets him. "You look flustered. Is all well?"

Cecil has not heard. He cannot believe it.

"No."

He sits, deboned.

"Gone?"

Walsingham nods. Cecil turns to look out of his window. After a while he turns back.

"Where?"

Where? Spain? France? The Low Countries?

"If I knew, do you not think I would be trying to get it back?"

They decide on a course of immediate action: Send messengers to Edward Clinton, the Lord High Admiral. Instruct him to put to sea every ship at his disposal: they must comb the sea lanes of the Narrow Sea; they must stop and search every ship. They must investigate every cove and inlet on every shore from Lincoln to Dorset, from Brill to La Rochelle. They must not lose that Greek fire. They *cannot* lose that Greek fire. Clinton must send it to the bottom of the sea rather than let it fall into the hands of the Spanish.

"Christ. We should never have kept it in the Tower. We should have kept it in Sheffield, right under Mary, Queen of Scots."

Messages are sent to every constable in Kent and Essex and Suffolk, too: they are to watch the roads as never before. Their searchers must examine every barrel. But for their own sake, do not use lamps or torches.

Christ. Christ. Christ.

"We have to cancel this procession of Her Majesty's. Tell people she is sick."

Cecil looks alarmed.

"It is not only the people who want it, Francis. You will have to tell her she is sick, too."

"We can't let her do it."

Cecil is silent for a moment, stroking his beard.

"Stop it, please, Sir William."

He means the beard. There is no time for this sort of thing.

Cecil stops.

"No, I was only thinking, Francis, that if you believe this Saelminck has stolen your Greek fire—"

"*Your* Greek fire?"

"Our Greek fire, then, then surely, he will have, as you say, set off for Artois or Hainault or wherever we believe he comes from. He will not linger to take a pop at Her Majesty, will he?"

Walsingham stops for a moment. He supposes that is true. If he had managed to steal this magical weapon, then he would not linger to be caught. He would want it home. Cecil pursues the thought.

"It is terrible news, Francis. But we might at least turn it to some advantage, surely? Saelminck is gone, so we may give Her Majesty the birthday she wishes, and then, tomorrow, we can come together and decide what it is we must do. You have secured the banks of the river, haven't you? Made them safe? And so let us, at least, enjoy this day."

Walsingham lets out a long, shaky sigh. He is not so sure. But Cecil is a reassuring figure, and, also, crucially, outranks him.

"Very well," he says. "If you are sure."

Cecil smiles.

"I am." Cecil does his best to laugh. "And it places you further in my debt, Francis, for in canceling your cancelation, I have saved you another lecture from Hatton on the meaning of the word *majesty*."

That is true.

"Majesty does not cower!" Cecil imitates.

"Thank you, Sir William, if only for that."

"My pleasure, Francis. Now go home, change your clothes, and make yourself ready. We will dance, for today at least, and deal with tomorrow as it comes."

"Sufficient unto the day is the evil thereof?"

"Precisely."

Walsingham nods a doubtful thanks and turns to go in search of a wherry downriver.

CHAPTER THIRTY-FOUR

Southwark, south of London,
the day of Her Majesty's birthday, September 7, 1578

Beale knows he is given charge of the south bank of the Thames as a punishment for what he has done, and what he has failed to do, and he knows he will have to accept many more of these sorts of jobs in the future if he is ever to regain Master Walsingham's trust, and so he is busy and ardent about the task, much to the dismay of the Yeomen who had hoped for a few days' rest, and perhaps, even, the chance to dip into Southwark to sample its fleshy delights. His second-in-command is resentful and from the northern parts, a man named Samuelson. He rides at a pace slower than Beale's, and whenever they ride somewhere together, he arrives a moment later than Beale, so that his men are uncertain whom to address. It has not stopped Beale riding up and down the river four or five times a day, from the dismal sludge of Rotherhithe, through Southwark and past the inns that line bankside: the Castle; the Bull; the Hart; the Elephant; the Bear; the Hartshorn; the Barge; the Unicorn; the

Boar's Head; the Cross Keys, and finally the Fleur-de-Lys. Theaters are being built among the bear gardens and the brothels and he has been careful to talk to the men on-site. None admit to knowing of any Jan Saelminck or Henk Poos.

Now it is nearing noon, and there has been nothing of note all morning. The crowds are beginning to gather, but it is supposed most of the interest will be on the other side of the river until the evening, when it will become very busy on this side, where licentiousness will flourish beyond the reach of the city authorities. By then, though, Her Majesty will have passed, and he—Beale—and Samuelson and his Yeomen will be gone about their business elsewhere.

"Some of them fucking playactors are setting up a stage on the bridge," Samuelson tells him. Samuelson has not time for playactors. He really hates them. So though the bridge is not their responsibility, Beale sends Samuelson to have a look, while he himself rides westward, to speak to the sunburned men posted into the fields and marshy inlets farther upriver. It is all quiet, and when he gets back Samuelson smells of drink and is reconciled to playactors.

"They've got George and the fucking dragon," Samuelson tells him. "The dragon'll sit in its cave and then when Saint George comes along, looking for it, it'll come out blowing fire and so on, and George'll cut his fucking head off. Where's the harm in that?"

It does sound pretty good.

"Won't they block the road, though?"

Samuelson shakes his head.

"They're using the frame of the new house going up, the one they've sent over from Holland."

Beale grunts.

"Let's go back," he says. "Look toward Rotherhithe."

CHAPTER THIRTY-FIVE

Whitehall Palace,
the day of Her Majesty's birthday, September 7, 1578

The morning has passed agreeably enough, with a game of cards at which she beat Mistress Parry and won sixpence, but Jane Frommond has concluded that she will ask to retire from court before Christmas. She has no clear idea what she will do, but her father left her a small income, and if she is honest, she is unhealthily bored by this life. Perhaps it was the time spent with Dr. Dee in Sulgrave? She wishes she had traveled, she thinks, as he has. She wishes she'd visited Leuven, Prague, Basel, and Geneva, and she thinks that perhaps now is the time.

But today is Her Majesty's birthday, and there is to be a masque, and dancing, at Westminster Hall, and so she must make her way there, but there are no wherries on the river, since they've been banned by Master Walsingham until the Queen has arrived in her royal barge, and so Jane decides that she will ride, perhaps, and see if she cannot shake off her lassitude that way, and so she makes her way to the stables.

"Hello, Mistress Frommond," the stableboy addresses her.

"John," she remembers. "God give you good day. How are you?"

She has not seen him since the day they rode to Stepney to see the pornographer.

"Fair to middling, mistress. Can't complain. Risen up."

He does look well and is wearing boots, she sees, of stout leather, and a doublet of the Queen's colors. He asks after Dr. Dee, whom he has not seen since that same day.

"I think fair to middling, too," she tells him, though she has not seen Dee since they came down from Sulgrave, so horrified and alarmed. She believed he had gone to Wales, which he claimed he always did every year, to seek King Arthur's treasure, though she was never to admit to anyone that this was what he was up to.

"Are you here for a horse, mistress?"

She is. He finds her the same pony she rode on that time before, and saddles it for her, and holds out his knee to help her up onto the saddle. When she is set she thanks him, and she is about to ride off when he clicks his fingers.

"Oh, miss," he says. "I saw your young gentleman today."

She is at a loss.

"The fellow you showed me the little picture of, all those months ago?"

She feels her hair rise on end.

"You saw Jan Saelminck?"

"If that's his name, miss, then yes."

"Where? Where did you see him?"

"He was on the bridge, just where they're putting up that new house. Didn't recognize him at first, since he was dressed in a funny way, and he was with a load of blokes who sounded a bit off, if you take my meaning?"

"When?"

"First thing this morning."

"By the bridge?"

"North side. Where they are setting up all the stages for Her Majesty's pageant and that."

The pony has picked up on her anxiety and she must walk it around.

"You are certain?"

"Well, no. But I saw him and I could've sworn I knew him, and then I remembered he was the one ambling around the yard that time, just after . . . just after my old man got himself shot? I helped you with Mistress Rutherford's coffer, and you showed me the limning, remember?"

She does, vividly.

"You did not . . . tell me you had seen him in the yard?"

"Ah. Well. He— To be honest miss, he gave a shilling not to mention him. It is why I remembered him. I'm sorry. I was that hard up."

She wonders how much trouble that might have saved. It is incalculable.

"Right," she says, "I must go."

"You'll bring her back?"

He means the horse, but Frommond is gone, out onto the Strand, riding as fast as the traffic on the thronged road will permit, eastward toward Ludgate. The streets are very crowded, with all sorts drifting idly toward the riverbank. Dozens of vendors and hawkers are out, praising their wares, and someone has managed to drive a last flock of sheep across the bridge and is driving them up to Smithfield. She wishes she had brought John to shout out, to

get people to clear the way, to mind their backs. W
people laugh.

Past Fleet Bridge, through Ludgate, past S
then along Cheapside. The crowds toward the br
already, and various companies of players are alr
their makeshift stages along the wayside. She cont

"Master Walsingham's house?"

"Just along there, dear."

She turns up into Seething Lane.

The porter is there, eating a pie.

"Tell him it is Jane Frommond. Tell him I h
Saelminck."

CHAPTER THIRTY-SIX

Greenwich Palace, east of London,
the day of Her Majesty's birthday, September 7, 1578

Dee has become wary of barges, so today he rents a horse and rides through the fields and commons to Green-ich, with Francis the lurcher at the horse's heels. It is a straight ne east, and they arrive a little after noon. On the way he tells ancis how he will endeavor to sell Frobisher's ore—more operly Walsingham's ore—for as much as five thousand ounds.

"I will make fifteen hundred pounds, Francis! Imagine what I n do with that? I will first repay all my—some of my—debts, and en I shall set about buying the rest of the books I need."

He has forced himself not to acknowledge that this is theft, d that in assisting de Lannoy he is become a thief, but instead is inking of owning Petrus Bonus's *Introductio in Divinam Chem-e Artem Integra* and Gildas's *De Calamitate Excidio, et Conquestu itanniae,* and Sebastian Münster's *Canones Super Novum Instru-*

mentum Luminarium for a start. These will be expensive and difficult to find, but worth it, he thinks, even if he has nothing left over.
If he does have something left over, well then, he will get at least
Giulio Cesare Scaligero's, *Exotericarum exercitationum*, which is
reply to Girolamo Cardano's encyclopaedic work *De Subtilitate*
and concerns the hidden nature of angels. He would also like to
buy something for Jane Frommond. He wonders about approach-
ing Points Hilliard.

Dee has not been to Greenwich Palace for perhaps five years,
but he has strong memories of its mirrored library, and the lawns
and gardens that sweep down to the decorative wooden wharf and
the river beyond. Today those lawns are covered in tents, of the
sort someone imagines King Arthur might sally from to joust with
Sir Tristan or Sir Lancelot or any of those other fools, and there
is a milling crowd of courtiers and their servants, waiting to greet
Her Majesty, and be with her at her side as she progresses up the
Thames to Westminster.

Dee feels very out of place among the extravagantly dressed
lords and their ladies, who fill the lawn in their taffetas and silks,
in vermilion and peacock blue, with each side seam beaded with
pearls, bright feathers nodding in wonderfully pointed hats, the
name of which he has temporarily forgotten—hennins, that is
it—as worn by Guinevere and her ladies, while he has more or less
come straight from his bed.

But he has had a long week of it, he thinks, first distilling the
naft to extract that top layer to provide the essence of Greek fire,
and then combining it with all the other ingredients, and finally
barreling the results and stowing them in the vaults. It has been
nasty, smelly work that has left him stained, strained, and somewhat breathless, and he got home so late last night that he might
as well have stayed in the Tower. He certainly looks as if he did:

dusty doublet, frayed breeches, and a worn scholars' cap. His boots are rather fine, it is true, but he wishes he had a sword like all the other men.

He wonders where Jane Frommond is, but before he can find her, there is a trumpet fanfare, and a great swirling reordering of the crowd as the Queen emerges from her palace to be admired by her assembled courtiers, and seeing her, Dee cannot help feel a twinge of autumnal sadness over the fate of Ness Overbury, and he wonders once again why anyone ever thought that Robert Beale's intrigue would end even half as well as it has.

Today Her Majesty is in pale silks, much roped about with pearls and studded in diamonds, and she is accompanied by Sir Christopher Hatton, who is very nearly her match for finery, in silver cloth of gold and vermilion velvet, dressed so that if you look at him with your eyes half closed, you might believe him to be in harness, as worn by King Arthur, had he lived just a hundred years ago. Courtiers bow before her.

"Your Majesty."

"Your Majesty."

But she passes them with a fixed absent smile, her eyes boring into Dee, and comes to a stop before him.

"John Dee," she says.

"B—"

"Don't."

"Your Majesty," he says and bends to kiss the proffered hand. Hatton looks at him and rounds his eyes, as if he has some message to impart. Dee feels a warm flush of mixed pleasure and pain. *The ore! He still wants the ore!*

"You look very smart, John, for our birthday."

"I have come as King Arthur," he tells her, "before he pulls the sword from the stone."

"He was a boy," Hatton says. "Not a dong farmer."

"So he was."

"But we are given to understand that you have been laboring on our behalf, anyway, John?"

She means: you certainly look as if you have.

"And it has been a pleasure," he lies. "As always."

"And so as a token of our appreciation, in a contravention of the usual practice, we gift you this, on our birthday."

She signals to a servant, who steps forward with a silver tray on which sits a familiar bundle of cloth: the scrying stone.

"You are too kind, Your Majesty."

He had hoped it would be a sword, or a new doublet. Still. He takes it up in both hands.

"It once belonged to Nostradamus," Hatton informs him. "And is of incalculable value."

Dee says nothing. Nor does the Queen. She smiles faintly. He is pleased to have it back in any event and bows in gratitude. He will have to return it to Bowes the goldsmith of course.

"Are you still suffering dreams of fire?" he asks her.

She admits she is.

"But that is because all your Greek fire has been stolen," Hatton snarls theatrically, "from right under Master Walsingham's nose!"

Dee steps back. Nearly treads on Francis, who yelps.

"Stolen?"

"Along with your apparatus for shooting it at our enemy."

"Th-th-that is . . . bad," Dee stammers.

Christ!

"Who by?" he wonders. "And how?"

"Her Majesty's enemies. They broke into the Tower through the hole you blew in the curtain wall," Hatton says.

"We are most displeased," the Queen adds. He can see her eyeing the scrying stone as if to take it back. He puts it behind his back.

"That was an accident," he says. "And I believed it had been repaired."

"Not well enough, apparently."

Well, that is not his fault, of course.

Elizabeth moves on. Dee finds a drink. He thinks about the Greek fire. He tries to think what its loss might mean. If the Spanish get hold of it, then they will reproduce it a hundredfold and burn Protestant Europe off the map. He can picture Leuven in flames, all those bodies; all those books—carbon black, blistered, the stink of roasting flesh and burning paper. *Christ.* He can see the Inquisition torching cities indiscriminately, locking the city gates and murdering everyone within, destroying everything. *Christ*, he thinks, *I have created a terrible, terrible thing. I have created Death.*

We must get it back, he resolves. *We must destroy it.*

He hurries to the river's edge where a line of barges is moored to the wharf, each swagged with lengths of linen so that they look like, well, he is not certain. Less like barges. Her Majesty's is at the back and has had its cabin removed and replaced with an old-fashioned tent, painted with the Queen's arms, in which she is to sit, presumably, as if in a glade, waiting for her questing knight.

"Where is Walsingham?" he asks one of the bargemen.

"Stayed in the city," he's told. "Only sent his wife and children."

Christ.

"When are we leaving?" he asks. The man looks at the tide. It is still rising. But they will need to time it right if they are to take the barges upriver and through the bridge: too early and it will be dangerous; too late, and it will be impossible.

"Have to be soon," the man says.

Dee paces.

"Come on, come on."

The shadows shift across the grass, the tide rises. It will be another hour, Dee supposes, and then there will come the moment when the water level is the same height on both sides of the bridge, and boats swing free on their moorings. After that the tide will turn, and run out, and the water on the inland side of the bridge will begin its twice daily buildup, and surge through its arches, and all the moored boats will turn their bows upriver to face the river's flow.

He is standing there when Hatton comes, trailed at a discreet distance by guards and servants.

"Dee," Hatton greets him. "Before we proceed to Westminster, I want to fix a final price for that ore."

Now is not the time, Dee thinks. News of the Greek fire's theft has driven away all pleasure in supposing himself a rich man. The titles of the books he was going to buy are forgotten. It gives him, he supposes, an edge in the negotiation. But the truth is, now it has come to naming sums and figures, he balks at the thought of perpetrating this swindle on Hatton. It will make him no better than de Lannoy. It will make him a fraud.

"Oh, I don't know, Hatton. I am not sure I want to sell it. As you say, if your man de Lannoy can get gold out of it, then why can't I?"

Hatton tenses.

"Do you know what your problem is, Dee?"

Dee is all ears.

"Your problem is that you are a third-rate alchemist, puffed up with pride and the sweet-talking blandishments of Cecil and Walsingham to believe yourself first-rate. You are a commoner masquerading as a gentleman, and there is nothing worse than that. You should step aside. Admit you are a failure and let your betters do better."

Dee could kiss him.

"Very well, Sir Christopher," he says. "You are right. Thank you for that lesson in proper humility. It is time I learned my place. So I will let you have it for—what?—fifty pounds a ton."

Even as he says it, he laughs. That is a vast sum of money. Hatton flinches. Dee is careless, really. This is not the time to be worrying about money, about alchemy. Something much more serious is unfolding. Nevertheless, that same slippery look comes into Hatton's eye as before, when Dee told him about Saelminck being in Ludgate. *Christ, he is going to accept it! De Lannoy must have persuaded him he could make him an absolute fortune!*

And he does.

"Fifty pounds a ton, Dee. Not a penny more."

Despite everything, Dee cannot help but grin. He extends his hand to shake and after a moment's hesitation, as if he risks contagion, Hatton takes it. His hand is wonderfully smooth.

"I will kick myself in the morning, Sir Christopher," he says. "And again when I see you plying the river on a golden barge."

Hatton laughs with pleasure at the thought.

"Let us not get ahead of ourselves, Doctor. There is many a slip between cup and lip."

"Quite so," Dee agrees.

"I will need a week to raise the gold," Hatton goes on, "and we may complete the exchange in the days subsequent thereafter."

Subsequent thereafter! Hatton is pretending to have done this sort of thing before. Dee nods. Just then a signal is made, another trumpet fanfare, some pompous shouting, and the crowd of courtiers moves toward the barges. Dee is assigned a place in the second to last, with Her Majesty's beautiful barge coming last, as the climax of the procession. Dee sits on a bench at the front of the cabin, behind the eight beefy oarsmen, with Francis curled under his feet, next to a man who—he stops listening after he mentions land in Shropshire. *These people*, he thinks. *At least he has a sword though.*

Come on. Come on.

Eventually—it seems—the barges are cast off, and out into the current. There are buglers in one who begin their fanfare as they round the bend past Limehouse, and Dee cannot help but peer over to see the house where the marksman Hamilton tried to shoot the Queen that first time. He cranes his head to see if the Queen points it out to Hatton: she does, and despite everything, he—Dee—is pleased.

But that was then. This is now.

CHAPTER THIRTY-SEVEN

Southwark, City of London,
the day of Her Majesty's birthday, September 7, 1578

There is nothing of any interest in Rotherhithe save mud and midges, and the threat of bestial violence, and now Samuelson's bonhomie has worn off and he is become wearingly fierce about the makeshift stages that line the shore. He would pull them all down if he could and throw their occupants in Bridewell, or worse.

"Shit, that is. How is she going to see that? Fucking playactors. Titting about like twats."

A walled-eyed woman from Kent tries to give him some flowers and he barks at her.

"Let's go back and see Saint George chop that fucking dragon's head off."

Beale thinks: *Christ, why not?*

They walk back along the shore, stopping to peer over their shoulders as the first of the barges in the procession appear around the headland. It is full of trumpeters.

"Bastards," Samuelson offers. "Blowing their horns while other fuckers do all the work. Tide's on the fucking turn, too. Rowing against it'll only get harder."

Beale and Samuelson make their way back past all the breweries and into Southwark and turn up the road toward the bridge. The drawbridge is lowered, of course, and across it is the framework of beams for the house that has been brought over from the Low Countries, which is to be made with treenails and thought to be such a marvel that it is already being called Nonsuch House, in that there is nonesuch in all the world to match it. Today, though, a broad floor of planks has been cunningly constructed in what may be the future servants' wing, raised up above head height on the west-facing side of the bridge.

"That didn't go up this morning?" Beale asks. It looks very solid.

"The chippies who've been working on the house made it," Samuelson tells him. "Do for a scaffold, wouldn't it?"

He mimes a beheading. Behind it is a cloth backdrop on which is painted a simple but effective landscape of sky and distant hills, and in the foreground some gray lumps that are intended to be rocks or boulders perhaps, and on the stage, before these rocks is placed a tent, likewise painted rock gray, in which is an aperture to represent a cave, from which, it is presumed, will emerge—when Her Majesty's barge comes into view—the dragon. A man in cloth armor, complete with a cloth helm, stands in the forefront of the stage, being mock-heroic and shouting that he is George of England, come to rid the world of a terrible dragon and asking the crowd that is gathered there whether they have seen it. Behind him, through various apertures in the back cloth, a painted dragon on a stick is stuck, bright red, and steadily getting larger, and the crowd cries out that the dragon is behind him, and he whips around to find it gone. Beale can see that everyone there is enjoying themselves, though, of course, it goes on for too long, because the physical dragon—who is probably hidden in the cave—must time his appearance with the arrival of Her Majesty's barge in the river below.

Beale fights his way through the crowd to the east side of the bridge and peers over heads and shoulders down the length of the river toward the Tower, where the mass of barges—perhaps twenty of them—are now rowing with the wavering tide in a broad arrowhead, with the Queen's barge coming last.

"Where is the dragon?" cries the actor onstage, swishing his sword. "Has anyone seen my dragon?"

"Behind you!" the crowd roars.

It is only then that Beale wonders how Her Majesty will ever be able to see the performance, if the stage is set on the west side of the bridge, facing west, while she is coming from the east? They must know she will never turn around to watch it, mustn't they?

Then why?

CHAPTER THIRTY-EIGHT

City of London,
the day of Her Majesty's birthday, September 7, 1578

Dee has so offended the minor lord from Shropshire that he is no longer being spoken to, and he prefers it that way, sitting mute, hearing the bells and watching the Tower come into view with Francis asleep under his feet, even though they—the feet—are jiggling with impatience. "Come on. Come on," he keeps whispering. He needs to be back. He needs to find Walsingham.

He has the scrying stone cupped in his hands. He cannot stop glancing down at it, and whenever he does, he experiences the strange sensation of having something drawn out of him, or up in him, from some depths. It is both physical and spiritual, a sort of summoning forth, but just when he thinks whatever is being summoned forth will come forth, the feeling dies, and he is left staring at a shiny stone. It seems as if he cannot commit completely, or he cannot get the stone to commit completely. He is on the outside of something, among its outer rings, he feels, but of what? What lies at the center? Perhaps a barge, surrounded by fools, is not the ideal place for the stone's effective use.

The oarsmen's blades flash in the late-afternoon sunshine and the shadow of the helmsman is long on the water behind the barge. He is a fine old fellow, Dee supposes—the helmsman—with a silver beard trimmed close, and he stands tall and erect, proud of his barge, and of his oarsmen who sweat away, but in the pink-flushed sunlight he cannot restrain himself casting anxious glances at the water's surface, where white rose petals float, scattered there for the Queen's arrival, and then back at the Queen's barge, which seems to be lagging behind. The sun is already low in the sky, shining in Dee's eyes as they round the foreland of Rotherhithe and slide toward the bulk of the Tower. Seeing it from this angle, he can see what he missed before: the hole he blew in its wall, magically reappeared. He feels a twist of guilt. What a fool he was. But it really was an accident, sort of.

From there on the crowds thicken along the wharves and quays that line both banks, and their cheering and shouting is heartening to hear, until the church bells drown it out with their peals. People on the boat start waving back, and Francis wakes up and starts barking, but Dee remains fixed. He sees things moving in the scrying stone. But then he stops and laughs. *Christ.* He is going mad. What he can see are the clouds above, reflected in the stone. He can see his own reflection if he holds it so. What a fool.

He looks up and about, and the helmsman is looking more concerned than ever. He keeps turning back to Her Majesty's boat, which lags farther behind, and Dee can see Her Majesty is wanting to slow it down so that she can see some of the vignettes that the mummers and the playactors have put on for her on the Rotherhithe shore. Were he, instead of Hatton, on the royal barge he would remind her that time and tide wait for no man, not even the Queen of England, and that if they are not through the bridge before the tide turns, she will miss her own procession. Dee feels a lurch of guilt when he thinks of Hatton, but really. What a fool. He hopes Hatton's innards are being pickled by anxiety: she will blame him if she is too late.

CHAPTER THIRTY-NINE

City of London,
the day of Her Majesty's birthday, September 7, 1578

Walsingham and Frommond find Sir John Jeffers standing in the sun on the steps of Saint Magnus the Martyr. "Bring your men. As many as are to hand."

Jeffers throws aside the cornet of strawberries he has bought and starts shouting and waving at the Yeomen who are gathered in knots nearby, staring downstream at the oncoming flotilla. They leave off and gather about Walsingham at the mouth of the bridge; they are young, bovine, well-armed and in most other circumstances, they'd be reassuring. Walsingham tells them that Saelminck has been seen this day.

"I believe he has some terrible thing planned for Her Majesty."

"She is coming now!" Jeffers says. "Look! Her barge!"

Quickly then.

Walsingham tells Frommond to wait there, but she won't.

He does not bother arguing. Her Majesty is his concern, not

Frommond. The Yeomen clear a path with their halberds, pushing and shoving and hoiking people aside. They enter into the tight confines of the bridge, darkened by overhanging buildings, and enclosed all around, the air is warm and moist and filled with midges and strong smells.

"What are we looking for, Master Walsingham?" Jeffers asks.

"I don't know," he admits. "Check any barrels you see."

Jeffers flinches.

"He's got the *Greek fire*?"

"Shhh."

Walsingham does not want the crowd panicking any more than they are by the sight, sounds, and feel of a dozen Yeomen beating a path through them. It is all small houses and shops and people packed in to see what they can. There doesn't seem to be anything especially odd or unusual or anything that shouldn't happen on a day such as this. Ahead it is brighter.

Someone has erected a stage just above head height in the frame of the new house being built, one of the new companies of playactors. Leicester has a company; the Lord High Admiral, too. Walsingham does not know who these fellows are. He supposes they must have a license, though who would have checked that? Not Beale, nor Jeffers. One of the actors is dressed as a knight of old, and swipes around a sword, making a fool of himself for laughs. The backdrop is of sky and rock and every now and then an unseen hand pokes a red dragon through and the— Well, it is what it is.

Then he sees Beale. He is peering over heads, looking eastward downriver toward where Her Majesty comes, with his back to the stage. He turns when he hears the fuss the Yeomen are causing. The knight on the stage, too, becomes distracted, and for a moment he stops playing his part.

At that moment the dragon emerges from the cave, a great red thing of cloth scales that should clank, but it is made of cloth, and it waggles its head to and fro, and the crowd gasp and cringe in delighted fright, and Walsingham can see the man's legs underneath, and see that he is holding the head on what might be the stand for an arquebus. The knight roars in fright, and pretends to flee, and the dragon pursues him across the stage, long tail twisting behind, and everyone laughs and jeers.

Beale has seen Walsingham across the crowd and touches his cap. He is looking puzzled.

Walsingham stands stock-still.

Christ! What is that smell?

CHAPTER FORTY

River Thames, east of London,
the day of Her Majesty's birthday, September 7, 1578

The oarsmen are pulling with real purpose now, and green river water is splashed over the guests' finery, but the oarsmen on the Queen's barge have pulled even harder and have brought her barge back in line, ten yards behind Dee's barge, but it may yet be too late. The tide has turned already. Rose petals on the river's surface have made up their minds and are flowing out to sea. The bridge is fifty yards ahead, thronged with people. Dee thinks he would have cleared them. *What if someone drops*—he worries—*a snake on Her Majesty?*

The bargemaster is leading them through the central arch, under the house that's being built by carpenters from the Low Countries. Dee tries to remember what had been said by the man taking down the old one, the day he rode across it with Frommond, before they were locked in the barge. *Skillful little fuckers.* It made him laugh, then.

The oarsmen pull harder still against the tide now, and the barge is suddenly clumsier than ever. You can feel the life go out of her, as if the bargemaster might be trying to steer a brick. Ordinarily this would not matter, oarsmen can row against the current, of course, but not through the bridge, where even the widest arch is not wide enough to permit a barge *and* its outspread oars, and also, because the starlings on which the arches stand are so broad, the river is pinched to almost half its width, and even at a moment when the tide is hovering between wax and wane, the water comes through at twice its normal speed. The only way to do it is for the oarsmen to dip and pull as fast as they can and, then, just as the barge enters the arch, they must draw in their oars and pray they have done enough: that the barge has enough impetus to slide under the bridge and out the other side, where they can once more extend their oars and start to pull again.

Dee is willing them on. He can see the oars bending with the strain and the oarsmen are taut with the effort. The bargemaster's hand is on the tiller. The barge seems to leap and then seems to stop, leap and then stop. The river flow is high. It must have rained in Somerset.

"Now!" the bargemaster bellows, and the oarsmen thrust their oars to one side, and the blades tuck in against the side of the barge as it slides into the shadow of the bridge and then into the central arch. The boat drifts, wavering in the increased flow against its bow, and it is at this moment that Dee looks down to check on Francis and seeing him unconcerned, he is about to look up again, to study the underside of the structure of the bridge, when he finds himself looking into the scrying stone, and at last, in this moment of curious crisis during which his emotions are heightened, he makes a connection with what the spirits have been trying to tell him since he was in that room in Whitehall Palace.

But what he sees is nothing angelic, or heavenly; he sees a face leering up at him, a man in visored helmet, such as knights wore to battle in his grandparents' time, though the visor is raised, and the face . . . the face is like a gargoyle, as you see at the corners of ca-thedral roofs, and he realizes it is just that, a gargoyle leering down at him, and that the barge has slipped from under the bridge, and that the oarsmen have done it, and that what he is seeing is not a reflection of a hidden world beyond man's comprehension, but a reflection of reality: a man really is leering over the edge of the bridge and he really is wearing an old-fashioned helmet, and the man is—*Saelminck*?

And at that moment he hears the noise: ten swans, choppy water.

He whirls around and sees something he never believed existed out of old wives' tales: a dragon, ugly, clumsy, red-painted, with dead eyes, but an open mouth and from it—he knows it for what it is—the nozzle of his contraption for shooting the Greek fire, and he can hear the swans' wings becoming louder and faster, and he sees that devil bead, the mouth of the nozzle, with its clever little flame that he spent so long developing, lit, and he can imagine the bladder in the barrel rapidly filling as the air is pumped in, and he knows that any moment the Greek fire will spurt from the hose, catch the flame, and drench him and the whole barge with boiling, inextinguishable lava.

He is on his feet even before the stern of the barge is hardly out from under the bridge. He wastes not a movement. Not a moment. He fells the bargemaster with a single blow and wrenches the tiller to the right. The rudder swings to the left. The barge turns sluggishly, but then the current catches it, and spins it in the river, so that it lies across the current. Everybody in the barge shouts in rage, especially the oarsmen, who face the bargemaster and see what Dee has done. But the current catches the barge and drives it back toward the bridge and they stagger and must look to hanging on before they can think of rescuing the barge from the madman who has seized its tiller. By then the barge hits the first stone-built starling, and then swings across to hit another. It is caught, jammed by water pressure between the two of them, blocking the arch. The water banks up against it, tipping it so that everyone on board must grab a new handhold, but it does not roll entirely. Everybody bellows or screams in fright.

The man from Shropshire catches Francis the lurcher, and Dee forgives him everything before he turns to look down the arch. The Queen's barge is framed by the underside of the bridge as it comes sliding into that central arch, its gilded prow aimed right at him. Behind him, upriver, Dee hears the woof of the stream of Greek fire catching light as the swans take flight. There is much new screaming. He feels the heat at his back. The roof of the arch flickers orange. He stands in the middle of his barge now, facing down the arch to where the Queen's boat drifts toward him, her oarsmen repeating the trick of laying their blades down. Dee has found the boat hook. As the Queen's barge comes on, losing momentum now, he slams the boat hook into the barge's gilded prow and tries to push it back, to stop its glide. Still everyone is screaming behind him and now the oarsmen in the Queen's barge are turning as if they have been attacked, but as they stand to come at him, they see the fire, spreading across the river beyond the bridge behind him. They stand amazed, confused, horrified. Dee clings onto the boat hook, pushing the Queen's barge back, stopping it coming farther, and then, in the reduced current, having to hold on to it for dear life as the Queen's barge falters, and then starts to slip away, and back out downriver. He must keep it under the width of the bridge. He must keep it safe. He must keep *her* safe.

CHAPTER FORTY-ONE

London Bridge,
the day of Her Majesty's birthday, September 7, 1578

The noise comes from within the cloth cave, or maybe from under the skirted stage, a great flapping and banging, and every man stands sore amazed, and startled, and the only movement is onstage, where Saint George has wrenched a length of what looks like a huge fat worm from the cloth cave and stands with the dragon holding it so that its curious brass nozzle points out over the river, and points it down, into the water, when suddenly it spurts into flame with a meaty woof, and there is a strong and hellish stink, and a pall of black smoke that blows back across the bridge to make everyone choke. Jane Frommond can feel the heat.

Walsingham knows what it is. So does Beale. They are up onto the stage, but as they do so, three men tear down the backdrop, and unlike Saint George, they have real swords and come at Walsingham and Beale, driving them back for a moment and there is that terrifying sound of steel ringing and sliding on steel. They exchange swipes and the three men drive the two back, but then the two are reinforced by two or three Yeomen with their halberds. The three should turn and run, but they do not. They are joined by three others, and they prepare to sell their lives dear.

"For God's sake, stop the fire!" Walsingham shouts at the Yeoman Frommond recognizes as Jeffers.

Jeffers is nonplussed. Frommond remembers Dee's description: bellows; hose; barrel; hose; nozzle; fire. She ducks under the stage. This is where the thundering noise comes from and in the semidarkness she makes out four men, hard at work on the bellows. They see her, but do not stop. What can a woman do? Especially one with no sword or gun. She doesn't even carry an eating knife. She grips the first length of hose in both hands. It is rigid, and made of greasy leather, double-walled and so full of forced air that she cannot bend it to pinch it shut. It snakes across to a barrel behind the stage, which is almost as tall as she. From there, the other hose, almost as thick, just as rigid, leads up to Saint George, who stands on the parapet of the bridge, still trying to tip the mechanism down so that he shoots the fire on something below, but the mechanism will not budge, and the fire squirts out into the river. Inches above Frommond's head, the stage reverberates under the stamping and scuffling of the fighting men. She ducks and makes her way to Saint George. She has a hairpin. Two of them. She is bent double and must fiddle her skirts through the struts of the new building and of the stage, but she gets there, and finds herself standing below him; his calves are at eye level, and he stands with his heels to her.

She looks up. Seeing her movement, he glances down.

It is him. Saelminck. The man who seduced, ruined, and then murdered Alice Rutherford. The man who caused Frommond's near death in the barge. They stare at each other. His eyes are watery blue, almost impossibly cold. In his hands is the leather hose, and from its nozzle a few feet away spurts molten fire. In her hands: two silver hairpins. Each is six inches long, each as thick as a poor woman's knitting needle, but each as sharp as a rich man's dagger. She holds them in her fists as you would the bars of a window in gaol. And then turns her fists sideways, and she rams the pins into Saelminck's calves.

He screams and flails. He drops the hose, and the nozzle springs into a life of its own, shooting fire out over the river in snaking curves. He tries to reach the pins in his legs, but as he dances on the parapet Frommond bats at him, and shoves his feet, and he loses his footing and his legs go out from under him. He lands heavily on the parapet but still manages to turn and grab her shoulders as he does; he clings on and tries to haul himself back, using her. They are howling face to howling face as she tries to wrench herself from his grasp. He has twice her strength. He claws at her and would bite her if he could. She pulls herself from him, twisting and writhing. Saelminck's legs still hang over the edge of the bridge, but now the Greek fire is running out. The barrel is empty, and Dee's design is not perfect, and when the liquid fire slows to a dribble, it drips down onto Saelminck's legs, and sets them flaming.

With a snarling scream, he arches backward, calculating in his agony that he must get to water, and she who had been pushing him now finds him pulling her, and with his grip like a vise on her arms he pulls her back with him, and she can do nothing to stop herself smashing against the parapet and toppling over, following him into the river below.

CHAPTER FORTY-TWO

London Bridge,
the day of Her Majesty's birthday, September 7, 1578

Dee sees the two bodies fall. A man and a woman. They hit the bottom of the half-turned barge, and they glance off it and vanish into the sea of flames that swirls through the arches either side of that which the barge has blocked. The fiery slick piles up against the barge's gunwale, threatening to spill over, but it doesn't quite: it parts, and flows around it, and slides down through the arches on either side. Everyone in the barge has been thrown to one side, and they are trying to untangle themselves from oars and other bodies, and Francis is there, barking and barking, and the bargemaster is coming around, too. A couple of the oarsmen have clambered onto the starlings, and they are retreating along them, inching past Her Majesty's barge.

Dee sees a flash of something burning under the water, under the archway, and then it's gone, downstream under the Queen's barge.

"Get out!" he shouts to those still in the barge. "Get out!"

He is sure the barge will soon go up in flames.

But then his mind catches up with his eye, and he knows what he has just seen: a man and a woman falling. Frommond.

"Take this!" he shouts at the bargemaster, who has roused himself and seen what is happening. He takes the boat hook and shouts to the oarsmen to tie the Queen's boat up to the starling. Dee leaps onto the bow of the Queen's barge, pushing aside more oarsmen as he hurtles its length. He jumps up onto the gunwale and his head hits the underside of the bridge. He carries on. Hatton looms before him.

"What the devil—"

Dee does not linger, but shoves him aside. He meets the Queen's eyes. She's sitting in her tent, frozen, watchful.

"Bess," he says, and keeps running.

The royal bargemaster is an old man, Sir Someone Someone, and he stands mute and immobile as Dee scrambles toward him and seizes a long loop of the red rope that is twisted especially for the queen's barge, and he dives headlong into the water, with the red rope trailing behind.

The water is murky, and tumbling, and for a moment he can see nothing. But Frommond is in pale silk—underwater it is the color of a fish's belly—and he sees her thrashing to escape the clutches of a man whose legs, even below the surface, are burning. Ever since he was forced to pluck Gerardus Mercator from a canal after breaking through thin ice while skating—this was before he was famous—Dee has thought about swimming, and the mechanics of fish, and of dolphins in particular, which he has never seen, but of which he has read much, and he has, away from the water, developed his own theory of swimming, which he now puts into practice for the first time.

It works, sort of, and he lays hands on Frommond just before the red rope runs out, and he gets an arm around her waist and holds her fast while the rope tightens around his left arm and then stretches as they are dragged downstream by the river. Then the rope stops him. He stops her. The burning man scrabbles to cling on, and she fights him off, wriggling and twisting, and all Dee can do is hold tight. Frommond fights and bites and kicks at the burning man, and at last she tears herself from his grasp, and though he lashes to stay with them, he cannot. He thrashes in the water, desperately swimming upstream, desperate to hold on, but the current is too strong, and after a moment he fades into the darkness downriver. Frommond makes a panicked lunge for the surface, and air, but Dee pulls her down: the water above is still puckered by orange flame, its surface corrupted by Greek fire. If they put their heads up there, now, their flesh will be burned from their skulls.

Dee must haul on the rope. With one arm he heaves and twists, so that the rope wraps itself around his arm, each time he moves a little farther upstream, a little farther from the confluence of burning rivers above.

At last, when he can stand it not another moment, he allows the rope to bring them up, and they surface together into hot scorching foul air. But it is not liquid flame. It is not Greek fire. They suck the stinking, foul air down as if it were ambrosia. After a while each looks around, and they are curtained by flames that burn on the river's surface as it drifts away downstream and out to sea.

Frommond clings to him, and he holds her tight. When the flames are gone, the water seems to smoke for a while, and then it passes, just as if it has never been.

A moment later they hear a scream of pure lasting agony from downstream.

"Saelminck?" he asks.

"Saelminck," she says.

"Strange," Dee says. "I did not have him down as a hothead."

"Oh Christ, Dee."

CHAPTER FORTY-THREE

Westminster Palace, west of London,
the day of Her Majesty's birthday, September 7, 1578

It is late in the evening—a fine one, thankfully—and Francis
Walsingham stands apart from the others under the stars and
watches the last of Hatton's fireworks shimmer in the night over
the river, wondering if Her Majesty has not had quite enough
pyrotechnics for one day. When they are done—astonishing, yes,
but also strangely frustrating—there is to be more dancing, and
more wine, but while in most hearts the relief of Her Majesty's
miraculous deliverance from the Greek fire has given way to wild
rapture, he finds himself in a mood that might loosely be described
as melancholic.

Perhaps it is because although everybody else is wildly
jubilant—the Queen lives! Her enemies are vanquished! Let us
have another drink! Another dance! Another kiss!—he cannot
share their joy because it seems that all his efforts over the last several years have been to leave him precisely where he was before this

year's events, save the Spanish are ever closer to taking the entirety of the Low Countries, and he has to admit—again—that if it were not for Dr. Dee, Her Majesty the Queen would now be dead.

That being so, he has to admit yet again that Hatton is right: he, Walsingham, has failed. He has failed his country, and his Queen. He cannot do so again. He tries to imagine what the Queen's father would have done to him if he had failed him as he has failed his daughter?

A shudder passes through him, and it is not because of the cold.

But this can't go on, he thinks. They cannot just go on like this, waiting for the enemy to come at them. They cannot just go on waiting to lose. They must change their tack. Perhaps it is time to follow Dee's advice. Perhaps it is time to listen to him and let him have his head. Perhaps he deserves that.

And he sees him now, Dr. Dee, in the Presence Room, the center of everyone's attention, even Her Majesty's, though he does not look as if he is enjoying it. He is nodding and smiling, but his gaze is drifting off elsewhere, looking for an escape perhaps, or, Walsingham must suppose, Jane Frommond. He knows Dee and knows how little the treacly drivel that courtiers serve up as flattery will mean to him, and he supposes that he, too, would rather pass a quiet hour or two with Mistress Frommond than endure the beady, calculating attentions of women such as Lettice Knollys. It is all fans, arch looks, and point-scoring. Dee is starting to look exquisitely uncomfortable, but at that moment, the music starts, and the dancers must take their places, and Dee looks up suddenly, and sees something—or someone—that sets an alarm bell to ringing. He moves with a curious flowing speed, and Walsingham turns to follow his trail and, through the windows, he watches Dee appear as if by magic at Mistress Frommond's side just as, with great swagger, Sir Christopher Hatton presents himself to the unfortunate girl with a predatory glint in his eye. Mistress Frommond's face when she sees Dee brings light to the room. Walsingham finds himself smiling despite himself, alone in the dark, and he stands and watches a moment. Then they start the galliard.

"Oh my God," he murmurs.

He watches as Dee disassembles the dance, removing from it all its habitual grace, and rearranges it in a strange and wonderful new form that he might describe as inimitable save as he watches, others start to join in, and the dance is transformed from a staid forward-and-back into something that is both riotous and joyous; a curious celebration of what it is to be alive; a strange sort of thanksgiving to God for all his benevolences. It makes him smile a deeper smile, though, my God, there is only so much he can stand to watch before it becomes concerning.

He hears a plate smash.

And a moment later, when he does not believe he can take any more, there is a voice from behind.

"Master Walsingham, sir?"

It is a Yeoman, come for him, sent by Her Majesty, who has retired to her private rooms for a short while and wishes to see him alone. He knew it would come: the summons. The postmortem. What he did. What he didn't do. If she knows about Ness Overbury, then this may be his last night on earth.

When he is brought before Elizabeth, he finds she is looking tired, and thoughtful, as well she might after the day she has had, and her diadem is placed on the table next to her chair, as if it were a normal hat that pinches, not an array of near-priceless jewels. There is a fire in the grate, a few candles dotted around, and she is drinking a cup of warm wine, mixed with ginger and verjuice.

"Not very nice," she tells him. "Have some."

He thanks her, and a servant pours him a cup. She is right.

She is silent for a while, gazing on the flames.

"So, Francis," she says. "Here we are again. Alive, by the skin of my teeth, and again it seems we have Dr. Dee to thank once more."

A week or so earlier and it would have pained Walsingham to admit that this may be so. Now he nods.

"Have you seen his dancing?" he wonders.

"He tried to teach me to do it, while we were in the Tower."

Walsingham laughs.

"Is he dancing with Jane Frommond?"

Walsingham nods again. The Queen pulls an unreadable face, which he reads as her being resigned to a loss that in another life, and at another time, would be insupportable.

"She wishes to leave court, did you hear?"

Walsingham has not.

"She wishes to go to Basel and Geneva, and Strasbourg and even Prague. All the places I never shall."

The tiara on the table is heavy both literally and metaphorically tonight.

"And perhaps John will go with her? Or she with him?"

Walsingham says nothing.

"Do you think they will marry?" the Queen goes on. There is an edge to her voice.

"They do seem to share the taste—or, well, the experience—of adventure. And neither is encumbered, unless I am wrong? Do you not wish them to?"

She pulls a little face.

"Not sure," she says.

She takes a sip of her drink. She is jealous, of course. As, really, why would she not be? All around her, men and women are finding love and marrying, while she . . . she remains lonely and aloof. Permitted nothing of the sort. He sighs for her, but she is looking more thoughtful than melancholic now.

"We are a small nation, as you know, Francis, with limited resources, in terms of almost everything, and we face across the battlefield a deadly enemy, with almost unlimited resources."

"Ma'am?"

"So we need to husband our resources very carefully, wouldn't you agree?"

Again, yes.

"And I think one of those resources that needs husbanding is trust."

"Trust?"

"Yes. You—we—are engaged in a dirty, rotten business, Master Walsingham, do not think I do not see that. I know the moral compromises you make on my behalf."

"You do?"

"I do. And I think this year you have made more than anyone's fair share of them."

She knows about Ness Overbury.

"And I believe you are distracted by them," she goes on. "You are becoming so used to dealing with double-dealers, the dishonest, the deceitful, and the corrupt that you are in some way becoming tainted."

"Your Majesty!"

"Don't stop me, please, Francis. I say this only out of concern. I know that were you not so invested in my person, and in our nation, you would never permit to flourish a plot that might see a woman take the throne in my place and rule as a puppet for who knows whom."

He hangs his head and drops to his knees.

"Ma'am," he says. He cannot ask for forgiveness. It is too much.

The silence lingers. He stares at the rug. At his own knees on it. He feels the Queen moving. He sees her skirt hem before him. He can hear her breathe. She sighs.

Christ. What does he do? Throw himself on the floor? Kiss her feet? Weep?

"Francis," she goes on, in a softer voice yet, filled, he thinks, with infinite sorrow. "Whatever Sir Christopher Hatton may say, however he imputes your motives, I know that your heart beats for me, and for England, and so Master Walsingham—"

He feels something placed on his shoulder. Not her hand. A sword.

"I knight you, Sir Francis Walsingham, for secret services done for your country."

And she taps him first on one shoulder, then on the other, and finally on the head.

"Arise, Sir Francis," she says.

And he does. Tears spill like rice. And he sees, standing beside her, emerged from behind a curtain, to hand her the sword, is Sir William Cecil, patting those soft little hands together in pleasure.

"Very nobly done, Your Majesty, very nobly done."

A servant has brought in a tray of gold cups, and there is proper wine, and the three stand together, and Sir Francis can hardly believe it and they toast him again and again, and then they toast Lady Ursula, and it seems the whole sorry day is forgotten.

"Before I let you go to tell your wife, Sir Francis, there are two further things you must do for me."

"Anything, Your Majesty."

"You have a book in your study, don't you? A humble little thing such as a wool merchant might keep?"

He does. It is the very first thing he will burn, come the day the

Spanish arrive, for it contains the names of his seven most secret, most unexpected, most valued servants.

"There is one more name I should like you to add to that list," she says. "The name of one who has proved infinitely resourceful, patient, and useful."

"Your Majesty?"

"I should like you to add Frommond, Lady Jane Frommond."

"Double oh eight, Your Majesty?"

"Double oh eight, Sir Francis, why not?"

Why not, indeed?

"And the other thing, Your Majesty?"

"The other thing is that I want you to let John Dee go. Let us listen to him, and give him his freedom to act as he wishes. Let him go abroad. Let him take the fight to Spain, to the Vatican, to the Holy Roman Emperor. Let us unleash him on them! Let us see how they like that."

"Very good, Your Majesty, yes. Let us see how they like that."

AUTHOR'S NOTE

The Queen's Men is obviously a work of fiction, but like all histori-
cal fiction it is based on a true story. That is not to say that in 1578
Dr. John Dee rediscovered the long-lost secret of Greek fire, and
that Queen Elizabeth was only saved from its devastating effects
by a piece of quick thinking under an arch of London Bridge, or
that Robert Beale groomed a royal look-alike from Suffolk who
was later secreted onto an Ottoman ship in return for thirty barrels of crude oil, or that there was such a guild as that of the Black
Madonna of Halle, but it is to say that this is the kind of thing that
could have happened, given the place there and the time then.

Well, maybe.

Perhaps it is more accurate to say that *The Queen's Men* is set
against the backdrop of a true story, because many of the bit parts
and the turning points of the novel are based in fact: Sir Christopher Hatton—aka the Dancing Chancellor—*did* promise Mary,
Queen of Scots, that on the death of Queen Elizabeth he would
bring her down to London in state to take up her throne (though
he subsequently gave Walsingham no cause for further suspicion
and was later involved in the prosecution of Queen Mary in her

shameful show trial), and Cornelius de Lannoy—the Dutch alchemist—likewise promised Queen Elizabeth extravagant gains and was imprisoned in the Tower only because she believed he was stealing his product, from where he "escaped" in 1566 (after bribing the guards with something that may or may not have been gold).

Anthony Jenkinson—here given somewhat unfair narrative treatment—was just as impressive a figure, traveling thousands of miles to befriend Russia's Ivan the Terrible before traveling south across the Caspian Sea to become the first Englishman to reach the court of Shah Tahmasp at Qazvin, in modern-day Iran, where he was not so lucky, for exactly the reasons described in the novel. The artist Nicholas Hilliard, too, is another name from history, who was just coming into the peak of his miniaturist powers in the late 1560s (having learned much of his trade from the great court painter Levina Teerlinc, daughter of Simon Bening, himself the last of the great Netherlandish painters) and whom we know acted as a spy in the French court for Francis Walsingham. There is no evidence Hilliard was nicknamed Points the Painter, of course, but he was perpetually hard up, despite his resonant success, and the old hesitate-to-adjust-your-clothing-at-the-pub-door trick is as old as time itself, so why not?

Elsewhere Nonsuch House (not to be confused with Nonsuch Palace)—so-called because there was nonesuch like it in the whole of the kingdom—was the first flat-pack house to be erected in England, brought over in 1577 from Holland and assembled by Dutch joiners on London Bridge (famously using no nails, which sounds improbably cool, but nail here means nail of iron, rather than of oak, which—wood being cheaper and easier to come by— is what were then used in most buildings). That year also saw the first navigation locks to be built on the river Lea, under the over-sight of the clerk to the Court of Sewers, in part to help William

Cecil ship building supplies to his lavish palace, Theobalds House, which he was having built in Hertfordshire, and again, by Dutch engineers, who often stayed in barges while they worked in teams. As then, so now; England's genius relied on her immigrants, while her rulers availed themselves of the public purse.

And talking of houses, I recommend anyone with time on their hands to visit Sulgrave Manor, in Buckinghamshire, once owned by George Washington's grandfather—who makes a cameo appearance here, though of course there is no evidence that he ever rented the house out to Robert Beale—the gable of which still carries the arms of Queen Elizabeth, complete with lion and dragon, with which Jane Frommond became so familiar during her summer under its roof. It is now a small museum dedicated to Anglo-American relations.

And it was about this time that the English began to reach out across other seas, too, to cement relations elsewhere, and particularly with her enemies' enemies, and specifically the Ottomans, and Queen Elizabeth's relations with the Ottoman Sultan Murad III became extremely friendly, so much so that the English came to see the Ottomans as the Protestants of the East, while the Ottomans came to see the English at the Moslems of the West, each an ally in the fight against Spain and the Catholic Church. Trade flourished and embassies were sent and more about this can be read in Jerry Brotton's fascinating book *The Sultan and the Queen* (Penguin), which lays out the little-known story of how vital relations with the Turks were for England's subsequent flourishing on the world stage.

There are other facts that have steered the narrative, some of which will have a familiar ring, too, such as the appearance of the Great Comet in 1577, just as the new star had appeared in 1572, leading in both cases to states of heightened awareness of doom, and to rashes of wild End Times speculation. And readers will note the continued, and constant, flow of the river Thames through both books. This is because the Thames was, until the nineteenth century, London's main thoroughfare, being far easier to traverse than the filth-clogged streets, though doing so required knowledge of the tide, especially under the city's only bridge, where at low tide, the starlings were so sturdy the river's flow was constricted into a torrent too powerful for all but the foolhardiest of pilots. Curiously, and ironically perhaps, the two hundred tons of ore that Martin Frobisher brought back from what is now Canada in the hope that from it Dee might distill gold was to lie worthless in a depot in Deptford for decades until it was finally used to construct—of all things—a road.

Oliver Clements
October 2020

ACKNOWLEDGMENTS

Eternal thanks to the secret ring of people behind this book and the rest of the Agents of the Crown series: Lisa Gallagher, who is our Bond; Libby McGuire, our Spymaster; Kaitlin Olson, our Q; as well as the fearless and talented Jade Hui, Claire Sullivan, Jason Chappell, Falon Kirby, and Raaga Rajagopala. Special thanks, too, to our very own alchemist, Toby Clements, for turning ideas into gold.

ABOUT THE AUTHOR

Oliver Clements is a writer and philosopher based in Mortlake, London.